PRAISE FOR JOSEPH FLYNN AND HIS NOVELS

"Flynn is an excellent storyteller." — *Booklist*

"Flynn propels his plot with potent but flexible force."
— *Publishers Weekly*

Digger
"A mystery cloaked as cleverly as (and perhaps better than) any John Grisham work." — *Denver Post*

"Surefooted, suspenseful and in its breathless final moments unexpectedly heartbreaking." — *Booklist*

The Next President
"*The Next President* bears favorable comparison to such classics as *The Best Man, Advise and Consent* and *The Manchurian Candidate.*"
— *Booklist*

"A thriller fast enough to read in one sitting."
— *Rocky Mountain News*

The President's Henchman (A Jim McGill Novel)
"Marvelously entertaining." — *ForeWord Magazine*

ALSO BY JOSEPH FLYNN

Part 2:
The Last Ballot Cast
by

Joseph Flynn

Stray Dog Press, Inc.
Springfield, IL
2012

Published by Stray Dog Press, Inc.
Springfield, IL 62704, U.S.A.

Originally published as an eBook, July, 2012
First Stray Dog Press, Inc. Printing, September, 2012
Copyright © kandrom, inc., 2012
All rights reserved

Visit the author's web site: *www.josephflynn.com*

Flynn, Joseph
　　Part 2: The Last Ballot Cast / Joseph Flynn
　　416 p.
　　ISBN 978-0-9837975-8-6
　　eBook ISBN 978-0-9837975-6-2

Printed in the United States of America

PUBLISHER'S NOTE
This is a work of fiction. Names, characters, places, and incidents are
either the product of the author's imagination or are used fictitiously; any
resemblance to actual persons, living or dead, events, or locales is entirely
coincidental.

Book design by Aha! Designs

DEDICATION

This book is dedicated to my proofreaders: Catherine, Caitie, Anne and Susan. Of course, some of my typos and other mistakes are so devious they defy human intervention. Any errors you may find in this novel are solely my responsibility.

ACKNOWLEDGEMENTS

My thanks to Jim Sullivan, instructor for Natural Spirit International, who shared with me some of his encyclopedic knowledge of the martial arts. And to Susan C. McIntyre, nurse practitioner, my senior go-to person on medical matters. If I got anything wrong in either of these areas, it's either a matter of literary license or I just messed up.

The Last Ballot Cast
Part 2

AUTHOR'S NOTE

This is a work of fiction. Some of it overlaps current realities, political and otherwise, but is in no way intended to mirror the real world. How could it? This novel, like the other Jim McGill books, feature a female U.S. president and her husband who's a private investigator. Some readers have told me they wish these characters were real but they aren't.

This book brings several story lines from previous McGill books to a conclusion, as well as telling the story of an imagined presidential campaign. That's a lot of ground to cover and took 900 pages to do so. In order to make the novel a more accessible buying and reading experience, I divided it into two approximately equal parts.

This is Part 2. Read Part 1 first.

CAST OF CHARACTERS

James J. (Jim) McGill, 2nd husband of President Patricia Darden Grant, *aka* The President's Henchman

Patricia Darden Grant, President of the United States, former Congresswoman, wife of Jim McGill, widow of Andrew Hudson Grant

Margaret "Sweetie" Sweeney, Jim McGill's investigative partner, former police partner

Putnam Shady, lobbyist, landlord and lover of Margaret Sweeney

Galia Mindel, Chief of Staff to President Grant

Stephen Norwood, Galia Mindel's Chief of Staff

Edwina Byington, the president's personal secretary

Mather Wyman, Vice President, Kira's Fahey Yates' uncle

Celsus Crogher, Secret Service Agent in charge of White House Security Detail

Elspeth Kendry, Secret Service Special Agent

Donald "Deke" Ky, McGill's Secret Service bodyguard

Leo Levy, McGill's armed driver, ex NASCAR

Carolyn [McGill] Enquist, first wife of Jim McGill

Lars Enquist, Carolyn's [McGill] second husband

Abbie McGill, oldest child of Jim McGill and his first wife Carolyn

Kenny McGill, middle child, only son of Jim McGill and his first wife Carolyn

Caitie McGill, youngest child of Jim McGill and his first wife Carolyn

Andrew Hudson Grant, President Grant's 1st husband [murdered]

Captain Welborn Yates, Air Force Office of Special Investigations

Kira Fahey Yates, wife of Welborn Yates

Artemus Nicolaides, White House physician

Clare Tracy, Jim McGill's college sweetheart

Dikran "Dikki" Missirian, McGill's business landlord

Sir Robert Reed, Welborn Yates' British father

Carina Linberg, USAF colonel, retired

CAST OF CHARACTERS
(continued)

Liesl Eberhardt, Kenny's first girlfriend
Chana Lochlan, television reporter; source of leaks from
  WorldWide News
Admiral David Dexter, Chairman of the Join Chiefs
Byron DeWitt, FBI Deputy Director
Daryl Cheveyo, CIA officer, Todd's agency contact
Michael Jaworsky, Attorney General
Linda Otani, Deputy Attorney General
Rev. Burke Godfrey, Pastor of Salvation's Path Church, husband of Erna
Erna Godfrey, anti-abortion activist, incarcerated murderer;
  wife of Rev. Burke Godfrey
Benton Williams, lawyer for Rev. Godfrey
Sir Edbert Bickford, CEO of global media empire WorldWide News
Hugh Collier, nephew of Sir Bickford, works for WorldWide News
Ellie Booker, producer for WorldWide News
Damon Todd, deranged psychotherapist, *aka Dan Templeton*
Arn Crosby, "retired" member of CIA
Olin Anderson, "retired" member of CIA
Linley Boland, auto thief [aka Jackie Richmond]
Alice Tompkins, [aka Mary] owner of Mango Mary's bar in Key West
Tom T. Wright, billionaire and Super Pac contributor
Reynard Dix, Chairman of the Republican National Committee
Henry Melchior, Chairman of the Democratic National Committee

Elected Officials and Staff
Charles Talbert, Senator from Indiana, Republican [retiring]
Sheryl Kimbrough, professor at Indiana University,
  Republican elector from Indiana
Cassidy Kimbrough, daughter of Sheryl Kimbrough
Howard Hurlbert, Senator from Mississippi, Republican,
  co-sponsor of SOMA
Merilee Parker, press secretary for Sen. Howard Hurlbert;
  one of Galia Mindel's spies
Bobby Beckley, Sen Hurlbert's campaign manager and chief of staff
Derek Geiger, deceased Republican Speaker of the House
Roger Michaelson, Senator from Oregon, Democrat

CAST OF CHARACTERS
(continued)

Bob Merriman, former Chief of Staff to Senator Michaelson; running for Senate

John Wexford, Senator from Michigan, Democrat, Senate Majority Leader

Richard Bergen, Senator from Illinois, Democrat, assistant to Senator Wexford

Marlene Berman, Representative from New York, Democrat, House minority leader

Diego Paz, Representative from California, Democrat, assistant to Marlene Berman

Peter Profitt, Representative from North Carolina, Republican, House Majority Leader

Darrin Neff, Senator from South Carolina, [Republican]

Jim McKee, Senator from North Carolina, [Republican]

Beau Brunelle, Senator from Louisiana, [Republican]

Dan Crockett, Senator from Tennessee, [Republican]

Jean Morrissey, Governor of Minnesota, [Democrat]

Frank Morrissey, Governor Morrissey's brother and lawyer

Eugene Rinaldo, Governor of New York [Democrat]

Edward Mulcahy, Governor of Illinois [Democrat]

Lara Chavez, Governor of California [Democrat]

John Patrick Granby, Secretary of State from New Hampshire

Paul Brandstetter, Secretary of State from Iowa

Charles Delmain, Secretary of State from South Carolina

Alberto Calendri, Chief Justice of the U.S. Supreme Court

Titus Hawkins, Associate Justice of the U.S. Supreme Court

1

November, 2011
McGill Investigations, Inc. — Washington, D.C.

It wasn't often, if ever, that the number two official in the FBI came calling at the offices of a private investigator. Byron DeWitt didn't come hat in hand because he wouldn't have dreamed of covering his locks with cloth, leather or fur. Sun streaks were the look for California surfers, not hat hair.

The deputy director left his entourage at street level where the ever genial Dikki Missirian, the building's owner and McGill's landlord, was serving them complimentary bottles of San Pellegrino under Cinzano umbrellas, the weather being unseasonably warm.

McGill was the one with the supporting cast. Sweetie was with him as his business partner and as a matter of course. Also present were Elspeth Kendry, Deke Ky and Leo Levy. The special agents from the Secret Service needed to be kept informed of any perceived threat they hadn't detected on their own, and Leo needed to know if any evasive or aggressive driving might be on the horizon.

DeWitt looked around, saw that there was an open chair next to Sweetie, guessed it was for him. Before sitting, though, he shook hands with all present and introduced himself to those he hadn't met. Shaking McGill's hand last, he began with his first item on his agenda, an apology.

"Sorry I screwed up. Responsibility is on me."

McGill said, "Anybody in this room can tell you how far from perfect I am. I'm grateful you saw your way clear to come here today. It would be awkward for all of us if you weren't feeling co-operative."

He sat behind his desk and gestured for DeWitt to take his seat.

DeWitt agreed. "Yeah, there are some hard chargers down-stairs who said the director and I should just tell you to butt out and dare the president to overrule us."

McGill gave DeWitt a look. Sweetie was the one to laugh.

She said, "Good thing cooler heads prevailed."

"What Ms. Sweeney is saying," McGill told DeWitt, "is we can't be muscled."

DeWitt said, "That's the last thing I want. My idea is, let's catch these SOBs and go out for a drink afterward."

"No worries about who gets credit when we do catch them?" Elspeth asked.

The deputy director shook his head. "I'm pretty insistent about taking blame when it's deserved; I'm less concerned about claiming credit."

DeWitt held his hands out to McGill. Peace, he was plainly asking.

McGill nodded and asked, "What's your takeaway from what happened with Todd?"

The deputy director said, "That he's smart and he probably still has Crosby and Anderson with him. They were loose cannons at the CIA, but they're tough and experienced."

"You think Langley might be holding anything back on us?" McGill asked.

"No, they'd be too afraid of what the president might do."

That was one big reason DeWitt's inclination to work with McGill had won out over the hard line advanced by not only his subordinates but the director as well. The president was clearly taking a special interest in finding Damon Todd; she'd made the

CIA come across with personnel records they'd undoubtedly have preferred remain their private reading. If she didn't want her husband — and company — working the case, she would have told them so, and passed the word to the FBI.

Sweetie said, "When I first read the files on Todd, Crosby and Anderson, it made me wonder what you'd get if you crossed a virus with bacteria."

"A lot of dead people," Deke told her.

Following up on that point, DeWitt asked McGill, "Are you sure Dr. Todd meant to kill you when he attacked you in your office?"

"Someone comes at you in the dark with a baseball bat, what would you think?" McGill said. "Todd told me he strangled a man. We also know that Dr. Evelyn Patanky, the therapist who helped him recover from a nervous breakdown, disappeared and has never been found."

Deke and Elspeth exchanged a look. Without saying a word, they'd passed sentence.

Almost like Crosby and Anderson might have done.

They weren't going to take any prisoners either.

McGill spotted the silent exchange. Didn't choose to comment. Wasn't sure he objected.

As if she were a mind reader, Sweetie gave voice to what the others were thinking. "So we're dealing with killers all the way around. Makes for a take-no-chances approach to the situation."

McGill pointed out, "The problem is, none of these guys has any record of committing any crimes. Correct me if I'm wrong, but there aren't even any arrest warrants out for them."

DeWitt said, "Consider them persons of interest to be brought in for questioning."

"Something best done by those of you who still have badges," Sweetie said.

DeWitt replied, "That would be ideal, yes, but under the law everyone has the right of self-defense. Given the fact that we all know how dangerous these men are, exercising that right to its full extent would be understandable."

Maybe in court, McGill thought, but if he or Sweetie popped Todd or one of his friends, it might not look too good in the context of a presidential election. He could practically hear the demands for the appointment of a special prosecutor. Better that than leaving a widow and fatherless children behind, but he and Margaret were going to have to be careful.

"Did you learn anything from the attempt to lure Todd to the house in Pennsylvania?" McGill asked DeWitt.

The deputy director said, "Yes, we were close to succeeding. From information we learned from the decoy we took into custody, we worked our way back to a bar in Wilmington, Delaware. Three men we believe to be Todd, Crosby and Anderson were there directing the efforts of the four people who spotted Lydell Martin leave work and followed him back to the safe house we were using.

"We believe Todd was using smart phone or tablet computer technology to receive video and voice reports from his scouts. Once Todd saw the house Martin entered and the coast was clear, we expected him to come in and find out what had gone wrong with one of his subjects. But he sent the decoy and I gave the premature order to grab the wrong guy. The decoy had a disposable phone he'd been given and used it to curse out the people who'd gotten him into the mess. That was all the warning they needed to get away."

Sweetie had the grace to admit, "I would've jumped the decoy, too."

"So would I," McGill said. "The thing to understand is you weren't the only one to make a mistake, Todd did. He screwed up somehow, but he recognized the mistake before it could hurt him. It's always a pain when a bad guy is smart."

DeWitt said, "He is that. We have a pretty good idea of what his mistake was. All the scouts he had watching Martin drove gray foreign made sedans. So did the decoy. It must have occurred to Todd at the last minute that he should run one last check to see if anyone else had noticed that pattern."

Leo spoke up for the first time. "These gray cars, were they stock models? Was any of them rigged for high speed?"

DeWitt said, "The Audi the decoy used wasn't a high performance vehicle. We haven't contacted any of the scouts or impounded their vehicles. From the video we have on them, they appear to be run of the line models. The background checks we ran on the scouts show no history of advanced driving skills."

Leo nodded. "How about these two fellas, Crosby and Todd, they have any special behind the wheel training?"

"Not that I saw," DeWitt said. "I'll double-check on that."

McGill said, "You haven't contacted any of Todd's scouts because you didn't think you could get the truth out of them? Maybe because they weren't even aware of what they'd done."

DeWitt said, "Yes, that and we wanted to leave just a bit of doubt in Todd's mind about the extent to which we're on to him. We're tapping the scouts' phones, hoping Todd might use disposable cell phones to call them. If he does, he'll learn his people haven't been contacted by law enforcement. If he's on the phone with them long enough, we'll get at least a general idea of his location."

"Good thinking," McGill said.

The deputy director nodded. "There was one thing that struck me that night. Just before I gave the order to grab the decoy, I noticed that the people Todd had used for his scouts were all socially prominent. I thought they looked like a cross-section of Who's Who in America. From reading about Todd's idea of crafting personalities to help people get the most out of themselves, and from meeting Lydell Martin, I got an idea."

Hearing DeWitt's words, McGill thought he knew where he was going.

Out of respect and a desire to keep things friendly, he didn't jump the man's idea.

But if he was right, he just thought of a way to play off it.

"What's your idea?" he asked.

"Well, part of it is that Todd, Crosby and Anderson wouldn't take the risk of hiding out anywhere close to where we tried to trap them. They had to take off for somewhere else."

"In a car," Leo said, "but not a gray one."

DeWitt said, "Exactly. It's almost certain that they went to stay with another of Todd's subjects, but how do we who those people are?"

Sweetie saw where DeWitt was going now, too. She also chose not to interrupt.

"Seems easy now," DeWitt said. "We look in Who's Who and we crossmatch the entries there against everyone we can find whom Todd knew as a classmate, student, colleague or friend. Any matches, especially people who experienced sudden leaps in achievement like Lydell Martin, we start watching. Tap their phones, if there's any justification. With luck we'll find him."

McGill liked the idea. It was smart and it was the kind of massive information collection chore for which the FBI was best suited. So was the job McGill had for the bureau.

"That's good," he told DeWitt. "Here's something else to consider. If Todd chooses not to stay with any of his subjects, he's still going to make use of them. Todd and his friends will need money to live on. They're not going to rob banks or get jobs. They're going to take donations from the people Todd has helped. The money won't come in cash-filled envelopes. It will be moved electronically."

DeWitt smiled. He liked the idea and appreciated that McGill was sending more work his way.

He said, "What we look for are money transfers from several widely dispersed accounts among Todd's crafted personalities to a single recipient account, his. We can follow the electronic trail right up to his doorstep."

Always practical, Sweetie told DeWitt, "Even for your people, that sounds like a big job. In the meantime, we've still got three very dangerous creeps on the loose. Assuming they have money, we also have to think they have guns."

McGill said, "You're right, Margaret." He looked around the room and told everyone, "So in the immortal words of Sergeant Phil Esterhaus, 'Let's be careful out there.'"

Starved Rock State Park — Utica, Illinois

Arn Crosby and Olin Anderson stood atop the sandstone butte that gave the park its name and looked out on the Illinois River one hundred and twenty-five feet below. The park was a great find: rock formations, canyons, woodland, riverfront. It was a wild world, set apart from all the placid cornfields that surrounded it.

The place had a bloody history, too. An Indian chief returning from a tribal council downriver was ambushed and killed by members of another tribe. In revenge, the chief's tribe and its allies caught several members of the hostile tribe on the spot where Crosby and Anderson stood. The chief's killers weren't attacked; they were besieged and starved. Hence the name.

Having read the sign that told the story, Anderson asked Crosby, "You know what this reminds me of?"

Crosby knew. He and Anderson had been all but married for the greater part of their lives.

"The Pali on Oahu" Crosby said. "Kamehameha and his army paddled ashore at Waikiki and drove the local studs up to the edge of the cliff and they jumped."

"Or were pushed, depending on who tells the story," Anderson said. "Either way, they died quickly. No prolonged agony, watching the meat disappear off their bones."

Crosby said, "You're right. What the Indians did here was crueler."

"Wonder why some of the tribe that got caught didn't die fighting."

"Or jump off the cliff," Crosby said.

He sat on the rock and looked down at the river. The water was gray on the chilly overcast day. Anderson sat next to him, his arms around an upraised right knee. The weather being what it was, school in session, people at work and no park ranger around, they had the place to themselves.

"Speaking of the Pali," Crosby said, "I've been thinking of Danny Kahanamoku lately."

Anderson smiled. "The Hawaiian. Wonder if that bastard's

still alive."

"Sure, if he hasn't made love to Pele yet."

Pele was the Hawaiian goddess of fire and volcanos. Danny K. had said when he got tired of living he was going to paddle his canoe from his home on Maui to the Big Island and make love to the goddess by throwing himself into the molten heart of Mount Kilauea.

Nobody who knew him doubted he was serious.

Danny K. had served in the Middle East with Crosby and Anderson and had been captured by hajis when he'd been knocked senseless by an IED that killed two other guys. The hajis figured it right that Danny K. worked for the Americans, but at six-four and two-sixty, brown skinned but not black, they were unsure of what kind of giant human being they'd caught.

"Never saw a Polynesian in their miserable lives," Anderson said.

"Sure didn't speak Hawaiian," Crosby said. "Couldn't find any-one who did."

"Bastards thought he was spouting gibberish."

"Didn't care for what he said when he finally told them in English he was preparing for death by talking to his gods."

Anderson said, "Sorta marked him as an infidel."

"If their threat to cut off his head was any clue, yeah."

"Good ol' Danny K., though, he came back with three haji heads in a canvas bag." Anderson enjoyed the reminiscence a moment and then asked Crosby, "You just happened to think of an old pal or was it more than that?"

"More. I talked to Danny the way he talked to his gods."

Anderson smirked. "Didn't know you're fluent in Hawaiian."

"Danny K. understood. I talked to him because I can't talk to you."

Anderson's forehead turned bright red. "What the hell do —"

Then it hit him. Crosby couldn't talk to him the same way he couldn't talk to Crosby. Because Todd had fucked with both their heads. But Crosby, devious bastard that he was, had looked for a work-around.

Anderson asked, "You and Danny K. have a nice little chat?"

"Sure. The guy has always been a good listener. Watch. I'll talk to him again. He won't even mind that I'm repeating myself."

Crosby stared out at a point somewhere above the river. Told the indomitable Danny Kahanamoku, wherever he might be, that a little mindfucker named Damon Todd had messed with his head, kept him from scheming with his best pal, Olin Anderson. The three of them were on the run from the Company but he and Olin had lost operational control.

Anderson jumped in, focusing on the same spot in midair.

"Hey, Danny, it's Olin. I'm in the same fix as Arn. What do we do?"

Almost immediately, the heads of the two former covert operatives jerked back and forth as if they'd been hit with a backhand, forehand combination. For a moment, they were stunned. Then they turned to look at each other and smiled.

As one, they told each other, "Make love to the goddess."

They wouldn't have to worry about any booby-traps going off in their heads if they beat the IEDs to the punch. If you didn't worry about dying, who could have any hold on you? They'd known that all along, of course. It had just taken Danny K. to remind them.

What was the point of continuing to live if you were stuck on a rock starving?

Maybe not for food but everything else that made life worth living.

Better to jump or die fighting.

The House on Gentleman Road — Ottawa, Illinois

The first three rules of real estate were: location, location, location. The same thinking applied to finding a hideout. The old house on the outskirts of the small central Illinois town was as close to perfect as a fugitive could ask. Set two hundred feet back from the road, it sat among stands of trees front, back and on both sides. True, almost all the leaves had fallen by now but the trees grew so closely together that their trunks and branches provided hardwood camouflage.

Beyond the trees, on the three adjacent sides and across the roads were empty farm fields. Todd didn't know if corn or soybeans would be planted there, but his expectation was that the land would lie idle until spring.

Todd had been the one to visit the Realtor; she'd brought him to the house. He'd never have found it on his own. He'd simply told the woman he wanted a secluded but comfortable house where he might work on a scholarly book he was writing.

The woman smiled at him and said, "I know just the place, quiet, out of the way, but in good repair. The late owner was something of a recluse. The heirs would like to sell the place, but I'm sure they'd let you rent rather than have no income at all and, who knows, if your writing goes well, maybe you'd like to buy it so you can write your next book there."

"Who knows?" Todd agreed with a smile of his own.

The house was farmstead plain but, as described, sound in all regards. The roof didn't leak, the windows didn't rattle and the electricity and heat were connected to the town's power grid. The furnishings of the late owner were still in place but in need of a dusting. The Realtor said she could have the house cleaned in a jiffy for a reasonable price.

Returning to her office, Todd signed a six-month lease and paid for the duration of the agreement in cash. He added a hundred dollars to have the cleaning done expeditiously. If the Realtor saw any incongruity in a scholar carrying cash instead of credit cards, she kept it to herself. But Todd noticed an increase in her normal blink rate.

Her pulse had undoubtedly quickened, too. The sight of a thick sheaf of hundred dollar bills had excited her. Within the context of a perfectly legitimate business transaction, she caught a whiff of something illicit and she liked it. Todd wondered, ever so briefly, if he should cultivate an acquaintance with her. He'd been a long time without a woman and …

He decided to be smart. There would be other, less revealing ways to meet his needs.

His best choice with the Realtor was to be polite, an academic gentleman too caught up in his work to have time for anything else. She'd see he wasn't interested, not in the way she might be. She'd stop regarding him as anything other than a pleasant client.

Or so he thought.

At the moment, with Crosby and Anderson out of the house, Todd was engaged in a matter of study. Sitting at the kitchen table with a glass of pomegranate juice, he was looking at a Google map of Illinois on his iPad. Ottawa, he saw, was little more than ninety miles southwest of Chicago.

Interstate 80 was only a few miles north of where he sat. You took that east to I-55 and it was a short drive northeast into the city. The highway ended at Lake Shore Drive. Turning north on that road, the first lakefront suburb you came to was Evanston — where the last he'd heard James J. McGill still owned a home. Travel just a bit further north along the shoreline of Lake Michigan and you came to Winnetka — where President Patricia Darden Grant had owned the estate that had been her home with her first husband Andrew Hudson Grant.

Would she have sold the site of a tragedy? He'd have to find out.

Todd looked out the window to let his eyes rest in a long-focus state.

The trees were all but leafless now, but come the spring they would bud again and fill with a dense cloak of green. Todd's plan to gain revenge on James J. McGill was as unembellished as the woodland outside. With the passage of time, though, it, too, would be filled out.

Stopping so close to McGill's natal home had to be more providence than coincidence.

Todd returned his attention to the tablet and pulled up everything he could find in the public record about McGill's life before he came to Washington. He also searched for Patti Grant's early career as a congresswoman from suburban Chicago. He was hours into his research and had compiled pages of notes next to the computer. The beginnings of a plan were forming in his mind when he heard the front door open.

Crosby and Anderson were back.

George Town — Grand Cayman Island

The idea that Linley Boland might have other adversaries pursuing him seemed perfectly logical to Welborn Yates. Once it was introduced, that was. Before that, it had never occurred to him. He was grateful Willa Pennyman had called him with the news.

Now, he had to catch Boland before these other guys — maulers, he'd been told —caught Boland's alter ego, Jackie Richmond.

"Eddie said these maulers with a white yacht are looking for the bloke you want," Willa had told him, and then she'd put her cousin, the taxi driver, on the phone to fill in the details.

Welborn listened to him and asked, "You're sure these guys aren't cops?"

"What cops you know travel on yachts?" Eddie replied.

Welborn couldn't think of any offhand.

As small as Grand Cayman was, Welborn also couldn't think of a way Boland/Richmond could remain at large for long. Not with two bounties on his head. Not with who knew how many locals looking to cash in on him. If Eddie had it right, the maulers would … do what? Feed Boland to the fishes? That wouldn't be an inappropriate fate for him. But it also wouldn't be nearly as satisfying as seeing Boland led into a federal courtroom in handcuffs and leg restraints to be tried, convicted and sentenced in front of the families of the guys he killed.

To make sure that happened, there was only one thing for Welborn to do.

Get rid of the competition. Drive off the maulers.

He decided it was time to go to the local cops, the Royal Cayman Island Police Service. He'd come clean about why he was on the island. He asked Eddie to pass the phone back to Willa and told her what he was going to do. Her reaction was understandable.

"This mean nobody's getting any reward?" she asked.

"No, not at all," Welborn said. His mother had instructed him that the worst thing to waste was the good will of others. He told Willa, "The police of any country always welcome appropriate help from a concerned citizenry. If someone you know were to provide a tip that leads to an arrest, there will still be a reward, at the same terms we previously discussed."

Willa told him, "You talk so pretty I want to hug you."

A sentiment Welborn had heard before.

"So you'll continue to help, you and your family?"

"Too right, we will."

Welborn cautioned, "But, Willa, by bringing the police in on this, it would look very bad for anyone who helped the maulers Eddie mentioned."

"We'll see everybody knows that, too."

Welborn thanked Willa for the warning again.

Then he lay down, trying to sleep in the master cabin of *Irish Grace*. Carina had told him she was certain Jackie Richmond would look for her boat. Jackie no doubt still wanted to get to South America and, the way she figured it now, try to sell her boat out from under her.

What she hadn't decided yet was whether he'd try to force her to bring the boat into harbor or try to dump her overboard while still at sea and attempt to steer himself into port under motor power. Either choice would present challenges for a villain.

From a storyteller's point of view, that is.

She also didn't know whether she'd want to see her character killed off.

Carina said she'd work on the story from her suite at the Ritz-Carlton.

Welborn could have the master cabin on her boat. She'd

changed the linens before arriving in Grand Cayman. If Jackie sneaked aboard during the night, he'd find Welborn instead of Carina and ... it'd be fun to figure out how that should end, too.

She gave him a kiss on the cheek and the keys to her boat.

Told him where he could find her LadySmith .38.

Said he *shouldn't* change the linens before he left the boat.

Welborn dozed only lightly through the night, and kept the gun close at hand.

Carina's clean sheets notwithstanding, her scent still filled the air.

With the arrival of the morning sun, Welborn got up, did a quick scrub and shave in a small but well appointed bathroom compartment. Satisfied that he made a presentable appearance for an officer in the United States Air Force, he locked up the .38 where Carina kept it and headed off to the central station of the RCIPS.

The official motto of the island cops was: We care, we listen and we act.

Welborn certainly hoped so.

Five minutes after he'd left the boat, Jackie Richmond found *Irish Grace*.

Welborn introduced himself at the Central Station of the RCIPS as a captain in the United States Air Force attached to its Office of Special Investigations. He showed his identification to prove his bona fides. As a colleague in law enforcement, he was given a polite reception from a desk sergeant.

When Welborn said he worked directly for the president of the United States and provided a White House phone number — which was duly checked out — he was ushered into the office of Deputy Commissioner Edison Graves.

Knowing there was still another step of the police hierarchy to be climbed, Welborn told the deputy commissioner that his father was Sir Robert Reed the former personal secretary to Her Majesty the Queen. The Cayman Islands were a British Overseas Territory. Welborn was quickly ushered into the office of Commissioner

Edward Peck.

Peck had worked for Scotland Yard before moving on to warmer climes.

He stood as Welborn entered his office and told him, "I've met Sir Robert more than once and —" Looking at Welborn closely he was forced to admit, "Yes, I see the resemblance. How may the police service be of help, Captain Yates?"

Always paid to have connections, Welborn thought.

The two men sat as Welborn told the story of Linley Boland, aka Jackie Richmond. Commissioner Peck's face tightened upon learning a killer had entered his jurisdiction and a crew of thugs was in pursuit of him. He was also annoyed that Welborn hadn't come to him straightaway.

"My mistake," Welborn said. "I apologize. The situation is an emotional one for me. The Air Force officers Boland killed were my friends, and I was in the car with them."

His narrative had held that fact back, hoping it would be a mitigating factor in his lapse of professional conduct. Peck saw it for the gambit it was, but was affected by it nevertheless. He'd have done the same thing in Welborn's place.

"You're sure you intended to contact my people once you found Boland?" Peck asked.

"Yes, sir. I'm looking for justice not revenge, and I'd never do anything to embarrass either the president or my parents."

Kira, too, he thought, adding her to his list.

Peck studied the younger man's face and nodded.

"Right," he said. "Let's find these yacht-going thugs and send them on their way. Then we'll put this Boland chap in custody. You'd like to come along, I take it."

"Yes, thank you, Commissioner. If your people arrest Boland as the result of a tip from a local person, please get that person's name. There's a reward that will be paid for providing the information."

Peck got to his feet; Welborn did the same.

"Decent of you to point that out. Speaks well of your upbringing. Give my regards to Sir Robert the next time you speak."

"I will," Welborn said.

The Oval Office

Jim McGill had been personally, emotionally and physically intimate with Patti Grant for almost four years, but sitting behind President Patricia Darden Grant's desk in the Oval Office made him feel as if he was taking indecent liberties — and when Galia Mindel bustled in, stopped short and tried to make sense of what she was seeing, he felt an overpowering urge to explain himself —

That he converted into a wisecrack. "The coup is not quite complete. Please take a seat while we decide your fate."

The great thing was, for just a second, he had her believing.

Then Galia scowled.

Then she remembered that he'd save her life.

"The president does know you're here?" Galia asked.

By that time, McGill had closed the briefing book he'd been reading and put it in a desk drawer. Galia looked displeased that he'd managed to distract her, but she didn't comment on it, and was far too smart to ask what he was hiding.

McGill said honestly, "The president *insisted* I sit here. She said I wouldn't be bothered. That leads me to think something urgent has caused you to rush in. You must have given Edwina a fit."

"No more than usual," the chief of staff said.

"She didn't even have the time to tell you the president is else-where. Must be quite the hoo-hah. What I need to know is whether it's a matter of national or political interest."

"Why do you need to know anything?" Galia asked.

"Because I'm one of the few people who knows where the president is."

The chief of staff frowned, but at the same time she felt pleased.

She and McGill were sparring again. The world was returning to some of its natural contours. She had to do her best not to let her gratitude to the man turn her into a mushy opponent.

"The president's schedule says she's supposed to be right where you're sitting."

"Her *official* schedule," McGill countered.

That shook Galia, the idea the president had a secret schedule. One she didn't know about but McGill did.

Then she saw him grin. He was yanking her chain again.

"It's a political matter," she told him curtly.

McGill glanced at his watch. "Can it keep another forty minutes?"

"Yes, but not much longer."

"In forty minutes, then, I'll tell Edwina and she can tell you."

The chief of staff turned to go, but McGill called her name.

He told her, "If Patti hasn't told you, I'm sorry I didn't get to Granby faster."

Galia's eyes began to fill. "You got there faster than anyone else."

She left and after waiting a minute McGill picked up the phone on the president's desk, hoping he was calling Edwina not the Kremlin or the Forbidden City.

"Yes, Mr. McGill?" the president's secretary said.

"Edwina, will you please have Secret Service agents with weapons drawn stand guard just outside this office? Tell them if anyone tries to storm in again not to spare the ammo."

"Certainly, sir, subject to presidential countermand."

"Of course."

McGill took the briefing book he'd been reading out of the drawer. He felt more relaxed about what he was doing now. Good old Galia.

He found the place where he left off. As he'd suspected, the CIA hadn't quite come clean about Arn Crosby and Olin Anderson. The spook-shop bureaucracy had passed along all the details of the missions the two covert operatives had led but … the Company had held back the psychological evaluations that had led to the men's confinement at The Funny Farm.

Both Crosby and Anderson had grown up in abusive family

settings. But neither of them had been materially or education-ally deprived. Crosby's father was the mayor of a small town, one whose town council he'd cowed, along with pretty much everyone else. Anderson's father had been a minister, one whose church, he thought, was losing its way, ignoring fundamental doctrine to make itself more salable to new recruits.

Both men beat their sons. Crosby's father did it simply because he saw himself as an authority figure who need not suffer contrary opinion from any quarter. Anderson's father saw corporal discipline as a religious mandate. Having no intention of spoiling his son, he did not spare him the rod.

As a result of their upbringings, Crosby and Anderson believed in both serving the powers that be and in subverting them.

The CIA had known of that dichotomy from the start. The agency had made cynical use of Crosby and Anderson's willingness to serve, doing work few others had the stomach for, and ignored their efforts at subversion. At least until the latter far outweighed the former. Then the Agency locked up the two of them.

The rationale for that was they could no longer be trusted not to disclose vital intelligence.

That and all the CIA shrinks thought they were headed for Technicolor self-destruction.

A post-escape addendum noted the opinion that both Crosby and Anderson would prefer to die rather than be returned to The Funny Farm.

McGill sat back and returned the report to the desk drawer.

Without going into detail, he'd have to tell everyone working with him that Crosby and Anderson had to be treated as candidates for suicide by cop.

Reading the CIA's evaluation of Crosby and Anderson made McGill wonder how much awful stuff Patti read routinely. All in a day's work. Probably a lot. Probably never stopped. He'd have to step up his game and be a more thoughtful husband.

He'd taken a step in that direction a little less than an hour ago.

McGill had gotten Patti to agree to a suggestion he'd been

making to her for over a year.

Take an hour for lunch away from your desk. Book time with one of the White House massage therapists. Let yourself relax a little. She'd said okay. Nothing like a health scare to make someone finally see sense.

For a moment, McGill wondered what the political tempest bothering Galia was.

Then he went back to thinking about Crosby and Anderson.

How Damon Todd might try to make use of them.

And how DeWitt would receive the new idea that had just occurred to McGill.

Aboard Irish Grace
Barcadere Marina, Grand Cayman Island

Jackie Richmond aka Linley Boland called out Carina Linberg's name before he set foot on *Irish Grace*. Even a desert rat like him knew that much about boat manners. If anybody on one of the other boats nearby saw him, they'd know he was behaving right. Getting no answer, he went aboard and tried calling out again. Got no response again.

But he *acted* like he had. Said loudly, "Sure, honey, I can wait a minute."

Using his body as a shield, he went to work picking the lock on the cabin door. Getting past it took less than thirty seconds. He went below and relocked the door from the inside.

He stood still and listened. Something electronic buzzed. If he'd triggered the timer on an alarm system, he'd go back outside and walk away like it had nothing to do with him. But after a minute there was no loud noise or flashing lights. Some other kind of doodad was drawing juice and humming about it. Nothing to concern him.

Of course, it was possible Carina had been out last night and thrown back some drinks. Might be sleeping it off, hadn't heard him call her name or felt the boat rock slightly when he'd come aboard. But he didn't think so. He had the feeling he was all by himself.

Before they'd arrived on Grand Cayman, he'd gotten Cap'n Thurlow to show him how he operated his boat. Wasn't anything to it. Just a throttle and a steering wheel really.

The hard part was figuring out which way to go.

Weren't any damn landmarks on the ocean.

He'd asked, "If you get lost out here, how the hell you know which way to go?"

"Use your GPS. That goes out, follow the birds," Thurlow said.

It was the second suggestion caught his attention. "Birds? What birds?"

He'd asked the questions with a smile on his face and a beer in his hand. He was no threat to anyone. Just a goober with money looking to learn a new thing or two.

"Seabirds," Thurlow said. "They can fly thousands of miles, but they got to find land sometime. They always know which way to go."

Jackie couldn't imagine any animal being able to walk that far, much less fly that distance, but he didn't see a hint that he was being kidded.

"Okay, then," he told the cap'n. "You see one of these birds, point him out to me, will you?"

Thurlow gave him a salute and another beer. After a while, sure enough, he pointed out one bird and then another. They followed the damn things straight to Grand Cayman.

Once they got there, Jackie had the cap'n go from one harbor and marina to the next, saying he couldn't remember the name of the damn boat his friend had chartered, but he'd sure as hell recognize him and his latest wife if they were out on deck.

"His wife's new, how you know her?" the cap'n asked.

Jackie said, "She'll be younger, blonder and bustier than the last one."

Thurlow liked that. He didn't really care if they were on a fool's errand. He'd already made his money. It was a nice day. The client wasn't any dumber than most, and he was easy going.

Jackie spotted *Irish Grace* at the next to last anchorage they visited, but he didn't say a word about it. Kept his face as straight as he could. Was glad Carina Linberg hadn't been on deck and seen him. The way he'd read her, she might have taken a shot at him.

When they tied up at the last stop, the cap'n said he was going to spend the night on Grand Cayman, visit family he had there. To show what a sport he was, Jackie gave Thurlow a tip. Said it wasn't the cap'n's fault his dumb friend was late showing up. What he'd do now was start a pub crawl. Maybe the jerk had decided to rent a house instead of a boat.

The two men said goodbye amiably, and that should have been that.

Should've been.

Though Jackie's thing was stealing cars, he had family and friends who burgled for a living. They told him where people kept things in their houses. Money and jewelry: bedroom, top drawer of a dresser, under lingerie or socks. Second choice: kitchen, cabinet within easy reach. Third choice: any room with artificial flowers or plants, under the flowers or plants.

There were other places for people who thought they were trickier, but Jackie's mentors had scoffed at all of them. They said if you were any kind of thief you should be able to *smell* money. If you were great, you should be able to *feel* where the money was.

Jackie didn't know if he was great but he was pretty good. He found Carina's .38 in a lock box made to look like an old fashioned computer processor. Damn thing didn't have any business on a boat where all the other electronics looked new.

He didn't touch the gun, though. Not yet.

He didn't see the need. Why transfer a fingerprint?

Besides, he was looking for money. People who worked straight jobs usually didn't keep cash in their cars, but the way he thought about it, it seemed like a good idea to bring a healthy amount of actual coin on your boat if you were sailing off to backwater countries where there wasn't an ATM on every corner.

Sure enough. Carina had ten grand worth of Uncle Sam's finest federal reserve notes stuffed inside a phony garbage disposal.

He was congratulating himself when he heard voices on the jetty outside approaching the boat. Sonofabitch, if one of them didn't sound like Cap'n Thurlow. Jackie took a quick peek out a window and saw he was right. Thurlow and three guys who looked like they ate bowls of anabolic steroids for breakfast. The cap'n was pointing right at *Irish Grace*.

Shit, Jackie thought. So much for being poker faced when he'd seen Carina's boat.

That dirty fucking bastard Thurlow had seen his interest and ratted him out.

After Jackie had *tipped* the prick.

But he hadn't given the cap'n nearly as much money as the biggest hulk was handing him.

So who the hell were those oversized ass — Oh, shit, the slavers. Alice had sold him out, too.

Thurlow smiled broadly, but not for long because there was a woo-waw, one of those police sirens you heard in foreign movies. The hulks looked at Thurlow like they might all grab a limb and make a wish. They didn't have the time. A dozen or so local cops appeared on the run and put all of them in handcuffs.

Marched them off like they were late for a hot date.

When the crowd moved on, Jackie saw two guys who'd stayed behind.

One was a local cop, probably *the* local cop, the uniform he had on.

It was the other one, though, who scared Jackie. He was that sonofabitch who'd caught him stealing his car in Baltimore. What the hell was he doing here?

Not waiting for an answer to come to mind, Jackie took possession of Carina's .38.

Either of those assholes outside came through the front door, he'd put him down.

Nobody came, though. They didn't know he was there.

Small comfort. Jackie knew the cops had to be looking for him. Maybe there were other guys he'd never seen before looking for him, too, and, goddamn, he'd never felt so trapped before.

He had nowhere to —

Wait a minute, he *did* have somewhere to go. Thurlow'd had his ass dragged away by the cops. He knew where the cap'n had docked his boat. Thurlow had showed him how to *operate* it. Okay, the boat used to belong to the cap'n. Pretty soon, though, it was going to be his.

He hoped the fucker had gassed it up. Jackie was going to … follow the damn birds someplace. Maybe they'd lead him to Venezuela.

He peeked out the window again.

No cops in sight. No anybody. He was about to leave *Irish Grace* when it hit him.

He had no way to prove it, but he *felt* where the money was.

The money that had been taken from his bank account.

That prick from Baltimore had stolen it. He had it.

The White House Residence

Galia was waiting for the president the moment she finished getting dressed after her massage. From the look on her chief of staff's face, Patricia Darden Grant knew something big was up. A crisis of some sort was about to become her concern and a part of the country's consciousness.

Only moments earlier so much of the tension the president had felt in her neck, shoulders and back had been dispelled that she'd felt like a new woman. Now, the tightness was creeping back and she decided there was only one way to deal with whatever headache Galia was about to share with her.

She held up a hand before Galia could get a word out and called for Blessing, the White House's head butler. She whispered a few words into his ear. He nodded and went off to carry out the president's wish.

"Sometimes, that man makes me think he's a genie," Galia said.

"He's better than that," the president said. "There are never any unintended consequences when Blessing does his work."

"May I ask what wonder he's off to perform now?"

"Galia," the president asked, "when was the last time you had a massage?"

The president and her chief of staff lay on adjacent massage tables, Galia still working on overcoming the embarrassment of being nude, under a cotton sheet, and being attended to by Antoinette Barrie, LMT. The president was receiving her second massage of the day from Devin Waters, also licensed to knead skin and muscle, whom the president had warned not to peek at the chief of staff.

That little joke had only made Galia more uneasy.

To prevent two innocent civilians from overhearing tales of political malevolence, both massage therapists had donned the ear buds attached to their iPods and turned the volume as high as they comfortably could bear.

The president had also insisted that she and Galia wait until they'd had their scalps, necks and shoulders massaged before getting down to business. Once that was accomplished, the president turned to her chief of staff and gave her a nod. Whatever it was Galia had come to tell her, she seemed far less anxious about it now.

Keeping her voice down, despite their precautions, Galia told the president, "Howard Hurlbert is about to make a fool of himself on CSPAN."

"And why should we do anything but cheer?" Patti asked.

"Because there are millions of fools who will take him at his word and swallow his lie whole."

"That lie being?"

Galia told the president.

Who frowned, drawing a look of concern from Devin. She waved it off. His sense of touch was perfect as always. The president pointed at Galia. All was well again.

"That's ridiculous," Patti told Galia, "but most big lies are."

"Absurd or not, we have to knock it down and fast."

"All right, but we'll do it with humor."

"What, mock people's paranoia? That's not nice," Galia said.

"Tough. If people want to act like dunces they should be seen for what they are."

The president had an idea on how to achieve their goal. She told Galia, who loved it.

Then Patti asked, "You learned of this through one of your sources?"

"Yes." Galia's answer held a note of anger.

That wasn't unusual; indignation was the chief of staff's favored emotional response.

Sensing something that went beyond her usual pique, though, Patti said, "I know better than to inquire about your sources, but is there anything you'd care to tell me?"

Galia took a beat and then said, "The woman I heard the news from is a formerly battered spouse. She heard it from a currently battered spouse."

The president had never had a man lay a hand on her in anger, but she knew other women who had, and she'd despised the men who'd hurt her friends. In the past, she hadn't been in a position to affect a legal remedy. Now, she was.

"Galia, I'd like to help."

"So would I, but … first, I'd have to persuade two women to go public with their humiliation and then you would have to deal with the political backlash."

The chief of staff explained what she meant.

Patti said, "I don't give a damn about that. If any man on the other side tries to give me grief about it, I'll destroy his career."

The president took a deep breath, exhaled slowly.

Tried to clear her mind, let herself relax.

Forget about all the bastards in the world for the next forty minutes.

United States Senate — Washington, D.C.

Senator Howard Hurlbert had the jitters as he waited his turn to enter the chamber and speak. His chief of staff, Bobby Beckley, waited with him, trying to keep the old man calm. In his third term as a senator, there was no reason for Hurlbert to have stage fright, Beckley thought. Especially, with only the presiding officer, Senator Grace Kalman (D-WA), and a few sleepy underlings nearby to watch him in person.

There was, however, one spectator present who did matter — a lot.

Up in the visitors gallery sat Tom T. Wright, chairman of the Do Right for America Foundation. He was one of the few people at that point who wanted to hear what Howard Hurlbert had to say. The rich old goat who'd ponied up the money for Hurlbert's original Super-PAC, Royce Selby, had turned tail and run when the Department of Justice had gone after him for the anti-Patti Grant commercial that it had labeled fraudulent.

The senator needed a new billionaire to bankroll his election efforts.

Tom T. more than qualified and had come to Washington to see if he wanted to buy in.

The Louisiana fat cat hadn't always been rich. He had grown up swamping out his daddy's bar in New Orleans every morning before school, after the local lowlifes had spilled their drinks, piss and blood in it the night before. Often as not, Tom T. would find teeth on the floor. A couple of times there were even glass eyes. He thought if he found enough glassies he could take them to school, get up a game of marbles with his friends that'd give the girls nightmares for years.

That hadn't worked out though. Most of Daddy's booze hounds managed to keep their orbs, real or fake, in their heads. What turned out to be Tom's greatest find was having his older sister, Marcella, run off and leave her six-year-old son, Jean Baptiste, behind. Tom's mother, Earleen, had run off, too — leaving Daddy alone and Tom T. to clean up the bar.

Tom T. hadn't missed his mother particularly, was indifferent to his sister's departure, but he praised Jesus she'd left J.B. behind. The kid, Tom T. guessed, was one-eighth black and a hundred and ten percent smart. Daddy liked the little guy, too, but it was Tom T. who raised him.

Rather than hand off his dirty work to J.B., Tom T. set him to being the bar's resident genius. The kind wagers got placed on. Things started simple, races to see who could recite the alphabet backward faster. Later in the night it would be who could say it *forward* faster. Bets were small at first, fifty cents, maybe a dollar. By the end of the night, though, there was usually about twenty-five dollars to split.

Daddy got ten percent off the top. Tom T. and J.B. split the remainder fifty-fifty. J.B. made sure the arithmetic worked out right.

Word of J.B.'s prowess spread from drinker to drinker, bar to bar.

Soon there were imitators. Then there were competitors.

For a period of four years, little smart guys matching wits got to be a bar sport in New Orleans. Drinkers would bring in their small fry, brag on them, tell everyone what their specialties were and turn 'em loose on each other, wagering question by question and best out of five. People of more refined sensibilities, who drank in nicer neighborhoods, heard stories of what was going on from their auto mechanics and such and complained to the newspapers and the police.

The chief of police investigated and concluded, "The kids ain't drinking nothin' but sody-pop, and they ain't chawin' on each other like dogs. Where the hell's the harm?"

The critics moved on to more tractable social problems.

What killed the sport was nobody could beat J.B. People started bringing in their high school kids toward the end and J.B., ten by then, still beat them. Some promoters wanted to match J.B. against college students, ones who attended class not just played football, but Tom said no.

Another group came to Tom offering to pay him a thousand dollars to have J.B. retire so the other kids would stand a chance. J.B. was tired of unequal competition by then and told Tom to take the money. He did and used it to buy saving bonds for J.B.

Thing was, without J.B., the sport died from lack of interest. There were plenty of regular smart kids around to play, but there was no one like J.B. who made people's jaws drop and say, "Sumbitch, no way in hell I coulda known that."

Watching kids whom they suspected — usually correctly — weren't much smarter than them wasn't any fun. The betting action dried up and that was that.

By the time J.B. was a junior in high school, Daddy had died, Tom T. took over the bar and J.B. demanded that he be the one to do the clean up. But he asked Tom T. would it be all right if he applied to go to college at MIT. The question of J.B. leaving for Cambridge, Massa-damn-chusetts hit Tom T. like a Nolan Ryan fastball. It made his heart hurt.

He still managed to say, "Anything you want, J.B."

J.B. was admitted to MIT, but even with a generous financial aid package the leftover expenses were more than Tom T. could meet. He said he'd take out a mortgage on the bar, but J.B. said no. He wrote a thank you letter to MIT and enrolled at L.S.U.

He studied petroleum engineering, graduated first in his class and turned down Exxon and every other oil company that offered him a job. He set up his own company, got venture capital backing from folks out in San Francisco and showed people he could find recoverable oil in places everyone else had missed.

He made Tom T. his partner and cut him in for half of every dollar that came his way.

Having raised one fantastic kid and gotten rich, Tom T. thought he had wisdom to share with everyone. Some of his ideas had merit. Others suggested that even starting out poor a man could be more than a little eccentric, and coming into money only made it obvious.

Bobby Beckley joined Tom T. in the visitors gallery of the

Senate.

Senator Howard Hurlbert stood at the lectern below and looked into the CSPAN camera.

"I am not a saintly man," Hurlbert said. "The best I can hope for is to be a good man and do the right things for America."

Tom T. cut a sharp look at Beckley, plainly thinking the senator was making fun of him. The senator's chief of staff held up a hand to counsel patience. All would be well.

Hurlbert continued, "If it hadn't been for my mother and father and the minister of the church we all went to every Sunday, I don't know if I'd even be a good man. I might be someone who doesn't even believe in God. I would never have known Jesus and my soul would be lost to eternal damnation. I wouldn't even know what was in store for me until it was too late and eternal fires were consuming me with pain that would never be extinguished."

Beckley thought his boss had started off well.

You didn't know better, you'd think he'd meant every word he'd said.

Hurlbert continued, "I reflect on how lucky I was, how lucky my family was, to have Preacher Curtiss show us the way to find heaven. We were lucky because he was the only man of God for thirty miles in any direction, and as hard as my father worked his farm, he didn't have the time, the money or the energy to find us another church. I shudder to think what would have become of us without Preacher Curtiss.

That was a lie. Hurlbert had grown up in a setting of minor wealth.

"That fearful thought came to my mind when I heard about Reverend Burke Godfrey dying — after the federal government sent the army in to take him out of his church."

That was another lie, of course. Godfrey had been snatched from his office building.

Had Godfrey claimed sanctuary in a house of worship, he would have presented Mather Wyman with a much stickier problem than he had by raising his own paramilitary force.

Ignoring the facts was no problem for Bobby Beckley. His political strategy was simplicity itself: Lie to the gullible. If that didn't work, lie some more. All you had to do to win an election was deceive more people than the other guy did, and it wasn't like you were dealing with a crowd of critical thinkers.

Ask the yahoos their opinion on any important issue and most of them would begin their responses with the same two words, "I feel." Feel not think. Thinking was hard work. They'd put all that behind them the moment they got out of school, if they'd even bothered trying to think in the classroom.

Hurlbert went on, "Where would I have been if the government had taken Preacher Curtiss from my mother, my father and me? I still might have done well in school. I might still have been the first person in my family lucky enough to graduate from college. But what sense of purpose would my life have had if I didn't know God?"

Hearing those words, not just reading them on a page, Bobby thought he might have laid it on a little thick there. The man was a *politician* after all. A lot of people would think a pest exterminator had a higher calling.

Still, Hurlbert was delivering a far better performance than Beckley would have thought possible less than half an hour ago. Tom T. was watching the senator closely, too. He appeared to be hanging on his every word. For that matter — and not necessarily a good thing — so was Senator Kalman, sitting in the presiding officer's chair.

She had taken a notepad and pen in hand and was making notes as her colleague spoke. Beckley didn't doubt for a minute that she had copied down the lies he'd written and Hurlbert had voiced about the army grabbing Godfrey.

Hurlbert continued, "Of course, I might have found God's word in the Bible whether I stayed home or went off to college. In fact, I did take the Bible that Momma and Daddy gave me when I went off to school. I would read it in private moments, whenever I felt myself in danger of taking a wrong turn."

That was fiction, too, but who could refute what someone did in his private moments?

"What has me worried now," Hurlbert said, "is if we were to reelect Patricia Grant or elect Mather Wyman as president, how do we know either of them wouldn't send the army after any minister, preacher or priest who got on the wrong side of them? If they can bring low a mighty figure like Reverend Burke Godfrey, how could any man of the cloth hold his ground and cleave to scripture?

"That thought is terrifying in itself, but what might follow could be far worse. If the government comes for our ministers, preachers and priests, how long will it be before Washington tries to take our *bibles* from us?"

That was where Bobby Beckley had stopped writing.

Where Senator Howard Hurlbert should have left things.

Even though he'd stuck priests in there with ministers and preachers when Bobby had left the Catholics out in the cold.

But no, goddamnit. Howard fucking Hurlbert had to leave *his* mark on the speech.

He said, "You might think all this is just the fear of a simple country boy, a cotton field Christian, but you mark my words, if the government comes for my bible, they'll soon come for your Torah and your Koran, too."

Your Torah and your Koran? Jesus! Beckley felt like someone just set his hair on fire.

Then Tom T. leaned over and told him. "I like your boy's style but we've got to get him some new material."

As Tom T. Wright was their only hope of landing a billionaire underwriter — and because Bobby hated it when any dumbass politician fucked up one of his speeches — the chief of staff nodded and said, "Damn right we do."

White House Press Room

In that afternoon's briefing, Press Secretary Aggie Wu executed the president's strategy to rebut Senator Hurlbert's claim that the government would soon be confiscating people's bibles.

She told the newsies, "In a moment of apparent hysteria, the senior senator from Mississippi, Howard Hurlbert, suggested today that the federal government might seize bibles from every Christian home in America. The president kindly requests everyone here to check the nightstand drawer of the next hotel you visit. See if there's a bible in it. If there is, all is well. Because even the federal government is smart enough to go after easy pickings first. If your favorite hotels still have their bibles, you can rest easy the one you have at home is safe, too."

The reporters, secular bastards that they were, laughed.

Anticipating a possible trouble point, Aggie added, "If someone starts stealing hotel bibles, we ask that the FBI be contacted. The culprits will be found."

Fair warning to anyone with dirty tricks in mind.

McGill Investigations, Inc. — Georgetown

McGill asked Special Agent Elspeth Kendry to step into his office and close the door.

He asked her to sit and offered her a soft drink.

She sat but declined the drink, regarding McGill with some suspicion.

Thinking she wasn't going to like whatever came next.

McGill said, "Would you mind if I ask you about the confrontation you were part of in Jordan?"

McGill had taken the time to read the personnel file on his new bodyguard.

She'd helped break up a counterfeiting ring in the Middle East.

Elspeth relaxed and said, "You mean the gunfight?"

"Yes."

"I don't mind," she said. "You want to know how it feels to get shot at or to kill someone?"

"Margaret Sweeney and I have both been shot. Her wound was more serious than mine."

"So it's killing someone you want to know about."

McGill said, "It was two someones, wasn't it?"

"Yes, it was. Might have been three if I'd been faster reloading. So what do you want to know, the in-the-moment experience or what comes afterward?"

McGill said, "I've been in some tense situations. I know you do what you have to, reflexively, if you want to walk away. But I've never killed anyone. What thoughts are you left with?"

"Don't you mean what regrets or at least *second* thoughts?"

"However you want to describe it."

Elspeth leaned forward. "My dad was a tough kid from Providence, Rhode Island. He caught a few breaks and got an appointment to West Point. The army showed him how to put all his energy to good use. My mother is Iranian by birth, Baha'i by faith. She had to be tougher than my dad just to survive."

Elspeth smiled.

"All this is the long way of saying I was raised not to take crap off anyone. Except for Mom, Dad and superior officers. When it comes to bad guys with guns … may I speak freely?"

McGill nodded.

"Fuck them. I shot those bastards before they could shoot me. My only regret was not being quicker seating that second magazine. That's what wakes me up shaking some nights. What if being too slow had cost me my life?"

"So you practiced," McGill said. "Now you can change clips no sweat."

Elspeth said, "In practice, sure. When people are shooting at me, who knows?"

McGill persisted. "No qualms about the men you killed?"

"None," Elspeth said. "Better them than me. But then having been in tight spots you already know that."

McGill did.

But he hadn't had to take a life to save his own.

Yet.

***

After thanking Elspeth for her candor and letting her return to the outer office, McGill called FBI Deputy Director Byron DeWitt.

McGill told him, "I've been thinking: If Damon Todd and his pals should decide not to seek shelter with one of Todd's special friends, he'll likely pay cash for a place to stay."

DeWitt agreed. "That or barter is the way the underground economy works."

"Would it be possible for the FBI to check with real estate agents around the country, the ones who rent houses, to see how many cash deals they've made? And were any of those deals made with guys matching the descriptions of the people we want?"

The deputy director considered the dimensions of the task. "I think we have the people and processing power to handle that. What if the bad guys bought a house or rented an apartment?"

McGill thought about that. "They might buy a house if they could do it inconspicuously. I don't see an apartment. They'd want more privacy."

"A house then, one that's out of the way," DeWitt said.

"Not in the middle of nowhere. Maybe in a city. If they have to run, they'll want some sort of cover."

"Forests make good hiding places," DeWitt said. "Mountains and ravines, too."

"Yeah, but if they start out by hunkering down in some remote place that means they're thinking of hiding not hunting."

"Good point. But maybe what they want right now is a place to rest and plan. Let us grow disinterested."

"Is that how Chairman Mao would do it?"

DeWitt said, "He went for the countryside first, then the cities."

"Split the difference," McGill said. "Maybe a city, maybe a wilderness area. But somewhere that offers some kind of concealment."

"That sounds more like doubling than splitting."

"I'm not being too big a pain in the ass, am I?" McGill asked.

"Just big enough," DeWitt said.

McGill laughed.

An FBI big shot with a sense of humor.
What would they think of next?

Office of the Press Secretary

Aggie Wu was doing her daily performance review — how the newsies had behaved and whether she'd handled them fairly — when her secretary said Ethan Judd was on the line.

Like everyone else in Washington, Aggie had been stunned when Sir Edbert Bickford had hired Judd. She figured it was a publicity move. The placement of a fig leaf of respectable journalism on the burlesque queen figure of WorldWide News.

As a fig leaf, though, Aggie thought you couldn't do better than Ethan Judd. She remembered sitting through a lecture he'd given at Medill. He'd made her proud she had decided to become a journalist. She wasn't so sure how the great man felt about press secretaries.

She took the call anyway.

"Mr. Judd, this is Aggie Wu. It's a pleasure to talk to you."

"Don't you mean talk to me again?"

"Sir?"

"When I spoke at Northwestern, you came up to me afterward and introduced yourself."

He remembered that? After what, eighteen years?

"Yes, I did," Aggie said. "That was a long time ago, and I'm sure you've had many J-students compliment you over the years. I can't imagine why you'd remember me."

Judd laughed. "You didn't compliment me. You told me I got two facts wrong in a recent column. I checked and you were right on one of them; the other was more open to interpretation. I meant to send a thank you note, but it got lost with so many other good intentions."

God, he was right. She remembered now. She'd corrected one of the giants of her time.

Aggie was glad he couldn't see her blush.

"Mr. Judd, my manners have improved greatly since those days."

"That's a shame."

It was Aggie's turn to laugh. "Not that I can't lash the crowd I face every day."

"Much better," Judd said.

"How may I help you, sir?"

"I'd like to do an hour-long interview with the president."

Patricia Darden Grant had never done an interview with WWN, not as a candidate, not as president. She'd come right out and said it wasn't a news organization, it was a propaganda organ. If anything, her distaste for Sir Edbert's crown jewel had grown over the years.

The feeling was mutual.

WWN had been expected to be one of the reelection campaign's biggest foes.

Until Sir Edbert had shocked the world and hired Ethan Judd.

He said, "Left you speechless, Ms. Wu?"

"Yes, but you shouldn't have. Why else would you have called?"

"You'll pass my request on to the president?"

"I will, but I can't make any promises."

"I wasn't expecting any. All I ask is that the president watches what I accomplish at WWN. If there come's a time when she feels it has become a forum for objective news, I'll be ready to do the interview at a moment's notice."

"I'll tell her, Mr. Judd. I've enjoyed talking with you, again."

He told her, "Feel free to let me know of any new mistakes."

Barcadere Marina — Grand Cayman Island

Jackie Richmond found a floppy hat, the kind military guys wore in movies, on *Irish Grace*. With ten thousand dollars of Carina Linberg's money in his pocket, he didn't think she'd even notice losing the hat. Wearing the hat over his sunglasses wasn't much of a disguise but it would let him blend in with half the other tourists on the island. Jackie took care to lock the cabin as he left the boat.

Wouldn't want just anybody making himself at home.

He went to the marina office and rented a thirty-five foot slip, paid cash for three days. The lady at the desk asked to see his ID and he brought out his Jackie Richmond driver's license. It had his picture on it, but the woman didn't ask him to take off the hat and glasses for a comparison. People hated giving cash back once they had it in hand.

She did ask, "You're renting the slip for a boat you've hired?"

"Right."

"You're sure you have the footage right?"

Jackie frowned.

"The slip will be big enough for the boat?" the lady clarified.

"It's a Whaler, thirty-two feet."

The woman smiled. "You're fine then. Is the boat coming from another country?"

"No, it's at this other place here on the island. Docked on a canal. I just thought your place looks nicer, you know, safer."

"Grand Cayman as a whole is quite safe, but we appreciate your business. Would you like a courtesy ride to meet your captain. I assume he's with his Whaler."

"Right. Yeah, that'd be great. Thank you."

She handed him a diagram of the marina and marked his slip with an X.

She told him if he waited outside a driver would be with him presently.

He said, "Thanks again."

He went outside and a minute later a kid driving a Jeep with a canvas top pulled up, took him where he wanted to go, didn't feel the need to talk. Jackie tipped him ten bucks. Kid smiled and took off.

Jackie spotted Cap'n Thurlow's boat right where the SOB had left it. He'd worried if the cops held Thurlow longer than the no good snitch had paid for his slip rental, the boatyard would impound the Whaler. Maybe chain and padlock it to the dock or something.

Not so far. Jackie paid for an extra three days rental at that place, too.

Lull people into thinking he was legit.

This office was manned by an old guy who was watching a replay of a soccer game. The guy stopped his video and like everyone else in the world was happy to have someone give him money. Before Jackie could get out of the office the TV was back on.

Guy had forgotten all about him.

He went to the Whaler and stepped aboard. If anyone asked what he was doing, he'd say he thought he dropped his wallet on the boat. He was the guy who chartered it; just ask the old man in the office.

Nobody said boo to him. He used a screwdriver and wire cutters he'd taken from a took kit on *Irish Grace* and hot-wired the ignition. The twin outboard engines fired. He untied the lines, got behind the wheel, dropped the twin props into the water and putt-putted out to sea. All ahead slow.

The ocean, thank God, was as flat as a pit boss' stare. But seeing the immensity of all that water in front him, not having anyone to back him up, sent a shiver through Jackie. Made him ask himself what the hell a car thief was doing out there.

The answer came right back at him — he'd just become a *boat* thief, that's what. He'd given himself a chance to stay a free man, and if he was lucky he'd get even with two guys who'd fucked him over, Cap'n Thurlow and that prick from Baltimore.

There had to be *some* way to get his four hundred thousand back.

How, he had no idea. He'd have to play everything by ear.

Whatever he did, though, he would go all out.

Let all the other assholes worry about him.

A horn sounded. So loud and so close it sounded like a goddamn *train* bearing down on him. He about shit. Whipping his head around all he saw coming his way was a freaking little motor boat, couldn't be more than twelve feet long with one dinky outboard motor. Guy driving the boat swerved around him. Gave another blast of that fucking horn — a Chihuahua sounding like a Rottweiler — and threw him the finger, too.

Jackie was about to curse the prick right back. Two thoughts stopped him. For all he knew, the other guy might have a gun on him. If that wasn't enough, he had the feeling he'd probably fucked up. The other guy must've had the right of way to get so ticked off.

Shit, he'd been able to steal the boat and get it going, but he didn't know jack about the right way to operate it when another boat was around.

All he could think was go slow and let the other assholes go first.

That's what he did, all the way back to the marina where *Irish Grace* was docked.

Eastbound Stevenson Expressway — Chicago, Illinois

The Buick Enclave carrying Damon Todd, Arn Crosby and Olin Anderson breezed along in the lull after the morning rush. Crosby was driving. He stuck the needle on the speedometer exactly at the speed limit and kept it there.

Back at the house in Ottawa, Crosby had looked over his shoulder and told Todd, "I know how to drive to avoid attention from the cops or anyone else. So if you don't see a plane coming in for a strafing run, keep any backseat comments to yourself, okay?"

Todd replied, "I'll count out-of-state license plates."

Anderson laughed at that. Even Crosby grinned. They set off, three good friends.

To outward appearances, Damon Todd was doing nothing more than looking out his window and watching the world go by, but he knew something was wrong. Crosby and Anderson had changed. They'd gone from being submissive to borderline assertive. They were no longer apprehensive that something terrible might happen to them if they questioned Todd's judgments or his decisions.

With the loss of that dread, Todd was the one who felt threatened. There had been no overt threats or gestures, but he thought the two former CIA operatives were plotting against him. They might have moved against him already if he hadn't told them of his plan to probe the security cordon surrounding James J. McGill's family in Evanston, Illinois.

The three of them had sat at the kitchen table of the house in Ottawa and Anderson had asked, "What're you thinking, Doc? Doing something nasty to bring the man on the run?"

Crosby said, "As a rule, we don't kill children."

"There were those two little shits up in the Hindu Kush," Anderson reminded him.

"True, but they were shooting at us with AKs. You pick up the gun …"

"You die by the gun," Anderson finished the thought.

They both saw the unspoken question on Todd's face.

Crosby told him, "We expect to go down fighting, too."

Anderson added, "You hang with us, Doc, you better plan on a violent end, too."

"What if we just go our separate ways now?" Todd asked. "Live quietly. Make it cost-ineffective to look for us, as you told me before."

"You know the problem with that," Crosby told him.

Anderson pointed to the research notes Todd had made. "That's not a retirement plan you've got there, Doc. That's an outline for vengeance. Think about it. From what Arn and I have seen, you'd have no problem tapping people for enough money to carry you comfortably until you're a hundred years old, but that's not what you want."

Crosby said, "You want to get McGill. If he was just some mope, okay, you could do it. Probably on your own. But McGill is good. He's had training. He has resources. You're not going to get him without our help."

"My money says you've got a few more people you'd like to

pop, too," Anderson said.

Todd couldn't help but keep Daryl Cheveyo from coming to mind. The psychiatrist who'd been his first contact with the CIA could have — should have — advocated more strongly for Todd to be allowed to join the Agency. If he'd done that, if Todd had been hired the way he should have been —

He saw Crosby and Anderson grinning like jackals.

They knew exactly what he'd been thinking.

Anderson said, "So there is another guy who needs killing. But tell us, Doc, is there some babe who's done you wrong, too?"

Chana Lochlan, he thought.

She'd been one of the first young people he'd ever helped. He'd crafted her so beautifully. She'd succeeded so wonderfully. She'd loved him in return — right up until the time she'd hired that bastard McGill to —

He saw Crosby and Anderson staring at him.

They were learning too much about him.

He told them, "I hear old age is a bitch."

They both laughed. Anderson told him, "We used to say that every time we started a new mission."

"Just our luck we kept coming back alive," Crosby said.

Approaching Chicago, they saw the skyline appear from forty miles out. Less than an hour later, they came to the lakefront. Crosby turned onto northbound Lake Shore Drive. The boats had been taken out of the city's harbors for the season but people were walking and running in Grant Park on the unseasonably mild late autumn day.

Chances were, Todd thought, on a pretty day like this, the people James J. McGill loved would be out and about too. Evanston was another thirty-minutes north in light traffic.

The mantle of fatalism Crosby and Anderson had draped over Todd began to settle more comfortably on his shoulders. He probably shouldn't have expected to live a long life. Everyone in his family had died relatively young. Why should he endure?

If he were able to take down McGill, Cheveyo and …

He still didn't know what to do about Chana. She should be made to understand the pain she had caused him, but he wasn't sure he could cause her death. If he saw her again, he'd probably fall in love with her all over again.

But McGill and Cheveyo, Crosby and Anderson, too, he'd be greatly pleased if they all died before he did. The two rogue CIA men thought they'd outsmarted him.

He'd have to prove them wrong.

George Town Harbor — Grand Cayman Island

Welborn had learned the name of the maulers' yacht, *Carcharodon,* and its anchorage, George Town Harbor, from Willa Pennyman. Who'd heard it from her cousin Eddie. Who'd seen the yacht arrive and had picked up Harry, Kurt and Wally at the harbor shortly after their arrival on Grand Cayman.

The three thugs knew they'd been betrayed, just as that fucking guy, Jackie Richmond, who kept getting away from their bosses, had been betrayed by the boat captain he'd hired. The whole goddamn island was full of snitches.

It wasn't going to be any fun for Harry, Kurt and Wally to go home and report that they'd failed. Fact was, it damn well might be fatal. The bosses wanted Jackie Richmond dead so bad it made their teeth hurt.

Being male chauvinists, they blamed Jackie rather than Alice for their troubles.

A platoon of the RCIPS's finest saw to it that Harry, Kurt and Wally were marched onto their craft and told they were no longer welcome in any of the Cayman Islands. Would never be welcome again. Would be locked up good and proper for a long time if they ever came back.

Commissioner Peck handed Harry a written order to that effect.

Peck asked, "Do you understand what I've just told you?"

Harry nodded, but said nothing.

He looked at Welborn. Pegged him for an American. Some

kind of cop, too.

He had to be looking for that prick Jackie, too. But hadn't found him yet.

Or there'd have been no reason to give him and the boys the boot.

You never knew, Harry thought.

All the cops chasing Jackie, he still might give them the slip.

If the little bastard found a way to fly off the island, Harry and his friends were screwed. But if Jackie left on the water ... hell, there wasn't anything short of a cigarette boat that could outrun them.

Commissioner Peck asked Harry if he needed to top off his fuel tank.

"No," Harry said.

"Have you left anyone ashore?"

"No."

"Right then, off with you."

Welborn stepped forward and whispered in Peck's ear. He nodded and told Harry, "I'm afraid we'll need just a minute more of your time."

The commissioner waved a sergeant and a sturdy constable forward, "Please go below. See if there's anyone else aboard. If there is bring him or her up on deck for a chat."

Harry glared at Peck. And Welborn.

"Frightful, the authority the police have in some places," the commissioner agreed.

The two cops went below, returned moments later shaking their heads.

Within minutes, the yacht was underway, leaving the harbor.

Once clear of slow-moving traffic, the *Carcharodon* rose on its hydrofoils and raced away, quickly becoming a speck in the distance.

"Predatory beast, that craft," Peck said. "Strange the owner didn't bother to complete the name."

"Pardon?" Welborn said.

The commissioner turned to look at his guest. "You weren't offered Latin in school?"

"Sure, I was, but I went with flower arranging instead."

Peck smiled and said, *"Carcharodon Carcharias.* Jagged-tooth one. Better known as the great white shark."

Welborn thought about that. Wondered if great whites were known to circle back.

The Oval Office

More often than not when McGill stopped by the Oval Office, Edwina Byington, the president's secretary, told him the president was busy with affairs of state and he'd have to come back later or wait until late at night when she returned to the residence. It could be trying to have to share your wife with the whole country on a good day, and the whole world on a bad day. McGill tried to keep a good attitude. If he had it tough, Patti had it far worse.

When she'd first told him she was going to run for president, he'd said, "Who better?"

That was before he'd known better. Now, having been through the drill for three years, he ran hot and cold about Patti's job. He'd been honest in telling the newsies he couldn't imagine anyone doing a better job. At the risk of feeling unpatriotic, though, he thought Mather Wyman might do a good enough job.

If only the country wasn't so damn divided, he might even secretly wish for an upset victory by Wyman so he and Patti could retire to private lives. Not that he wanted to stop working, not for a few more years anyway. When he wanted to amuse himself, he imagined continuing to work cases as a private investigator and having Patti work for him.

That'd be a hoot, having a former president, movie star and model as his secretary.

"Mr. McGill? Sir?"

Edwina's voice cut through his reverie. He looked at her.

"Yes?" McGill said.

"The president will see you now."

"No waiting?"

"I suppose the president might find something to do if you'd like to keep me company."

McGill smiled. "Would you like to go to work for me, Edwina, after you're done here at the White House?"

"I don't think I could stand the excitement, sir."

"You'd probably have the time to write your memoirs on the job."

Edwina thought about that. "Possibly, I'll reconsider."

McGill grinned and went into the Oval Office to see his wife. She came out from behind her desk and gave him a hug and a kiss and another hug. McGill didn't remember saving the Republic that day, which led him to wonder …

"Did I do something right?"

Patti looked at him and said, "You do so many things right, I don't have the time to tell you."

"Tonight then. We'll take the phone off the hook."

The president laughed at the idea. "Wouldn't that be great?"

She sat on one of the office sofas and patted the cushion to her right. McGill took his cue and sat next to his wife. He knew Patti's affection was real, but he also was sure she had something important to tell him.

"I need to find a private investigator, but it can't be you," the president said.

"And it can't be one of the many people with badges who work for you?"

The president shook her head. McGill began to understand.

"It's something political. I'm too close to you. That means Sweetie is out, too."

The president nodded.

"Is this something that could get a guy in trouble?" McGill asked. "Hauled before Congress or worse?"

Patti said, "It would be best if you could find someone highly competent who is quite close to retirement, but there would be no need to do anything illegal."

"The money would be good enough to offset any risk?"

The president nodded again.

"If I'm going to sell this job to someone, I'll have to know what it is."

Patti scooted closer to McGill and spoke softly. "Galia has a spy in Howard Hurlbert's office. The spy's husband is Bobby Beckley, Hurlbert's chief of staff. Beckley likes to beat his wife; he used to beat his ex-wife as well."

McGill's jaw tightened. He hated bullies. Wife beaters ran a dead heat with child beaters at the top of his list.

"You want proof Beckley's a monster?" McGill asked. "Most of these bastards work behind closed doors, especially the white-collar creeps."

"Can it be done?" Patti asked.

"The question is, can it be done in time? Any one beating might be fatal. A hard slap from a strong man can break a woman's neck. I know someone who can do the job, but getting a little help from inside might be the thing that saves a life."

"What kind of help?" Patti asked.

"Could be as simple as leaving the curtains open and making sure there's enough light in a room for clear pictures to be taken. If that's not possible and the woman feels she's going to catch a beating when she gets home, she has to provoke the guy to go off in public. In any case, she has to be in on the plan, willing to do as much as she can to help, if you want the best chance for her to survive."

"I do. I'll talk with Galia. I'll let you know. If we go forward, you'll have to find a way to handle things confidentially."

McGill nodded. "No comebacks."

The way to do that, McGill knew, was to hire someone with whom his communications would be shielded by law. A lawyer. Putnam Shady came to mind. The late speaker of the House of Representatives, Derek Geiger, had tried to hire Putnam to be his firewall for a scheme to consolidate the lobbying community in

Washington under his thumb.

That hadn't worked out because Putnam had talked to the speaker about the job only as a ruse to thwart his plan. If Putnam were to help McGill, he'd be doing a good deed, and if he ever thought to violate his professional code of ethics and McGill's confidence, he'd know it would cost him Sweetie's love and companionship.

McGill was positive Putnam wouldn't risk that. So the plan would be to have Putnam hire Brad Lewis, a former colleague of McGill's on the CPD, currently working on a private license in Chicago and, in his sixties, somewhere near retirement. Brad might have a suspicion of who was hiring him, but he wouldn't know and wouldn't ask.

Putnam would know, but he couldn't be made to tell.

McGill thought it was a good thing he had an honest nature because he might have made a successful criminal.

Patti put a hand on his arm, bringing him back to the moment. "There's something else I've been thinking about. I wanted to ask you first, before I acted."

"Okay," McGill said, wondering what might be coming.

"I'm thinking of reopening the house in Winnetka."

The lakefront estate she'd shared with Andy Grant, where Andy had been killed by Erna Godfrey. McGill knew the damage that had been done to the house had been repaired long ago. Even so, neither of them had set foot in the place since the night Andy had died.

McGill would have been less surprised if Patti had told him she'd decided to sell the place.

Patti read his feelings accurately. "I know, when the idea first came to me it was a surprise."

"You think it would be … helpful?" he asked.

"Yes. What happened to me in the hospital, coming closer to dying than either of us ever would have expected, made me start reviewing things, if only subconsciously at first. Staying away from where Andy died was a way of denying that he was gone. How can I do that now, after Erna Godfrey told me she saw Andy with Jesus?"

Patti's eyes started to fill. McGill put an arm around her shoulders.

"I think," she said, "we could honor his memory better by filling the house with life rather than letting it sit empty and, who knows, we might need a new place to live before too long."

"Whatever you want," McGill told Patti.

She kissed him again.

"Are you going to let Erna have her prison ministry?" he asked.

"I think I am," Patti said.

Capital Yacht Club — Washington, D.C.

Hugh Collier saw that Uncle Edbert's yacht, *Poseidon,* didn't fit into the club's largest docking space — two hundred and twenty feet — by more than a whisker. He wondered if Uncle had specified the length to the Amels Shipyard in Vissingen, Holland. It was like the old boy to have his life tailored just so.

Hugh turned to Ellie Booker and asked, "Well, what do you think?"

"The boat?" she asked. "Looks like a wedding cake that got caught in the wind."

Hugh laughed, thinking of how Uncle would react to such a description of one of his favorite toys. Despite having finally struck a deal with Ellie, she was still in a bit of a pout. He'd learned through WWN's publishing contacts that Ellie's book deal had been put on hold. The canny souls in New York publishing were waiting to see if there was going to be a legal action, civil or criminal, captioned *U.S. v. Sir Edbert Bickford.*

If so, the publishing world's preferred outcome would be one in which Ellie got to stick the knife into the media mogul in a courtroom. That would result in a blockbuster book deal and a Hollywood bidding war for the movie rights. The dustcover for the book would be an illustration of Ellie on the witness stand pointing a damning finger at the accused.

Problem for Ellie was, she didn't know dick about Sir Edbert's bribes to politicians and cops around the world. What she knew was how he and Hugh had screwed her at Salvation's Path, leaving her alone in the middle of a pack of religious madmen. That had been a best-selling concept, too. Until goddamn Burke Godfrey had to go and die, and his jailbird wife decided to get all holy and forgiving about the whole thing.

Erna's refusal to look for payback had been good for Ellie in one way. She was no longer sweating the possibility a prosecutor might be looking into her story that she'd conked Godfrey in self-defense. But the lack of Godfreys as antagonists sure as hell made her story yesterday's news. Sit tight, she was told. If there was some way she could take down Sir Edbert at trial, she'd be back in business.

Fucking vulture publishers.

Then Hugh had dropped by her condo unannounced with a contract for another book deal: what it was like to be a woman in television news, loyal to an embattled media titan — Sir Edbert — in his darkest hour. Hugh had heard, of course, that the bottom had fallen out on the market for Ellie's name on a hardcover tome. He no longer offered multiples of any other offers she might come by someday.

Still, the contract he had with him would pay a million-dollar advance.

Other than the dollar amount, there was a curious absence of detail to the contract. It lacked any completion date for a manuscript to be submitted. Not only that, it didn't mention the number of words for the floor or ceiling of the first draft. The only requirement was that the tone of the book must be in no way disrespectful of or unflattering to its subject, Sir Edbert Bickford.

And it was signed by the great man himself

Ellie said to Hugh, "Tone, huh? So it'd be acceptable to say he's the nicest sonofabitch you'd ever want to meet?"

"Probably wouldn't make it past the lawyers," Hugh said.

"They're the ones going to edit this thing?"

"A million dollars ought to buy some authorial forbearance."

He was right, the money was nothing to take lightly. At least not for her just then. Out of a job with no book deal. Christ!

Then she had an idea, one she certainly wasn't going to share with Hugh.

He saw her smile, though. That encouraged him enough to ask her to accompany him to the *Poseidon*. He thought she might like to see how the truly rich traveled.

"Bullshit. You just want that old bastard to focus his anger on me."

Hugh tried his best to look innocent. It wasn't good enough.

"What's the bad news you've got for him?" Ellie asked.

Hugh took an envelope out of a coat pocket.

"The Department of Justice has advised Uncle that they've opened an investigation into his business practices both in this country and internationally."

"That's why he's on his boat? He's going to skip on the feds? He must be nuts."

That was when Ellie thought it might be a good idea to accompany Hugh. Sir Edbert couldn't personally cause her any harm. He tried, she'd kick his ass. She didn't think he'd sic some seagoing thug on her. Might be wrong about that, but it was an acceptable risk. What was a much better bet was the old shit would lose his temper and say something incriminating in front of her.

That would be something she could testify about in court.

Which would fit neatly with the idea inspired by the contract Hugh had offered her. Sir Edbert's publishing company was offering her a million dollars while demanding nothing specific in return for its money. Some people might consider that a bribe.

Better yet, she knew where she could take the bribe angle to amp up the publicity.

To Ethan Judd, the new face of Sir Edbert's news organization.

How would that be for sweet? She tossed the contract Hugh had brought her on a pile of unopened mail. Let him think she was unimpressed.

But she told him, "Sure, let's go see your uncle's boat."

Now, that she was about to go aboard, she was beginning to get nervous. Her goddamn old man had been in the Navy and the pictures she'd seen of the ship he'd served on didn't look as big as this one. And wouldn't you know it, the rich old bastard himself had just appeared at the railing of the yacht.

He wasn't smiling either.

Fuck it, Ellie thought. She'd told Hugh she wouldn't forgive him and his uncle.

What she would do was con the both of them.

Stick it to them from the witness stand just the way those publishing assholes wanted.

She smiled at Sir Edbert. Called up to him, "Hey, it's me again."

Aboard *Irish Grace*
Barcadere Marina, Grand Cayman Island

Welborn Yates had a fighter pilot's eyesight, good for spotting even the smallest details in the larger environment. In this case, he noticed scratch marks on the lock of the cabin door to Carina Linberg's boat. He hadn't caused them. Fitting a key neatly into a lock had never been a problem for him. The scratches hadn't been there before, so …

He called the number of the Ritz-Carlton and asked for Ms. Linberg's suite.

She answered in a gruff tone, "Hello."

"I've called at a bad time?" Welborn asked.

He thought maybe he'd interrupted an intimate moment.

"I was really going strong, working out an idea for my story."

"Why don't you make a note and call me back?"

"Why don't I keep writing and *you* call me back in a few hours?"

Writers, Welborn thought.

"I could do that, but I think someone might have broken into your boat." Thinking things through, he said, "Someone might even be below deck right now."

"Damn!"

"By all means, jot down some notes, but then you might want to come by."

"You'll be there?"

Welborn thought about that. Carina's gun was inside the cabin. If there was an intruder below deck, and he'd found the gun, he might not want to leave any witnesses to his misdeeds.

"I'll be nearby," he told Carina.

He stepped off the boat onto the jetty and headed toward the marina office.

He sat on a bench next to the office and called Willa Pennyman. "Any word on that fellow I'm looking for?"

"You sure he's not a ghost? Nobody's seen him anywhere, and *lots* of people are looking."

"Keep at it," Welborn said.

But looking out at *Irish Grace,* he thought he knew where Linley Boland might be.

As wonderful as Welborn's vision was, he couldn't see through the cabin cruiser that was docked between him and the thirty-two foot Whaler on which Jackie Richmond lounged wearing his hat and sunglasses. Cap'n Thurlow, searching high and low in every marina on the island for his boat, happened upon a much better vantage point.

Running along the jetty, pointing a finger at Jackie as he sat in the captain's chair, the cap'n said, "You poxy son of a blind whore, you stole my boat."

He stopped just short of boarding, though, when instinct told him a boat thief could be a dangerous person. He looked around, hoping to see a cop, but whenever you needed one ... There wasn't even another boater in sight.

Jackie saw they were alone, too. He said, "I didn't steal any-thing. Just moved it to a nicer location. After you sold me out to the cops. Anybody should be calling people names, it's me."

Hearing that his treachery had been discovered, Cap'n Thurlow started to back off. Jackie didn't want him to run. He wanted him to come aboard. The cap'n drove the boat way better than he did. What the prick needed was a reason to think he was the top dog.

Jackie tossed the cap'n the long-bladed knife he used to cut up fish.

Thurlow caught it neatly, surprised at first but then wearing a big smile.

"You must be crazy," he said stepping aboard the Whaler, "but I'm gonna cut you some anyway and then turn you into the cops. There's a hundred thousand dollar reward for you."

That prick from Baltimore, Jackie thought. He *had* to be some kind of cop.

But who the hell offered that kind of reward for a car thief?

Nobody, he thought. Then it all came clear to him. A young guy who was a cop tracking him all the way down to Grand Cayman? There was only one thing he'd ever done that would make somebody chase him so far and offer so much money for his hide.

Killing those three Air Force guys in that goddamn accident in Vegas.

Fuck, it *was* an accident.

What'd they expect, someone like him was going to stick around?

Say, "Oops, sorry."

Catching the sun glint off the knife blade, snapped Jackie back into the moment at hand. Cap'n Thurlow was coming his way, intent on making good on his promise to cut him some.

The guy was no end of a scumbag.

Jackie took out the .38 he'd stolen from *Irish Grace* and hidden under his thigh. Seeing the gun backed the cap'n off real fast.

Jackie told him, "Stop. Get your ass up here and drive. Maybe I'll let you live."

The cap'n hesitated and then started forward.

Still had that big knife in his hands. Was looking at how little

Jackie's gun was. Had to be thinking maybe he'd have a chance here after all. He got in the first cut and —

Jackie said, "This is just an itty-bitty .38. Might not kill you. But I'll be shooting for your balls. Sure to ruin your love life if nothing else."

The cap'n couldn't keep a look of fear off his face.

Jackie told him, "Put the knife down easy, and get up here and drive."

Cap'n Thurlow did as he was told.

Once the cap'n had his hands on the wheel, Jackie slipped past him and took a seat in the stern.

The cap'n asked, "Where you want me to go? Back to Cayman Brac?"

"No," Jackie said. No point giving the cap'n home-island advantage. There was still time left on the slip he'd paid for on the canal. He told the cap'n to head back there. It'd be as good a place as any to hide out.

On the way out of the harbor, Jackie asked Cap'n Thurlow how he knew which boat had the right of way. The cap'n explained that, generally, a boat on your left was supposed to give way; a boat on your right, you were supposed to give way. There weren't any lane markers on the water but there were buoys. The cap'n told him which side of the buoys you were supposed to be on.

Shit, Jackie thought. You knew that stuff, it made everything a lot easier.

He had one more question, and he waited until there were no other boats around to ask. "This boat have the gas to make it to Venezuela?"

Cap'n Thurlow laughed loudly.

Seemed Jackie had asked a dumb question.

But Thurlow laughing so hard let Jackie sneak up behind him and put a round into the cap'n's skull. The guy might not have been entirely dead when Jackie threw him overboard, but he figured drowning or sharks would finish the job. He wiped up the little bit of blood on the boat with an old piece of cloth and tossed that into the sea, too.

He made his way back to the marina on the canal, driving with much more confidence.

Didn't piss off a single boater.

He was disappointed the Whaler couldn't make it to South America.

All that did, though, was make Jackie more determined to get his money back from that prick cop who'd ripped him off.

Welborn had four members of the RCIPS waiting when Carina Linberg showed up at the marina. The cops boarded *Irish Grace* with guns drawn and using Carina's key went below deck. Finding no one aboard, the cops told Carina and Welborn they could come aboard.

Carina didn't report anything missing — to the cops.

After they'd left, she did a more thorough search and told Welborn that ten thousand dollars, her LadySmith .38 and an old boonie hat had been taken. It was mention of the hat that caught Welborn's attention. He asked if it had been Air Force blue.

"What else?" Carina asked. "Did you see it while you were aboard?"

Welborn shook his head. He remembered seeing a guy on a white boat leaving the harbor shortly before Carina arrived. The guy was wearing a blue boonie hat.

"What kind of a white boat?" Carina asked.

Welborn described it.

"A Whaler. Shit. If it had been a sailboat, we could have gone after it."

"How far can a Whaler travel?" Welborn asked.

"Not very, not without refueling."

Welborn nodded. "I think the bastard will be back then."

Carina gave Welborn a long look and said, "You've got something he wants, but you're not going to tell me what it is, are you?"

Welborn smiled and said, "Have to leave something to the writer's imagination."

The Alibi Club — Washington, D.C.

Tom T. Wright, Senator Howard Hurlbert and Bobby Beckley were sitting around a table in a private room, a drink in front of each of them, when Tom T. slapped a check for ten million dollars down on the table. The check faced the senator and his chief of staff so they'd have no trouble getting a good look at the amount tendered. Maybe it was all the zeros but Hurlbert and Beckley took their time reading the check.

The Alibi Club had been founded in 1884. Its name came from the practice of providing members with corroboration to claims of their whereabouts when questioned by their families. Its *stated* founding purpose was to provide mutual improvement, education and enlightenment. It was just the place for what Tom T. had in mind.

Hurlbert and Beckley looked up at Tom T. Maybe it wasn't the amount payable that had stopped them cold. It might have been the fact that the check was unsigned.

"Okay, Tom," Beckley said, "what's the *quid pro quo*? Neither the senator nor I have any children so we can't give you our first born."

The billionaire smiled. "I already raised one boy, as you surely know, so I'm not looking to bring up another child, and before we get to what I want, you should know I'm willing to put another ninety million into the pot. That should go a long way to rounding up the petition signatures the senator will need to get his name on the ballot in all fifty states. Might even be enough to buy TV time in all the big markets."

Beckley said, "In other words, you're going to want as much as you give."

"Fair's fair. I look at Senator Hurlbert's presidential ambitions as a startup venture, something that could pay off for at least eight years and maybe a whole lot longer, if we play our cards right."

"What is it you'd like, Mr. Wright?" Hurlbert asked. "Your own key to the Treasury?"

Tom T. laughed and sipped his drink.

"That what you think I have in mind, Senator? Backing a truck up to the Bureau of Printing and Engraving, filling it with new hundred dollar bills?"

The senator was about to answer when Beckley held up a hand.

He said, "For a hundred million dollars, Tom, we expect you'll want something big."

"Oh, I do. You got that part right, but it's not about me. I've got more money than I'll ever need, and the only person I truly love has even more than me. What I want to do is change a few things. I thought somebody who had the gumption to start a whole new party and name it for my part of the country might be just the man. Now, with the senator acting like all I've come to do is some horse trading, I've got my doubts."

"I apologize," Hurlbert said. "I've gotten too used to the way things are done around here."

Tom T. nodded his acceptance. Beckley stayed focused on the matter at hand.

"How can we help you, Tom?" he asked.

"Start by telling me who you think was the most important politician ever to hold office in the South. You might be tempted to say the senator here, and I'd give you a pass on that, loyalty to your employer and all. But I mean history-book important."

Beckley ran the question through his mind. He felt sure Tom T. meant someone from his home state, Louisiana. Many of the big political names from down there had wound up serving federal time. Only New Jersey and Illinois came close to matching the Bayou State for political corruption. Putting the convicted felons aside, the only big name from Louisiana politics that came to memory was …

"Are you talking about Huey Long, Tom?" Beckley asked.

"I am," he said with a smile.

"He was a Democrat," Hurlbert objected.

Tom T. replied, "And you were a Republican. Things change. The important thing to remember here is that Huey Long was a true *Southerner*. Who better for a True South candidate to liken himself to?"

The senator leaned forward. "Huey Long believed in the *redistribution* of wealth."

"You say that like it's a bad thing, Senator. I'm talking about redistributing a hundred million dollars of *my* money to *your* campaign's interests. I haven't heard you complain about that."

Affronted and stuck for an answer, Hurlbert downed his drink. Beckley pushed his drink over to his boss.

He said to Tom T., "If I remember right, Huey Long wanted to tax corporations during the Depression to relieve poverty and homelessness."

"That's right."

"He wanted the federal government to spend money on public works, build schools and colleges. Provide old age pensions."

"Right again. He was a man of vision, and we know who did all those things: Mr. Franklin D. Roosevelt. Think how different the United States would be today if a Southerner had done all that. We'd be the part of the country everybody looks up to, turns to for leadership."

Hurlbert leaned forward and hissed, "Huey Long was *assassinated*."

Tom T. shrugged. "He was shot just the one time in the belly. Died of it, that's true. But if he'd had a bulletproof vest the way we do today, he'd have been fine. Now, the fella that shot Huey got plugged sixty-two times. I don't think there'd be any helping him."

"How do you feel about social issues?" Beckley asked.

"Ten commandments about cover that for me."

"You'd like to see them taught in school?"

"Sunday school."

"Abortion?"

"Never had one. What I hear is they're no fun at all. Best way to prevent them is to give kids the education and the means to keep girls from getting knocked up."

This time Tom T. raised a hand to keep Beckley from speaking.

"Is there a man at this table who hasn't wanted and had sex with a young lady he'd never care to marry?" The silence that followed was all the answer he needed. "I didn't think so. Now, maybe we all got lucky and those girls didn't get pregnant. Maybe one of them did and she took care of it on her own. Maybe one of us even helped her take care of it.

"When we talk about birth control and abortion, we're talking about burdens that weigh heaviest on women, but all us folks with tallywhackers are involved, too. We kept our peckers in our pants ninety-nine times out of a hundred, the abortion debate would be over. Of course, nobody'd be having any fun except the blue noses, and that's pretty much the way they want it."

Tom T. finished his drink and pocketed his check.

"So, here's what I'm thinking, gentlemen. I'm looking for a southern man of the people. Someone who'll lend a hand to folks in trouble, not give them the back of his hand. I was poor once. I know how much it hurts. I'd have loved to see another Huey Long coming down the road to help my daddy and me. I got lucky and now I'm rich. It's my turn to come down the road to help those as poor as I was. Y'all let me know if you want to be the ones to help me."

Tom T. got to his feet, but he had one last thing to say.

"I do want to thank you for one thing even if you say no. Your idea about starting new political parties, that's a winner. Things don't work out between us, I just might start one of my own. Y'all won't mind if I call it the Real True South Party?"

2

December, 2011
Indiana University — Bloomington, Indiana

"We're going to begin today with an assignment," Sheryl Kimbrough told her class. "The Democratic Party was founded in principle in 1792 and came to be known by its current name in 1828. The Republican Party was founded in 1854. One week from today, I'll expect to see five pages from each of you outlining and analyzing how our two most prominent political parties were regarded by American newspapers when the parties were brand new. Did the only mass communications medium of the time take them seriously? Who were their supporters? Who were their detractors? How much did the journalists of the time rely on truth to advance their points of view and how much bull-puckey did they fling?

"Once you've got all that sorted out, take a look at the new True South Party that Senator Howard Hurlbert has started. See if there are any parallels between how True South is being treated by contemporary media and how the Democrats and Republicans were treated at the times they were new kids on the block. This paper will count for half of your final grade."

A young woman in the front row raised her hand.

"Yes?" Sheryl asked.

"Each of us has the copyright on our papers, right? Because if we do a good job ..." She looked around at her classmates and said, "And I'm sure we all will." That drew laughs, including Sheryl's. "What we'll be turning in to you would also make really cool book proposals."

"I hope you'll mention me in the acknowledgments," Sheryl said, "whichever of you hits it big. You have the copyright on everything you write from the moment you finish writing it. If you wish to sue someone for violating your copyright, however, you have to register your work with the U.S. Copyright Office. You can do that online for a thirty-five dollar fee. If you can manage all that by the deadline I've set, more power to you."

"How do you spell your name again?" the girl in the front row asked. "For the acknowledgement, you know."

Playing along, Sheryl printed her name on the board at the front of the class.

"I have to tell you, though," she said, "that I've already cut a deal with *The Indiana Daily Student.*" The university newspaper. "They've agreed to publish the best papers. If you want your work to appear there, you'll have to consult with them about retaining your rights."

The class went on to discuss whether True South would be the last new party to appear and field candidates before the next election. The students thought there might be one more. They guessed each major party would have serious competitors before the 2016 elections, and by 2020 coalitions of smaller parties might govern Congress in the fashion of a parliamentary system.

By the end of the period, Sheryl was dazzled by the way bright young minds could leap about from one idea to the next. It gave her hope for the future. God help the country if political thinking ever stopped evolving and became —

Static. Adversarial. Dug in. Us against them.

The way it really was outside of university classrooms.

It was enough to depress a saint. That was, someone far closer to the divine than she was. She wondered whether she'd be doing the right thing to cast her Electoral ballot, unthinkingly, the way she'd pledged to do.

On the other hand, if people couldn't be counted on to keep their word, where would we be?

Having no answer to the conundrum, she packed her brief-case. Cassidy was meeting her on campus today. The two of them planned to do some clothes shopping and go to dinner, talking all the while they were together about any number of things. She cherished such times and—

Sheryl heard Cassidy's scream through the closed classroom windows.

She knew that sound from the first time she'd heard it from her baby.

It terrorized her, and then things got so much worse.

The scream was followed by the metallic sounds of a horrible crash.

And more screams.

20° North, 82° West — Caribbean Sea

For a while there, Jackie Richmond thought he was in clover.

Or whatever the hell was the right thing to say when you were out on the water.

Looking at his situation as he'd hunkered down on the Whaler the past few days, he'd considered his goals and his opportunities. What he wanted to do was get to South America and have a good chunk of money to back up his next play. What he needed to do was kidnap Carina Linberg and steal her boat. That or kidnap that fucking cop and hold him for ransom.

If he went with Carina, she'd said her boat could make it to Isla de Margarita, and it would bring a good price even if the buyer knew it was hot. If he kidnapped the cop, that prick would be a lot more trouble. He probably wouldn't have the four hundred grand with him and … fuck that.

Carina, it was. He'd settle up with the cop later. Would *not* forget that guy.

Having made his choice, Jackie took the chance of going out and buying a new disguise. A Landshark Lager baseball cap, a flowered shirt and cargo shorts. But no goddamn sandals. He got a pair of running shoes, in case he had to lay down tracks.

Then he stretched out on the Whaler under a sheen of tanning lotion and deepened the color he already had. Looked like a new man. Fit right in down around Venezuela. Only thing left to do now was to go grab Ms Snoot and her *Irish Grace*.

Damn, he was going to be pissed if she'd gone back to Key West.

All he could do was hope her boat was still in the local marina.

Only it wasn't. He didn't have to go that far.

Irish Grace was anchored at sea. Not too far out. Just a little farther than where he was. Just beyond the coastal boat traffic. Carina Linberg was lying out on top, looking to him like she was naked.

He motored a little closer and saw she had on a real *small* bikini that was just about the color of her own tanned skin. He knew she was no kid but, damn, she'd kept everything right where it belonged. Without making a conscious decision, he kept the Whaler moving closer.

She must've heard the motor because she lifted her head and then got to her feet.

With her back to him, she undid the strings that held her top in place.

Then she turned his way and let the top fall.

Jackie knew right then it had to be a trap. The woman had never taken to him at all. Well, maybe that first day at Mango Mary's when they'd tag-teamed that chump the slavers had sent. They'd gotten along okay that day. Right now, seeing what she was made of, he couldn't help but wonder what it'd be like sailing off with her and staying tight for a good long time.

He moved in a little closer. Got a *good* look. Hoped she'd drop her bottoms.

Maybe it wasn't a trap.

He edged the Whaler closer, sure he could outrun a sailboat.

You know, if someone did try to grab him.

She put her hands on her hips. Daring him to come get her.

God, he was tempted … just looking at her was great.

Touching her would be —

Something he'd never know. That fucking cop came roaring out from behind *Irish Grace* in some kind of big black inner-tube with a monster outboard stuck on the back of it. Jackie did the only thing he could. He opened fire with the LadySmith. He was aiming for the cop, but the black rubber boat was bobbing up and down like a teeter-totter.

Jackie didn't hit the cop, but he put at least two big holes in the inner-tube.

Damn thing started going flat like a blown tire. The cop had to kill his motor or it would have driven him right under the water. Jackie slammed his throttle to full speed and steered around the cop and *Irish Grace*. He wanted to give Carina goddamn Linberg the finger as he passed, but he saw she not only had her top back on, she had a rifle in her hands and looked like —

Shit! She hit the Whaler with her first shot.

Jackie crouched on the far side of the console, steered with one hand and kept going.

He'd gone maybe a quarter mile straight out to sea before he dared to get back in the captain's chair and look behind him.

Goddamnit, *Irish Grace* was chasing him. Didn't look like it was gaining on him, but it was sure as hell keeping up. How the hell could it do that? Then he remembered, the sailboat had a motor, too. With the combination of the sails and the motor, it might be able to keep him in sight.

If the wind picked up, maybe it'd even be able to catch him. No, it definitely would catch him because if the wind rose the sea would, too. No way was Jackie going to try to go fast in big waves. As it was, he couldn't hide around a bend in the road or duck into an alley. He fucking hated trying to make a getaway on the goddamn ocean.

The only thing he could do was, what? Get over the horizon

maybe?

Then Jackie saw a boat way the hell off to his left. It was moving fast, getting bigger every time he blinked his eyes. Which he had to do because the Whaler was moving fast enough to make his eyes water. Every time he cleared his eyes, the damn boat on his left looked bigger.

He knew about speed; that sucker was really moving. What scared him was it looked like it was coming straight at him. Like he was a goddamn target.

No, like he was a *meal*.

Now, he could see the color and the lines of the boat bearing down on him. It was white with a big dark space in the middle of the bow. Looked like an open mouth. He half-expected to see teeth flashing any minute. The fucking thing was going to eat him alive.

And there was not a damn thing he could do about it.

Jump over the side? The way he swam, he'd maybe go twenty yards before he went under.

He could see two of the pricks on the deck of the white boat now. Those fucking slavers Cap'n Thurlow had ratted him out to. Why hadn't the cops locked them up? Why were they so hellbent on making him pay? It should have been fucking Alice they were after. He'd just been a guy who stopped into a bar, tried to do a favor for a broad. He was *innocent,* goddamnit.

He hadn't done *anything* to deserve this.

The last thing Jackie Richmond, aka Linley Boland, ever did was throw an empty revolver weighing less than two pounds at a fifty-five-foot yacht weighing twenty tons and moving at forty-five knots. The *Carcharodon* crushed the Whaler like it was a Dixie cup, turned a homicidal car thief into a bloody pulp and then flew a hundred feet through the air.

Mass and velocity were both on the side of the yacht but a hydrofoil catamaran running on plane was not designed to ram a solid object weighing over four tons without suffering its own fatal consequences. Spectacularly deficient seamanship was on rampant display that day in the waters off Grand Cayman Island.

Welborn Yates and Carina Linberg saw the stunning collision and regarded the aftermath for a length of time neither of them would later be able to specify.

Carina spoke first. "That *was* the bastard who killed your friends, right?"

"Yes."

"Did you know the madmen on that yacht?"

"Only saw them once."

"If I wrote something like what just happened, what would you think?"

"That I'd rather see it on the page than on the water."

Carina leaned against Welborn and he put an arm around her. Thinking she might need a moment of comfort.

But she said, "I don't know. Might make a good movie sequence."

When they got back to the marina, Welborn's phone rang and he got another shock.

Kira was calling to tell him, "I'm pregnant."

Indiana University — Bloomington, Indiana

Cassidy Kimbrough and two friends from high school, Jeff Banks and Lindsay Fitzpatrick, were walking through the IU campus on their way to meet Sheryl Kimbrough. They stole glances at the college students and checked out classroom buildings. Jeff and Lindsay wanted to enroll at the state's flagship university.

The three of them tried to be inconspicuous. Hoped they didn't get pegged as high school kids and teased about it. Told to get their backpacks back where they belonged.

They needn't have worried. Either they were beneath notice or their educational betters were feeling charitable. They were allowed to pass freely through the college environs as if they belonged. The day was sunny but the first nip of real coolness was in the air. Not cold enough to cause shivers but sufficiently chilly to put a spring in your step.

By Midwestern standards, it was a great day to be outside.

That thought had no sooner occurred to Cassidy than Jeff pointed to a vehicle coming toward them on the adjacent campus road and asked, "What the heck is that car doing?"

It was a 50s Chevy, restored to a showroom finish. That was eye-catching enough. But it was the way the car moved that had everyone looking at it.

Lindsay said, "It looks like it's dancing."

There were three kids in the front seat of the car, two girls and the boy behind the wheel. Maybe they were IU students, maybe other high school kids on campus and goofing off. They were bouncing up and down, snapping their fingers and swaying back and forth, listening to music sealed inside the car by its raised windows.

The cool thing was, the car had as many moves as the kids did. Dipping its front end. Doing a side to side shimmy. Jumping ahead a few feet, then backing up the same distance. Like the "D" on its transmission stood for dance instead of drive. People on the sidewalk started dancing, too, clapping their hands in rhythm with the car as it passed. Then someone opened up a residence hall window and started cranking out tunes.

The car responded like it had *heard* the music and its movements became more exaggerated.

Then the rear windows slid down and fireworks shot out.

People cheered and Cassidy was about to say, "Cool!"

But that was when she saw a look of fear come over the face of the kid behind the wheel. A ball of fire erupted in the back seat, the Chevy shot forward and the girls inside screamed. This wasn't part of the act. Cassidy felt the terror of the kids in the Chevy and screamed in sympathy with them.

A heartbeat later the car slammed into the back of a parked delivery van and in seconds the whole thing was engulfed in flames.

Still screaming, Cassidy ran toward the car. Jeff tried to grab her, hold her back, but she pulled free. She was the second person to get to the Chevy. A tall guy with blonde hair edged her out.

The interior of the car was a furnace. The blonde guy yanked the driver's door open and jumped back as flames shot out at him.

Cassidy had to keep him from falling as he stepped on her foot. He gave her a look and then went right back to the car. He reached in and grabbed the driver, had him halfway out when Cassidy took over and pulled the driver the rest of the way. The two girls were screaming and scrambling to crawl out the open door, getting in each other's way.

Both girls' hair was on fire.

The blonde guy got the two of them out with one big tug.

Cassidy somehow caught one of the girls, let her fall to the ground and began beating out the flames in the girl's hair with her bare hands. Then somebody picked *Cassidy* up and was running with her like he had a football under his arm. Before she could ask him what the hell he was doing, she heard people yelling, "Get back, get back!"

Then she was on the grass with someone lying on top of her and she *felt* a clap of thunder, loud and hot, like maybe she'd been hit by lightning, too.

She didn't know what the heck was going on, but when she heard a swarm of sirens shrieking, she knew things had to be bad. Then whoever had been on top of her rolled off and there was Mom, her eyes filled with tears and a look of horror on her face.

That was the moment Cassidy first felt fear.

Seeing her mother's shocked reaction.

"Mom?" she asked.

Meier's Tavern — Glenview, Illinois

The place on Lake Avenue looked like an old-fashioned road house and it caught Anderson's eye. He told Crosby and Todd, "I need a cold brew, some hot beef and a place to tap a kidney."

Needing no further justification, he pulled into the gravel parking lot.

Crosby and Anderson had exchanged their Red Sox caps for

White Sox caps. Both of them knew Cubs caps were more prevalent on Chicago's North Side and the city's northern suburbs, but they thought the blue caps with the red C looked lame, and what self-respecting team would have a cute little cubbie-wubbie for its mascot? Pathetic.

Todd stuck with his Nike cap.

They asked for and got a table off to themselves. The waitress didn't seem to care what team they rooted for and was happy to take their orders. Anderson was delighted the place had beer from Dortmund, Germany.

Todd, Crosby and Anderson had done a casual single-pass drive-by of James J. McGill's house in nearby Evanston and Patti Grant's walled mansion in slightly more distant Winnetka.

A sign on McGill's lawn warned that a security firm protected the premises.

The Grant mansion's wall was unmarred by commercial signage.

The Secret Service didn't advertise.

As they'd passed McGill's house, Anderson said, "You can bet your ass no other house in town will get a faster response from the local cops."

Todd thought about that. "Maybe we should throw a rock through a window and see just how fast that response is."

"They'd know it was us," Crosby said. "You want to let them know we're reconnoitering?"

"Who's McGill's wife?" Todd asked.

Crosby and Anderson looked at each other.

"You want to make it look like it's a political thing?" Crosby asked.

"The woman must have made some enemies leaving the Republicans and joining the Democrats," Todd said.

They'd all read everything they could find on McGill, the president and McGill's family.

Knowing your enemy was always the first step.

Anderson said, "Maybe I should go to a novelty shop, see if I can find a nice smooth stone they could put an elephant decal on."

Todd liked that.

"They'd still suspect us," Crosby said.

Todd replied, "They'd suspect but they couldn't know. It would be a little psychological jab."

"That's not bad," Anderson said, "and we might learn something."

Todd said, "Gathering information is the purpose of this little excursion, right? We might even divide our forces and see if a rock through McGill's window rings an alarm at the president's home."

The two former covert operatives looked at each other.

Despite their initial misgivings and knowing that Todd had fucked with their heads, their respect for the little bastard continued to grow.

Anderson said, "Tell me something, Doc. You think you'll be happy if we get McGill?"

Todd etched a bleak smile on his face.

"Will I take pleasure in the doing of it? No. The satisfaction will be in knowing he'll never thwart me again."

Meaning he wouldn't have to look over his shoulder as he pursued Chana Lochlan once more.

Crosby spoiled Todd's mood by saying, "There's always someone ready to fuck with you."

"That's just the way the world is," Anderson added. "You finish killing commies, up pop the jihadis."

Todd didn't want to hear it. He got up and went to tap a kidney.

In the wee hours of the morning, Anderson threw a rock through McGill's living room window. The response was very quick. But not quick enough to catch Anderson.

There was no response at the president's lakeside mansion that Todd and Crosby could see.

They were back in their Ottawa hideout by dawn.

Calder Road — McLean, Virginia

Senator Howard Hurlbert's second home, the one he used

while Congress was in session, sat on a two-acre lot in the upper-most reaches of the northernmost state of the former Confederacy. To some Southerners, it might as well have been Newfoundland. Especially the way nearby stretches of the Old Dominion had been infested by Yankees and had taken to voting for the goddamn Democrats.

Hurlbert took pains to point out to his constituents in Missis-sippi that Robert E. Lee, the most revered general the South had ever known, had been born just (eighty-nine miles) down the road at Stratford Hall. Hurlbert's residence also had the pleasing look of a southern gentleman's property with a white picket fence, green lawns, a curving flagstone driveway and a pale yellow house with powder blue shutters. Out back was a four-car garage, converted from a coach-house.

An apartment above the garage served as the living quarters for the African American couple who cooked and cleaned for the senator.

Appearances were everything for Hurlbert. He believed people voted with their eyes. If they liked what they saw — that was, if you looked like what they wished they looked like — you were in. Look good and you could get away with spouting all sorts of hokum.

Within limits.

The senator believed the wishes of Tom T. Wright exceeded those limits.

He told Bobby Beckley, "You read a Huey Long speech to most of the people back home, they'd think it was Karl Marx talking. There is *no* way I can do what that man wants."

The senator's color was high, but that was due to more than a hot temper. He'd finished his third Woodford single barrel bourbon and was pouring his fourth. Beckley knew he'd have to cut him off soon or there would be no talking to him.

He took the senator's glass from him with a polite, "Thank you, don't mind if I do."

Hurlbert understood his old friend was exercising a measure of judgment he lacked.

He still didn't like it, though, and sat pouting on a nearby sofa. Beckley lowered himself into a facing armchair.

"Senator, how did your family come into its money?"

"Reginald Hurlbert made our fortune in the early nineteenth century."

"Yes, but how did he do that?"

"He was a —" Hurlbert bit his tongue. He'd been about to say a progressive farmer. "He was ahead of his time in the production of cotton."

Beckley smiled, sipped his bourbon and spoke in a soft voice. "Senator, your esteemed ancestor was one of the many cotton farmers in the South who *stole* the design of Eli Whitney's cotton gin."

"He did no such thing!"

"Mrs. Hurlbert told me he did. Said she heard it from you."

The senator reached for the glass in Beckley's hand. He pulled it back.

Falling back on the sofa, Hurlbert said, "You haven't told anyone, have you?"

"No."

"What I told Bettina was he *improved* on Whitney's design."

"Ah, well, that makes all the difference. But let's look at his source of inspiration. Eli Whitney was born in Massachusetts. He was a graduate of Yale. By the standards of his day or any other, I doubt he was a good ol' boy. But that didn't stop Reginald from taking a good idea and running with it, did it?"

"No."

"After the Civil War, Reginald's son, Denton, took over the land holdings and while others were bemoaning the loss of their slaves and failing to bribe the Yankees so they could hold on to their land, he moved ahead as a pioneer of new methods of cultivation, didn't he?"

"Yes."

"So both men took chances with something new."

"They did."

"In your own way, you've followed in their footsteps by starting a new political party."

Hurlbert knew he was being flattered. Didn't need to hear any more puffery. He got straight to the point.

"You really think we could get away with peddling southern populism?" he asked. "In this day and age?"

"I think it's a damn fascinating idea, especially when it's backed up by a hundred million dollars. I also think smart people make a sharp turn when they see others running straight off a cliff."

Beyond that, Beckley thought their little chat with Tom T. Wright might have been an elaborate trap set up by Galia Mindel. God only knew how she could get a New Orleans billionaire to play her little game, but there wasn't much he would count as out of reach for that woman.

Hell, he'd have loved to come up with an idea that devious.

So what he was going to do was spend a small chunk of the senator's leftover campaign funds from his last election on a raft of private investigators. He was going to cover everyone he could think of from Galia Mindel right on up to James J. McGill. Have them followed and photographed. Point some directional microphones their way, too.

That'd be damn risky, of course. Especially with McGill having Secret Service protection. But, hell, he was running an empty suit as the presidential candidate from a new party. His career was already a hot rod racing toward the railroad tracks. Seeing if he could get across before the train nailed him. Funny damn thing, that was just the way he liked it.

Not that he'd share either his thoughts or his sentiments with the senator.

He tossed the bourbon down his throat and got to his feet.

He had to start the ball rolling, but he left the old man with one last thing to chew on.

"You don't feel comfortable trying to sell Tom T.'s ideas, Senator, you let me know who else wants to give you his kind of money."

WorldWide News — *Washington, D.C.*

A security guard accompanied Ellie Booker to her old office. She'd told the drone at the lobby desk that she'd like to talk with Ethan Judd. She was sure every tight-assed little J-School grad with clean fingernails and untarnished ideals was trying to see the man these days. She'd read about Judd shit-canning most of the old staff. Not just the on-air talent, but the producers, the writers, even some of the hair and make-up people.

It had come as something of a surprise that she hadn't received a termination notice.

The humanoid at the lobby desk made a phone call. Whether it went to Judd was another question. Putting the phone down, the unsmiling creature told Ellie, "You may enter the building to pick up the personal effects you left behind."

So she had been fired.

Judd, being an old school guy, had probably sent the pink slip by postal mail. Media rate. Ought to be in her mailbox any week now.

Keeping her tone civil, Ellie asked, "Will Mr. Judd see me?"

"If he's interested, you'll see him."

Great. This android probably communicated with another just like it that screened Judd's unwanted calls. Ellie asked herself if she'd left anything in her office she really cared to retrieve. Thought of the voodoo doll featuring the face of a late president of Haiti she'd picked up on a visit to the island. That was too cool to leave behind. She could always paste a photo image of her current least favorite person on the doll's face.

Stick it a few good ones when the mood took her.

Ethan Judd might be a place to start.

The security guy was big enough to play lineman for the Redskins, but he at least was human. Had the decency to smile at her and say, "Will you please come with me, Miss?"

Guy didn't have a gun or look like he'd ever need one.

Ellie resisted an impulse to take his hand like she was some waif he'd found on the street.

She nodded and followed along a half-step behind him. They took the elevator to the tenth floor and stepped out into a room that should have been familiar, but wasn't. The walls had been painted. The carpet had been replaced. The furniture was new. Even the air smelled better.

Sure, Judd wouldn't tolerate any big on-camera egos flouting the no-smoking laws.

The only two familiar faces Ellie saw belonged to video archivists.

You wanted a clip of any moving image, in-house or outside, starting from the days Louis Lumiere first shot movie film, they'd find it for you and fast. Ellie had always valued their skills. Now, they repaid her with smiles of acknowledgment, not giving a damn if it was the politically incorrect thing to do.

Almost made her feel warm and fuzzy.

She and the security guy came to her office and he told her, "You can have five minutes, Miss. I'll wait right out here. Please leave the door open."

Ellie nodded and stepped inside. Her old office had been re-decorated, too. She liked it. Businesslike but relaxed. She thought she might do good work in the space, once the new carpet smell faded.

All of her possessions had been put in boxes and set on a trolley. She looked inside. Each box had been neatly filled. Fragile items had been covered with bubble-wrap. The voodoo doll even had a stick-on note: *Neat!*

So they were putting her on the street but weren't being jerks about it.

Only thing left to do was push the trolley down to her car.

Then she heard a gruff baritone voice say, "We'll be out in a few minutes, Bill."

"Yes, sir."

Ethan Judd entered the office and closed the door behind him. He extended his hand to Ellie and introduced himself. Didn't waste time with any attempt at empty chitchat.

"You were a close call, Ms. Booker. Highly competent but closely linked with the old power structure. I was leaning toward keeping you, but Hugh Collier said it would be better to let you go. He told me I could keep you but doing so would make it harder for Sir Edbert to keep his promise not to interfere with my operation."

"Sonofabitch," Ellie said.

"Hugh, Sir Edbert or me?" Judd asked.

Ellie laughed. She knew about Judd, had read about him often enough, but this was their first meeting. She kind of liked the first impression he made.

"I'll get around to judging you," she told Judd. "The jury's already in on the other two."

Judd smiled. "I heard you speak your mind. Was there anything other than asking to keep your job that you wanted to see me about?"

Ellie opened the courier bag she carried. It'd had to go through a metal detector so Judd didn't look worried about what she might have inside. She handed him an envelope.

Without opening it, he asked, "What's this?"

"A copy of an unsigned publishing contract. Well, I didn't sign it, but Sir Edbert Bickford did. Hugh Collier gave it to me. It would pay me a million dollars for basically doing nothing."

Judd gave her a look. He gestured her to a guest chair and sat behind the desk that in other circumstances might have been hers. The new managing editor of WorldWide News read the contract.

He looked up at Ellie and said, "Easy money, and the reason you haven't signed the contract?"

"The way I read it, the only thing I have to do is shut up about Sir Edbert. It's a bribe."

Judd said, "Might be interpreted that way."

"Sir Edbert is being investigated by the Department of Justice. He seemed quite agitated about it when Hugh and I visited him on his yacht."

That got a flicker of reaction from Judd.

Ellie went on, "He seemed particularly sensitive when Hugh

brought up the subject of paying bribes to officials in other countries and how that might be viewed under the lens of the Foreign
Corrupt Practices Act."

"And here you have documentary evidence of what *might* be
considered a bribe."

Judd tossed the contract on the desk.

"I thought I'd let a U.S. attorney make that decision," Ellie said.

"You brought it to me for a second opinion?"

"I heard you play the news straight, and damn the consequences."

Judd finally smiled. "You've roped me into your game. I ignore
this, you can tell the world I'm just another of Sir Edbert's lackies.
Nicely done, Ms. Booker. Has it occurred to you that —"

"The contract is a ploy Hugh has devised? Sure. I'll leave it up
to you to work that out. He's *your* colleague now."

Judd shook his head in admiration.

"You know I could never hire you now. That would look like I
was trying to buy you off. But this has been the most enjoyable job
interview I've ever conducted. We'll have to work together sometime in the future."

Ellie left the copy of the contract on the desk. "I'll look forward
to it."

She got up, shook Judd's hand, opened the door and pushed
the trolley toward the elevator.

She'd know if *she* would ever want to work with Judd based on
one thing.

What he did with the story she'd just handed him.

SAC Crogher's Office — the White House

Celsus Crogher was at his desk at 3:00 a.m. when Elspeth
Kendry knocked at his door. There was nothing unusual about
that. He made sure that he was on hand for at least part of the
three shifts that worked the presidential security detail each day.
He took primary responsibility for only one shift per day, delegat-

ing the other two to senior special agents. If anybody needed him, though, he was never far away for long.

Rather than spend the night in bed, Crogher had taught himself to sleep in short stretches through the times he didn't have primary responsibility. He called in every two hours to make sure all was well. Crogher had heard that McGill had once said he plugged himself into an electrical recharger for a couple hours in the dead of the night. He wished.

That would've been the way he wanted it.

Especially, if he could have recharged with his eyes open.

When he wasn't catching catnaps, he'd do paperwork during off hours. Scan reports that evaluated the threats made against Holly G, ranging from crackpot to red alert. He also evaluated every person who worked for him. When your job was to keep the president alive, well and functioning at top form, you could *not* abide screw-ups.

Hard as it was for him to acknowledge, there had been Secret Service personnel who'd disgraced their brothers-and-sisters-in-arms with unprofessional behavior. That had happened before his time, and it was a damn good thing it had. He got steamed just thinking about it.

When Crogher was a kid, his old man had told him and his brother, Cormac, "Don't make me angry. If I ever hit you, you'll die bouncing." That from a man who taught high school Latin. The brothers took his warning seriously, though. Following the rules, all the rules, was seen as the surest way to avoid grief in life.

SAC Crogher would have been more inclined to warn his subordinates, "You'll die looking like Swiss cheese," had they failed to observe all the rules laid down to protect the president. Such an exhortation from a man who carried an Uzi wouldn't be taken lightly. Unfortunately, it wouldn't be tolerated by his superiors.

So Crogher had to work subliminally, giving the impression that any breach of the president's safety would be considered a capital offense. His visage, his demeanor, his body language all carried a threat of great bodily harm. Woe betide anyone who crossed the SAC.

Anyone except Holmes.

McGill was a force unlike any other.

He was smart, charming and knew when and how to fight.

He also had the president backstopping him every step of the way.

The sonofabitch.

Then there was Holly G herself. He'd have been happier safeguarding a male president. Women were unpredictable. Coming up with that idea he take dance lessons. He'd loved that it would give him the chance to put McGill's nose out of joint. He'd thrown himself into the lessons as hard as he'd ever done anything, but as he actually started getting good on the dance floor he found it was softening him.

Not physically or mentally. It was just taking the ... not the edge off his attitude exactly, but maybe the corners off his thinking. He didn't see everything in straight lines and right angles anymore. You sure as hell couldn't dance that way. You'd look like a damn fool, if you tried.

He'd tried, so he knew.

When his dance instructor, who had the patience of a saint and the body of a goddess, and had told him explicitly she was partial to other women, finally got him to loosen up, to *flow* with the music, God, it was like a whole new world had opened up before his eyes. Not only did he move better, he started thinking differently.

He saw subtlety, nuance, intuition.

He understood how all those qualities could help him to do his job better. Thing was, he kept getting the feeling he was ready for something new. Finish out Holly G's first term, dance with her at an inaugural ball, smirk at McGill and move on.

When Elspeth Kendry knocked at his door early that morning, SAC Crogher was in a state of mind that no one would ever have thought him capable of: He was mellowed out.

He even refused to get tense when he saw Kendry had the only kind of news anyone ever got at three in the morning: bad.

He simply asked, "Is someone down?"

Kendry shook her head.

"Good. What is it then?"

"Somebody tossed a rock through the living room window of Holmes' house in Evanston, Illinois."

"You got the word from the local cops?"

Kendry said, "Yes, sir. They said they arrived less than three minutes after the alarm on the window went off. They didn't make an arrest or even a stop. Said by the time they started a grid search, they didn't find a single person on the street within a radius of a mile."

"The locals responded to Mrs. Enquist's residence, too?"

"Per the plan we agreed on with them. Holmes' daughter, Caitie, was safely tucked in bed. The former Mrs. McGill and her husband Mr. Enquist were also safe. I doubt they'll get much sleep the rest of the night, though."

Crogher shrugged, something he never used to do.

"No one was picked up lurking near the Enquist home?" he asked.

"No, sir. Again, the police report seeing nobody on the street for several blocks."

"Peaceful town. Our people are working the crime scene?"

"Yes, sir. The Evanston PD did a visual scan to see if anyone was inside the house and then secured it. Our people went in armored but found no one inside. They did find the rock that went through the window. It had a decal of a red, white and blue elephant on it."

Crogher thought about that. He said, "You could hit Holmes' house with a rock from the sidewalk; the president's house in Winnetka, behind that big wall and on the far side of an acre of lawn, you'd need a catapult. Could be a peeved conservative going for the easy target or it could be Damon Todd trying to get cute. What do you think, Kendry?"

"Todd. We know about him. Some pissed off political partisan is just a shadow. There's no point chasing that."

"I think you're right. Holmes' neighbors had to see all the commotion outside his house; some of them probably put in on video. But the cops have kept the stone with the elephant quiet, haven't they?"

Elspeth nodded. "Should we let Holly G and Holmes know what happened?"

"Now? No."

Crogher didn't have a date to go dancing with Carolyn Enquist. Causing her a few sleepless hours was her tough luck. But no way was he going to blow his big moment with Holly G.

"The president's an early riser," Crogher said. "I'll have our people in the residence let me know as soon as she's awake."

Elspeth had expected SAC Crogher to respond with a much greater sense of urgency. At the very least, she'd thought he'd enjoy the opportunity to roust Holmes from his bed. Crogher had said he agreed with her that Damon Todd was probably behind the vandalism, but he was acting like it had been nothing but a boneheaded act of vandalism.

"Are you all right, sir?" Elspeth asked.

"Fine, why?"

He knew why: He wasn't acting like his old self.

But he wanted to hear what Kendry had to say.

She surprised Crogher and gave him a straight answer: "Seems to me like someone hijacked all your piss and vinegar."

Crogher did something no one had ever seen him do in the White House before.

He laughed.

The Oval Office

The president invited Senate Majority Leader John Wexford and Assistant Majority Leader Richard Bergen to the Oval Office to discuss filling the vacancies on the Supreme Court. Galia Mindel was present to be a second set of eyes for the president. Overt political discussions weren't allowed on government property, but matters of substance such as the nomination of two justices were permissible, even though the process would inevitably involve political considerations.

Once the two top Democrats in the Senate had been comfortably seated and each had accepted a glass of water to sip, the president got down to business.

"I'm going to nominate a new chief justice and a new associate justice simultaneously. I'd like them to be considered seamlessly. If possible, I'd like to have the hearings for the chief justice to be in the morning and the hearings for the associate justice to be in the afternoon on as few consecutive days as the Senate can manage, before bringing the nominations to a vote. Will that be doable?"

Wexford and Bergen looked at each other.

Nothing of the sort had ever been done or even contemplated.

The Senate was the home of governmental sclerosis.

The lifeblood of democracy flowed slowly there, if at all.

Then, again, this president seemed to be a precedent setter by nature. If the Democrats in Congress were going to work with her and be successful, they'd have to learn a new trick or two. Sprint just to keep up with her.

"We can certainly try," Wexford said. Turning to his assistant, he asked, "Can't we, Dick?"

Senator Bergen had a gleam in his eye; he had more of a natural political affinity with the president.

He said to her, "You'll want us to employ some mechanism for cutting off Republican filibusters, won't you, Madam President?"

"Chief of Staff Mindel, will you please tell the senators what my thinking is?"

Galia said, "If the Republicans or Senator Hurlbert of True South should choose to stall the nominations, the president would like you to use the nuclear option, most recently threatened by Senator Bill Frist."

"Madam President," Senator Wexford said, "the so-called nuclear option is not provided for in the formal rules of the Senate."

Patti had done her homework. "No, it's not, but the possibility of using such a measure was endorsed in a parliamentary opinion by Vice President Richard Nixon in 1957 and by the Senate itself in a series of votes in 1975. Gentlemen, the Republicans were prepared to use this option without apology when they thought it necessary. We can do no less. There's no place left for timidity in Washington — wouldn't you agree?"

Wexford had to think about that; Bergen didn't.

"I agree," he said. "The rationale for using the nuclear option is the same now as it was then. The Constitution requires that the will of the majority be effective on specific Senate duties and procedures. The option allows a simple majority to override the rules of the Senate and end a filibuster or other delaying tactic."

Wexford gave his number two a cutting glance, but he wasn't going to chide him for speaking out of turn in front of the president and her chief of staff. For one thing, Dick was going to run for reelection and he was going to retire. For another he didn't want it getting back to their caucus that he had been the timid guy in the room.

"I concur, Madam President," Wexford said. "The Democrats in the Senate will expedite whatever nominations you send to us. If any members of our caucus are hesitant about your choices, I'm sure Dick will whip them into line."

Bergen nodded, accepting both the reproof and the burden.

Wexford asked, "Are you ready at this time to tell us whom you'll nominate?"

"I am, if you gentlemen promise to keep both names confidential."

The two senators saw Galia staring at them. If there was a leak from either of them, she'd have no trouble tracing it. Federal funds due to their states might encounter unexpected bottlenecks of long duration.

Wexford and Bergen looked at each other and exchanged a silent message.

"Perhaps it would be better to wait for that information,"

Wexford said.

"As you like," the president said. "Thank you for coming, gentlemen."

She shook hands with both men on their way out. Unless he was a dolt, and he wasn't, Senator Bergen recognized that his handshake had been a bit longer and warmer. He'd just been recruited as the president's eyes and ears in the Senate.

After the door to the Oval Office had closed behind the senators and Galia had silently counted to ten to make sure no one poked his head back in, she said, "Well done, Madam President. Wexford needed to have his courage bucked up a little; Bergen will be ready for the fight. You handled each of them just right."

Patti nodded, her mind already elsewhere.

"Something I should know?" Galia asked, reading her.

"Jim and I heard from SAC Crogher this morning. Someone broke a window at Jim's house in Evanston. The rock had a decal on it, an elephant."

"That's not good," Galia said.

The president nodded.

"Whoever did it is going to find out I'm ready for a fight, too."

McGill Investigations, Inc.

McGill and Sweetie had the inner office to themselves. Elspeth and Leo had been left to occupy themselves in the outer office. McGill was relying on Sweetie's Mother Superior sense of proximate mischief to sniff out anyone — Elspeth — eavesdropping just the other side of the door.

Sweetie stared at the door as if she could see through it. She turned to McGill and nodded. All clear.

He'd told her about the rock being thrown through the window of his home in Evanston.

"I think one of Damon Todd's new CIA pals did it."

"While Todd and the other one are somewhere around here?" Sweetie asked.

"Yeah, that's what I think, if they're going to make a move anytime soon. That's their style: create a diversion one place, hit another."

"If they're smart," Sweetie said, "they have to know you've read the files the government kept on them. Maybe what happened with the rock was just a way to psych the security people out and see how they responded, back in Illinois and right here."

"Gathering their own intelligence, that would make sense. They could see how the security details were reinforced and then watch as they're drawn down. If they 'cry wolf' a few times, they could lull the people watching out for my family into a sense of complacency."

"Your family and you, Jim. You're the one Todd wants."

"What about the CIA guys?" McGill asked. "What do you think they want?"

"Hard to say. They probably aren't interested in buying a condo in a retirement community."

McGill grinned. "Yeah, I'd say that's a safe bet. What they might think will happen is I'll rush home."

Sweetie said, "But I'll take care of that."

"Take no risks, Margaret. If one or the other of us has to cross the line and put somebody down, we'll trust in Saint Peter to sort things out."

"No temporal worries? We've got the local courts greased?"

"Presidential pardons will be forthcoming as necessary. I've been assured."

"Good to know people in high places," Sweetie said.

McGill told her, "Good but not always easy."

"What do you mean?" Sweetie asked.

"You know how the Federal Election Commission says political campaigns aren't supposed to coordinate their efforts with Super-PACs?"

"Not really," Sweetie said, "but I'll take your word for it."

"Thank you. Thing is, I'm married to someone who's going to be campaigning for president, and you're engaged to marry someone who is running a Super-PAC. And you and I —"

"Work together," Sweetie said.

"Right. Suspicious minds with partisan motives might think we're acting as a conduit for our respective better halves."

Sweetie scowled. "Putnam and I never talk politics. Other than in moral terms."

McGill raised a fist. "Great. Please keep it that way. Now, if it's all right with you, I'd like to ask if it would be all right for me to hire Putnam as my lawyer."

Sweetie said, "You're not about to turn to a life of crime?"

"No," McGill said.

"If you can afford him and he's willing, be my guest."

Under the present circumstances, Sweetie thought it best not to ask why McGill might need Putnam's services.

"You want his mobile number?" she asked.

"It would be better if I got it from another source," McGill said.

Sweetie's scowl returned. The idea that the two of them had to permit subterfuge to enter their relationship after all this time did not sit well. Sweetie stood up to go.

"It's all right if I call from Evanston to let you know what I find?" she asked.

"Of course, and please be careful."

"You, too."

"Yeah," McGill said.

After Sweetie left, McGill called Byron DeWitt at the FBI to make sure he hadn't been left out of the loop on the broken window in Illinois. He told McGill he'd heard from Special Agent Kendry, and thanked McGill for the courtesy call. His people were still tracking down Todd's personal and professional acquaintances and cross-matching them against directories of prominent people. That and looking for Realtors who'd dealt with cash customers. It was labor intensive work, he told McGill. Might be a while before they had anything to act on.

McGill placed one more call.

"Hello," a woman's voice answered.

"Chana, it's Jim McGill."

A hopeful tone entered Chana Lochlan's voice. "Have you caught them yet?"

McGill sighed, answer enough.

But he said, "No. I'm still looking and so are a lot of other people."

McGill's original reason for making the call was simply to see how Chana was holding up but now, with Damon Todd playing head games, McGill came up with an idea of his own.

"Are you getting restless?" he asked Chana.

"I love all the time Graham and I have had together, but I'm going crazy from not being able to do any work."

McGill said, "Graham's okay?"

"As long as he has his computer and a connection to the Internet, he can work anywhere. He's fine."

Graham Keough, Chana's husband, was the Manager of All Things Creative for a video game company called MindGames. He also owned a controlling interest in the company. There was no reason why he couldn't work anywhere he wanted.

McGill said to Chana, "How would you like to spend some of your free time helping me drive Damon Todd to distraction?"

"I'd love to," Chana told him. "Can we do it from a safe distance?"

Aboard the Poseidon — Capital Yacht Club

Mike O'Dell, former loudmouth-in-chief at WorldWide News, was still so pissed off about being fired he almost told Sir Edbert Bickford to get fucked when the old man called to invite him to his yacht. Then he thought of demanding a written apology before he'd even *consider* responding to the invitation. But with an effort that caused his whole face to contort, reason elbowed ego aside, and what he said was, "What time would you like to see me, Sir Edbert?"

O'Dell chose accommodation instead of rebuke because he

knew that Sir Edbert, whether he was in legal trouble or not, could still see to it that O'Dell never worked in conservative media again. Where else could he find another job? PBS? Not likely.

Beyond that, O'Dell had the feeling Sir Edbert had a trick up his sleeve. Firing him and all the lesser on-air creatures at WWN and hiring that self-righteous prick Ethan Judd had to be a ploy. A con. Now, the boss was calling him back to be in on the payback.

Hearing the good news on a yacht that he'd been told had cost a million dollars per foot to build was the icing on the cake. God, he loved tough, rich old bastards. The tougher and richer the better. O'Dell thought it would be great sport if they could set up heavy machine guns on the deck of the *Poseidon*, cruise off to the Indian Ocean and blast Somali pirates like they were ducks in a video arcade.

They got tired of that, they could turn around and bag wind-surfers off Martha's Vineyard.

When O'Dell arrived at the yacht, Sir Edbert had him piped aboard with a bosun's call.

How cool was that? He almost got a hard-on.

The old man invited him into the salon, poured him a drink and got right down to business.

"You're too good a man to let lie idle, Mike."

O'Dell sat tall in his chair. Had he been on his feet, he might have stood five-seven.

"Thank you, sir."

O'Dell expected the next thing he heard would be that he was back in and Ethan Judd was out. That wasn't it, but it was almost as good. Maybe better, if he played his cards right.

"Mike, I'm thinking of starting a new network, one that will run parallel to the new format at WorldWide News. I don't know if you've heard but Ethan Judd has eliminated all forms of commentary over there. There will be no analysts, no spin doctors. There will be journalists only, simple messengers of the facts."

O'Dell's mouth fell open. He hadn't heard the news.

The reason for that was simple; Sir Edbert had learned of it only hours ago.

Had decided things had gone farther at WWN than he could abide.

"How the hell will people know what to think if we don't tell them?" O'Dell asked.

"Exactly, Mike, exactly."

O'Dell was a natural street fighter — except he'd never bruised a knuckle or suffered a split lip — and had the instinct to know what was coming next.

"Your new network, Sir Edbert? That's the answer to the problem?"

"Indeed it will be. I'm going to call it WorldWide News in Review. If the original franchise will be strictly journalism, the new effort will be exclusively opinion."

O'Dell all but swooned. There would be no need to pretend they were objective. They could rant and vent and shout around the clock. Facts would not only not be checked, they'd be beside the point. Whatever they felt was right would be right. Their ratings would skyrocket.

Leave the solar system entirely.

And he —

O'Dell felt a sudden flutter in his stomach.

He was going to be in on the whole thing, right?

The old man hadn't called him just to yank his chain?

Sir Edbert saw his minion's moment of doubt and reassured him.

"Mike, I want you to lead the effort. You'll get two hours in prime time, Monday through Friday, and any time there's a marquee news story, you'll go on the air from wherever you are. And I want you to choose every member of a conservative all-star supporting cast."

Sir Edbert's words were the realization of a dream O'Dell hadn't dared to conceive. He felt giddy. Like a kid in a — No, he felt as if he were Harvey Korman in *Blazing Saddles*. Recruiting every vile desperado in the Old West to further his evil plans.

His eyes filled with tears of joy. He got to his feet and hugged Sir Edbert.

Who thought, happily, they hadn't even talked money yet.

He patted O'Dell on the back and counseled him, "This will take some time to set up, Mike, and we must keep things quiet until we're ready to make our big splash."

O'Dell blubbered, "Of course."

But Sir Edbert's secret was already under assault.

The bosun who'd piped O'Dell aboard was on Hugh Collier's payroll.

3

January, 2012
Reserve Drive — Dublin, Ohio

Vice President Mather Wyman got weekends off. Weekdays, too, lately, if he wanted them. He couldn't blame the president for taking all his responsibilities away from him. He would soon be trying to take the presidency away from her. She would have looked foolish to her new Democratic colleagues if she'd let him maintain a portfolio of even ceremonial duties.

If some foreign dignitary died anytime soon, the secretary of state would have to go to the funeral.

That being the case, Wyman had taken to spending less and less time in his White House office. The estrangement from the power he'd enjoyed as acting president began to make him bitter. His mind kept churning out ways he could make sure he would be the next person to take the oath of office as president.

Most of his ideas were so melodramatic they couldn't have sustained a B-movie. Not that they made those things anymore. But they might like the high concept of a closeted widower getting elected and revealing he was gay during his inaugural speech.

More than one gay man had shielded himself with an unsuspecting wife and children. Wyman had always thought that was a terrible thing to do. He understood well the impulse to protect oneself, but to do so at the expense of deceiving others was just not right. He and his dear Elvie had revealed themselves to each other before they had wed. They had been willing and informed coconspirators.

They'd been able to pull off the masquerade because they'd gotten along so well when they had both pretended to be straight. Carrying on with that affection and having it ripen into true if platonic love had been easy. They'd both delighted their parents when they'd announced their engagement. Everyone on both sides of the family thought the two young people couldn't have made a better match.

Except for the small matter of a mutual lack of sexual attraction, those people were right. When Mather and Elvie had explained that she wouldn't be able to conceive — they'd gone to the best specialists in New York, they said — they'd been told they should adopt. But that would have meant deceiving a child, along with everyone else, and they wouldn't do that.

Mather Wyman had come home to Ohio for the new year because for the moment he had nowhere else to hang his hat. He'd decided he would return to the White House only on such occasions as the president requested his presence. That being the case, his official residence at Number One Observatory Circle had lost its charm and even its legitimacy.

Moving back into the last home he'd shared with Elvie had been bittersweet. Walking through the old familiar rooms both brought her back to him in a rush of memory and broke his heart all over again. He wondered, had Elvie lived, if they could have come out together.

Come out together, stay married and have separate discreet affairs.

As he continued to hold public office.

The very idea brought a smile to Wyman's face.

That would be a high concept for a *French* movie.

When Kira came to visit with Welborn and told him she was pregnant, the news brought tears to his eyes. Learning from Welborn how the bastard who'd killed his Air Force friends had died reassured him that his daughter in all but name would have a good man to share her life. He felt happier than he had since losing Elvie.

The bliss he felt made him wonder if he, too, should take his secret to his grave.

What purpose would be served by revealing the truth?

None at all, if it was a matter of telling the man who just arrived at his front door.

The Oval Office

Aggie Wu, in addition to all her other duties as White House press secretary, scanned as many national and global media outlets as she could in a given day. She looked for news of any sort that might not only have an impact on the way the president did her job but also stories that would catch the president's personal interest … and, if possible, be of political benefit.

She'd found one of the latter, a good one, too.

But she was not about to bury her lead.

The first thing she told the president was, "Ethan Judd would like to do an hour-long interview with you, Madam President."

Patti thought about that. She'd long admired Judd's objectivity, in-depth research and elegant writing when he'd been at the *New York Times* and other papers that made an honest effort to maintain a sense of professional ethics. It had come as a surprise to her to learn that he taken over the news operation at WWN.

"What's your take on this, Aggie?" the president asked.

"He's cleaning house at WorldWide News, Madam President. I think what has happened over there is Sir Edbert Bickford is busy with his international legal problems. His nephew, Hugh Collier, has taken over day-to-day management of the company. Either as a public relations move, a different point of view by Collier or a combination of the two, the focus of the company has changed, at least for the short term. It would be hard for them to fire the new crew and round up the old gang. I'd say you've got at least six months of a new WWN."

"Is that reason enough to think that one of my favorite journalists hasn't decided to cash in? Mr. Judd can't be too far from thinking about retirement."

"I wouldn't know his personal plans about that, but my guess is he'll work until he drops. He knew you wouldn't say yes quickly. What he asks is that you keep an eye on what he does with the network. Whenever you feel you can trust him, if that day comes, he says he'll be ready to do the interview at a moment's notice."

"That's both fair and noncommittal. Please let Mr. Judd know I'll be keeping an eye on his work. Meaning you'll do that for me, Aggie."

"Of course."

"Is there anything else?" the president asked.

"Yes, Madam President. I have a video clip from WTHR, the NBC affiliate in Indianapolis, I thought you might like to see."

"Good news or bad?" the president asked.

"Heroic, Madam President. With a connection to Senator Talbert."

Patti Grant, in her former life as a congresswoman, had co-sponsored three bills with Senator Charles Talbert. She had a warm spot in her heart for him. She took the iPad Aggie offered her and played the video.

It started with a shot of a burned out car on the campus of Indiana University. The young female reporter informed her audience that three teenagers had been in the car when it crashed into a parked truck and burst into flames. All three young people had been seriously burned but all of them were alive thanks to the heroic efforts of Terry Pickford and Cassidy Kimbrough who pulled them from the burning wreck.

Pickford had suffered second degree burns on his face, hands, arms and shoulders. Kimbrough had suffered first and second degree burns on her hands and arms. The three passengers in the car had suffered second and third degree burns over more than fifty percent of their bodies.

All the burn victims were being treated at the Burn Center of Wishard Hospital in Indianapolis. The video came to an end and the president looked at Aggie.

"Cassidy Kimbrough is Sheryl Kimbrough's daughter?"

As with any first-rate politician, Patricia Darden Grant had an extraordinary recall of people and their names.

"Yes, Madam President."

The president put a hand to her mouth as she absorbed the shock, horror and pain the victims and their families in Indiana must be feeling.

She said to Aggie, "Please have Edwina set up calls for me. Start with the families of the young people in the car, then Terry Pickford's family, then Sheryl Kimbrough. Cassidy, too, if she's up to it. I'll finish with Senator Talbert. Thank you for bringing this to my attention, Aggie."

"I thought you should know, Madam President."

Aggie went to relay her instructions to Edwina Byington.

Proud that the president had her call priorities right.

Reserve Drive — Dublin, Ohio

Mather Wyman welcomed Senator Daniel Crockett into his home. The two men took their ease in Wyman's home office, sitting in facing wing chairs. Crockett had a measure of the Tennessee sipping whiskey the vice president had offered him. Wyman contented himself with sparkling water and a slice of lime.

The vice president asked, "So how is New Mexico at this time of year?"

"Surprisingly chilly at night, but then I haven't spent much time there. I forgot how high up in the mountains Santa Fe is," Crockett said.

"Governor Fuentes' hospitality was warm, I hope."

Crockett took a sip of his drink. "It was, up to a point. She's interested, but she hasn't committed."

"She has other opportunities?"

"She was very open about that. Rosalinda Fuentes has been keeping a sharp eye on Patti Grant. She thinks if the president does a good job, not even a great one, in a second term, the country might be open to putting another woman in the White House. If the president should have a disappointing second term, however, Governor Fuentes is sure the next president would be a man, an 'old white guy' to restore a sense of comfort."

Wyman said, "So she isn't interested in the old white guy from Ohio this time around."

"No, that's not the case. She has great admiration for the way you handled your tenure as acting president."

"So we can trust that she won't turn up on the True South ticket?" Wyman asked.

Crockett laughed. "The thought would never cross Howard Hurlbert's mind."

"So what are Governor Fuentes' concerns?"

"That you are too identified with the Grant administration. She liked what she saw when you were running things, but she feels you've got to show the country more of who you are."

Wyman kept a feeling of acute irony off his face.

"That will happen soon. The Iowa caucus, diminished though its importance is, is next week, and I leave for Des Moines tomorrow," he said.

"I trust you've lined up your donors and surrogates."

"I have," Wyman told him, "and I'm happy with the results."

Crockett finished his drink, got up and poured another tot.

He looked at Wyman and said, "There's one thing you could do, going into the primaries, to show the country you are your own man."

Wyman felt a chill as he guessed where Crockett was heading.

Still, he pushed the senator to say it by asking, "What's that?"

"Mr. Vice President, you should resign from office. Effective immediately."

The House on Gentleman Road — Ottawa, Illinois

Damon Todd sat in the kitchen reading the *Washington Post* on his iPad. There had been no mention of the vandalism at James

J. McGill's house in Evanston. The same had been true in the *Chicago Tribune* and the *New York Times*. Wanting to be thorough, Todd had also checked CNN, Google News and WWN online. He'd saved the *Post* for last, thinking if any paper would have news concerning the president's husband, it would be the Washington paper.

It had been over a week now, and he was disappointed to find no mention of the incident.

He'd thought a broken window, even at McGill's house, wouldn't rate top of the news coverage. So he'd searched the depths of the news sites and still had found nothing. He decided to click on every link on the site before he conceded that the cops had kept the story out of the media.

He even looked at the *Post's* Celebritology blog, thinking the way fame was measured these days a presidential spouse's petty annoyances must qualify as news in some way. He didn't find any reference to McGill, but what he happened upon made the blood drain from his face.

Some time later, he didn't know if it had been minutes or hours, he heard a door open and Anderson say, "Look at that. Doc died where he sat. We could leave the windows open and he'd keep right where he is all winter."

"He's got that iPad of his in his hands," Crosby said. "Maybe we should see if there's something on it that did him in."

The day's temperature was below freezing, and Todd thought with the door open he could well freeze in place if he didn't start moving. He began with his eyes, looking over at the two rogue agents. Crosby had his Vietnam tomahawks in hand.

Todd knew that Crosby and Anderson had been out practicing with the unusual weapons. A little thing like cold weather didn't deter them. They also practiced knife fighting, light cuts allowed, no deep slashing or stabbing.

They'd also practiced these skills with Todd. He proved surprisingly good at throwing the tomahawks, but had less of a stomach for the knife work. On the other hand, being younger than Crosby and Anderson and more dedicated to his strength training, he was in better physical condition than the other two.

Anderson's comment on that had been, "Strong is good. Quick and ruthless are much better. You'll never kill a badass by showing him how many chin-ups you can do."

"Push-ups either," Crosby added.

Now, the senior CIA fugitive stepped over to Todd, extended his hand and asked, "You mind?"

Todd let Crosby take the tablet computer.

He read from the screen, "Chana Lochlan and Graham Keough attend Kennedy Center gala. Story says Ms. Lochlan was once known as 'the most fabulous face on television.'"

Anderson had to see that, and took the iPad. "Still looks fine to me," he said. "And Mr. Keough is a Silicon Valley multimillionaire."

"A very handsome couple," Crosby said.

Todd snatched the computer back from Anderson.

Crosby and Anderson sat at the kitchen table with Todd, stared at him.

"Reacting like that tells us all we need to know, Doc," Anderson said.

"You once had it bad for Ms. Lochlan," Crosby made clear.

"You ever get some of that, Doc?" Anderson asked.

Crosby said, "Of course, he did. Only question is, *how* did he get it?"

Anderson feigned shock. "You mean, Arn, did Doc hypnotize a poor girl to have his way with her?"

"I'm sure he did, with some poor girl. Think how tempting that would be. He's going to give some little sweetheart the kind of life she could only dream of, it's only fair he takes a taste for his time and effort."

Anderson nodded, certain that was the way things had been.

"That was some racket you had going, Doc."

Crosby said, "Another thing to think about is whether Ms. Lochlan is our new friend's all-time heartthrob. Because if she is, you know what that might mean."

Anderson gestured to Todd. "Come on, Doc, play along. What do you think Arn means?"

Barely moving his lips, Todd replied, "McGill is using her as bait. The same way he did with Lydell Martin."

"Very good," Crosby said.

"Play it out a little more for us, Doc. What else does it mean?"

"That I've been looking for Chana since we broke out, but I haven't been able to find her until now."

"Sort of underlines that McGill is behind all this, doesn't it?"

"Yes," Todd says.

Crosby continued the thread. "No way McGill doesn't give you credit for being smart enough to see that, but he knows you won't be able to help yourself. You'll go after her anyway."

"The story says Graham Keough is your girl's husband," Anderson said in quiet voice, "so you'll have to get rid of him. He's kind of a mild, peaceful looking guy. You might be able to handle him by yourself. Or you could ask Arn and me to dispose of him. We'd be —"

Both of Damon Todd's hands shot out and he grabbed the two Vietnam tomahawks that lay on the kitchen table. For a second, fear flashed in the eyes of both former CIA men.

Todd saw it, but took no joy from it.

He stalked outside holding the two weapons.

Crosby looked at his friend, both of them knowing they'd just had a very close call.

"Olin, we'd better be a little more careful around that guy."

"Yeah, I think he could use some therapy."

Wishard Hospital Burn Center — Indianapolis, Indiana

Cassidy Kimbrough lay asleep in a private room when the call came through. Her mother, Sheryl, sat in the chair next to her daughter's bed, dozing. The room was filled with mylar balloons, stuffed animals, flowers and cards expressing admiration and wishes for quick healing. Sheryl grabbed the phone before it could ring a second time.

She was pissed. The phone had rung incessantly after Cassidy had been brought into the room. Media outlets from across the country and around the world wanted to talk with Cassidy. The former press secretary to a United States senator was who they got. She told them tersely that her daughter was not available for comment. She was just beginning to heal from a serious physical and emotional trauma. They should respect her needs, goddamnit!

Fucking reporters, Sheryl thought.

She'd gone to the hospital's CEO and wrung a promise out of him that the only phone call that would be put through to Cassidy's room would be from her father.

So, Sheryl thought as she picked up the receiver, it had better be Blake on the line.

It wasn't. In a very gentle voice, Edwina Byington asked, "Am I speaking with Ms. Sheryl Kimbrough?"

The motherly tone disarmed Sheryl. "Yes."

Edwina said, "The president of the United States would like to know if this is a suitable time for you and your daughter to take a call."

"Mom?" Cassidy said, groggy from sleep and her pain meds, "Is that Dad?"

Sheryl said into the phone, "Can you hold for just a moment?"

"Of course," Edwina told her.

Sheryl said to her daughter, "No, honey, it's —"

Tears welled in Cassidy's eyes. "It's not one of the others?"

Cassidy had made every doctor and nurse she'd met in the hospital promise to keep her informed about the status of the other burn victims with whom she'd arrived.

"No news on that front," Sheryl told her.

"Another reporter?" Cassidy asked with a moan.

"Not that either. It's the president calling."

Cassidy's eyes went wide. She'd lost her eyebrows in her efforts to help Terry Pickford save the others. Her face was bright red, as if she'd been out in the sun far too long. Both of her hands were bandaged from using them to extinguish the flames in one of the victim's hair.

There were the usual worries about shock and infection.

Still, there was no question Cassidy had suffered less than anyone else involved.

"Let me talk to her, Mom. Please."

Sheryl said into the phone, "My daughter would like to speak with the president now."

She held the phone up to Cassidy's ear. Patricia Darden Grant came on the line; Sheryl could hear the president's voice but not distinguish her words. Sheryl had no trouble seeing the effect the call had on her daughter. Cassidy's poor wounded face filled with joy — and then tears.

"Oh, no, Madam President. I wasn't the brave one. I just helped Terry. Somebody had to."

Cassidy's tears continued to flow as she listened to the president's response.

"That's good, that's good. Yes. We'll be there for each other, especially Terry. Thank you so much for this call. I'd love to meet you sometime. I'm just bummed I won't be old enough to vote for you."

Cassidy listened to the president speak for a moment and then laughed.

You didn't hear much of that in the burn ward, Sheryl thought. Whatever the president had said to inspire her daughter's joy, Sheryl was deeply grateful to her.

"You will?" Cassidy asked. "That is so cool. Yes, I will. Goodbye."

"Call's over?" Sheryl asked.

Cassidy nodded and her mother put the phone receiver down.

"The president told me to say hello to you."

"She's a very nice person. You can't imagine how many things she has to do. Taking the time to call you was something special."

"She called all of us, Mom. Well, the parents of the others. The president said it will be very important for all of us to continue to support each other. Especially the kids who were in the car. They're going to have the hardest time of all."

Cassidy's chin started to quiver as she thought about that.

Sheryl tried to distract her daughter.

"What was so cool that the president said?"

Nudging her sadness aside, Cassidy said, "The president told me I should call her and let her know how I'm doing. She said the next time you and I are in Washington to let her know and we'll have lunch at the White House. How cool is that?"

"Very," Sheryl said. "And what was it that made you laugh?"

"The president said she could probably find a friend in Congress to introduce a bill that would lower the voting age just for me, but she didn't think the Republicans would let it pass."

"I believe there's one of those evil people in the room right now," Sheryl said.

"You're never evil, Mom." Cassidy leaned forward and puckered her lips.

Sheryl kissed Cassidy, glad beyond words that she hadn't lost her.

"You know what the best thing was?" Cassidy asked.

"What?"

"The president called me last. She called all the others first, tried to help them feel better because they need it more. That was the right thing to do."

"Yes, it was."

Cassidy let her eyes close, a smile on her face, and drifted back off to sleep.

Sheryl looked at her. She had wondered, at first, if the president's call had been just a political gesture. She had worked for Senator Charles Talbert, who had sponsored legislation with former Congresswoman Grant. Smart politicians never overlooked an opportunity to do a good turn for a colleague, even one who'd soon be retiring.

But as far as Sheryl knew none of the other burn victims' families had any political connections, and as Cassidy had said the president had called those suffering the most first. That had been the right thing to do. Of course, Patti Grant had also been a bone marrow donor for her stepson Kenny McGill not all that long ago. Doing that might have cost the president her life.

Sheryl sat back in her chair, closing her eyes.

Once again, she ran the nature of the president's call past a former reporter's skeptical view of life. Came up with only an act of kindness that had helped her daughter.

No bull-puckey at all.

Galia Mindel's Office — The White House

Everybody knew that the main reason there was a vice president was to have a warm body ready to step up if anything bad ever happened to the president. What people didn't think about nearly as often was that the president or, more often, her top staff people also had to think about who would fill the vice president's slot if he went down. You didn't just draw up a shopping list after the fact.

Not after the Spiro Agnew debacle anyway.

Richard Nixon's vice president — Agnew — resigned after he *pled nolo contendere*, no contest, to a charge of not reporting more than twenty-nine thousand dollars in income. The *quid pro quo* for what amounted to a sweetheart deal was that Spiro had to quit his job. Otherwise he'd be charged with accepting bribes in three public offices: Baltimore County Executive, Governor of Maryland and Vice President of the United States.

Agnew was replaced by the minority leader of the House of Representatives, Gerald R. Ford, who, after Nixon resigned in disgrace, went on to become the nation's only president who'd never been elected to either that post or the vice presidency. Ford chose as his vice president Nelson Rockefeller, a *liberal* Republican. Conservatives all across the country prayed that Ford didn't break his neck in one of the stumbles for which he became famous.

Ford survived his twenty-nine months in office and conservatives became more convinced than ever that God was on their side.

Galia Mindel's list of preferred candidates to replace Mather Wyman ran ten deep, but that didn't keep her from feeling a chill when Wyman stepped into her office unannounced. She knew that such a surprise appearance could portend only one thing.

"You're quitting, aren't you?" she asked Wyman.

He closed the door behind him and said, "I am."

Galia chose to react as a professional. "I know I advised against it before, but having seen you banished from the White House, I've changed my mind. It's the smart thing to do."

"Thank you. I thought by tendering my resignation to you privately there would be no media notice, allowing the president and you to have a few quiet days to make your plans."

"Very kind of you."

Wyman took a sealed envelope from a pocket inside his suit coat and handed it to Galia.

He said, "Please tell the president I remain deeply honored that she chose me to be her running mate.."

"I will."

Galia put Wyman's letter of resignation into a desk drawer. She was tempted to tell Wyman that he wouldn't beat the president in the election, but she didn't want her hubris to bring any divine reproof down on the president. She resolved to take Mather Wyman very seriously.

She contented herself to say, "As you are no longer employed at the White House, Mr. Wyman, I'd better walk you out of the building."

"That's very kind of you, Ms. Mindel."

Wyman offered his hand to Galia and she shook it.

Wouldn't that make a fine picture for the history books, she thought.

Political enemies observing the best of manners.

The founding fathers would be smiling. Or laughing.

McGill Investigations, Inc.

Putnam Shady was back from Omaha and other points west and sat with McGill in his inner office. Sweetie, neither needing nor wanting to know what the two of them had to discuss, waited in the outer office with Elspeth Kendry and Leo Levy.

Putnam had just accepted a check from McGill, making him McGill's lawyer. With the check went the task of hiring private investigator Brad Lewis of Chicago to keep an eye on Mrs. Robert Beckley of Jackson, Mississippi and, if possible, to obtain photographs of Mr. Beckley beating his wife. Then, of course, Mr. Lewis should call the police, anonymously.

Putnam understood without having to ask that McGill didn't want the PI to know who hired him, other than a lawyer he'd never met before. What Putnam didn't tell McGill was that he would hire a Chicago lawyer he knew, a guy McGill had never met, to hire Lewis. Another cutout might be helpful.

What Putnam said was, "Pretty ironic, don't you think?"

"You mean we're doing the same thing Derek Geiger wanted to do?"

"Yeah, without the taking over the government part."

McGill wanted the lawyer-client confidentiality privilege to protect him from any Congressional inquiry that might come his way. With Patti moving over to the Democrats and that party controlling the Senate, he was safe there. The House of Representatives, however, was in Republican hands, and the way presidential races were going in the U.S. it was easy to imagine a partisan panel trying to get at the president through him.

As McGill's ambitions were purely defensive, he trusted that his life expectancy would be greater than the late Speaker Derek Geiger's had proved to be.

That hopeful thought had no sooner crossed his mind than there was a knock at his door.

Receiving McGill's permission to enter, Elspeth Kendry stepped into the office.

"We just caught someone taking pictures of your car," she told him. "Leo is checking it out to make sure there was no tampering with it."

"Who's the photographer?" McGill asked.

"A professional colleague of yours. A local PI by the name of Maxwell Kern."

McGill shook his head. "Never heard of him."

"He asked for a lawyer and refuses to talk with us, but we'll find out everything there is to know about him."

"You already know he can't be too smart, trying to snoop my car while the Secret Service is watching it," McGill said.

"Yes, sir. Leo's concerns are understandable, but the special agents who grabbed him don't think he was trying to do anything to sabotage your vehicle. They watched him a minute or two before taking him into custody. Their judgment is he was looking to see if any personal property or papers of yours might have been left in the car where they might be photographed."

McGill and Putnam exchanged a look.

Elspeth didn't miss the silent exchange.

She said, "Mr. Kern took pictures of Mr. Shady and Ms. Sweeney entering the building. His camera has the functionality to upload photos to the Internet. We'll find out where he sent them, if he did, but it looks like someone is invading your privacy, sir."

Putnam shrugged. "My client has done nothing wrong and any communication he has with me is confidential."

So was any communication McGill had with his wife, the president.

Any Congressional committee that might subpoena him was in for a tough time.

Bridal Suite, Four Seasons Hotel — Boston Massachusetts

After leaving McGill's office, Putnam and Sweetie caught the first flight leaving Washington for Boston. It was Putnam's considered legal opinion, as well as his heart's fondest desire, that he and Sweetie not waste another minute before they got married.

Hearing her fiancé's reasoning, that he wanted to protect both of them from possible Congressional or legal snooping, Sweetie agreed.

But she still wouldn't consent to being married in Las Vegas.

She was agreeable to having Pastor Francis Nguyen perform the ceremony in Massachusetts. A quick smart phone check of that state's marriage laws showed them that they would: both have to appear at the Boston City Clerk's Office, present a valid photo ID, report their Social Security numbers, file an intention to marry form, wait three days and pay a fifty-dollar fee.

They called Pastor Nguyen and confirmed his availability.

Then it was pack lightly and wing off to Boston.

After getting the red tape out of the way, Sweetie and Putnam hid out at the Four Seasons.

Seventy-two hours later they got themselves to the church on time.

Putnam in his best navy blue suit, Sweetie radiant in a pearl white knee-length dress.

Though no longer a Catholic priest, Francis Nguyen still counseled each of them, separately and together, about the seriousness of the step they were about to undertake.

In Pastor Nguyen's own words, "I like to make sure people get it right the first time. I don't do do-overs."

Satisfied that their love was more than mere infatuation and their dedication to each other's well-being was sincere, Francis Nguyen performed the ceremony he'd learned in the seminary, leaving out the reference to the newlyweds living their lives according to the laws of the church.

For Pastor Nguyen, living according to the teachings of Christ was more than enough.

Putnam vowed: "I, Putnam, take you, Margaret, to be my wife. I promise to be true to you in good times and bad, in sickness and in health. I will love you and honor you all the days of my life."

Sweetie vowed: "I, Margaret, take you, Putnam, to be my husband. I promise to be true to you in good times and in bad, in sickness and in health. I will love you and honor you all the days of my life."

In the case of a younger couple, Francis Nguyen would have asked, as part of the ceremony, if they would lovingly accept and nurture any children God might give to them. In her private counseling, Sweetie had mentioned that it would take more than your average miracle for her to have a child, but if a miracle happened, she would certainly love and nurture any child who came her way.

Putnam would, too, she said.

The rings were exchanged, Pastor Nguyen gave the new couple his blessing and that was that. Francis Nguyen's wife, Harriet, and his housekeeper, Janet, were the only two witnesses in the church.

Back at the Four Season, Sweetie dismissed with a brief laugh the idea of being carried across the threshold of the bridal suite.

"Thought I should ask just for the sake of form," Putnam told her.

"Your respect for etiquette is duly noted and appreciated."

"I also thought I might show you how hard I've been working out."

Sweetie smiled. "As your personal trainer, I've noticed that, too."

"*And* appreciated it?"

"You'll see."

Sweetie and Putnam walked into the bridal suite.

Before braving the first night of married life for either of them, Putnam took Sweetie in his arms and asked, "No regrets?"

"None."

"After you told me about Kenny McGill's interest, that was another reason I knew I had to move fast."

Sweetie kissed Putnam and led him off to the bedroom.

No announcement of the wedding had been published in any newspaper.

Or posted online. The gossip columnists had missed the scoop.

Putnam and Sweetie intended to tell all the people who mattered personally — and before too very long they were going to throw one heckuva party to celebrate what they'd just done.

H-329, The Capitol — Washington, D.C.

Peter Profitt, Republican, eight-term congressman from the 4th District of North Carolina, sat in his Capitol office and reviewed the information that had been presented to him and decided on January 23, 2012, the first day of the second session of the 212th Congress, the time had come. After allowing the office of the speaker to remain vacant for one hundred and fifty-six days, a period of unprecedented length, and beating back ambitious colleagues who sought to usurp his place at the head of the line of succession, he decided it was time for him to become the new speaker.

At first, nobody wanted to go near the most powerful political position in the legislative branch of the federal government. The late Derek Geiger had made a toxic wasteland of that office. There had been no shame in Geiger's trying to consolidate power in his hands, except that he had failed. Making a bad situation far worse, he'd even tried to murder a lobbyist, Putnam Shady, for betraying him. His mania had even extended to making his failed murder attempt at the wedding of Vice President Wyman's niece, Kira Fahey.

It was said, though never proved, that Geiger, as long as he was in a homicidal frame of mind, also decided he would put an end to Congressman Zachary Garner and the president's husband, James J. McGill.

Had Geiger succeeded, he would have fallen short of John Wilkes Booth in a rogue's gallery of American political assassins, but he certainly would have received an honorable mention.

Just his making the attempt had been a terrible cross for his fellow Republicans to bear. It was thought that temporarily leaving the speaker's post unoccupied was the smart move. All of Geiger's possessions and furnishings had been removed from his offices, which were cleaned, painted and decked out with new furniture, all at party expense.

A Catholic member of the caucus even suggested a spiritual cleansing and blessing of those spaces, but there was a dispute over the wording and in the end nobody thought it was a good idea to suggest that a member of the party had actually been in league with Satan.

The GOP saved that kind of assertion for Democrats.

Time being the great healer and politicians not having any great respect for their constituents' long-term memory, members of the Republican caucus, a month after Geiger's interment, started pestering Profitt about voting for a new speaker. If he didn't want the job, plenty of them did.

After two months, restless political minds had started plotting against him.

With the passing of three months, he knew it would soon take more than threats and bribes to keep the caucus together under his leadership.

Then, today, one hundred and fifty-six days after Geiger's death, a sealed envelope arrived from Senator Howard Hurlbert's office. In it were photographs of Vice President Wyman entering the White House grounds. Everyone in political Washington knew that Mather Wyman had abandoned any pretense of continuing to do his job. So what had he been doing at the White House that day?

The photo of Wyman exiting the building in the company of Galia Mindel seemed to answer the question. He'd submitted his resignation. He'd done so on the sly. Or so he thought.

With the offices of both the vice president and the speaker of the House vacant, the next man in line to become president was the President Pro Tem of the Senate, Senator George Mossman of Hawaii, a Democrat.

Peter Profitt would have been derelict in his duties to his party if he allowed that to happen. He put out a call to his caucus, and with only a few grumbles, and no direct challenges, his fellow Republicans elected him the new speaker of the House.

A press release alerted the media.

Being a true believer in a better life after this one, Profitt did not want to have to explain himself to the Almighty for wishing another person ill. He didn't hope to see Patricia Darden Grant taken before her time. He just wanted to be in the right place in case she was.

He didn't think the Lord would have any problem with that.

4

February, 2012
The Oval Office

In the president's opinion, the prospect of Howard Hurlbert defeating both her and Mather Wyman was so remote that she hadn't lost a minute's sleep worrying about it. Whether her former vice president might beat her was another matter. He'd never lost an election, having been elected to four consecutive terms in the Ohio legislature, two terms as that state's governor and as her running mate in the last presidential election.

Mather was smart, experienced and successful — and he was a man.

His gender still counted with many voters and not all of them men. There were countless women who preferred to have a man do the heavy lifting for them. Perhaps an even greater number of women would choose to have a man do such dirty work as sending young military personnel into harm's way. Knowing they would *never* risk the lives of their own sons or daughters in a foreign conflict, many of these women, if only subconsciously, excluded a member of their own gender from doing the same.

The way the president read the electoral landscape, though, the voters with traditional sensibilities were being supplanted by the rising generations, young-to-middle-aged men and women who had matured with a truer sense of gender equity.

It was to this segment of the electorate that the president's thoughts turned, and even to a large number of the baby boomers. That demographic leviathan was rapidly graying, but in their heart of hearts many of them considered themselves to be "forever young." What the president had in mind should appeal to their sense of sticking it to the man.

The president paid her chief of staff the respect she was due for compiling a comprehensive list of vice presidential possibilities. She read the file on each candidate thoroughly. Then, in keeping with the idea she'd formulated earlier, the president asked Galia the obvious question.

"Where is Jean Morrissey's name?"

"Madam President?"

"The woman I want as my running mate, remember?"

Of course, Galia remembered. She'd merely been hoping that —

"Galia," the president said, "not only is Jean my preference as a running mate, it makes political sense to bring her on board now. Doing so will eliminate one of my primary opponents, leaving only Roger Michaelson for both Jean and me to beat up on."

Galia had to nod grudgingly.

"Giving Jean several months of White House experience would also make her a more formidable running mate in the general election, and there's no way I could ask someone else simply to fill in until November, and then have Jean on the ballot with me."

"No, you couldn't. You'd look foolish."

The president said, "I really did read through your list of possible VPs carefully. I didn't see anybody I liked better than Jean."

Galia said, "It's just such a *big* risk, *two* women."

"It's also the next logical step. More important, it's what I think would be best for the country. Can you trust me on this?"

What choice did she have, Galia thought. Resign?

That would look great, wouldn't it? First Wyman going and then her.

It would give the entirely incorrect impression that she thought the Grant Administration was a sinking ship. And she was a rat leaving it.

Galia couldn't abide either of those perceptions.

"Yes, Madam President," she said. "You have my complete trust."

Then she added, "It will likely be three women running, not just two. Mather Wyman has feelers out to Governor Rosalinda Fuentes of New Mexico to be his running mate. Initial word is she's lukewarm about the idea. But if you bring Governor Morrissey on board, she'll look like your heir. Governor Fuentes wouldn't be able to claim your mantle."

"No, she wouldn't. So what do you think, Galia?"

"I think it boggles my mind, women holding three out of four top spots on the two major party tickets."

"Makes up for lost time," the president said. "Now, if we can only coax Howard Hurlbert to add a belle to the True South ticket."

Galia laughed … but she couldn't rule out the possibility.

FBI Headquarters — Washington, D.C.

McGill and Sweetie brought Daryl Cheveyo with them when they stopped in to see Deputy Director DeWitt. The former CIA shrink grinned when he saw the Andy Warhol rendering of Chairman Mao on the deputy director's office wall.

Cheveyo shook hands with the deputy director and told him, "It'd be funny if that print of Mao was a Chinese counterfeit."

"Not when you consider its price tag," DeWitt said, but he smiled as he said it.

He got everyone seated around a small conference table and provided each of them with a bottle of Poland Spring water and a glass.

McGill took a sip and told DeWitt, "I recently asked Chana Lochlan to help me mess with Damon Todd's head. Then it occurred to me to ask an expert if that was a good idea. I got in touch with

Dr. Cheveyo and he agreed to help me."

DeWitt nodded and asked, "Your opinion, Doctor? A good idea?"

"Todd is very smart. He'll see it for the provocation it is. None-theless, he'll respond."

"If he knows he's being baited, why would he respond?" DeWitt asked.

"You know that Todd lost his parents and sister to a series of tragedies?" Cheveyo asked.

"I do," DeWitt said.

Cheveyo told him, "As far as I was able to learn, Chana Lochlan was the most significant relationship Todd has ever had outside of his family. He thinks, accurately, that Mr. McGill took her away from him. Not for any romantic interest of his own, but his actions led to Ms. Lochlan's marriage to another man."

DeWitt picked up the ball. "That's a strong lure, getting your old flame back and, what, whacking the guy who caused all your troubles?"

McGill said, "Both those things and proving to the CIA they made a big mistake not hiring you when they had the chance."

"A three-fer, then," De Witt agreed.

"There's probably one more grudge to settle," Cheveyo said, "me. I was Todd's first point of contact with the Agency. He probably thinks if I'd been more supportive of his efforts to sell himself to my superiors, he'd be happily toiling at Langley today."

"Why didn't you push harder for him?" DeWitt asked.

"He seemed just a touch erratic," Cheveyo said deadpan.

"Certainly can't have nonconformists doing government work," DeWitt said. "So has Mr. McGill persuaded you to offer yourself as bait, too, Doctor?"

Cheveyo said, "He makes a good case that it would be preferable to have Damon Todd come out of hiding at our urging, when we're prepared for him, than at some future moment when we might be looking the other way."

McGill told DeWitt, "We're starting out by raising Ms. Lochlan's and Dr. Cheveyo's media profiles."

"Have they been offered federal protection? Say from the Secret Service?"

"They have. We hope that Todd will make a move on one of them before coming for me."

DeWitt looked at Cheveyo. "Very charitable of you and Ms. Lochlan."

He said, "We've both spoken to SAC Crogher and Special Agent Kendry. We're comfortable with the measures they're taking to protect us."

McGill continued, "If Todd plays it cagey, we're going to put out the biggest prize we can: Ms. Lochlan, Dr. Cheveyo and me, live, all in the same place, one night only. If it comes to that, we thought your people might like to collaborate with the Secret Service."

"The Secret Service has agreed to your idea?" DeWitt asked.

"The president has talked with them; you'll be hearing from her, too."

McGill was usually reluctant to invoke the power of the presidency, but there were times when you didn't want anyone dragging his heels.

"Well, then, that's settled. Will I be working formally with SAC Crogher?"

"Him or Elspeth Kendry. You'll hear from them as details are worked out."

"Would you care for any input on our part?"

"On *your* part, sure," McGill said. "After you filter out any FBI ideas you don't like."

DeWitt grinned. "I'm not nearly as high up the food chain as you are, Mr. McGill. Sometimes ideas are presented to me from on high. They're not easily disregarded."

"Some revolutionary you are," Sweetie told him.

DeWitt told her in a conspiratorial tone, "I'm biding my time."

"Let me make things a little easier for you," McGill said. "While Ms. Lochlan and Dr. Cheveyo will be on hand for the grand finale, should there be one, they will have only cameo appearances. At that point, I'll be the center of hostile attention, and I'll have lots of help. Anything goes wrong, it's on me."

DeWitt turned back to Sweetie. "You'll be there, of course, Ms. Sweeney."

Sweetie nodded.

"If something unfortunate were to happen to Mr. McGill," DeWitt asked her, "would you concede he was solely responsible?"

"No."

"I'm afraid I wouldn't either." Turning to McGill, DeWitt said, "Sorry, sir, but I just don't like the idea of any civilian personnel placing themselves on the front lines, especially when they're near and dear to the president."

You and Celsus Crogher, both, McGill thought. Welcome to the club.

What he said was, "So save us all the trouble. Catch these guys before I do."

Wishard Hospital Billing Office — Indianapolis, Indiana

Sheryl Kimbrough thought the hospital billing lady, Joan Miller according to the nameplate on her desk, was pulling her leg.

"I'm sorry, what did you say?" Sheryl asked.

"Your daughter's bill has been paid in full, Ms. Kimbrough. You have a zero balance."

Joan had articulated each word clearly, as if speaking to someone for whom English was a second language.

Sheryl saw no sign that she was being jerked around.

Joan Miller didn't look like she was about to guffaw, slap her thigh and say, "Just kidding!"

"My insurance has a deductible and a co-pay," Sheryl said.

"I know," Joan agreed.

"Will you bear with me just a minute?"

"Of course."

As Joan waited patiently, Sheryl sent a text message to Cassidy's father, Blake, asking if he'd paid the balance of Cassidy's hospital bill.

The response was all but instantaneous. HOSP BILL? FOR WHAT?

Blake's alarm, indicated by the upper-case shout, was palpable.

Damn, he was right, Sheryl realized. She hadn't told him.

He was working on his new book. On his typewriter. Listening to jazz on vinyl. Away from all forms of twenty-first century communication, except his smart phone.

Sheryl texted back, even though she now knew he hadn't paid the bill.

Minor burns. (Comparatively, Sheryl thought.) Discharged today. Going home.

ON MY WAY.

Sheryl was stunned. Blake never interrupted his writing for anything. Except his daughter, apparently. His concern made her eyes mist over.

"Ms. Kimbrough, are you all right?" Joan asked.

Sheryl backhanded the emotional display from her face.

Returned to the matter at hand.

"Yes, I am, thank you. I was trying to see if I knew who paid the balance of my daughter's bill."

"Oh." Now, Joan looked nervous.

"Are *you* all right, Ms. Miller?"

"I thought you'd be happy," the billing lady said.

"You paid the bill?" Sheryl asked.

"No, no. I couldn't afford to do that."

Sheryl switched from being a concerned mother to a bulldog reporter.

"But you know who did pay it," she told Joan.

"No, I don't."

"Yes, you do. If you don't tell me, I'll go to your boss. If that doesn't work, well, I've already talked to the hospital's CEO once. If I have to, I'll do it again."

Joan Miller was agog.

She'd have been doing pirouettes if someone covered a big bill for her.

"I *can't* tell you," she told Sheryl.

"Why not?"

"Because I don't know." As Sheryl started to rise from her chair, Joan added, "Look!"

She turned the hard copy of the billing form in front of her around. As expected, Sheryl's insurance had covered most of the hospital charges, but a not insubstantial amount was noted as ... *paid by anonymous benefactor.*

What the hell?

Sheryl settled back onto her chair. "You really don't know who this person is?"

Joan told her, "No. I guess I'd be upset, too, if I thought this was just a mean trick, but it isn't. Your bill has been paid. The hospital has received the funds. It's a true act of kindness. Isn't that enough?"

Sheryl explained, "I used to be a newspaper reporter."

"Oh," Joan said, as if that explained everything.

Who paid her charges was just the first of Sheryl's questions. Right behind it was: Did Terry Pickford have his charges covered by the anonymous benefactor? What about the kids in the car? You added the costs of treatment for those four kids to Cassidy's you were talking big money.

There was a story here.

Not that Joan was going to be any help.

Sheryl said, "Thank you, Ms. Miller. I'm sorry I got upset. I am happy some goodhearted person has helped me out."

The billing lady nodded and smiled.

Sanity had been restored to her domain.

Sheryl went up to Cassidy's room. She was going take her daughter home. Baby her as much as she'd allow. Tell her that her dad was coming to see her.

If Cassidy looked like she was up to answering a question or two, Sheryl would ask if she heard any good news about the other kids with whom her life had become intertwined.

Turned out Sheryl didn't have to ask.

Cassidy gave her a bigger smile than usual upon seeing her.

Followed that with a hug that almost squeezed the breath out of her.

"Oh, Mom, wait till you hear. Somebody's picking up the hospital bills for all of us. No matter how high it goes."

That forced Sheryl to ask, "Where'd you hear that?"

"Mr. and Mrs. Henderson. They're Nancy's mom and dad; she's the girl whose hair was on fire. You know, that I put out with my hands. They told me. They came by to thank me for what I did, and they told me. We were all crying."

Sheryl embraced her daughter and added her tears to the others that had been shed.

Still wondering who the anonymous benefactor was, and determined to find out.

McGill Investigations, Inc.

"I should have thought of that," McGill told Sweetie.

"Of course, you should have," she agreed.

The two of them were in McGill's office. Elspeth and Leo occupied the reception area.

McGill had been discussing the meeting they'd had with Byron DeWitt. On the way back to the office they'd dropped Daryl Cheveyo off at Georgetown University. His Secret Service detail was already in place. As long as they were at the campus, McGill and Sweetie caught Abbie between classes and had lunch with her.

Never hurt to see your child, be reassured she was alive and well.

Returning to the office and getting back to business, the two former Chicago coppers were evaluating the new fed they had to deal with. Sweetie had pointed out that DeWitt was far more socially and psychologically deft than SAC Crogher.

The deputy director had scored a direct hit by equating his concern for McGill's welfare with Sweetie's. His motivation was different, but his point of view was, if not identical, at least similar. As McGill had just been forced to admit.

"You think DeWitt will be able to capture Todd and those other two?" McGill asked.

"Cheveyo confirmed he has a good rep, even among CIA people."

McGill said, "I don't get the feeling he's holding back on us. He's sharing the information he has. For a fed, that's damn rare."

"It is, but what does he have to lose? You've already come up with one idea that almost bagged Todd. Why wouldn't DeWitt want you to keep your thinking cap on? Even if you're directly responsible for catching Todd, everyone's going to think you just got credit because you're married to the president."

McGill laughed. "Yeah, that's true. And if everything blows up in my face, I'll get the blame for that, too."

"We're not going to let anything blow up around either of us, are we?"

McGill shook his head. "No. We've both got too much to live for."

Neither of them carried the idea any further, but they both felt they were working on an existential plane this time: Somebody wasn't going to come out of this situation alive. Better it was the other guys than them.

Sweetie had talked to her old cop contacts in Chicago and the North Shore suburbs when she went to Evanston to check out the rock that had been thrown through McGill's living room window. There had been no record of partisan political rock throwing on any police blotter in the area or even the whole state.

In Illinois, elections could be pitched battles, but they were fought with political wiles and bags of unmarked cash far more often than blunt objects. John F. Kennedy's 1960 election to the presidency was often credited to the late Mayor Richard J. Daley's vote stealing in Chicago. What usually went unremarked was that downstate Republicans had been stealing votes for Nixon as hard as they could.

But nobody threw any rocks through any windows.

Certainly not rocks with party icons on them.

Given their knowledge of the local culture of political corruption, both McGill and Sweetie were convinced the elephant on the rock that shattered McGill's window was the work of an outsider who thought he was being tricky. Say a former CIA agent who hadn't done his homework. One of Todd's new pals.

Sweetie had informed the Evanston cops and Secret Service agents what they could be facing, and made sure there were no holes in the armor. She even took Carolyn out to the firing range to sharpen her skills — and Lars came with her. He hadn't done any of his own shooting, but Sweetie saw he was leaning that way.

Now, McGill and Sweetie pored over the binders DeWitt had given them.

They held copies of the compilation of all the people with whom Damon Todd had more than passing contact in his life — at least those the Bureau had been able to dig up and verify thus far. The thoroughness of the FBI effort had produced a printout with the thickness of a small town phone book.

If a name was also found in *Who's Who in America,* it was highlighted and cross-referenced. The agents hadn't stopped there, though. Social prominence was one thing. Achievements in education, science, medicine, business and agriculture were also recognized in corresponding reference publications.

Sometimes hunting down wanted men could give a person eyestrain.

McGill decided he and Sweetie shouldn't have all the fun.

He called Elspeth and Leo in, gave them reading assignments, too.

The Beverly Hills Hotel — Beverly Hills, California

Politicians of both major parties and more than a few minor ones had long used the affluent and politically active residents of California as a vast ATM machine. Patti Grant didn't need anyone else's money, but she had flown west to see if she might persuade some old friends from her movie days to donate their time and talents to her reelection campaign.

Arriving at the grand old pink hotel on Sunset Boulevard, she quickly made her way to the presidential suite. It was impossible for her arrival not to be noticed, but with the Secret Service, Beverly Hills cops and the hotel's staff escorting her not a single person got to ask for an autograph. Everybody she saw, many of them doing double-takes, got a brilliant smile and a friendly wave.

Everyone thus graced was able to think Patricia Darden Grant had specifically singled out him or her for a greeting. Such was the talent of both the politically and theatrically gifted.

Waiting for her in the presidential suite were her former talent agent, the legendary Dorie McBride, retired and now nearing eighty years old, but as feisty as ever; Tom Gorman, a television writer and producer and the winner of three Emmy Awards and two Peabody Awards, and Edward Cabot, the witty, intellectual public television host who divided his work schedule between KCET in Los Angeles and WNET in New York.

All three of Patti's invited guests stood as she entered the suite. Dorie stepped forward and extended her hands to the president. Patti took them and kissed her former agent on both cheeks.

"Patricia, you look wonderful. Stick with me and you may go far."

"You don't think I'm too old to land a leading role?" the president asked.

"Of course not, but we'll have to make sure you and Meryl aren't working the same year."

The president laughed. Avoiding competition with La Streep was a strategy many an actress hoping for an Academy Award followed. Patti said, "I'm just glad she won't be running against me for the presidency."

The president stepped forward to greet Gorman and Cabot. They were given friendly handshakes and smiles that would have left lesser men bedazzled. The principal players sat around a table with a view of the Hollywood Hills. Food and drink were provided by the suite's butler and his staff.

When everyone indicated all their needs were met, the staff withdrew and the Secret Service stepped out of sight.

Cabot asked the president, "Do you ever get used to all the security presence, Madam President?"

Patti smiled. "They're wonderful people. Brave beyond understanding, considerate of when Jim and I need personal space and they make sure I can find a parking spot wherever I go."

Gorman grinned and said, "I know Dorie would never let us think of you as less than a movie star, Madam President, but I'm a fan of the way you come across on television, always have been."

Dorie McBride shrugged, "Maybe we can find Patricia a sitcom after she retires from politics."

Patti took one of Dorie's hands in hers. "I'm afraid Jim has other plans for us."

"Don't worry," the agent said, "we'll find a part for him." With a sly look at Gorman she added, "Or we can let him produce."

Patti knew the banter was all good-natured ribbing, but she thought there was a germ of an idea worth pursuing. She said, "Who knows? Maybe Jim would be interested in sharing his experiences as the president's henchman."

"On PBS," Cabot said, "working with Ken Burns."

"Or HBO working with me," Gorman said.

"I could work a deal either way," Dorie said.

Patti took a sip of orange juice.

"Before we get ahead of ourselves," she said, "I'd like to discuss a plan to keep both Mr. McGill and me in the White House for another four years. I know that all of you have wonderful sources of information, but I don't think it's leaked yet that I'm not going to do any TV commercials for my campaign."

Wide smiles appeared on all three members of the president's audience.

They were savvy enough to make the inference.

Patricia Darden Grant had come up with a more compelling way to reach the public.

One that involved them.

"What I'd like to do is this: Come up with three nights of must see Web TV each week."

"The format of this programming being?" Cabot asked.

"Lively, intelligent, funny, free-flowing debates between two three-person panels. One side would represent the points of view of my administration, the other side would represent Mather Wyman and maybe, on occasion, Howard Hurlbert. We could set a nominal length of one hour for each show, while allowing Edward to extend the Webcast up to ninety minutes if the situation demands more time."

"You're talking celebrity panels, Patricia?" Dorie asked.

"I'm thinking of smart, articulate well known people who don't need to use profanity to make a point. Yes, that would include actors from both movies and television, but it would also include writers, directors, composers, painters, scientists and others."

"Journalists?" Cabot asked.

Patti said, "They're problematic. You don't want them to be overt advocates, but when they pretend each party is equally responsible for the country's problems, it sets my teeth on edge."

Dorie said, "Patricia's right. Journalists would make it just like any other news show. People from the arts and sciences would make the show distinctive, and say what you want about actors, they'd be a much bigger draw."

"That's part of my thinking," Patti admitted, "but you'd have to use people who are informed on the issues and able to express their ideas without a script. That being the case, I'd like to cast as big a net as possible. Let's use some people who are well known but haven't worked on camera lately because, oh my, they might have some gray hair."

Gorman, whose hair was a tumbleweed of gray, raised a fist.

"That's wonderful, Madam President. You'll be offering opportunities to revive careers."

"And extend mine, I hope. What I was thinking was to use two celebrities, one contemporary, one classic, if you will, and an accomplished but lesser known figure from the arts or sciences."

Cabot said, "That would give you good trans-generational coverage and you could mix and match ethnicity and gender. What I'd like to suggest, though, is a bit more fluidity in your casting."

"What do you mean, Ed?" the president asked.

"Well, you could sandwich your non-entertainment figure between classic or contemporary actors, as you've put it. Or you could skew the celebrities older or younger and have your third person be on one end or the other. On the older end you could have the country's poet laureate and a middle-aged actor and a newcomer; on the other end you could have your classic actor, a middle-aged colleague and, say, a young creator of a new iPhone app."

Gorman said, "That's great. I like that a lot."

"So do I," Patti said. "Another thing I was thinking of was to do one week of taping here in Los Angeles and the next in New York."

"No," Dorie said.

The president turned to her and said, "No?"

"Patricia, what is my hometown?"

"Brattleboro, Vermont."

"Exactly."

Cabot asked, "You'd like us to do all the shows from Brattleboro?"

Dorie gave him a cutting look. She said, "Do a week in L.A. and another in New York, yes. But in between do a week in regional hubs: Chicago, Boston, Atlanta, Denver, Portland. You do need more than two big states to win the election, don't you?"

"I do," Patti said. She gave her former agent's hand a squeeze.

"Thank you, Dorie."

The president turned to Gorman and Cabot. "I was thinking each new show should first go up on the Net at ten p.m. Eastern time. Does that make sense to everyone?"

It did.

"I guess the only question I have left to ask," Patti said, "is whether all of you are interested in participating and will be free to do so."

"How long do you see this enterprise running?" Gorman asked.

"From Monday, March 2, 2012 to Monday, November 5, 2012."

"The eve of the election," Gorman said. "That would have to be a special show."

"I'm sure we could think of something," Patti said.

"I'm in, Madam President," Gorman said.

"As am I," Cabot said.

The president turned to Dorie.

Who told her, "Oh, Patricia, don't be foolish. I won't even ask for my usual commission."

"We will have a reasonable production budget?" Gorman asked.

"You'll all have everything you need. I'm paying for this campaign out of pocket."

"I'd like to make a suggestion," Dorie said.

"And I have one question," Cabot added, "but ladies first."

"Your suggestion, Dorie?" Patti asked.

"Everyone who comes on the show from our side? I'd like to give each of them, say, a minute to look right into the camera and say: 'I'm going to vote for Patricia Darden Grant and this is why.' If we have them on hand, why not get an up close and personal pitch?"

"I like it," Patti said. "Thank you, Dorie. You have a question, Ed?"

"Two, now that I think of it. Assuming you're the unofficial executive producer, Madam President, if one of us has a question calling for your guidance, and you're busy saving the nation, whom do we call?"

"Galia Mindel." The president gave Dorie's hand another squeeze. Her former agent and her present chief of staff were not the best of friends. Their personalities were too much alike. "She'll either be able to reach me or will have the authority to speak for me. What's the other question?"

Cabot said, "We'll be picking the guests for our side."

"Yes, each of you has a vote, majority decides. Unanimity would be better."

"Great, but who's going to pick the opposing teams?"

The president smiled. "I have just the person in mind."

Cheltenham Drive — Bethesda, Maryland

Reynard Dix, the former RNC chairman, had never thought he would live in the North. He never thought his daughter would be born in China of Chinese parents. He never thought he'd be without gainful employment. He never thought he'd entertain thoughts of suicide — at least before he got so old he couldn't stop drooling or started to think maybe the damn Democrats had a good idea or two.

It was true that Virginia — the South — wasn't much more than a good peg from center field to home plate away. Dix had been a star outfielder and a solid C+ student at Georgia Tech. But his wife, Miranda, had him living in Maryland which had stayed in the Union, even though it was south of the Mason-Dixon Line.

Miranda also had decided she didn't want to ruin her figure with a pregnancy.

She'd told Dix, " Reynard, do you know what can happen to a girl's boobies from getting pregnant and giving birth? They can get stretch marks and droop and maybe even shrink right down to little buttons. Is that what you want?"

Dix thought his wife was perfect — physically — and didn't want to see her change at all. Ever. He sometimes wondered if she'd hang on to her looks longer if he covered her in plastic like his mama had done with the living room furniture. He could leave little spaces so she could breathe all right until he took her out of the house and showed her off.

So he agreed to go for an adoption.

He thought the ideal would be a little boy who looked at least somewhat like him, had a good throwing arm and, unlike his adoptive daddy, could hit a breaking pitch.

Miranda told him he was crazy.

"You think someone who has a kid like that is going to give him up? What we have to do is get a baby from a foreign country."

"All right," Dix said. "How about Canada?"

If the kid couldn't swing a baseball bat, a hockey stick would have to do.

Miranda thought that was hilarious.

"China, Reynard. That's where we'll get our baby *girl*. The fools over there don't value them. They keep giving away these beautiful little girls who are smarter than Einstein just so they can take another shot at having a boy."

That sounded like a plan to Dix, but he fell in love with Li-hua, Pearl Blossom, the moment he saw her. Miranda had insisted on keeping the baby's Chinese name, but Dix just called her Lee, and dared his wife to argue with him. She didn't. Miranda fought only battles she knew in advance that she'd win.

As predicted, Dix's daughter was scary smart. What was really strange was having the little girl in their lives seemed to be making Miranda smarter, too. To help Lee maintain a sense of her ethnic heritage, Miranda enrolled both of them in Chinese language classes. Which was where they were at that very moment.

Dix had begged off. He thought learning Chinese would be way too hard.

Didn't think speaking Mandarin would endear him to his political cronies either.

Not that he seemed to have any friends in politics anymore. That was why he was out of a job. First, the damn president left the

GOP, but she was just a RINO, Republican in name only, anyway. Then, when the party had the chance to replace the president with a real conservative in the next election, the fix was put in for the vice president, Mather Wyman, another RINO.

So, though the irony pained him, he left the Republicans, too, signing up with True South. How could a party with that name be anything but colorfast conservative? The bitter answer was by being bought off by a crazed billionaire. Sure, every candidate — except damn Patti Grant, who had her own billions — had to have at least one fat cat bankrolling him. But why had Senator Hurlbert thrown in with Tom T. Wright?

And why was Wright so obsessed with Huey Long?

Because the man had been from Louisiana like him? So what? Long's motto had been "Every man a king." If that wasn't pure bullshit, it at least had to be communism. It sure wasn't the way Dix had been raised. You took care of the rich, they'd take care of you. By and by you'd get to be rich, too, at least in a small way.

A few generations went by, your offspring — if your wife didn't mind getting pregnant — they'd be respectably rich, too. The bastards who didn't play along, they could vote for Democrats and pray for socialism.

Not that most of them bothered to pray at all.

When Dix had seen Hurlbert abandon all conservative principles to become a populist, he'd had to quit True South, even though he badly needed the paycheck. The way Miranda spent money, he could have used *three* paychecks.

All he had left was his life insurance policy. The payout from that would see Lee through college. After that, he was sure she'd invent a cure for cancer that would be part of a sensible weight-loss plan and clear up acne, too.

Dix would have killed himself already, if he'd been able to think of a way to do it that wouldn't invalidate his life insurance policy. He was working on that knotty problem when the phone rang. He thought it might be —

Anybody but a sweet-voiced old lady who said, "Mr. Dix?

Please hold for the president of the United States."

Then the woman herself, Patricia Darden Grant, came on the line and told him all about an Internet TV show she had planned. She asked him, "Mr. Dix, how would you like to be the person who selects the celebrities for the conservative side of the debate?"

How would he like that? He'd like it even better than the first time he'd seen Miranda take off her bikini.

The president told him, "It's a volunteer position, Mr. Dix, but all your travel, meals and lodging will be paid for and everything will be first class."

"Madam President," Dix said, "I'll be happy to serve my country."

She thanked him for his service and said a courier would deliver all the paperwork.

He was busy figuring out how to play this windfall — he couldn't simply *sell* slots on the show to people on his extreme end of the political spectrum, but he could choose persons who had other means to express their gratitude to him. Book deals. Speaking dates. Think tank fellowships.

Long as they didn't want him to think too hard.

Dix laughed at his private joke.

Then the phone rang again. Sir Edbert Bickford was on the line. He was the first person to hear Reynard Dix's good news. He'd called to offer Dix an off-camera spot on WorldWide News in Review. That offer came with a lot of money attached. But after Sir Edbert heard of the president's offer, he doubled the amount, as long as Dix let Sir Edbert pick the conservative lineup for him.

Dix didn't hesitate a heartbeat before agreeing.

Wilson/West Realty — Ottawa, Illinois

Deanna Wilson picked up her office phone and thought she'd received a prank call. A male voice told her, "This is Special Agent Vincent Gallo of the FBI calling. May I speak with the person in charge of your office, please?"

The FBI? Come on, Deanna thought. Nobody in Ottawa ever did anything to deserve their attention. The IRS, maybe. She knew half-a-dozen people she thought were fudging on their taxes, but —

"Ma'am, are you there?"

"Are you really with the FBI?" The guy had a nice deep voice. Maybe she wouldn't mind meeting him, prankster or not. "Can you stop by and show me your badge?"

"I could, but that would mean driving down from Chicago and I might be cranky by the time I get there."

"I could save you the drive and meet you up in Chicago."

She was the one having fun now. Let's see how he liked a joke.

"That's very kind of you. We're at 2111 West Roosevelt Road. I have to tell you, though, that some people feel a little uncomfortable visiting us."

Still thinking it was a gag, albeit an elaborate one, Deanna asked, "Why is that? They have something to hide?"

"Funny you should put it that way. What I need to mention is that for security reasons we do full body scans, like they do at airports. Only our machines show more detail."

"What?" Deanna asked, not liking that idea, even if it was a joke.

"It's true. As a further precaution, we check our records to see if we have an open file on anyone who visits. May I have your name, please?"

Retreating to formality, thinking now maybe she was really talking with the FBI, Deanna gave her name and said she was the co-owner of the realty office with her friend Suzie West.

"Maybe we'd better talk over the phone," Deanna said.

"That would be fine, Ms. Wilson," Gallo said. "I need to inform you that what I have to say is part of an official investigation so I'll ask you to keep this conversation confidential and you need to answer my questions truthfully because lying to a special agent of the FBI is a crime punishable by up to five years in prison."

Deanna swallowed hard. If this *was* a joke, she was going to scratch someone's eyes out.

"Do you understand what I've told you, Ms. Wilson?"

"Yes," she said in a small voice.

Now, having become submissive, was the time she half expected to hear a bunch of people laughing at her.

But Gallo said, "Good, thank you. What I'd like to know is whether at any time over the past year you've acted as the Realtor for a client who paid you in cash to rent an apartment or a house. Have you done business with anyone like that?"

Deanna had, just once. She hoped she wasn't in trouble.

"Yes," she said, her voice even smaller now.

"Was that one client or more than one?"

"No, just one."

"What was that client's name, please?"

"I'll have to look it up. Hold on." Deanna kept all her records on her computer so it didn't take long. "His name is Thomas Gower." She spelled the last name.

"Did Mr. Gower have anyone with him?"

"No, he was alone."

"What occupation did he give you?"

"He said he was a college professor; he needed a place to write a book."

"Did he tell you the name of the school where he teaches?"

Deanna winced. "No, he didn't."

"Did he tell you the subject of the book he's writing?"

She felt better about answering that. "I didn't even think to ask. I mean, writing is a personal thing, isn't it? Nobody gets to know until the book comes out."

Deanna thought she heard the FBI man sigh.

"Can you describe Mr. Gower's physical appearance for me? You did see him, didn't you?"

Now, she thought the FBI man was getting snotty. "Of course, I saw him. He came to my office to sign the lease. I'd say he was nice looking. Not a movie star, but if you met him on the street, you'd be happy if he smiled at you."

"Did he smile at you, Ms. West?"

"Only politely," she said, the regret in her voice clear.

"Can you tell me the color of his hair and eyes and any other distinguishing feature?"

"Dark brown hair, brushed forward. I didn't get the impression he was losing it, though. His eyes? Kind of blue but with some gray in them, too. His nose was just a bit large, but it was nice and straight. His mouth was kind of big, too, but it worked with the nose."

"Height and weight?" Gallo asked.

"He was just a bit taller than me when I'm wearing heels. So I'd say about five-ten. His weight, I don't know. He wasn't fat or skinny. So whatever's medium for his height."

"Age?"

"Now, that I'm terrible at guessing. He was no kid, but I didn't see any gray hair, and he didn't color his hair. That's something I do know."

"How much money did Mr. Gower pay for his rental?"

"Three thousand dollars."

"Which paid for what kind of shelter?"

"A well-maintained old family farmhouse. Three bedrooms, two baths. Six months."

"Is this house located in Ottawa?"

"Just a bit out in the country. It's real quiet out there. Ideal for writing, I remember him telling me."

"Will you give me the address, please?"

She gave him the number on Gentleman Road.

Deanna asked, "Is that all?"

"If I have anything more, I'll call back."

"May I ask you something now?"

"You may. I don't know if I'll be able to answer, though."

"This shouldn't be too tough. Are you for real?"

Special Agent Gallo laughed. "Yes, I am."

"Well, if that's the case and it wouldn't be against any rules, could you send me a picture of you holding up your badge just so

I'll know for sure this hasn't been one big joke?"

There was a pause before Gallo said, "I'll do that, Ms. Wilson, but only if you promise to keep it to yourself until I tell you otherwise."

"Cross my heart," Deanna said. "I know I'll get in trouble if I'm not good."

Gallo assured her she would. Then, after hanging up, he faxed a photo of himself holding up his FBI credential.

"Oh, my," Deanna said. The man looked as good as he sounded. She should have gone up to Chicago.

Maybe she'd remember something she'd forgotten to tell Special Agent Gallo.

She'd definitely put his picture in the drawer of her nightstand.

Special Agent Gallo reviewed the information he'd taken from Deanna Wilson. He rated it as credible. The woman was basically honest and more than a little frightened by the consequences of lying to him. As to the substance of her answers, he deemed the situation worthy of a follow up visit to Ottawa by a special agent. Then he went on to call the next Realtor on his list. It was a boring job, but he'd been shot in the line of duty last year.

For the time being, boring was okay.

He made no official notation that he'd sent his picture to Ms. Wilson.

The House on Gentleman Road — Ottawa, Illinois

Olin Anderson knocked Damon Todd for a loop, but Anderson was wearing sixteen-ounce gloves, and Arn Crosby caught Todd before he hit the floor, so no great damage was done. Except to Todd's pride. That was his own damn fault. He took his eye off the more immediate threat. In real life if he'd done that, he'd be dead.

The three men had been doing close quarters combat exercises in the living room with the curtains drawn. It would have been more realistic to go through the drills outside, but with the trees bare they didn't want to take the least chance of attracting any attention.

As soon as Todd looked like his head had stopped spinning, Anderson asked, "Okay, Doc, what was your big mistake?"

Shrugging off Crosby's supporting hands, Todd said sullenly, "I looked for the man I heard coming up from behind me."

Crosby moved past Todd to stand next to Anderson, who was taking off his gloves.

He asked Todd, "What should you have done?"

"Attacked Anderson. Put him between me and you."

Both former covert ops men nodded.

"What would have been your best point of attack on me?" Anderson asked.

Todd reviewed Anderson's approach to him. "You had your left leg forward. I could have kicked your shin or knee and slipped behind you."

"Then what?" Crosby asked.

Todd worked out a strategy. "Kick the back of Anderson's left knee. Get him stumbling forward. Shove him into you. He wasn't holding any weapon I could take from him and turn on you. So I should have run."

Anderson said, "You've got the theory down pat, Doc. Now, you have to replay it in your head until it becomes automatic."

Crosby gestured to Todd to follow as he and Anderson headed to the kitchen.

Todd let them go, suspecting an ambush.

Anderson looked over his shoulder and grinned. He used his hands to form a T: timeout. He said, "Come on, we all worked up a sweat. Let's get something to drink."

Crosby was already in the kitchen and out of sight.

Todd let Anderson follow.

No way he was walking into that room like some witless fool. He began moving the living room furniture. Not back to its usual positions. He put it between himself and the kitchen doorway. Those two assholes came charging out of the kitchen at him they'd have to hurdle two chairs and the sofa. At the end of the obstacle course, Todd waited with the knife he took out from under one of the sofa's cushions.

They'd practiced knife work using soft plastic facsimiles.

The knife Todd held, though, was the real thing.

Problem was, he still wasn't ready for the pros. Anderson took a quick peek from the kitchen and pulled his head back. Then he stepped into the doorway and pointed a gun, also the real thing, at Todd. And that was just the half of it.

Crosby had slipped into the living room through the house's front door; Todd felt the cold air from outside a second after Crosby put the barrel of another gun to the back of his head.

"Shit," Todd said.

His shoulders sagged and he let the knife drop to the floor.

Then he spun to his left as fast as he could, trying to get behind Crosby. His plan was to do just what he should have done the last time. Get behind his opponent. He'd grab Crosby's gun and use it on — well, point it at Anderson. It would have been a good idea, if Crosby hadn't been ready for it.

Fast as Todd had moved, Crosby still found the time to retreat six feet, have his gun leveled at Todd's chest. Todd would have been killed again. But Crosby put his gun in his waistband and applauded. So did Anderson, his gun now also at his waist, as he walked around the furniture.

"Good reaction, Doc. If we weren't the guys who taught you what you should do — and knew what was coming — you'd have had us."

Todd took a deep breath and let it out.

"I'm still not ready for McGill," he said.

Crosby started putting the furniture back in place. "No, you're not, but you'll get better."

Anderson shoved the sofa to where it belonged. "Now, let's really get something to eat. We need to talk. Arn and I have the idea we'd like to spend the rest of the winter somewhere warm."

Putting a hand on Todd's shoulder, Crosby said, "We also need to ask how you'd feel about jumping out of an airplane."

Reserve Drive — Dublin, Ohio

Governor Rosalinda Fuentes (R-NM), according to her official schedule was taking personal time to travel to New York City to see a play or two and do some shopping for her family. She was flying commercial with her husband, David Ramsey.

The governor had a reputation as the hardest working public servant in her state and if she and her husband, an architect, needed some time to relax, and it wasn't costing the people of her state a dime, nobody could complain. They were entitled. No one from the media paid them the least attention as they drove up to Denver for their flight east.

Mr. Ramsey settled into their suite at the Waldorf-Astoria. Governor Fuentes left the hotel fifteen minutes after checking in, got into a limo and traveled to Teterboro Airport. A chartered jet flew her to Columbus, Ohio. Another limo took her to Mather Wyman's home in Dublin.

The former vice president met her at the door. He shook her hand and quickly ushered her in from the cold night.

"Governor Fuentes, I'm so pleased to welcome you into my home."

"My pleasure, Mr. Vice President."

Wyman had a gas fire was lit in the living room fireplace. Kira Fahey Yates, radiant at the start of her second trimester of pregnancy, stood just behind her uncle with a smile on her face.

"May I present my niece, Kira," Wyman said. "Kira, we're honored to have Governor Rosalinda Fuentes of the great state of New Mexico as our guest tonight."

Kira stepped forward and extended a hand. "Madam Governor, it's a pleasure."

Rosalinda Fuentes took Kira's hand in both of hers. She smiled warmly and said, "You are beautiful, Mrs. Yates. My congratulations to you and your husband."

"Thank you."

Mather Wyman guided the women into the living room.

He said, "I hope you won't mind Kira joining us tonight. She's become my confidant and my closest adviser."

Kira told the governor, "Of course, if you'd be more comfortable speaking privately with Uncle Mather, I'll excuse myself."

Very smooth, Rosalinda thought. These two know how to work together.

That still left a question to be asked.

"Pardon me, Mrs. Yates, but I'm someone who's always believed in doing her homework. Isn't your husband on President Grant's staff? Doesn't he work quite closely with her?"

"He is and he does, and we talk about everything, except our respective politics. I have to tell you, though, that my uncle is the only person I'd prefer to see as president to Patricia Darden Grant. But anything you say tonight will never get back to the president because of me."

The governor turned to look at her host. Raised an eyebrow a millimeter.

"I'd trust Kira with my life," he said. "Her word is her bond."

That left the governor with the choice of whether to cross the bridge that lay in front of her. If she were to become Mather Wyman's vice president, she would have to trust the people he trusted. Asking Kira Yates to excuse herself now would be an impolite way of saying she'd made a long trip for no good reason.

Allowing her to stay, on the other hand, would give the governor a chance to see how the man who would be president related to women.

"I'm happy to have Mrs. Yates join us," the governor said.

"Please call me Kira."

"Thank you, Kira. My friends call me Rosa." Turning to Wyman, she asked, "Would it be all right if I had a drink? In your kitchen maybe? That's the one room in any house where I feel like I can both relax and talk business."

"Of course," Wyman said. "What should I grab a bottle of on

the way?"

"Scotch for me."

"I'll have the same," Wyman said.

Kira told the others, "I'll pour and content myself with a glass of water."

Governor Fuentes opened the discussion with a bombshell.

"The president has asked Jean Morrissey to replace you, Mr. Vice President."

Wyman and Kira looked at each other.

Kira asked the question her uncle wanted to ask but didn't.

"How did you find out?"

"Take a guess," Rosa said.

Mather Wyman had an idea, but he was still playing things close to his vest.

Kira having a moment to think said, "You're a governor and so is Jean Morrissey. You wouldn't talk directly to each other about politics … but people on your staffs might. If they'd met, say, at the national governors conference. Maybe two staffers who hit it off after hours and didn't think there'd be any harm sharing some juicy news that would become public soon anyway."

Rosa looked at Kira with genuine admiration.

She told Wyman, "Your niece is *very* good."

"A jewel in all respects," Wyman said.

"Can you see what your uncle is thinking now?" Rosa asked Kira.

The younger woman looked at Mather Wyman as if she was trying to peer into his mind. Apparently, she could. She turned to the governor and said, "Governor Morrissey told the president yes … and that's why you're here tonight."

Rosa took a tiny sip of Scotch. She said, "A Fuentes has to work hard to keep up with a Morrissey."

"Possibly," Wyman said, "but that doesn't mean you've already decided to say yes, too."

"With respect, I haven't. Not yet."

"Because?" Wyman asked.

"Because I think we should see where each of us stands on the big issues, and I have one condition for joining you on the Republican ticket."

"Maybe I should go," Kira said.

Rosa put a hand on Kira's arm. "Please stay. I don't think what I want is too outrageous. Certainly, hearing it will be of no harm to your little one."

"Twins," Wyman told her. "Girls."

"*Maravillosa,*" the governor said.

"Now, what might your condition be, Madam Governor?" Wyman asked.

"I would ask you to pledge to learn to speak Spanish, Mr. Vice President, with the goal of being able to carry on a conversation in that language by the end of your first term."

Wyman looked nonplussed, as if that had been the last thing he was expecting.

"Think about it, sir," the governor said. "The president speaks Spanish and French."

"What about Jean Morrissey?" Wyman asked.

"Governor Morrissey speaks Spanish, French and Swedish. I grew up speaking English; I learned Spanish as a second language."

Mather Wyman bunched up his face as he sorted through the matter.

Tossed back his Scotch to help his thinking.

Wanted to light a cigar, but he smoked only when he was alone.

Finally, he said, "I don't suppose it would look good if I were the only one on either major ticket who was limited to one language."

"*No bueno en absoluto,*" Kira said. Not good at all.

Wyman gave his niece a look; Rosa gave her a smile.

"*Aprendí en la escuela,*" Kira explained. "I learned at school."

Keeping a straight face, the governor saw she would have an ally in Kira.

In certain matters anyway. Still it was a good sign.

"Very well," Wyman said, "if I do it my way."

"What way is that?" Rosa asked.

"My way is to let the question come to me. Some precious little newsie will notice the fluency everyone but me has in other languages and will ask me about it. I'll respond truthfully that I'm studying Spanish. I'll let you find a tutor for me. I won't make a big deal of it. I certainly won't try to make it an obligation for any future candidate for the presidency."

Kira said, "With some candidates, it would be nice if they could speak English properly."

Everyone laughed.

Rosalinda Fuentes agreed to the vice president's condition to her condition.

She knew how things worked. Once you learned a new language, got good at it, you liked to show it off. And men, especially, liked to show off, didn't they?

Besides that, if Mather Wyman won the election, there was no way in the world he wouldn't take political advantage of an opponent who spoke only English.

Before the night was over, Governor Fuentes agreed to join Mather Wyman on the ticket.

Once he got the nomination.

I-80 Westbound — Iowa

The last thing Damon Todd did before leaving Ottawa with Crosby and Anderson was drop an envelope containing a brief message to Deanna Wilson in the mail at the local post office. He informed her that he'd be doing some traveling to further the research for his new book. He planned to return before his lease expired. He left the heat on low so the pipes wouldn't freeze. The lights were set on timers so the house wouldn't look empty. The doors and windows, of course, were shut and locked. If she wished to inspect the house or arrange for snow removal, he'd be happy to pay for any additional expenses upon his return.

Crosby and Anderson had an easy time of it, persuading Todd they had to move on.

They'd put a Google Alert out on Chana Lochlan, wanting to see if she popped up in the media again. She had, and this time it was at a fundraiser for Georgetown University. Standing next to her in the *Washington Post* picture was Dr. Daryl Cheveyo, the Agency's point man for its contacts with Todd, and now a professor at Georgetown.

"All a big coincidence, right, Doc?" Anderson had asked.

Todd didn't bother to respond; he was fixated on the image on the iPad.

He wanted to reach right through the screen.

Throw an arm around Chana's waist.

Grab Cheveyo by his throat.

But there wasn't an app for that.

"They're working us hard, Doc," Anderson told him.

Crosby added, "In more ways than one. The pictures might be bait, hoping that you'll react in a stupid way and make things easy for them. But getting you worked up can also serve as a distraction so you, or we, don't notice them sneaking up on us."

"The thing is," Anderson said, "the longer we're on the loose the greater the glory will be for the sonofabitch who catches us."

Crosby amended that notion. "Up to a certain point, that's true. If all we do is keep our heads down, then they'll reevaluate. Decide we've lost our will to fight, and like we said before they'll think we're not worth the trouble or money of continuing an all out search."

Todd said, "We're not at that point yet."

"No we're not," Crosby agreed.

Anderson said, "They might be damn close to catching us, Doc. Some people make fun of the FBI, but they have some hard cases with real smarts working for them. They have manpower. They're methodical as hell, too. The bastards just love solving puzzles."

"Olin's saying it's time to hit the road, and I agree."

"But we'll fuck with them because it's fun and it's to our advantage. We'll make them think we're coming back here."

"Which we might do, if they're not as close as we think," Crosby said.

"How can we know if they're close?" Todd asked.

"With these," Anderson said.

He held up two plastic coat hooks and the face plate for an electrical outlet.

"There are cameras in each of these things," Crosby told Todd. "They're never going to fool pros, but they don't have to. These are security devices normal people use. Fits with your cover. Why shouldn't you use them? Really, all we want to do is get one good look at anyone who enters the house besides the real estate lady."

Anderson completed the tutorial. "Any FBI agents come in, we'll see it right here." He tapped the iPad. There was an app for that.

So now the Buick Enclave was carrying them west.

They were headed for the desert, either Arizona or California.

They wanted wide open spaces with room to run and endless places to hide.

Having the border with Mexico nearby was another good thing.

They'd also need a small airport where they could practice sky-diving.

Todd had never had a fear of flying but neither had he imagined jumping out of a plane.

"Is that really necessary?" he asked.

"We don't know yet," Crosby said, "but sometimes the only way to get to someone is by dropping in."

"Unannounced," Anderson added.

Capitol Street Café — Jackson, Mississippi

Brad Lewis had been a Chicago cop for twenty-five years before retiring. He'd lasted only six months sitting in his basement recreation room with his feet up watching SportsCenter all day before he knew he'd either have to get another job or have a lobotomy. He'd been working since he was eight years old, started out sweeping the floor in his dad's butcher shop. He wasn't cut out for having time on his hands.

He was tired of all the political aggravation that came with being a Chicago copper, but he loved serving a heaping plate of grief to any kind of shit-heel you could name, strong-arm robbers to white collar hackers. He didn't care. Putting the cuffs on them, hearing a guilty verdict returned, it was like having sex. Some times it was good, most times it was great.

When a judge came down with a maximum sentence on one of the mopes he'd arrested it was all he could do not to jump up and cheer in the courtroom.

So he went back to work doing what most closely approximated his old job.

He became a private investigator. Most times, his cases kept him right in Chicago, the place he knew the best. Occasionally, he'd get up to Milwaukee on a job or down to Saint Louis. He hardly ever traveled outside the Midwest.

This was the first time he'd been to Mississippi. He hadn't been crazy about the idea of going south. His grandparents had moved north from Alabama almost a hundred years ago, but Brad remembered hearing their stories about the things that could happen to black people in Dixie. They sure weren't tales of the good old days.

When he heard the details of the case, however, he decided to take it.

A lady was getting beaten by her husband. A friend of the woman wanted to see the brutality stopped before the lady got killed. Lewis remembered that very same thing happening to his favorite aunt, and that was after his father and two other men had given the bastard his own whipping. The cops caught the killer and he got locked up for a long time, but that didn't keep Mama from grieving the loss of her baby sister.

What it had done was get Lewis on track to become a police officer.

And now a private investigator.

A lawyer named Alvin Topman had hired him to take the case, but Brad Lewis wondered who'd hired Topman to be his front man. Seemed to Brad like it had to be someone who knew his personal history. Most likely someone he'd worked with as a cop.

He knew better than to ask. It was probably smarter that he didn't know.

He bought three new suits to take with him on the job. He was dressed to the nines every day he stepped out of his hotel room. He had his haircut touched up every other day. He presented himself as a man of means. His experience as a cop had taught him that even the bigots with badges, in Chicago or elsewhere, were less likely to throw their weight around when dealing with someone who looked like he had a fat wallet and friends with connections.

Lewis added a congenial manner to his prosperous appearance. He was always polite and usually smiling. Most of the people he met, black and white, seemed happy to see him coming. With the way he tipped, the staff at the Capitol Street Café certainly did.

He always got a good table. Sometimes it was right next to the one favored by Mrs. Robert Beckley. Other times he was a few tables away. Lewis would acknowledge Nella Beckley with a gentlemanly nod and a minimalist smile. Then he'd go back to reading, either a copy of the *Wall Street Journal* or a paperback edition of a Shakespeare play.

Upscale reading material was a good cover, too.

It wasn't long before he and Nella had become acquaintances.

They'd say good morning and comment on the day's weather.

The first time Lewis had seen Nella Beckley she'd worn sunglasses. The bruise on the left side of her face, though, was only partially concealed by the dark glasses, her hair and makeup. The former Chicago cop made sure he didn't stare or even look twice, but he knew what he'd seen. The mark left by a fist.

He took it as a good sign that the woman wasn't going to let her abuse keep her a prisoner in her own home. She'd cover up to be polite to others, but she still went about her business. It was a good way to see how people reacted, Lewis knew, find out who might stand by her if things got life threatening.

Lewis had been told Nella's husband spent a lot of time working out of town. As the days passed and her bruises faded, she started to relax. The private investigator thought there would be an arc to her emotional well being. The farther away she moved from the last beating, the happier she would be; the closer she got to her husband's next visit home, and her next beating, the more anxious she'd become.

The morning she came into the café without wearing her sunglasses, Lewis saw that Nella had bright green eyes. Perfect for her auburn hair and pale skin. A man took his hand to her, he wasn't only hurting another person, he was marring God's own artistry.

That was the day she asked him, "Are you visiting Jackson without your wife?"

Lewis answered truthfully. "I lost her five years ago."

Another reason he couldn't stand to have idle time.

"I'm so sorry."

"Me, too." He tapped his chest. "She's still in here."

Lewis let Nella think the memory choked him up. Which it did. He asked her to excuse him and got up from his table. He left a cell phone behind, Nella saw. She kept her eye on it to make sure nobody made off with it.

Ten minutes later, she decided her new friend wasn't coming back that day. Her question must have upset him too much. She felt terrible about that. She didn't even know his name or where he was staying.

The only polite thing to do would be to apologize the next time she saw him. She'd hold his phone for him until then. That'd be the right thing to do, too. She stepped over to his table. It surprised her to see that the phone was a cheap little knockoff, something you might pick up for a few dollars at a drugstore. It didn't fit at all with the way the gentleman dressed.

Oh, well, she'd still tuck it in her purse and —

She saw the business card that the phone had covered.

Thinking she might learn her new friend's name, she picked it up. Her throat tightened when she saw what was on the card. No name, no address, no place of employment.

Just a printed message. Meant for her.

The next time you need help, hit #1 on the phone.

Don't wait until it's too late.

Her heart racing now, she looked up to see if Bobby was anywhere nearby.

He wasn't. Wouldn't be home for another week. The party for Senator Hurlbert's birthday.

Nella's first impulse was to throw away the card and the phone.

She'd decided to do just that when she noticed there was a message on the back of the card.

If necessary, provoke a public fight. Subtly.

That thought jolted her as hard as any blow she'd suffered. She'd been taught to keep all her troubles private … as Bobby well knew. He counted on it. She had no doubt she could make him lose control in public. He'd never see it coming. She knew all his triggers, had learned them at considerable cost. She could set up a trip wire neither he nor anyone else would ever see.

The question was, did she dare do it?

She turned the card over: *Don't wait until it's too late.*

Nella paid her bill. She walked down the street, tore the card to bits and tossed the pieces into a trash bin. She kept the phone and remembered the speed dial instruction. Considered where the best place to have Bobby beat her in public might be.

The idea that she might have to endure only one more beating put a bounce in her step.

At that moment, Brad Lewis was reviewing the files he'd been given on Bobby Beckley, Howard Hurlbert, senatorial staffers, friends, hangers-on and their respective spouses. Lewis made note of one name, someone he thought might be a great help to him.

The Oval Office

Galia informed the president, "I've been told that Governor Jean Morrissey did everything but turn a cartwheel when you called and asked her to become your new vice president."

Stephen Norwood, the head of Patti's presidential campaign, added, "The deciding factor in not doing the cartwheel wasn't a lack of enthusiasm, it was a matter of the governor wearing a skirt when she got the news."

Patti grinned, "Good to know the woman has a sense of self-restraint."

"Nothing's official yet," Galia said, still trying to hedge the president's bet. "You're *sure*, Madam President, that Governor Morrissey is your best choice."

Patti was, but she was also politician enough to ask Norwood, "What do you think, Stephen?"

Sparing a glance at Galia, he said, "I like her on her own merits. I like her even better paired with you."

"How might I help improve the governor's sterling qualities?" the president asked.

"You have three years of Oval Office experience, Madam President. You can help the governor benefit from the lessons you learned. Except with the former prime minister of the U.K., you've been a model of patience, a trait the governor might emulate."

"That was an accident, Stephen, the unfortunate incident with the prime minister."

"Of course, Madam President."

Turning an ankle on an uneven walkway at Chequers, the prime minister's summer home, the president had lost her balance, spun and inadvertently planted a flying elbow on the prime minister's face, breaking his jaw and displacing a number of teeth.

That was the official story.

With the passage of time and endless review of the video, a growing number of people were coming to believe the prime minister had groped the president's bottom and had gotten exactly what he deserved.

Keeping a secret in the face of advancing technology grew ever harder.

The president pushed on, "Aside from what I might do for Governor Morrissey, Stephen, what might she do for me?"

"By virtue of her gender, and yours, she shakes up the status quo in a way that picking a man wouldn't do. Governor Morrissey becoming vice president is an invitation —"

"Or a taunt," Galia said.

"Possibly a taunt," Norwood agreed, "to traditionalists to criticize or even lampoon a ticket with two women on it."

"Meanwhile, it's giving Congressional Democrats fainting spells," Galia said.

Norwood said with a smile, "Only the men, and there's no one better able to defend both herself and the party against any and all critics than Jean Morrissey. You've bought yourself a fireball, Madam President."

The president said, "I'm not sure that's what I was aiming for."

"Wait until you see how she defends *you* against any critics, Madam President."

Galia said, "Stephen sounds as if *he* might turn a cartwheel."

"I can, you know," Norwood said, "in the appropriate place."

"More admirable restraint," the president said. "How does the schedule for the general election campaign look, Stephen?"

The president had already won the primaries in California, Illinois and New York. She'd even eked out a win in New Hampshire. She'd also won the Iowa caucuses. Roger Michaelson had taken South Carolina. Might win at home in Oregon down the road, but even that was looking iffy. He had no money to go on and stayed in the race only in the hope that Patricia Grant might be struck by lightning.

Mather Wyman was having similar success in the Republican

primaries.

The only candidates running against him were hard right conservatives who had been too stubborn to move over to Howard Hurlbert's new party. Their chances of success were similar to Roger Michaelson's.

Stephen Norwood reported that, in accordance with the president's wishes, the general election machine was up, running and well oiled.

Their meeting was just about to end when Edwina Byington buzzed the president. "Please forgive the interruption, Madam President, but Mr. McGill is here and he says it's on a very important matter."

Patti Grant's heart lodged in her throat and she thought: Kenny?

Finding her voice, she said, "Please send Jim in, Edwina."

McGill entered the Oval Office. His face was grim. Galia and Stephen Norwood started to rise to give the president and her husband their privacy, but McGill waved them back into their chairs.

He told Patti, "I'm sorry to interrupt, but I just heard from Aggie Wu. She's fielding calls from every reporter in the country."

"What happened, Jim?" the president asked.

"John Patrick Granby died," McGill said, "from the injuries I caused him."

"Oh, my God," Galia said.

McGill nodded but kept his eyes on Patti.

"I've killed a man and the world wants to know how I feel about it. I thought you should know first."

Via Las Palmas — Palm Springs, California

Crosby and Anderson opted to go with the California desert over the Arizona sandbox. If they needed to evacuate by air, Palm Springs had its own airport for executive jets and LA/Ontario International Airport was just sixty-nine miles west on I-10. It was a considerably longer drive to San Francisco and back, but Crosby made the trip and rented a modest Bay Area studio apartment as both an emergency hideout and as an address to open a bank account.

Todd had a score of *friends* from around the country make deposits ranging between eight and nine thousand dollars to the account. Crosby explained to the bank that investors in a new high-tech startup would be responsible for the inflow of cash. With Silicon Valley nearby the people at the bank didn't think there was anything peculiar about the story.

It was hardly less plausible than the idea of people starting companies in their garages and going on to make billions while their dreams became global icons.

Meanwhile, Anderson took on the chore of finding a suitable house in Palm Springs. That task was made challenging by the facts that it was high season in the desert, Anderson had no intention of using a Realtor and the desired landlord had to be someone who was used to living and working in the cash-only economy. Someone who could be trusted to honor his agreement.

It took Anderson two days to succeed. He landed them a four bedroom house with a large pool, Jacuzzi, weight room and home theater. Dense landscaping kept the outside world from seeing anything that occurred on the property.

Anderson being who he was got the owner to swear on his life that the house was not currently under surveillance by any law enforcement agency and its phones weren't being tapped. The term of the lease was for a three-month rental with the option to extend for another three months.

Upon Crosby's return, he, Anderson and Todd took occupancy of the house, chose their bedrooms and went out to the pool area wearing large brim straw hats. The hats were helpful both to keep the desert sun off their faces and to shield them from being recognized by any satellites passing overhead. It was unlikely the National Reconnaissance Office had been recruited to help in the search for them, but you never knew.

Crosby liked to be careful — when he wasn't charging an enemy head on.

Anderson said, "I'd have figured if we don't sunbathe in turbans and long beards we should be okay."

Crosby told him, "Wear the hat. Leave your AK-47 inside, too."

Todd paid his compatriots and their chatter no attention. He found a lounge chair in the shade and turned on his iPad. Having learned about Google Alerts, he'd become inseparable from the device. He had alerts set up for McGill, the president, the two of them in combination, Chana Lochlan and Daryl Cheveyo.

There was always news about the president, far too much for anyone to read all of it. But when there was no news about the others, Todd felt cheated, deprived. He especially looked forward to seeing new photos of Chana. Her looks had matured since the last time he'd seen her in person, but to his eye that had only made her more beautiful.

His desire to see her, hold her, have her again was a compulsion that grew more intense by the day. It grated on him no end that Chana had married once more. The thought of another man usurping his place was not to be borne lightly. He'd made that point to Chana's first husband, Michael Raleigh, arranging a fatal hang-gliding accident for him — and that was after Raleigh and Chana had divorced.

Todd had wanted to avoid any chance of a reconciliation. Now, she had married again and her second husband would also have to —

Wait while Todd read the new alert that popped up in his email.

This one was about McGill.

He had … killed someone?

The headline said: *Fatal Injury to N.H. Secretary of State Caused by President's Husband.*

Todd was stunned, to an extent that was evident to his companions.

Anderson called to him, "Hey, Doc, what's wrong? You find

your own obituary?"

He and Crosby walked over to Todd, who yielded the iPad to them.

The two former covert operatives read the headline.

"Whaddya know?" Anderson said. "As far as we've been able to find out McGill had never aced anybody. He finally broke his cherry."

Crosby said, "Question is, how does he feel about it?"

Todd thought about that, remembering the night he'd confronted McGill in his office. The president's husband had pointed a gun at him. Instead of shooting Todd, though, McGill had asked him not to force the issue — because he had gone to confession that day and didn't want to sully his newly purified soul.

No doubt McGill would need to seek absolution now.

Only this time, given the media coverage and the politics involved, McGill would have to confess publicly as well as privately. It didn't matter that he'd acted to save a life. He'd still have to outflank the president's enemies and their accusations.

Did you really have to hit the poor man so hard, Mr. McGill?

The idea of his nemesis being persecuted by the media pleased Todd.

He said, "McGill will have to tell us how he feels."

"Only one thing he can say," Anderson told Todd. "Same thing Arn and I always do."

"Sonofabitch brought it on himself," Crosby said.

Arlington National Cemetery — Arlington, Virginia

Keith Quinn, Tommy Bauer and Joe Eddy had been laid to rest side by side.

Captain Welborn Yates, Kira Fahey Yates and the parents of the fallen Air Force pilots stood before the graves. With them were the president and James J. McGill. Also present were Air Force Chief of Staff General Bertram Kinney, Colonel Carina Linberg, retired, an honor guard and a bugler.

The bugler played "Taps." The military personnel stood in a posture of salute; the civilians placed hands over their hearts. Tears flowed without embarrassment. The bugler's last note lingered in the unseasonably warm February air.

The honor guard fired no volley because the occasion was a memorial not a burial, but because the deceased had all been fighter pilots General Kinney had ordered the flyover of a missing man formation. All eyes turned upward as more tears fell to earth. When the last reverberation of the thundering jet engines faded, the president hugged the parents of the fallen pilots; McGill shook their hands.

Before leaving, the president told Welborn, "I'm so sorry this tragedy happened, Captain Yates, but my administration is much the better for having you in the White House."

Kira took her husband's arm, the one that wasn't saluting his commander in chief.

McGill shook Welborn's hand, told him, "Well done."

After the First Couple departed, Welborn and Kira exchanged hugs with the parents of his late friends. All of them expressed their gratitude to Welborn for bringing them a measure of closure. Joe Eddy's father summed up their feelings, "My Sally gave me the best gift I ever got when Joe was born, but your making sure that bastard got what he deserved comes pretty damn close."

The other dads nodded. The mothers asked Welborn to stay in touch. All of them requested pictures of the babies. Kira promised they would be sent without delay.

General Kinney congratulated Captain Yates on a mission accomplished. The chief of staff told Welborn to expect his personal letter of commendation to be added to his personnel file. He graciously added his thanks to Carina Linberg for her help in the matter.

After the general left, Carina introduced herself to Kira and congratulated her on her prospective motherhood. Then she gave Welborn a salute and said, "Thank you for sharing the credit with me. I can't remember the last time a man did that."

Welborn returned the salute and told Carina, "It was the right thing to do. That's the way my mother raised me. Good luck with your new TV show."

Carina Linberg smiled and walked off. Kira watched her go.

She asked, "The colonel is going to star in a TV show?"

"Write and produce," Welborn answered.

"She should do well in Hollywood."

Welborn nodded. If anyone gave Carina Linberg trouble, she'd call in an airstrike.

He and Kira walked arm in arm to their car, and he said, "It's the damnedest thing."

"What is?" Kira said.

"Thinking about Keith, Tommy and Joe, knowing the man who killed them has paid the price. I thought I might be hunting him the rest of my life. My greatest fear was I'd never catch him. Now, it's all behind me. I even got to see Linley Boland die."

A shudder passed through Welborn as that memory skated across his mind.

"I feel like a chapter of my life has come to an end," he said.

Kira pulled him closer. Kissed his cheek.

"I'm at a crossroads now," he told her.

Kira said, "I'm not sure those are comforting words to a new wife and expectant mother."

Welborn returned Kira's kiss. "You, Mrs. Yates, have no worries. I not only want to spend sleepless nights comforting colicky babies with you, I want to bounce our grandchildren on my arthritic knees."

"I'll keep your knees and all your other parts in top working order," Kira told him. "Were you speaking, then, of a professional turning point? You'd consider leaving the Air Force? The White House?"

"After honoring my military obligations … I might ask James J. McGill for a job."

"I married a gumshoe?"

"I could ask my father if anyone at Buckingham Palace needs

a personal secretary."

Kira laughed. "Go with the private eye idea."

"We'll see, but one thing is certain."

"What's that?"

"With the two of us soon to become the four of us, we'll need more than his and hers sport cars."

Kira grinned and told him, "Lucky for all of us, Porsche makes an SUV."

The Grant Estate — Winnetka, Illinois

A cleaning and gardening crew, carefully monitored by twice their number of Secret Service agents, made the house sparkle and groomed the grounds. A small army of government technicians installed the wiring, hardware and software for the security and communications infrastructure a president required. A helipad was built, after obtaining a zoning variance from town hall and making the promise it would be removed within a month of the president leaving office.

Strategies for defending the house Andy Grant had built were devised. Patrol schedules for the neighboring streets and lakeshore were established. Coast Guard cutters would observe and if necessary interdict any watercraft approaching within a mile of the estate's private beach.

No one would be allowed to duplicate Erna Godfrey's water-borne attack on the house.

The president had two dozen of her most immediate neighbors over for dinner and apologized to them for all the fuss she was causing. She expressed the hope that they would understand her need to come home again. Everyone was gracious in respecting her feelings, though one little boy with spunk raised his hand and said he'd feel better about things if the president provided pony rides on the grounds.

"I'll tell you what," Patti told him with a gleam in her eye, "let's see if we can have a Fourth of July picnic here."

The president glanced at SAC Celsus Crogher. He gave a small nod.

"If I hear good reports about you children, we'll bring in a pony or two."

Ethan Judd was brought in well before that. The president's curiosity had compelled her to watch the metamorphosis of WorldWide News under Judd's management. Galia had watched out of professional necessity. Both of them were impressed. Judd seemed to be doing the impossible, providing objective in-depth journalism without a hint of favoritism or sensationalism.

WWN was coming to serve as a measuring stick against which other news organizations could compare themselves. Spin doctors and other propagandists hated that the network eschewed their services and called its programming deadly dull. The critics, however, couldn't keep ever larger numbers of viewers from tuning in.

McGill trusted both Patti and Galia to put him in the best position to defend what he'd done to John Patrick Granby in the White House Press Room.

He and Ethan Judd sat in facing chairs in what had been Andy Grant's study. The chairs, at both men's insistence, were positioned so neither man would have to worry about bumping knees with the other fellow. Their comfort was more important than any particular camera angle the director might have wanted.

WWN was providing a live pool feed to the other broadcast and cable networks, and streamed the interview online. McGill wore a sport coat, a shirt with an open collar and casual slacks. He'd vetoed a blue suit as something a guy with a guilty conscience would wear.

As soon as the camera's red light came on, Ethan Judd got straight to the point.

"Thank you for taking the time to speak with us, Mr. McGill. Will you tell us, please, what was your intent the moment you left your chair on the morning John Patrick Granby attacked Galia Mindel?"

McGill said, "My intention was to keep Mr. Granby from killing Ms. Mindel with a garrote."

"How was it that you were able to act in such a timely manner?"

"I shook hands with Mr. Granby when I entered the room. His hand was sweating. At first I thought he might be nervous about appearing before the national press. Then I thought maybe he was going to castigate Ms. Mindel for diminishing New Hampshire's place in the primaries. Mr. Granby kept displaying nervous mannerisms. He played with his tie, the place where he'd hidden the length of fishing line with which he intended to choke Ms. Mindel. He also wiped his hands on his pants as he stood up."

"You sound as if you were watching Mr. Granby quite closely. As it turns out, you were correct to do so. Was there anything else beside what you mentioned just now to call your attention to him?"

McGill said, "I didn't know what he was going to do, but I knew Mr. Granby was on edge. More so than he had any apparent reason to be. In a situation like that, you have to ask what you're missing. It's a good idea to keep looking until you find out."

"Do you think that's what most people would do?"

"I can't speak for most people. I do think most street cops and others who face dangerous situations on a regular basis would be watchful."

"Was there any final deciding factor that spurred you to action?"

"Yes, the expression on Mr. Granby's face as he put the garrote around Ms. Mindel's throat. It was in a real sense the most murderous look I'd ever seen."

Judd paused to look at his notes and then said, "The law permits the use of deadly force when a person is faced with a deadly threat or to save the life of another person faced with a deadly threat. Mr. Granby died from complications caused by the paralysis he suffered from a broken neck. Was it your intent not only to save Ms. Mindel but also to kill Mr. Granby?"

"No," McGill said. "That thought never entered my mind."

In a quiet voice Judd asked, "Other than taking your word for that, sir, is there any way for someone who doubts you to be persuaded that you didn't intend to kill Mr. Granby?"

McGill took a moment to think.

Then he said, "I haven't looked at the video of what happened that day. I have no desire to see it. But I think if you look at the event in real time you'll see I didn't stop to think about anything. I reacted as fast as I could to save a life. That was instinctive. The only way I could hope to persuade an unbiased person is to ask that he or she think of a situation that demanded an immediate response on their part. If you see a falling child, for example, you don't stop to think about what the best way to catch him will be. You just reach out as fast as you can. Grab whatever's available."

"A moment ago you referred to your career as a police officer. Is it correct that you never shot anyone while you wore a badge?"

"That's correct," McGill said.

"But there was a time when someone else shot you, is that right?"

"Yes, it is."

"How did you respond to being shot?"

"I took the gun from the assailant and slapped his face. Placed him under arrest."

"Would you have felt justified in using greater force against the man who shot you?"

"I didn't think about that at the time. I just reacted then, too. Looking back now, I'm glad I didn't use greater force."

"What you did back then is something you can live with now?"

"Yes."

"How will it be for you to live with what you did to Mr. Granby?"

"Harder," McGill said.

After Judd had shaken McGill's hand and he and his crew had left, Patti embraced her husband. Some moments later, he asked, "Did I do okay?"

"You were great."

"Judd was fair with me."

"Yes, but he knew he was being tested to see how he'd do with me. Thanks for being my guinea pig."

"What's a henchman for?" McGill asked. "Galia approved of my performance?"

"She said she hates the way she keeps sinking deeper into your debt."

"Always the sweet-talker. So we're as good as we can be with this?"

"Galia said after Burke Godfrey and John Patrick Granby it would be better if anyone else we place in custody survives through his trial."

Hillside Drive, Bloomington, Indiana

With Cassidy Kimbrough healing from her burns, her mother, Sheryl, held her class at her home. The living room was packed as the students watched Jim McGill's interview with Ethan Judd. The floor, as well as the furniture, was used as a seating area. Cassidy had asked to be present and by unanimous consent of the class she was welcomed.

The high schooler sat between two of Sheryl's brightest students. The coeds took turns whispering to Cassidy and making her giggle. Sheryl couldn't help but wonder if their humor was at her expense. That concern was fleeting as she and the others became caught up in an interview whose subject was life and death and the measure of responsibility a person took upon himself by becoming involved in such a situation.

As the interview concluded with the president's husband tacitly admitting that having caused a man's death would weigh upon him, Cassidy offered her unsolicited opinion.

"He did the right thing," she said.

"Cassidy?" Sheryl said.

The elder Kimbrough wasn't objecting to her daughter's participation in class discussion, but Cassidy was off point.

The question was whether James J. McGill had been honest and straightforward in his responses, not if he had or hadn't acted properly.

Such academic precision was lost on the youngest person in the room.

Getting to her feet and becoming emotional, Cassidy elaborated, "I would have done the same thing he did, if I could have. I did the best I could. I wish I could have helped those poor kids more, but ..."

Cassidy burst into tears. She hopped over students on the floor and ran upstairs to her bedroom. Sheryl followed, stopping at the foot of the stairs.

She turned to look at her students. "Please give me ten minutes. If I'm not back by then, feel free to leave. But please write a brief analysis of Mr. McGill's responses to Mr. Judd's questions."

Having done her best to hold up both her personal and professional responsibilities, Sheryl ran up the stairs and found her daughter in her bed with the covers pulled up to her nose. Her eyes were red and overflowing, but she made no sound.

Sheryl did her best to stay calm. She sat on the edge of the bed and stroked her daughter's cheek. She asked, "Honey, what's wrong? Was it the interview that upset you?"

Cassidy bobbed her head. She reached out and pulled her mother down to her.

Sobbing now, she told Sheryl, "I did my best, Mom, honest. I don't know what more I could have done."

"You mean helping the kids in that car? Nobody could have done more."

"Terry did."

"Oh, honey."

Sheryl wouldn't say so, not for years, if ever, but she thanked God that Cassidy hadn't been the first one to reach the car. If she'd been burned as badly as Terry Pickford —

As if reading her mind, Cassidy said, "Mom, I'm so worried

that Terry or one of the other kids is going to die. I worry all the time."

That was still a possibility so Sheryl didn't try to pretend it wasn't.

Cassidy continued, "Mr. McGill *saved* Ms. Mindel. He doesn't have to worry about that, but you could see it still hurt him that the other man died. If he feels bad about that, how am I going to feel if …"

She couldn't bring herself to complete the thought.

Sheryl couldn't think of a way to comfort her.

The door to the bedroom opened and a shadow fell across both of them. Sheryl thought it might have been a student, come to ask if any help might be offered, but it wasn't. Blake was there. He'd come to see Cassidy in the hospital, then he'd returned to D.C. to clean up loose ends. And now he was back.

"Dad!" Cassidy said. She extended an arm to him. He knelt next to the bed and kissed his daughter's forehead. For a moment, they huddled in silence. Sometimes there was comfort in numbers.

Easing away, Sheryl said, "I better get back to —"

Blake shook his head. "I dismissed your class. Told them you'd send an email."

Sheryl squeezed his hand. "Thank you."

Cassidy asked, "Dad, can you stay a while?"

"You bet, kiddo," he said.

He looked to Sheryl for confirmation. She nodded.

Jackson Hilton — Jackson, Mississippi

Other than taking a sip of champagne as part of a toast that described Senator Howard Hurlbert as the next president of the United States and wished him a happy birthday, Nella Beckley refused to drink anything with alcohol in it. At first, that had amused Bobby Beckley. He'd whispered to his wife, "That's okay. The way I recall things, you were never a girl who needed liquor to get hot, wet and short of breath."

That was true, Nella thought, before you started beating me, you sonofabitch.

In front of the three hundred people in the Hilton ballroom, however, Nella didn't think it was the time to make that point to her husband.

Then again, maybe it was exactly the time.

She'd been advised by her nameless friend at the Capitol Café to provoke a public fight. Not that she thought there was any black man in Mississippi so foolish as to defend a white woman at the birthday party of the figurehead of the new True South party. Even so, if she got Bobby to start in on her in a crowd this big, there'd have to be some witnesses willing to testify on her behalf.

One or two of the women, anyway.

Steeling herself, Nella said, "One of us needs to be sober to drive home. You wouldn't want to embarrass the senator with a DUI."

Bobby sat back and grinned at her. "Ain't a cop in this state would give me a ticket for any damn reason. Precious few in Washington, D.C. would for that matter."

Nella told her husband, "There's always one who just doesn't know any better."

That gave Bobby Beckley pause, the idea that his home-state armor had even the least chink in it. He almost felt he had to put the notion to the test. Show both Nella and himself that it couldn't be true. Then a more rational, less macho part of his mind asserted itself.

He'd had only one drink at the moment.

Bobby said, "It wouldn't matter if that bitch in the White House called out federal troops to keep me off the road. I got us a room for the night."

Bobby's slur of the president had been loud enough to reach ears for a radius of several banquet tables. Nobody particularly minded his characterization of Patricia Darden Grant, but raising your voice in a rude way was frowned upon.

Nella helped stoke Bobby's temper by responding in little less than a shout, "A room? That was the best you could do? Not even a suite?"

Brad Lewis sat on a sofa outside the ballroom in the Hilton that night in the same fashion he'd become a regular at the Capitol Café. Well dressed with impeccable manners. He was already a guest at the hotel, had been booked into it since he got to town. When he saw the sign outside the ballroom stating that Senator Howard Hurlbert's birthday party was taking place there, Lewis knew he'd picked just the right place to wait.

A pretty white woman approached wearing a very tight dress that didn't cover anything more than the law demanded. Lewis had contacted her the day before. He wasn't certain she'd have the courage to show up. But there she was, looking like she could steal a man's heart and break it with a single glance.

She was Lewis' backup plan in case Nella didn't have the pluck to take advantage of a golden opportunity.

"Pardon me, sir," the woman said. "Would you mind if I sit down? I'm supposed to meet someone here in a little while."

Lewis didn't see how she could sit anywhere without putting on a real show.

He got to his feet to be polite.

"Please sit anywhere you like," Lewis said, gesturing to the sofa. She chose the far corner. He took the seat he'd already warmed.

Now all the two of them had to do was see how things went at the party.

Nella's crack about Bobby not springing for a suite drew a few laughs. Not all that many. But the way Bobby saw it nobody was supposed to laugh at him. He was the guy who poked fun at other people. To show that he was a sport, he made a point of sending a local toady to "get me the biggest suite in the place."

Unless Bobby passed out early or she sneaked off to sleep at another hotel, Nella was sure she was already in for a beating. Not to her face, the two of them being out in public. But somewhere between the knees and shoulders, under her clothes, she'd be bruised purple.

Before he got around to the rough stuff, though, Bobby thought the proper thing to do was humiliate Nella. So he drank and he danced. He was light on his feet, had a fair sense of rhythm and even in his late forties still had a thick enough head of hair to shake without looking totally foolish.

He picked the youngest and best looking women as his dance partners. Only one male objected to his spouse being poached, a young fellow not five years out of Ole Miss and a former starting lineman on the football team. Bobby waved a finger at him in a good natured way. Nella knew what that meant. Bobby would be back and next time he wouldn't be denied.

To aid Bobby in having his way, as he made off to the dance floor with another man's wife, his toady whispered to the big young man. Words to the effect of, "Don't be stupid. You want to get ahead in business or politics around here, let the man have his dance."

It was a contemporary take on the *droit de seigneur*. The feudal lord's right to have sex with a vassal's bride on her wedding night. Some of the men who had yielded thought one dance was no big deal, but Bobby often came back for more than a tango later. Depending on what favors the men wanted from the federal government, that would be overlooked, too.

Not in this case, though. While Bobby was off dancing, the big guy shoved the toady out of his way and took his lady fair out of the room. Good for you, Nella thought. Didn't make Bobby happy, though. He was pissed. Sloppy drunk by now, too.

Nella had watched the last four of Bobby's dance partners wince as he stepped on their feet. He wasn't Elvis out on the dance floor any longer. Women all over the room were refusing to meet his eyes or finding a sudden need to visit the ladies room with three of their best friends.

About the only woman who didn't turn away from Bobby was Nella. She stared right at him with a mocking smile. Bobby didn't like that much either. He stomped over to her. As if the band leader sensed trouble coming, he had the boys play a slow song, "Wonderful Tonight."

Eric Clapton's love song to his beautiful lady.

Bobby thrust his hand out to Nella, knowing she wouldn't dare refuse.

She didn't. She knew from experience the least serious beating she'd ever taken from her husband had been when he was falling down drunk and tired. He could barely land a punch, and the ones that connected did little more than sting. Nella got to her feet and let herself be led onto the dance floor.

Bobby took her in his arms and held her close. His breath was foul and his body was rank with sweat. His hair hung down into bloodshot eyes, making him blink ceaselessly. Despite his dissipated condition, the predatory smile he directed at Nella made her shiver.

Then she felt Bobby's right arm tighten around her torso. The pressure was more than uncomfortable. She felt like her ribs might crack. A jolt of pain hit her backbone, too. It didn't seem possible that he might try to kill her right there in front of everyone, but if a fractured rib punctured a lung, she might die. If he damaged her spine she might be paralyzed.

Was the bastard even aware of what he was doing to her, Nella thought.

Then she looked in his eyes and saw that he did. He knew exactly what he was doing.

His smile grew wider with every moment of pain he caused her.

Nella did the only thing she could. Bobby had been stepping on his dance partners' feet? She brought her three-inch stiletto heel down hard on his right instep. Bobby's howl of pain stopped the band cold.

He growled, "Bitch!" and threw a right hand at Nella's head.

Nella had seen that punch before. Several of them had landed on her face. But Bobby was slow and clumsy now. She ducked the blow easily, and turned to run. She hadn't gone a step before he grabbed her hair with his other hand.

He didn't have a real good hank of it, though. With a shriek of pain, Nella pulled free, leaving Bobby to look dumbly at the hair in his hand. He threw it to the floor and took up the chase. Everyone in the room looked on in horror, especially Senator Howard Hurlbert.

But no one tried to stop Bobby.

Brad Lewis tensed as he heard shouting and screaming coming from the birthday party. He turned his head toward the ball room doors, dreading the thought that he might hear gunfire next. The pretty woman on the sofa, following her instructions, scooted over close to Lewis. The Chicago private investigator could feel her tremble against him.

Lewis heard the sharp clickety-clack of footsteps approaching. A woman in high heels was running as if her life —

Nella Beckley burst out of the room, panic on her face and her hair standing on end. She turned left toward the hotel bar, the front desk and the main entrance to the building.

Lewis looked that way. The big young white guy who'd left the party earlier with his wife was standing with her just outside the bar. Lewis gave him a nod and got one in return.

The big young man's face turned hard with anger as he saw Nella run past him.

Nella had noticed neither him nor Lewis as she made her escape.

A moment later, Bobby Beckley ran from the room, clearly in pursuit of his wife. He, too, passed the spot where Lewis sat, but Bobby got a good look at him. The two men had never met, but Bobby saw something that brought him to an abrupt, stumbling halt.

Bobby's face twisted, first in surprise, then in recognition, finally in rage.

The man who intended to make Howard Hurlbert the president said, "Merrilee, goddamnit, you're stepping out on me in public? With some old nigger?"

Brad Lewis knew exactly who Beckley was chastising.

His *ex*-wife, Merrilee Parker. Whom Beckley used to beat before Nella. He seemed to think he still had some kind of claim on her.

Bobby Beckley came for Brad Lewis now.

That gave Lewis only two choices, defend himself or cover up.

Lewis might have had a lot of gray in his hair, but he was strong, worked out three times a week. He'd been in his share of fights arresting tough guys on the street, too. Handling a drunk like Beckley would not be hard.

Not physically, that was. Dealing with the cops afterward, that might be a lot tougher. If it turned out he broke the jaw of a white man with political connections, he'd see the inside of a jail cell for sure. After that, in Mississippi, who knew what might happen?

Lewis just turtled up. Covered his face and head with his arms, pointed his elbows forward, the direction from which he was most likely to be punched. He pulled his knees up to his chest.

If the man took some shots at him now all he'd hit would be bone and muscle.

Probably bust a knuckle or two.

Unless the big young man with the pretty young wife got there fast.

The way Lewis had paid him to do.

Lewis counted three punches hit him. One on each shoulder, another on a forearm. None of them hurt worth mentioning. He doubted they'd even leave a mark. He did hear a loud yelp of dismay though. Not his own.

He opened his eyes and peeked out though the slit between his upraised arms.

The big young man had grabbed Beckley by the lapels of his suit coat and lifted him clean off the ground. Walked him over to a wall as Beckley started yelling at him. Whatever Beckley had to say stopped abruptly when the young man slammed him into the wall a time or two.

Then he let Beckley collapse into a heap on the floor and came over to Lewis.

He asked, "Are you all right, sir? Did that man hurt you?"

Lewis knew his role and played it well, "He surely tried to, but you saved me, young fella. You have my heartfelt thanks."

The cops showed up a minute later, and Lewis gave the young man credit for saving him from a beating. He said he was a guest of the hotel and he'd been sitting down on the sofa minding his own business when he'd been attacked.

It helped his credibility when he told the local police he was a retired cop.

After things settled down and Beckley was hauled off, Lewis was told he could return to his room. Merrilee Parker was long gone by then. She'd been the bait, and she disappeared as soon as Bobby had started in on Lewis.

The private investigator went to his room and started packing for his trip back to Chicago. The files he'd received, to be returned upon reaching home, had given him all the information he'd needed to set up his trap.

If the files had been any more detailed, they would have been step-by-step instructions.

The big young man who'd *saved* Lewis had been looking to move to New York. Now, he'd find a job waiting for him, and lots of new friends to help him succeed in business. Just for standing up to Beckley, a jerk the young man had hated since he'd impregnated the young man's sister while she was still in high school.

Whoever had hired Lewis had counted on him to see the opportunities he'd been handed.

Thinking about who knew him that well and who might send this job to him without leaving so much as a fingerprint, he could come up with only one name.

Jimmy McGill, the smartest rookie cop Lewis had ever trained.

That boy grew up and married the president. That's how slick he was.

5

March, 2012
20,000 Feet Above Ground Level — Mojave Desert, California

Damon Todd, Arn Crosby and Olin Anderson jumped out of
the plane in the last moments of daylight. Todd was making his
ninth jump, having started training less than a week earlier. It was
his first jump after being licensed, under his alias, by the United
States Parachute Association. Crosby and Anderson had long ago
lost count of how many times they'd exited an airplane in flight.

Todd had been taught that in a Superman posture, belly to
earth arms extended, he'd fall at one hundred and fifteen miles per
hour. If he went vertical, head or feet first, he'd fall much faster.
If he wore a wing-suit, he'd cut his rate of descent to half of the
Superman speed.

Todd had learned all this and more from his certified instructor.

Making no apologies to either Crosby or Anderson, he'd declined having either of them teach him a skill on which his life
would depend. He'd paid close attention to Angeline Woods, the
handsome forty-something former stuntwoman who'd drilled him
in all the finer points of hurtling through the air without leaving
a splat on the ground. He took detailed notes and watched the
training videos repeatedly.

He also paid her the high compliment of relating to her in
strictly a professional manner.

Didn't try to hit on her, the way so many jerks did.

With unknowing insight, she told Crosby and Anderson, "This guy is dedicated. It's like he's on a mission or something."

Neither of them wanted Angeline to think Todd was a terrorist.

Crosby said, "He's trying to prove his ex-wife wrong."

Anderson added, "Impress his fiancée, too."

What they didn't tell her was Todd had spent hours under self-hypnosis to dismiss the normal fear that something would go wrong and his first jump would be his last. That and focusing on doing things right to make sure he did get a second jump. By the time that night rolled around, it looked to all concerned like Damon Todd was actually having fun.

The altitude from which the three men jumped was high enough for Angeline to strongly recommend the use of bottled oxygen. Todd followed her advice without a quibble. Crosby and Anderson politely declined, but they wore small transceivers with microphones and earbuds so they could talk to each other above the roar of the wind as they fell.

Todd jumped first and quickly angled head down, as if he hoped to enter a swimming pool more than three miles below without raising a splash of water. Crosby and Anderson followed, each doing a Superman, falling like autumn leaves compared to Todd. Angeline was the last to jump, using an oxygen bottle.

She knew by now that Crosby and Anderson were accomplished jumpers, probably ex-military and better than her if she wanted to be honest. But neither of them was still the kid he thought he was. If one or both of the heroes blacked out from oxygen deprivation, she wanted to be close enough to pop their chutes. They broke their legs while landing unconscious that was their tough luck, but she'd never lost a jumper and didn't want to start now.

Turned out they both still knew what they could do, waggled their fingers at her and grinned.

She gave them a wave and went into a vertical dive, wanting to close the distance with Todd as much as she could. Make sure he opened his chute at twenty-five hundred feet.

"Nice lady," Crosby said, watching her go.

"Too nice for us."

"True. Give us a girl who's part scorpion, we're happy."

"Where's the fun without a hint of treachery?"

The two of them laughed watching the world grow closer.

Anderson said, "Doc's surprised me in a lot of ways. Jumping out of planes is just one thing. But I don't think he's ever going to get into a fight with McGill and walk away from it."

"McGill won't let him tap out again?"

"I wouldn't and neither would you. McGill? This time, I think he'd end it."

"Me, too."

"You think either of us could take him?" Anderson asked.

The sun was all but gone now. They were rushing toward impact as fast as ever, but visual reference was down to points of light on the ground. No, wait, two chutes just opened. Todd and Angeline were drifting earthward at a mere twenty miles per hour now. Nearly as safe as a baby in Mom's arms.

"I think it'd be real close for either of us," Crosby said, "but, yeah, I think we'd both win. McGill's good, he's got lots of natural talent but —"

Anderson shook his head. "He's on the board now. Got his first kill."

"Yeah, but he feels bad about it. Where you and I've got him cold is we're both fucking merciless. We get an opening, we won't hesitate."

"That's true. So let's go after him. We'll tell Todd it's just to soften McGill up for him."

Crosby said, "Okay, who gets first shot?"

"The guy who pops his chute last."

Playing aerial chicken wasn't a new game, but it was one in which either player or both could die testing his nerve. Invariably, in either military or civilian circumstances, equipment failure was blamed for such fatalities. Nobody wanted to give parachuting a bad name.

Everybody wanted their beneficiaries to collect on the life insurance.

Crosby and Anderson zipped past Todd and Angeline softly settling toward the earth. Each of the special ops crazies had his eyes on the luminescent face of his wrist altimeter. Todd and Angeline had opened their chutes at a safe, conservative altitude. Crosby and Anderson had experience *starting* jumps below two thousand feet. BASE (buildings, antennae, spans, aka bridges, and earth, aka cliffs) jumpers used very fast opening chutes to take flight starting below two hundred feet.

At the speed Crosby and Anderson were approaching their doom, neither man could risk looking at the other; he might not get back to reading his altimeter in time. The only thing each of them could do was pull the rip cord at the very last second he thought he had any chance of survival, and hope if the other guy waited a nanosecond longer the SOB would at least break his ankles for making his friend look like a pussy.

Crosby, feeling his greater age, popped his chute at four hundred feet.

Anderson kept going. For the blink of an eye, Crosby thought Anderson hadn't been able to get either his main chute or the reserve to deploy. Would leave a round hole in the desert floor. Then, if not at the last second pretty damn close to it, Anderson's chute billowed.

He still hit hard, but he had his knees bent and went into a roll.

He was still moving when Crosby made his own rough landing.

Both of them were on their feet before Todd and Angeline arrived.

"You okay?" Crosby called to Anderson.

"Dinged my right wrist on the roll. How about you?"

"Once I clean my drawers, I'll be fine."

The two of them were laughing like madmen when Todd and Angeline touched down. Angeline shed her harness and sprinted over to them. He face was twisted in rage.

"You assholes! I know what you did. Get the hell out of my jump zone. You cocksuckers are never going to jump anywhere around here again."

Crosby and Anderson looked at each other.

"I believe we're no longer wanted," Anderson said.

"We're definitely an acquired taste," Crosby agreed.

They dropped their harnesses. Left their chutes on the ground and walked off.

Todd, who'd overheard Angeline, approached and said in a quiet voice, "I'm very sorry for what happened. I'll see that they don't bother you again."

He tried to offer Angeline extra money but she refused it.

Todd took off his harness, handed it to Angeline and headed to the Buick SUV.

He wasn't happy with the spectacle Crosby and Anderson had made of themselves.

He was thrilled, however, by what he'd seen the two fools do.

He wondered if he could pull off the same thing.

On the way back to Palm Springs, when Todd told Crosby and Anderson what he had in mind, pushing his own sky diving to the limits, Anderson said, "Maybe we can drop down to Baja for a week or two, do some wing-suit flying. They're not so tight-assed down there."

Crosby told Todd, "You check out, they raise a glass to your memory."

"If you were a good tipper while you were still around," Anderson said.

"Maybe we can get into the real spirit of things and plug a bandito or two," Crosby added.

Todd glanced from one of them to the other to see if they were joking.

Without bothering to look at Todd, Anderson said, "He thinks we're pulling his leg, Arn."

Crosby turned to look at Todd and said, "You know what a real ass-tickler is? Shooting at targets on the ground on full auto under your canopy as you come in for a landing. Just like Grandpa did on D-Day."

"Lucky for us, we know where to buy assault weapons in Mexico," Anderson said.

With a shudder, Todd wondered when and how he'd lost control.

When he'd become every bit as crazy as Crosby and Anderson.

Most of all he wanted to know when they could get started.

The Beverly Hills Hotel — Beverly Hills, California

The president was tired from a long day, five hours of work in the Oval Office and then the long flight across the country. She spent half-an-hour talking with her husband. McGill had told her not to neglect her rest, but don't let any Hollywood singer croon her to sleep.

Patti met with her former agent, Dorie McBride and Tom Gorman, the producer of that night's premiere celebrity Internet debate. She wanted to be on hand and watch from the wings.

Patti's people had made their choice in response to the list of picks Reynard Dix had made for the opposition. Dix had been given a deadline for presenting his choices that allowed Patti's side time to line up a panel they thought would prevail.

A more savvy political operative would have demanded the choices for each side be submitted at the same time.

Dix, being cocksure of his side's popular appeal, hadn't.

The president approved of Dorie and Tom's picks.

She thanked them and then realizing how short the time would be before she had to fly back to Washington, changed her mind and decided to watch the webcast from the bedroom of her suite.

The White House

The last time McGill had occasion to use the White House workout room to give martial art instructions he'd been showing Patti a few basic Dark Alley moves. She'd used her newly earned defensive skills to leave an indelible impression on the facial structure of the prime minister of the United Kingdom. The man had undergone reconstructive surgery, but had retired from public life, never quite regaining his old take charge personality.

Having learned where the prime minister had placed a hand on the president's person, McGill thought it was a good thing the man had become a recluse.

Now, McGill was in the room with Sweetie. They folded up the padded mats that covered the wooden floor and stacked them in a corner. McGill swept the floor so neither he nor Sweetie would slip on a sheen of dust and turn an ankle. Wouldn't do to be in less than top shape in the coming weeks and months.

By now Sweetie had heard the stories of McGill giving his children lessons in Dark Alley and how he'd fared sparring against two Marines. Hearing that McGill had used an Irish fighting stick, aka a shillelagh, against his military opponents, Margaret Mary Sweeney thought she should get in touch with this part of her heritage.

As luck would have it, McGill had a spare stick.

He brought one other item with him, but Sweetie was the patient type.

She could wait to find out what McGill had in mind for it.

Using the two shillelaghs, McGill showed Sweetie how to hold it, how to defend against someone swinging another long, weighty object by using windshield wiper strokes originating from either hand. Showed her how to build a roof against a strike directed at the crown of her head. Demonstrated the parry for a direct thrust to the torso.

Each defensive move was followed by an offensive counterstrike. Once an opponent's lunge or slash was deflected, there was a moment when he was vulnerable. If the opponent was quick, that opportunity would be short-lived. But if your timing was right, he'd be shorter lived.

McGill and Sweetie worked through the series of offensive, defensive and counteroffensive moves with Sweetie gaining speed and fluidity. It didn't surprise McGill that Sweetie would make a formidable nemesis. The smile on her face said she liked practicing with the stick and if a time ever came to use it in earnest, she'd be ready.

After thirty minutes, McGill called for a break.

They were both breathing hard by now.

"That was fun," Sweetie said. "Of course, it's so much easier just to shoot someone."

McGill sighed and nodded.

Knowing him for as long and well as she did, Sweetie had no problem guessing what was on his mind. "You're still scourging your soul about John Patrick Granby."

"I am," McGill said.

"That's despite the fact that you did nothing wrong and would be far harder on yourself if you'd sat back and let Galia Mindel die."

"It is."

Sweetie took McGill's shillelagh away from him and leaned it and her stick against a wall. She put a hand on each of his shoulders and looked him in the eye.

"Would you be suffering as deeply if it had been Patti's life or the life of one of your kids you'd saved?"

McGill looked abashed, and shook his head.

"How about Carolyn or even me?"

"Carolyn and you are right there with the others."

"How about you? Did you ever think you might have broken your own neck doing what you did?"

"Never occurred to me."

"Still you risked your own health if not life for someone who maybe isn't your favorite person. How do you think that will be weighed on Judgment Day?"

McGill summoned a small smile. "As a mitigating circumstance?"

Sweetie laughed and gently pushed him away from her.

"You're going to be all right, and here's one more thing to think about. However John Patrick Granby is judged, here or above, you saved him from becoming a murderer."

McGill nodded. Sweetie's words of wisdom had helped. As usual.

"Refraining from taking another life is why I feel the need to work hard on sublethal techniques these days." He told her about the political necessity of preventing further bloodshed, what with Burke Godfrey and now Granby already on the mortality scoreboard. "Being limited in my options makes things harder with Damon Todd and the two ex-CIA crazies on the loose."

Sweetie looked at the other object McGill had brought with him.

To those with an uncritical eye it looked like an umbrella.

"Does that thing fire bullets?" Sweetie asked.

McGill shook his head.

"Is there a sword sheathed inside?"

"No."

"So what's the plan?" Sweetie asked. "You get in trouble, you open your brolly and sail off over the rooftops like Mary Poppins?"

Before McGill could answer, there was a knock at the door and Elspeth Kendry poked her head in. She said, "Sorry to interrupt, but I was told all the racket in here had ceased. Is there anything going on I, maybe, should know about?"

McGill smiled and said, "Come in, Special Agent."

Central Jail — Jackson, Mississippi

Bobby Beckley had been left to sit in his jail cell for four days. He'd been kept in a one-man cell so he hadn't been cornholed but that was about the only indignity he'd been spared. He was told he'd been charged with assault and battery as a state charge; the feds, though, were looking at the possibility of hitting him with a hate crime indictment, as he'd characterized his victim with a racial epithet.

That little indiscretion seemed to be common knowledge among the inmate population. That meant, of course, the word had been passed to the cons by the powers that be. If Bobby got all high and mighty with one of his jailers or anyone else, why, he might find himself in the close company of people of color. Very large people who didn't care to have their ethnicity disparaged.

Bobby knew if he wasn't careful he might never know freedom or another birthday again. He had to get out of jail as fast as he could. He was rewarded for his good manners with a call to his lawyer, one of the top movers and shakers in town. If anyone could spring him, it was —

Sawyer Middleton's secretary told Bobby the attorney would no longer be representing him on any matter, now or ever.

Bobby was momentarily dumbfounded. When he regained his voice, he responded politely, "I have Sawyer on retainer. He's already been paid. We also hold common interests in a number of business ventures."

"Mr. Middleton has already refunded the balance of the retainer. The business holdings have been sold off and your share of the proceeds have been electronically transferred to your account."

"Huh," Bobby said. He could only hope the money was sent to his *offshore* account.

The way he'd become everybody's whipping boy, though, it probably hadn't been.

"Mr. Middleton recommends the public defender's office to help you in your present situation, and he asks that you not attempt to make contact with him again."

The goddamn public defender? Who was he now, just another nig—

Whoa. He better stop thinking like that. He sure couldn't say that word in jail.

The important point was, that treacherous bastard, Sawyer, had just told him no other big name defense lawyer in the state was going to argue or even plead his case. He had to count on some poor overworked kid or old burnout, either of whom might have gone to night classes at a law school that advertised itself on matchbooks.

Shit! He was in real trouble.

Then he got head lice. Took to scratching his scalp like a madman. The jail authorities weren't about to take any chances of the infestation spreading to other inmates. They carted Bobby off to the infirmary, shaved his head to the bone and while they were at it took the rest of his body hair right off him. Put him in a shower that would have scalded the devil's backside. Made him rub some vile lotion over every last inch of his body.

Naked and with all his hair gone, the final indignity visited on him was making sure he got a good look at himself in a full-length mirror. His scalp was lumpy and red. His jowls drooped with no mutton-chop sideburns to hide them. His chest and belly sagged without a jungle of hair to cover their slide toward his shrunken knob. His shaved legs looked like they might've come off a chicken.

As a way to make a man humble, seeing his reflection as presently constituted was hard to beat. The best he could say for himself was he was bug free, no longer itched and had been given a clean jail jumpsuit. Returning to his cell, he curled up on his bunk, closed his eyes and prayed that when he woke up it had all been a bad, bad dream.

It wasn't, but a young woman from the public defender's office came to see him. She'd had a preliminary phone conversation with an assistant U.S. attorney and it looked like the feds would be going ahead with the hate crime prosecution. If that wasn't bad enough, Bobby's victim was going to file a civil action against him.

That was when Bobby was *sure* his money from Sawyer Middleton had been sent to his local bank, where it could be seized with the greatest of ease.

The public defender had one more gift to give him.

Nella Beckley had filed for divorce.

More than anything else, at that moment, Bobby wanted to give the snotty woman in front of him a good beating. Luckily for him, there was a slab of polycarbonate resin between them and they were talking by phone. He hung his up gently, stood quietly and waited to be taken back to his cell.

He was fucked. In desperation, he thought if he begged real hard, Senator Hurlbert might take his call and pull a few strings for him. Get him out of jail quick as a whistle and —

Sure, that old gasbag was always a profile in courage.

The way things were stacking up for Bobby, that bastard Hurlbert would probably say his former chief of staff and campaign manager had been a temporary employee, who somehow had managed to hang around the past twenty years.

Bobby's thoughts turned to suicide.

He was working out ways to meet his end as painlessly as possible when a jailer came and told him to get up. His bail had been reduced and he'd been bailed out. The man looked pained to say those words.

Bobby suspected a trap. All the way out to the street, dressed in the stale, stiff, sour from sweat and spilled booze suit in which he'd been arrested, he thought he would be yanked back inside, returned to his cell, with every last prisoner and guard parading by to laugh at him.

Nobody grabbed Bobby. Nobody stopped him from going his own way.

The only person waiting to greet him was a black kid, maybe twelve years old.

"You Mr. Beckley?" the kid asked.

Suspicious of everyone by now, Bobby only nodded.

"This is for you then," the kid said.

He stuck a hand in his pocket and Bobby froze, thinking the kid would come out with a gun and shoot him dead right in front of the jail.

But all the kid took out of his pocket was an envelope with

Bobby's name on it.

He handed it to him and walked away.

Bobby's hands shook as he opened the envelope. He expected more bad news. Who on earth would have a kind word for him now?

Reynard Dix, as it turned out.

Not just a kind word, but a job offer.

And a thousand dollars cash money.

Bobby caught the first flight north to Washington, D.C.

The White House

Special Agent Elspeth Kendry asked if she could try her hand at Irish stick fighting, saying, "I always wanted to say I had to beat somebody off with a stick."

McGill was willing to give another demonstration but deferred to Sweetie who told him she'd like to get in more practice. With a sharp memory and a keen eye for detail, Sweetie instructed Elspeth exactly the way McGill had taught her. In a matter of minutes, the two women were going at it harder and faster than he had with Sweetie.

Some guys, those who hadn't been raised right, might have found an element of titillation in the spectacle of two women whacking at each other with sticks. McGill had other things in mind. He was examining the technical skills being presented. Spotting strengths and weaknesses.

Deciding how he would counter the strengths and exploit the weaknesses.

Not that he expected to fight either woman.

You never knew, though, McGill thought, when you might face someone with a similar style.

After a last flurry of attempted strikes, parries, further attempted strikes and parries, Sweetie and Elspeth grinned wearily at each other, stepped back and lowered their sticks. Then they shook hands.

"Very cool," Elspeth said, handing her shillelagh back to McGill. "So what's with the umbrella? You have a weapon hidden in there?"

"Just what I asked," Sweetie said.

McGill put the shillelagh down and picked up the umbrella.

"You can use this the same way you use the stick, with a few extra moves thrown in."

"It's sturdy enough?" Sweetie asked.

He tossed the umbrella to her. She caught it and said, "It's light."

"Less than a pound. But you could whack a heavy bag with it until your arms fell off and it would be good as new. It's called an unbreakable umbrella."

"You've tried breaking it?" Elspeth asked as Sweetie handed the umbrella to her.

"Yeah." McGill grabbed the shillelagh he'd put down. He asked Elspeth, "Ready?"

She raised the umbrella as if it was a fighting stick. She parried the attacks directed at her upper body and head, but then McGill gently rapped her knuckles. And grinned.

"Sorry, I forgot to show Sweetie what you do if someone goes after your hands," he said.

"An oversight, I'm sure," Elspeth said, looking like she'd like to whack McGill.

"You want to show us now?" Sweetie asked.

"Sure, but let's put the floor mats back in place first."

They did. Then McGill showed them how to protect their hands and their legs.

He also showed them ways you could use the umbrella's curved handle.

"Where'd you get that thing?" Elspeth asked when she saw how dangerous the umbrella could be.

McGill beamed with paternal pride. "Kenny found it online for me, after I started teaching him Dark Alley."

He then informed Sweetie and Elspeth that the White House physician would soon be announcing that McGill was suffering from a flare up of traumatic arthritis in his right knee and would be using a walking aid to help him get about.

Sweetie said, "Let me guess, a shillelagh."

"An umbrella on rainy days," Elspeth added.

McGill nodded.

Just because he couldn't shoot an antagonist didn't mean he had to go unarmed.

U.S. Capitol

The Republican caucus in the Senate thought it would have a little fun at the president's expense and filibuster her nomination of Governor Jean Morrissey to become vice president. That would leave the position of first in line to succeed the president vacant for an indefinite period, giving the Almighty a chance to reconsider whether he might like to give Patti Grant a mortal heart problem, and put the new speaker of the House, Peter Profitt, into the Oval Office. The Republicans were unanimous in thinking this was a swell idea, but there were only forty-seven of them.

Roger Michaelson, feeling betrayed that he hadn't been chosen to replace Mather Wyman and having his primary challenge to win the Democratic nomination to be president die in New York, Illinois and California, chose to vote with the Republicans on the filibuster. Even with his support, though, that made only forty-eight senators in favor of jabbing a finger into the president's eye.

Normally, it would have taken only forty votes to sustain a veto.

But Majority Leader John Wexford, giving no warning, invoked the nuclear option and ruled the filibuster out of order. He raised his voice above the shouts of outrage that filled the chamber and said, "The Constitution requires that the will of the majority be effective on specific Senate duties and procedures. This option allows a simple majority to override the rules of the Senate and end a filibuster or other delaying tactic."

Further, Wexford ruled, as the Republicans were trying to

delay confirming a new vice president solely in the hope of gaining political advantage, the vote to confirm Governor Morrissey as the new vice president would be called immediately. There would be no hearings on the matter. Also meaning there would be no chances for hostile senators to ask the nominee potentially embarrassing questions.

The Republicans howled in rage, vowing to bring the matter to the —

Supreme Court. Which was no longer their last lever of power. Having no alternative, the Republicans and Roger Michaelson stomped out of the chamber, retreating to parts unknown their vengeance to plan. Those plans became far more problematic when Mather Wyman, later that day, having heard what had happened, said the party he nominally led had been wrong to attempt to filibuster the nomination of Governor Morrissey.

The reactions to Wyman's declaration divided Republicans sharply. While Wyman's popularity jumped by an average of ten percent in national polls, the GOP suffered thirty-six Congressional defections, seventeen in the Senate, to True South.

Governor Jean Morrissey was confirmed as the country's new vice president unanimously — by a vote of 52-0.

For the first time, the United States had two women running the country.

United States Penitentiary — Hazelton, West Virginia

Erna Godfrey was led into the warden's office not knowing what to expect. The man was busy when she arrived, reading a typed document that lay on his desk and frowning as he did. Erna knew that look. She'd seen it before. Someone had just given the warden an order he had to follow, but he didn't like it.

We all have our crosses to bear, Erna thought.

There was only one way to go about such a chore, Erna knew. Remember it was better to carry a cross than to be nailed to it.

The warden came to the end of the document, picked up his

pen and scrawled his name across the bottom. Dated it, too. Then he looked up at Erna.

"Mrs. Godfrey, I've just acquiesced to a presidential order assigning you to another correctional facility, a medium security housing site. That is where you'll serve the remainder of your sentence."

Erna thought that was a nice way to put it. She was serving a life sentence. The warden might have said this is where you'll go to die. But a medium security facility would be a luxury hotel compared to Hazelton. It was almost enough to give Erna hope that —

"The president has directed that you will be allowed to initiate a ministry to serve other federal inmates," the warden told her.

Hallelujah. Erna's prayers had been answered.

"This ministry will not begin immediately," the warden said, responding to the smile that lit the inmate's face.

Erna's joy vanished.

She asked, "May I ask when it might start?"

"Yes. It will begin when you complete your doctorate of divinity."

Erna rocked back on her heels. The correctional officer who'd brought her into the warden's office had to place a hand on her back to steady her.

"But I'm a four-year Bible school graduate. I've read the Good Book cover to cover more times than I can remember. I've memorized most of scripture," she said.

"The president has taken that into account. You'll start your studies as a master's degree candidate and then pursue your doctorate."

Erna thought about that for a moment.

"Who will I study with?"

"With volunteer faculty members of the Northwestern Theological Seminary. Once you've received your doctorate, you'll be allowed to record videos and podcasts to be distributed to other federal inmates who are interested in receiving them."

The warden had finished his spiel, still not liking what he'd had to do.

He looked at Erna impassively. It was her move now.

Take it or leave it.

Erna realized what she'd just been offered. Patricia Grant was so incredibly smart. She was making Erna work for what she wanted. Making her study with academics whose understanding of the Lord's teachings likely weren't the same as her own. To earn her doctorate, she'd have to defend her thesis, her understanding of the Gospels.

Still, the president wasn't setting her up to fail.

Patricia Grant was making her test her ideas against … people whose faith had never led them to take anyone's life.

That was more than fair. It was an act of faith on Patricia Grant's part. That things would work out for the best in the end.

Erna asked the warden, "Is there any way I might express my thanks to the president?"

"In my opinion, yes." And he told her what he thought she could do.

Senator Charles Talbert's House — Bloomington, Indiana

Sheryl Kimbrough was admitted to the senator's house by Dorothy, the housekeeper. The two women were old friends. Sheryl had spoken to Tal when Dorothy hadn't felt it proper to ask her employer to nominate her nephew, Dwayne, for admission to the United States Military Academy. She hadn't even wanted to talk to Sheryl about it, but the former press secretary, who had learned of the matter only by snooping, had pried it out of her. Captain Dwayne Williams had graduated with honors and gone on to win a silver star and lose an eye in Iraq. He now taught at West Point.

Always polite but formal with the senator's guests, Dorothy nonetheless allowed Sheryl to kiss her cheek.

She said, "It's so good to see you again, Ms. Kimbrough. Please tell me Cassidy is recovering well."

Sheryl bobbed her head. "The doctors say she won't need any plastic surgery, but Cassidy told me the least she should get out of the whole thing is a boob job."

Dorothy's mouth fell open, but then she stifled a laugh.

"Yeah, kids these days," Sheryl said. "What are you going to do? Is Senator Talbert ready to see me?"

"He is, Ms. Kimbrough. I'll just give a little knock on his door. Make sure he hasn't nodded off."

Sheryl followed Dorothy to the office her former boss maintained at the back of the house. It looked out on his backyard and, in season, a riot of flowers. The space was also adjacent to the kitchen, and the lawmaker believed in frequent recesses for snacking. Sheryl had been just one of the women in his employ who tried to keep him from putting on too much weight.

He still moved like a ballroom dancer, though, stepping out from behind his desk, gliding over to embrace Sheryl and kiss her on both cheeks.

Sheryl told him, "Better watch that, boss. That kind of greeting looks positively European. Maybe even a touch Socialist."

Talbert laughed. "Nobody saw us except Dorothy, and she's not talking."

"It's always the quiet ones who write the most sensational memoirs," Sheryl warned.

Dorothy blushed and quickly backed out of the room, closing the door behind her.

Sheryl arched her eyebrows and said, "Who knows, maybe I guessed right."

Taking his seat behind his desk, Talbert said, "Dorothy will take our love match to her grave."

Sheryl laughed and sat opposite the senator. He was a long-time widower, but if she remembered right, Dorothy had started working for the senator shortly before his wife died. If the two of them had an illicit relationship dating back to … she didn't want to know.

What she'd come to find out, though, was if Senator Talbert

could use his clout to discover the identity of the mysterious benefactor who had paid the balance of the medical bills Cassidy had incurred, and by extension the far larger bills the other victims had run up.

Sheryl had tried everything she could think of to pry the information out of the hospital and all the doctors involved. She'd been stonewalled. Hadn't even been able to coax a hint out of any of the nurses treating the victims. Such uniform, intractable discipline bespoke two possible motivators, admiration or fear.

Fear didn't make any sense, really. Why would somebody both powerful and dangerous enough to scare people act so charitably to the burn victims? Didn't seem plausible.

So that left a good soul with a lot of money.

Someone like that should hear from a grateful parent, her.

It was driving her nuts that she couldn't say thank you.

That and satisfying her professional busybody's curiosity.

She explained all this to Senator Talbert and asked if there was any way he could help.

He said, "I can help. I'll personally convey your gratitude to the appropriate person."

"You know?" Sheryl asked, incredulous.

"You don't have to sound so surprised. I'm still a member of a rather exclusive club."

"It wasn't you, was it, Tal?"

The senator laughed. "I'm quite comfortable, and I'll have a shamefully good pension, but I'm not wealthy. My charitable impulses are far smaller."

"But you won't tell me who?"

"I gave my word."

"Damn!"

"Tell you what. You insist on paying all your bills personally, persuade the others to do the same, get that bundle of money returned to the donor, and I'll ask if I might be released from my pledge."

Sheryl gritted her teeth. If only her money had been part of the bargain, she'd have gone for it, and Tal knew it. But she couldn't ask the others to do it. They'd be financially ruined ... and Cassidy would never forgive her.

With a large sigh, Sheryl decided she'd have to accept the hand she'd been dealt and act like a grown up. "Very well. Please tell this mystery man I will do my best, within my limited means, to emulate his generosity at every possible opportunity."

As she'd made her statement, Sheryl had kept close watch on Talbert when she twice used the word his. He hadn't blinked, twitched or shown any other tell. She still didn't know whether the angel who'd showered money on Cassidy and the others was male or female.

"How's university life?" the senator asked, hoping to distract his friend.

Sheryl told him she loved it. The students in her class gave her hope for the future.

"Maybe I should see if I can catch on there," Talbert said. "I could use some hope."

"I heard about the defections to True South. Three dozen, wasn't it?"

Talbert nodded. "That actually gives me hope. Our party and the Democrats have been doing business at the same old stands for far too long. I'd like to see all of us evolve before we kill the government."

"It's not that bad, is it?"

"Not if we're smart, but I don't think we are. Not if we're lucky, which we just might be. But when you have a sitting president leave her own party, the body politic is running a high fever. Damn, I wish we had Patti Grant back, especially now with that pack of hotheads gone."

Sheryl nodded in sympathy.

And thought to herself how close Tal and the president were in political outlook and temperament. They were friends socially, too, both of them having been in the federal government for a long time and coming from neighboring states.

Charles Talbert and Patti Grant. Good friends. Maybe even confidants?

People who might share a secret knowing it would be kept.

Patti Grant richer than many small nations.

A woman who took time out from running the country to call Cassidy.

You couldn't publish a story on a hunch.

But Sheryl was very glad she'd come to see her old boss.

The White House

McGill tapped on the door to Galia Mindel's office and was told to come in. The chief of staff was annoyed by the unexpected interruption, but she couldn't even wear a snug collar anymore without thinking of how McGill had saved her life. She put aside professional pique and asked him to have a seat.

"How may I help you, Mr. McGill?"

"I'm sorry to intrude, Galia. I'd have called to ask for a moment, but I thought you must be busy all the time, so I just dropped by."

"Your reason being?"

"I want to get involved in the campaign, but in a specific way and for my own reasons. That being said, I don't want to do anything to harm the cause."

Galia frowned. One of McGill's charms for the political creatures in the Grant administration was that he didn't think he knew better than they did about presenting the president and her policies to the public. That was a great relief. The man could have caused all sorts of headaches if he'd wanted to.

As the administration had gotten under way, he'd respond to any question a reporter might ask with the stock answer, "I support the president wholeheartedly." That response was above criticism for a devoted husband, and that was exactly what the man was. By repeating those five words time and again, McGill also bored the newsies so much they stopped bothering him.

As a man who worked at his career full time, he also wasn't

pestered about why he hadn't taken on the do-gooder projects a first lady was expected to assume.

But now he wanted to get involved in a presidential campaign. In a specific way? For his own reasons?

"Would you care to elaborate, Mr. McGill?"

"Sure. I'm tired of Damon Todd and his two pals lurking in the weeds somewhere. I've worked with the FBI to catch them, but that hasn't panned out. It's time to take a leading role. So I'm going to make myself a target. Well, *appear* to make myself a target."

Galia blanched. The Grant administration had become one of historic firsts. Becoming the first president to have a spouse assassinated, however, wasn't on anybody's to-do list.

Rather than shout at McGill that he had to be crazy, Galia focused on practical matters.

"You've discussed this idea with the president?" she asked.

"Not yet. I've talked to Elspeth Kendry. Now, I'm talking with you. I want to get all the nuts and bolts in place before I talk with Patti."

The man was serious. He was going to do what he said. From what Galia had seen during the past three years, McGill could exert an amazing influence on the otherwise rational and highly intelligent woman who was the president. Almost bend her to his will when he wanted.

For a fleeting moment, Galia wondered how much political advantage might be wrung from a McGill assassination.

She discarded the thought as unworthy, possibly even a sign that she'd been in politics too long. The president loved this man. He was the father to three young children. Better that Mather Wyman should become president than —

"Galia, I'm going to be all right," McGill said, just as if he'd been reading her mind. "The idea is to bag the other guys. I'll be working with the Secret Service on this one. In fact, I'd like to bring Deke Ky back for the job. We'll find a suitable replacement to watch Abbie."

"You'll do what the Secret Service tells you?"

"I'll listen to their advice. Believe me, I'm not going out on any limbs. I want to spend a long time with my wife after she leaves office, and I'd love to become a grandfather."

Grandpa McGill, there was an idea Galia had never entertained.

She supposed it was somewhat reassuring.

"What is it you'd like to know from me?"

"Where I should speak on the president's behalf that would leave a lot of space between the two of us. What I should say that might sound good coming from me. How I should dress, if that's important. Whether to answer any questions that are off topic or just smile and shine the newsies on. Things like that."

Galia took McGill's points seriously. He'd clearly given the matter some thought. If the president backed his idea, there would be nothing she could do to stop him. So she might as well have him be an asset not a liability.

The man was attractive, had a certain charm, but …

"You really think you can be an effective surrogate for the president?"

McGill shrugged. "I do a decent press conference, don't I?"

Galia had to concede that with a nod.

Then she asked, "If you're successful in your personal goal, is there any possible way you might be discreet about it?"

McGill said, "I'll keep the mayhem to a minimum."

God willing, he thought.

Penrose House — Charlottesville, Virginia

Professor Fletcher Penrose was mildly amused to receive a call from the deputy director of the FBI.

"The jig is up?" Penrose asked.

"Which jig might that be?" Byron DeWitt responded.

"The one that led to this call."

What led to the call was a theory DeWitt had come up with far later than he should have. Asking himself how he would have disappeared had he been the one to escape the Funny Farm possessing the resources Damon Todd had, he arrived at the answer he would have gone to ground with the nearest *friend* who lived in an out of the way place.

Applying that logic to the database of names and addresses of people whose lives had intersected with that of Damon Todd and had experienced sudden leaps of fortune, the FBI had come up with the names of fourteen people who lived within a radius of one hundred miles of the CIA's training and confinement facility.

University of Virginia professor of economics Fletcher Penrose had been one of those people. His background check revealed that as a boy he'd been a severe stutterer. His speech impediment had caused him to evade any form of social engagement including participating in class discussions. After one egregious instance of verbal bullying in middle school, Penrose, who was also mocked for his name, was removed from school and educated by his parents.

Knowing their teaching abilities would not be a substitute for a college education, Penrose's parents brought him to Damon Todd, a psychiatrist whom they'd heard could work wonders. Work one for young Fletcher, he did, though he wouldn't explain exactly how other than to say his methods involved hypnotherapy.

Not only had Penrose's stutter disappeared, he became a winning extrovert. His natural intelligence carried him through his undergraduate and grad school years, and his social graces won him influential friends who aided his rise every step along the way. He was currently on his way to the chairmanship of the economics department of one of the country's top universities.

It was said Penrose was one of those rare lecturers and writers who could make the dismal science entertaining.

Along with his stunning professional success — and in keeping with James J. McGill's thinking that Todd would tap his friends for funds — Penrose had experienced recent outflows of three hundred thousand dollars from his personal accounts.

The place he called home, however, was hardly inconspicuous.

It was a pillared mansion within sight of a road that carried hundreds of vehicles every day. Looking beyond the obvious, though, DeWitt took into account the fact that the Penrose property covered three hundred acres, including woodland, river frontage and —

Why, lookit there, a cabin nestled among the trees, as viewed by Google Earth.

The trees were bare when the mapping satellite had snapped its picture, but when Todd and friends had slipped the bonds of the CIA the trees would have been in full leaf. The cabin would have been as well concealed as a slipper kicked under a bed. Who could ask for anything more?

DeWitt said, "Professor, do you know a man named Damon Todd?"

"Of course, I do. He turned my life around. I owe him everything."

Couldn't be any more frank than that, DeWitt thought.

"Have you heard from him in the past year?"

"No, I wish I had. He's one of those people you long to repay, but as far as I know he's off helping other people. If you hear from him, please ask him to call me."

"Sure," DeWitt said.

Like the deputy director was just another old chum of both Penrose and Todd. No worries that he was with the FBI. Most people got a call from a federal cop, they either wondered what they might have done wrong or how they got caught. Penrose carried on as if DeWitt was just someone who'd called to shoot the breeze.

The deputy director wanted to see how far the professor's cooperation would extend.

"Would you mind if I stopped by for a visit, Professor Penrose?"

"Not at all. This is getting interesting. Might make a good lecture series story."

There was that possibility, DeWitt realized. He wouldn't want the man blabbing in public.

"I'd appreciate your keeping my call and visit confidential for the time being."

"Of course," Penrose said.

Too damn cooperative. DeWitt pushed a little more.

"Would it be all right if I brought some bloodhounds with me?"

"I'll *have* to write about this. When the time is appropriate."

"Right. See you soon."

DeWitt had agents watching Penrose's house from conceal-ment at that very moment. They had been waiting for a court order to search the property. But now they had the owner's permission, recorded for posterity. The deputy director gave the agents an order to stop Penrose from going to the cabin. He didn't want any last-minute housecleaning done.

Penrose never made the attempt. He stayed inside his grand house until DeWitt arrived. He waved the FBI men on as they asked again if they might search the cabin. The dogs found the scents of Todd, Anderson and Crosby inside, as compared to bedding they'd left behind at the Funny Farm.

So now the FBI would have to talk to the professor and find out what he knew.

DeWitt didn't think that would be an easy task.

He called James J. McGill and asked if he'd like to help.

Wilson/West Realty — Ottawa, Illinois

Special Agent Vincent Gallo would have kept working his desk job, stir crazy though it made him, if the late winter weather in Chicago had been anything near normal. Cold enough to chill an Eskimo and bleak enough to make Edvard Munch break out his paint brush. But it was sunny and sixty. He'd have liked to go to a ball game or even play catch with his son. Instead, he settled for a drive in the country. He motored down I-55 to the turnoff for Ottawa, where Realtor Deanna Wilson plied her trade.

Gallo always wore his wedding band. Somedays he buffed the

ring so it would be impossible to miss. Today was one of those days. He remembered Deanna Wilson's voice when she'd spoken with him. The lady may have been a cop groupie. She might have liked his voice. She could have been lonely just a bit too long.

In any case, he didn't want her to think he was anything but a man doing his job.

Turned out, he needn't have worried. Deanna was spending the week in St. John, USVI.

Her partner, Suzie West, was holding down the fort at Wilson/West Realty when he arrived and identified himself. Suzie couldn't be more than twenty-five. The smile she gave Gallo was more mischievous than amorous. Still, her expression was unusual enough to make a G-man take notice.

"Is there something I should know, Ms. West?"

"You are cute for an older guy."

"Thank you. My wife says pretty much the same thing."

Suzi grinned. "I'm not hitting on you. I've got my own hunk. But you've made Deanna all moony."

"I have?"

"Yeah, but it's harmless. She keeps talking about moving somewhere with more men. Interesting men. But we do a nice business here so she keeps on saving for the day when she can buy a condo somewhere warm and live off her money."

"Not a bad plan," Gallo said.

"It's a good plan, but she gets pretty horny in the meantime. So she goes on her little vacations, looking for fun. I always give her a dozen condoms. Different colors and textures, you know. Tell her not to do the deed unless her knight wears his shining armor."

"*Okay*," Gallo said. "Do you think you could show me the house on Gentleman Road that Ms. Wilson and I discussed?"

"Absolutely, but there's something else I've got to show you first."

Gallo was about to hold up a hand, but Suzie saw the apprehension on his face and laughed.

"Not me, silly. I really do have my own guy. I'm going to show you what Deanna did for you."

Suzie opened the file drawer of the unoccupied desk in the office. She withdrew a manila folder and offered it to Gallo.

"Deanna put this together in case you or one of your people came by. She's gonna kick herself when she finds out she missed you. Aside from being married, you are about the right age for her."

Gallo chose not to comment. With Suzie's permission, he sat down at Deanna Wilson's desk. He opened the folder and said, "Holy shit!"

"The good kind or the bad?" Suzi asked.

Gallo held up a hand, asking for a moment's indulgence.

The folder was a gift that kept on giving. Deanna Wilson had written down the license plate number of the car driven by client "Thomas Gower." Not only that, she'd clipped a picture of the type of vehicle it was. A Buick Enclave in pale gold.

The big prize, though, was the first thing he'd seen: a pencil sketch. It was a dead bang match for the picture of Damon Todd that had been circulated to every FBI office in the country. There could be no question now that Todd had been the man who rented the Ottawa house.

"Is that someone you want?" Suzie asked, looking on over Gallo's shoulder. "He's not some sort of crazy killer, is he?"

From the way Gallo had read Todd's file, that was exactly how he'd characterize the guy.

What he told Suzie was, "You and Ms. Wilson are going to have a couple new people in your office for a while."

"You? Deanna would love that."

"Female agents," Gallo told her. "With others nearby. Probably not me."

"So this guy is a killer."

"He's dangerous," the special agent conceded. "Did Ms. Wilson draw this likeness?"

Suzie shook her head. "She hired the art teacher at Ottawa High School."

Damn, Gallo thought. Limiting knowledge of the situation

was going to be hard.

He made a phone call to Chicago from his car. Photographed the sketch of Todd and e-mailed it. Texted the information about the license plate and the car. He had Suzie West ride with him to the house on Gentleman Road.

The support team arrived by helicopter forty minutes later.

A plan was laid to trap Todd, Crosby and Anderson, should any of them return.

As the spy cams Crosby and Anderson had set up caught the FBI's arrival on the scene and transmitted video to Todd's iPad, that wasn't going to happen.

New York Times Homepage — www.nytimes.com

The banner ad in the electronic edition of the *New York Times* bore the headline: *The United States Government — Love It or Leave It.* Clicking on the expand button revealed an image of the U.S. Capitol and the ad's body copy:

How many politicians do you hear these days blaming all our problems on Washington? For most people, the answer is too many to count. The way the blame-Washington-first crowd acts, it makes a person wonder why any of them would ever set foot within its city limits. Much less want to spend their careers there.

Would you compete to work in a place you reviled?

Would you raise funds so you could keep working in that place?

Would you work for an institution you insist is destroying our country?

Of course, you wouldn't. That's why it makes no sense to vote for anyone who claims that Washington is the problem not the solution. If all you do is bad-mouth the place where you work, you'll never make it any better.

A private sector business would never hire a disgruntled job applicant. Any company that recruited and retained employees who consciously thwarted the way it was supposed to work would soon crash and burn. If you think about that, it becomes clear exactly what the problem with Washington is.

Our government is being sabotaged by people who hate it and say so proudly.

The way to solve that problem is simple. Vote for candidates who honor and respect the government that the patriots of the Revolutionary War sacrificed their lives to give us. Would those first Americans have voted for a candidate who said, "You know, on second thought, this whole idea of representative democracy is a big mistake."

That might sound funny, but what the hate-Washington-first crowd is doing to our country is a tragedy in the making. Tell them to go home and stay home. Vote for candidates who value government as an indispensable tool for making your life better.

The ad also ran in the online editions of the one hundred biggest circulation newspapers in the country. Social media sharing sent it viral within an hour of its first appearance. Print newspapers and television stations gave it headline coverage. Talking-head shows talked of little else. Bumper stickers quickly appeared on cars nationwide.

The U.S. Government. Love It or Leave It.

For emphasis, some stickers appended the word motherfucker.

In a matter of days, the idea of expressing contempt for Washington became political suicide. That sent a sizable number of political strategists scrambling for a new way to keep the average American from joining with his compatriots to push the federal government to work on their behalf. The monied special interests couldn't have that.

Putnam Shady was ready for the push-back with his next ad.

Capital Yacht Club — Washington, D.C.

"Uncle, Uncle, Uncle," Hugh Collier said, sitting drink in hand opposite Sir Edbert Bickford in the salon of the *Poseidon*. "You really can't help yourself, can you?"

Sir Edbert looked three weeks dead, left out in a warm dry place, his desiccated flesh holding no appeal for the usual scavengers. His mood was worse than his appearance. There was no reason it shouldn't be. Sir Edbert and his lawyers had spent the day reviewing the case the Department of Justice would be bringing against him.

At Sir Edbert's age, conviction on even one count of the many the government was contemplating might result in a life sentence. Such harsh justice wasn't supposed to be meted out against men of his stature. He was a *nobleman*, by God! At worst, he was supposed to be allowed to buy his way out of a difficult situation with a fine, set at a price that was within reason.

"I'll outlast her," Sir Edbert muttered.

"The president, you mean?"

A pronoun was as far as the old man would go. *"Her,* damnit."

Hugh sighed. "If that's your plan, Uncle, you should trade in this floating palace for the *Nautilus* because your only hiding place will be twenty thousand leagues under the sea."

"You're fired," Sir Edbert said. "Leave this vessel at once."

Hugh replied, "After I finish my drink. Have one of your crew try to remove me and I'll break both his neck and yours. Quite possibly yours first."

"I made you what you are," Sir Edbert reminded his nephew.

"Then you'll know I'm not having you on. Uncle, if I was able to find out about this new television channel you're planning, so will others. Others include the government and the administration that mean to lock you up. You're only making things worse for yourself. The wise course is to take shelter behind what WorldWide News has become, the most respected source of televised journalism in the world. Its transformation, and its increase in ad revenue, have been nothing short of staggering. You plead guilty to the least charge against you. You negotiate the shortest sentence and largest fine you can bear to pay. You do a year or two in a minimum security prison, and you come out still filthy rich. You live a quiet, comfortable life, leaving behind you a monument to —"

"I don't *only* want to be respected, I don't *only* want to be rich,"

Sir Edbert growled. "Damn you to hell, I want to be *feared*."

Hugh stared at the old man. He finished his drink and stood. He said, "I'll see myself out. Please let me know if you come to your senses. Be quick about it, though, you don't have much time left."

As soon as Hugh got to his car, he called Ethan Judd.

"You might as well go ahead. The old bastard wouldn't budge."

Penrose House — Charlottesville, Virginia

Leaving his house to travel to Washington was where Fletcher Penrose finally dug in his heels. He refused to go unless placed under arrest. If he was arrested, he would invoke his right to remain silent and have his attorney represent him. That being the case, McGill agreed to Byron DeWitt's request to travel to Virginia.

He brought Daryl Cheveyo with him.

DeWitt made the introductions.

The presence of another academic seemed to calm Penrose.

"Would you like to talk with Dr. Cheveyo alone?" McGill asked.

"He won't shrink my head, will he?" Penrose asked.

"Only if it gets too big, I suppose," McGill said.

Penrose grinned. "I use humor in my work, too. You've never stuttered, have you?"

McGill shook his head. "For the most part, I've been very fortunate."

"So have I, since Damon Todd helped me. I won't do anything to hurt him."

McGill was tempted to lie, say nobody would hurt Todd, but he didn't. Penrose would see through that. How Penrose would deal with the truth might make dealing with the professor harder for Daryl Cheveyo or it could be a good place for the two of them to start their conversation about Todd.

McGill took a seat opposite Penrose and told him, "Damon

Todd tried, one night, to club me to death with a baseball bat. I had a gun and could have shot him but I didn't. I've come to think that might have been a mistake. If you can help us find him, maybe we can work things out so no one will have to shoot him."

McGill got to his feet and gestured to DeWitt to leave the room with him.

Closing the door, McGill heard Penrose ask Cheveyo, "How can I know if he was telling me the truth?"

Cheveyo said, "I was there at the end. Mr. McGill had a gun. Dr. Todd didn't and —

The door closed.

DeWitt asked McGill, "You think Dr. Cheveyo will get anything out of him?"

"I don't know. My guess is Todd's instruction set for Penrose will hold up only if it doesn't violate deeper beliefs. That's the way I've seen it work."

"You think about it, Todd could have helped the CIA and a lot of other people."

"Todd never helped anyone without exacting a price."

Sex or money, McGill knew, depending on the circumstances.

DeWitt told him, "I probably would have shot the guy, if I'd been in your shoes."

McGill said, "If you wear the right size, I'll lend you a pair."

Department of Justice Building — Washington, D.C.

Attorney General Michael Jaworsky read through the contract Ethan Judd had brought him. When he finished he laid it on his desk and placed his reading glasses atop it. He looked at the newsman sitting opposite him.

"What do you think I should do with this, Mr. Judd?" Jaworsky asked.

"Whatever your professional ethics dictate, Mr. Attorney General."

"You're just being a good citizen here?"

"I'm being a good reporter. Ms. Ellie Booker brought that contract to me. She said she construes it to be an attempted bribe. She also said she was going to bring it to the attention of your office. Whether she has, I don't know and won't ask — for now. I only wanted to make sure you are aware of it."

"Why now? Because the investigation into Sir Edbert's business dealings is about to conclude?"

"Yes. If I'd brought this to you sooner, it might have been just another snowflake in a blizzard."

Jaworsky chuckled. "So you think Sir Edbert might soon be facing an array of charges brought by the federal government?"

"If you're asking whether I have any inside information about what you're going to do, the answer is no. You run a tight ship here."

"We try, Mr. Judd. Are you planning to leave your new job so soon?"

Judd leaned forward, "Mr. Attorney General, talking to you and bringing you that contract will be the least of my offenses against Sir Edbert. I'm going to air the story of my employer offering a million-dollars-for-nothing contract to Ms. Booker. I thought I'd time my story to run in concert with the conclusion of your investigation of Sir Edbert."

"No doubt, you'll be fired for that," Jaworsky said.

"No doubt at all, but I've already shown the country what a return to objective television news looks like. My guess is I've whetted the public's appetite for more. If I'm to be a part of the renaissance, bully for me. If not, I'll write a book."

Jaworsky nodded. "I've enjoyed what you've done with WWN. I wish you luck. May I hold on to this contract or should I have copies made? I'd like to get a few opinions on its relevance to our investigation."

Judd stood and said, "It's all yours. I've made all the copies I need. Oh, there's one more thing. You might want to pass it along to the president."

"What's that?" Jaworsky asked.

Judd told him about the coming launch of WorldWide News in Review and how Mike O'Dell would be its leading voice.

"I'm sure you won't let it influence your legal judgment, but Sir Edbert and friends don't mean to go down without taking the president down with them."

Penrose House — Charlottesville, Virginia

Daryl Cheveyo found McGill and DeWitt outside, leaning against McGill's Chevy.

Leo Levy stood twenty yards away talking to an FBI agent who was into cars.

"Anything?" McGill asked.

Cheveyo shook his head. Not evincing a lack of success, but a sense of wonder.

"It was like nothing I've experienced."

"Penrose is okay, though, right?" DeWitt asked.

"He's sleeping like a baby. I'm the one who's going to need a sedative tonight."

"What happened?" McGill said.

"Well, I injected him with ketamine hydrochloride, a small dose to reduce the risk of emergence delirium. He seemed to tolerate it well. I'll go back inside in a few minutes to make sure he doesn't have any problems."

"Did he open up to you?" DeWitt asked.

"He was happy to talk. I brought out my iPad. It can play a series of video loops that help a subject enter a hypnotic state. There's a flickering flame dancing up and down, a row of tulips swaying back and forth in a breeze, and other things like that. I asked the professor to tell me when he saw one he liked. He went with highway lane divider stripes passing under a car from a driver's perspective."

"Highway hypnosis," McGill said.

"Right. When he was nice and relaxed, receptive to my voice, I asked him to go back to the first time he'd met Todd. He began to stutter and get very anxious. Told me he never wanted to go through that again. I brought him forward to the time when he'd overcome the speech impediment. I asked how Todd knew what to do to help him.

"He said, 'Doctor Todd just knew what I needed.' He couldn't explain it any better than that. He told me his parents had brought him to Todd, and I'm sure they gave Todd their take on their son's life, but that narrative would have been biased, edited and untutored in psychological understanding. For Todd to have elicited information from a fearful young man that would allow him to construct a stable, well-integrated personality able not only to cope with a previously frightening world, but also succeed in it while overcoming a lifelong handicap … that's a masterful achievement."

Cheveyo sighed. "When I first met Damon Todd, I thought he was a crank. Now, I'd like to gather all his subjects in one room and listen to how he managed to assist them."

McGill said, "Don't forget he kills people. You might ask why he couldn't help himself."

DeWitt, not having any history with Todd, was able to keep his eye on the ball.

"Did Penrose tell you anything that might help us catch Todd?"

"Maybe. He said Todd told him he would probably need more money from him."

McGill liked that. "Then all we'll have to do is follow the money."

Wingsuit Flying — 12,000 Feet Above Baja California

Damon Todd followed his instructor, Jaime Martinez, out of the plane. Crosby and Anderson jumped after Todd. Martinez was an old friend of the covert operatives and they'd all paid close attention to his instructions. There'd be no screwing around here like there was up in the Mojave Desert.

Wingsuit flying was both trickier and more exhilarating than normal skydiving.

The wingsuit was sewn with areas of fabric between the legs

and from the arms to the torso. When the flyer's arms and legs were extended the surface areas adjacent to his body expanded, making him look like a flying squirrel. That significantly decreased the speed at which a belly-to-earth flyer fell and extended the range he could glide. The standard ratio was two point five meters forward for every meter downward.

But you couldn't just spread your arms and legs as you left the plane. There was a little matter called relative wind to consider. Relative wind was generated by the forward speed of the aircraft. If the wind popped open the flying suit's gliding surfaces, it could propel a flyer into a collision with the plane. Even if that fatal mishap didn't occur, the thrust of relative wind could launch a flyer into an unstable start to his flight.

Because a flying suit lacked a vertical stabilizer even poor technique could send a flier into a spin from which it would be difficult to emerge and regain control.

Despite these potentially mortal hazards, Todd had never done anything so thrilling in his life. It was addictive from the first moment. He saw the world from the perspective of a god. The speed of the flight and the rush of cold air stimulated every nerve ending in his body. He didn't say anything to the others about it, but he got hard as he flew.

It was all he could do not to ejaculate.

Below was the blue Pacific and the dun dangle of the Baja California peninsula. Details of ocean and earth were flattened by the great height of the jump altitude, but they came into progressively sharper relief as Todd streaked downward.

More than the view was breathtaking, though. The way the world became ever more clear to his eyes bore an uncanny resemblance to the way the minds of Todd's subjects became progressively more clear to him.

What started as an undifferentiated mass of anxieties, inhibitions and even self-loathing resolved itself into a neat sequence of traumas, abuse and misfortunes. Discovering where the fault lines of the mind intersected and how deeply they cut gave him the clues he needed to rebuild and if necessary reroute the ways his subjects saw themselves. It was never easy, but when the patients told him what their goals were he had an intuitive sense of how to start the therapy. From there, it was a matter of seeing —

Jaime tapping the altimeter on his wrist.

Todd looked at his own altimeter. It was time to open his parachute. He did so, thinking it wasn't at all a good idea to get distracted while falling out of the sky. Even in a wingsuit, you'd still become a blob to be sponged up by some poor soul who'd curse you for a fool.

The planned landing zone was the beach directly below. Drifting to earth, Todd watched Jaime, who still hadn't opened his chute. The man all but danced on air. The way he maneuvered in flight was a sight to behold, both artistic and athletic. At so low an altitude that Todd would have been yelling for help, Jaime's parachute blossomed and he hit the beach running.

He stopped just short of the water, turned and spotted his companions about to land safely. A good jump for everyone. Jaime stepped over to a cooler ten feet from where he'd touched down. He'd left it on the beach before takeoff. He lifted the lid and had a cold bottle of beer open for everyone by the time they joined him.

The four men toasted each other's skill and bravery.

The *gringos* were fortunate to have reached Jaime Martinez while he was still alive. He was in robust physical health, but he was a man on a suicide mission. His beloved wife, Nalda, had left him for a lieutenant in the Baja Cartel named Elvio Mora.

She hadn't left Jaime because she loved Mora. She left because Mora was a man who got whatever he wanted, and he wanted Nalda. He told her that if she didn't live with him and please him greatly he would kill Jaime, everyone who shared a bloodline with him and all their animals.

Of course, Mora told Nalda, if Jaime were truly a man he would try to take his woman back.

That was close to what Jaime had in mind. His plan was to

buy a plane and a bomb, and now he had nearly all the money he needed. He would fly the plane over Mora's hilltop fortress on the night of the great fiesta the drug boss gave to celebrate his birthday. The *narco-trafficantes* were enthusiastic participants in any form of savagery that might come to mind, but as of yet they hadn't thought to use airplanes for bombing missions.

But Jaime had.

He didn't intend to drop his bomb from his plane nor did he intend to crash the plane into Mora's hacienda. He planned to strap the bomb to his chest and fall from the sky like a comet. There would be no need for a parachute on this jump. He would spot Mora from above and take him like a raptor seizing a rabbit, detonating his bomb as he sank his teeth into the coward's stinking flesh.

"I like it," Anderson said, hearing the plan.

"Calls for great intel and pinpoint execution," Crosby opined.

"I can help you with the focus you'll need for the execution," Todd told him.

Jaime looked at Todd. He liked the way the new *gringo* paid respect to him and careful attention to his instructions. For one so new to wingsuit flying, Todd had shown no fear and save for letting his mind wander for a moment he had done well.

"What do you want for helping me?"

Todd said, "I have someone I'd like to see die, too. Crosby and Anderson have told me they'd like to try to get the job done. If either of them succeeds, I'll help you free of charge. If they fail, I'll see if I can do it. If that's the case, I think you might be able to help me."

"A favor for a favor. *Bueno.*"

The bargain was sealed with an embrace.

Everyone felt good until the *americanos* tried to find their shiny gold truck.

It was gone. All that remained were its license plates.

Front Page — Washington Post

The photo showed James J. McGill stepping out of the White House, walking with the aid of a cane. The headline said, "President's Husband Suffers from Old Knee Injury." The accompanying story detailed how years earlier as a captain of the Chicago Police Department McGill had given chase to and caught a purse snatcher while off duty and visiting the Lincoln Park Zoo with his children and former wife, Carolyn Enquist.

In tackling the thief, McGill suffered an injury to his right knee.

The story had all of that right. In making the arrest, while wearing walking shorts, McGill had skinned his knee. In a moment of overzealousness, the rookie paramedic attending to him that day had bandaged the scrape as if her binding was the only thing keeping his leg in one piece. McGill had taken a good deal of ribbing after a photo had been snapped of his over-wrapped leg.

Now, that image appeared on an inside page of the *Post's* front section.

Only the description of the injury McGill had suffered was now an avulsion of the patellar tendon, an injury that had required surgery and physical therapy to repair. Government disinformation. It went unchallenged, for the most part, because McGill's medical history, just like anyone else's, was protected by the privacy rules of the Health Insurance Portability and Accountability Act of 1996.

The lie might have been contested by anyone who had seen McGill's bare, unscarred knee in the intervening years, but there was no great worry on McGill's part that a whistle-blower would come forward, and he didn't intend to drop his pants for anyone except the president.

The story would have been beneath media notice for anyone without first rank celebrity standing. Even for McGill, it was only a few paragraphs and a couple of small photos, but it was widely distributed and briefly commented upon by the mainstream media. That was good enough to make the jump to the Internet.

One blogger even guessed the truth. It was all a fake-out. But that anti-administration voice ascribed the wrong motive to McGill's gambit. He thought it was a ploy for sympathy on the part of the president's husband. To show the public what a trooper he was as he went on his political rounds speaking as Patti Grant's chief surrogate.

Look at him up there with his bum leg. What a guy. I'll vote for his wife.

It was unfortunate that anyone would question the authenticity of the illusion, but the blogger had the reputation as a crackpot and wasn't widely read. Some critics simply had to be ignored.

The people who were in on the gag, Carolyn and the kids especially, had been briefed to go along with it or better yet to say a person's medical history was nobody else's business.

In any event, McGill would be presenting himself to the world with either a curved handle cane or curved handle unbreakable umbrella in hand until Damon Todd and friends were no longer a threat.

Elspeth and Sweetie had seen what McGill could do with the umbrella.

He also gave a demonstration to Deke, who was back on board, and to Celsus Crogher.

Crogher had asked, "Can you bat away bullets with either of those things?"

McGill conceded he probably wasn't that quick.

He added, "It gets down to shooting, I'll leave things to Deke or Elspeth."

"Or me," Sweetie said.

She was present to see more of her old friend's Dark Alley magic.

"Or Margaret," McGill said.

6

April, 2012
White House Press Room

Aggie Wu announced the arrival of the president and the newsies got to their feet just like they'd all been raised indoors by parents who valued good manners. Such propriety was a now and then thing when reporters questioned most public figures. What was constant at the White House was their fear of the press secretary.

You were on your best manners when speaking to the president or you looked for another beat to work. Some editors and publishers complained that Aggie had a chilling effect on the free press. Informed of that evaluation, the president had her own take.

"Don't think of Aggie as chilling, think of her as air conditioning. She keeps the press room from overheating." Aggie had a plaque made from those words.

Now, the president said, "Good morning. As you all know, there are two vacancies on the Supreme Court. Some people think *any* reduction of the federal government is a good thing ..."

The president paused for and got a laugh.

"I feel, however, the court operates best with a full complement of justices. With that thought in mind, I'm here to inform the country of my nominations to fill the Supreme Court's vacancies. I'm sure my choices will not please everyone. Given our current state of political disharmony, I doubt there breathes a soul who could please us all.

"What I looked for in making my choices was to find two individuals who understand that the Constitution is a body of law that must be as vibrantly alive as the country itself. The principles articulated in the Constitution must be interpreted to deal with situations that its authors never could have imagined.

"These interpretations inevitably are arrived at through the filters of personal experience, education and thinking. The decisions that flow from the interpretations of the Supreme Court are not subject to further review — except by future courts with new justices. A court with new justices may choose to reverse completely what had been thought of as settled law. Such reversals necessarily cast doubt upon the original decision and by implication the wisdom of the justices who rendered it.

"Such reversals might also make a new court susceptible to suspicions that maybe they got things wrong and their predecessors had it right. Right and wrong, of course, are often subjective judgments. Here again, individual differences come into play, including the nature of the politics one favors.

"Many of my predecessors have hewed close to their own politics when nominating justices to the Supreme Court. Conservative presidents want to stack the court with justices who reflect their own thinking. Liberals take the same tack from their point of view. As I see things, this endangers the public perception of a court that will be impartial in its decisions.

"It also engenders the idea that one side might have the upper hand for now, but don't you worry, we'll have our guy — or gal — in the White House again and then we'll put our people on the Supreme Court and reverse the decisions the other party's justices made.

"I think politicizing the Court, any more than it already is, would be a terrible mistake. The Constitution, as it is interpreted for us, should not veer back and forth like a shuttlecock. To the greatest extent possible, the core truths of the laws that govern us should remain clear. The only way I see to do this is by balancing the makeup of the court, not by stacking it with justices whose views neatly align with one party or the other.

"Of course, the Founders in their wisdom dictated that the number of justices on the court be odd not even to allow for majority decisions. But I suspect the Founders also thought presidents would nominate and Congress would advise and consent to nominees with open minds, and not have to deal with ideologues who think they know every answer to every question that might ever confront them because it is right there in their political catechism.

"I have chosen two nominees, one conservative, one liberal, both open minded and both critical legal thinkers of the first order. For the position of associate justice, I nominate Senator Daniel Crockett of Tennessee and for chief justice of the United States I nominate the chief judge of the Ninth United States Circuit Court of Appeals, Craig MacLaren."

The two men joined the president at the front of the room.

They nodded and smiled politely for the cameras.

The president said, "Senator Crockett and Judge MacLaren will not be taking any questions today. They will save their answers for the questions they will hear from the Senate. Majority Leader Wexford assures me the Senate will take up these nominations quickly and concurrently and votes on confirming the nominations will take place on the same day."

Turning to her nominees, the president said, "Thank you, gentlemen."

Crockett and MacLaren left the room, with every reporter present dying to shout out questions to them. But the president had spoken. And Aggie Wu's glare was even fiercer than ever.

To reinforce Aggie's terrible power, the president said, "I will take just a few questions now. Aggie will point out who she'd like to hear from."

A reporter from *The Christian Science Monitor* got the first opportunity.

"Madam President, in light of the extraordinary confirmation of Vice President Morrissey, would you say you are now ramming your choices for the Supreme Court through the Senate?"

Of course, I am, Patti thought.

What she said was, "I'm *asking* the Senate, a body that never thinks of itself as anybody's doormat, to expedite its consideration of two nominees whose records of public service are both extraordinary and well known. I'm *asking* the Senate to proceed in a deliberate but not dilatory manner. This is a time for public servants to serve the public, not distract themselves with any political shenanigans."

A wise guy from the *San Jose Mercury News,* who had bought Apple Computers at six dollars a share and was about to retire, piped up without Aggie's permission. "Madam President, is there ever a time for public servants *not* to serve the public?"

Patti Grant didn't miss a beat. "Only when they've been granted eternal rest and are busy listening to their eulogies."

The newsies laughed, all the more so when Patti added, "I'll be here all week, be sure to tip the wait staff well."

Aggie gave the president a look. Was she done?

She was and waved farewell to the press corps.

Café Lulu — San Diego, California

Todd, Crosby and Anderson sat at an outdoor table, shortly before the three a.m. closing time with their check paid and no one nearby. Todd, the designated driver, contented himself with a club soda. Crosby and Anderson were drinking Scotch and sharing a hookah burning what was supposed to be a blend of exotic tobaccos but smelled to Todd as if his companions had added at least a pinch of hashish.

"Fucking Mexicans," Anderson said, "bastards will steal the shine off your shoes."

He was still angry about losing the Buick to a car thief. They'd had to ask Jaime Martinez for a lift back to Tijuana and walked across the border to the U.S. In San Diego, Crosby bought a new car for them, a black BMW 550i sedan with a 400 horsepower engine.

They were close to going operational now. It was time to have muscle under the hood.

Crosby replied. "Some Mexicans are crooked, but you can say the same about any nationality, even Swedes."

Anderson grinned. "Yeah, that's true, the berserker Viking lives on in a lot of us."

Todd watched his companions with clinical detachment. He could almost see them shift gears mentally and emotionally. They were preparing to do battle. In the months they'd spent together, he'd never seen either of them have more than an occasional beer. They'd never been drunk in his presence.

The only time they'd taken any drugs was when he'd injected them with Special K.

The ketamine hydrochloride he used in hypnotizing his subjects.

Now, though, they were indulging themselves with alcohol and hash.

One last good time before they risked their lives. Well, before Anderson did. He was going to take the first shot at McGill. Crosby was indulging to be sociable with an old comrade. Todd wondered if Crosby hoped for Anderson to succeed or fail. If he had to guess, he'd say Crosby wanted Anderson to succeed, spare him from having to face McGill himself.

Anderson was younger, bigger, stronger.

If McGill dispatched him, Crosby would have to wonder what chance he stood.

Of course, Todd wondered, if McGill overcame both of them … what chance would he have?

Well, without his two new friends around to keep him honest, maybe doing a vanishing act would be the wiser course. Todd saw their waitress looking at them. They were the only customers left, and a glance at his watch showed Todd it was closing time.

They didn't want to leave an unfavorable memory of their presence at the café.

Certainly didn't want anyone calling the cops on them.

Todd stood up and smiled at the waitress. She gave him a nod. After he held up three twenties as a tip and put them on the table, she smiled back.

Anderson said to Crosby, "Doc's telling us it's time to go."

Crosby helped his friend to his feet.

"You know how I'd like to finish up the night?" Anderson asked.

"With a hooker," Crosby said.

Anderson grinned and asked Todd, "You think he's right, Doc?"

"I'd have said two hookers," Todd told him.

Anderson pointed a finger at him and said, "Bingo."

"Of course, one or the other of you knows where to indulge."

Crosby said, "This is a Navy town. There's no shortage of places."

"I believe they mention that in Fodor's," Todd said.

Crosby and Anderson both laughed, but they were stoned and easily amused.

"Tell me one thing before I drop the two of you off wherever it is you wish to go," Todd said. "Have you figured out how and where Anderson will take McGill's life?"

Anderson smiled broadly and said, "You tell him, Arn."

Crosby nodded. "Olin is going to use that big blonde of McGill's as his bird-dog."

"Margaret Sweeney?"

"Right. McGill's got Secret Service protection. She doesn't. Our bet is there are times those two get together without any federal company."

"You think they're lovers?"

"Don't know about that, but we have a strong feeling the two of them, just like Olin and me, have secrets they share."

Anderson said with a leer, "What I'm hoping is I can have a

little time with her before he drops by."

"And you'll kill them both without drawing the attention of the Secret Service?"

"Doc, I can be oh so quiet when I want to, and my favorite weapon is a knife."

Crosby added, "You clamp a hand over their mouths as the blade goes in and nobody hears a thing."

Todd had no doubt they'd both done just that.

He dropped them off at a chain motel where they assured Todd they'd be able to find all the nookie a man could want. Todd drove on to a higher end hostelry, quiet at that hour of the morning. He went to his room, showered and slipped into bed.

Should have gone straight to sleep, but checked his iPad to see if there was any new photo of Chana. There wasn't, but there was video from the house in Ottawa, Illinois. The FBI had found it. They were getting closer and thus encouraged wouldn't give up the chase anytime soon.

Crosby and Anderson were right, it was time to strike while they still could.

Manouch Hot Dog Stand — Washington, D.C.

Speaker of the House Peter Profitt, like most politicians, wanted things both ways. He was a man of high principle, who'd stop at nothing to be on the winning side. He was a tireless servant of the people, who kept a year 'round golf tan. He insisted on transparency in government, except when he was eating lunch from a hot dog stand with a private eye on a bench near George Washington University.

His dining companion, Maxwell Kern, twice spilled toppings from his own hot dog down the front of his shirt.

Each time, Kern said, "Excuse me."

And ate from his fingers what he'd spilled on himself.

"Hate to waste food," he explained.

The speaker wore both a hat and sunglasses to his lunch

meeting.

He hadn't fobbed off the meeting on a staffer for two reasons. Kern had said to him on the phone, "Bobby Beckley told me to call." Name dropping mattered in Washington. And, "Bobby thinks we've got a way for you to screw James J. McGill."

If McGill's fate was in play, the president's own political fortunes might take a turn for the worse. Then again, the last speaker who'd tried his luck against McGill — Derek Geiger — wound up getting his neck broken and went home to Florida in an urn. Profitt, however, would never be so foolish as to wave a gun around in McGill's presence. He also wouldn't trust the judgment of an underling if there was a real opportunity to damage the president's chances of being reelected.

"What happens now?" Profitt asked.

For all he knew Kern was wearing a wire for the FBI, but after the man had made a Jackson Pollock knockoff of his shirt, the speaker wasn't about to pat him down. He also wasn't going to say anything that might incriminate himself. His syntax would be as content free as light beer.

Kern said, "Now, I tell you I have pictures of a guy named Putnam Shady going to see the president's old man. Shady's a lawyer, used to hustle votes in Congress for his clients. Now, he runs something called ShareAmerica and is partners with that billionaire, Darren Drucker, in what you people call a Super-PAC by the name of Americans for Equity."

Profitt knew about ShareAmerica, a pool of lobbying funds created by small donations from mobs of ordinary people. He thought the idea was subversive. Was ShareAmerica going to offer him a multi-million-dollar sinecure when he left office, the way Wall Street bankers would? No way in hell. Horseshit ideas like ShareAmerica had to be stopped.

Americans for Equity sounded like more of the same.

"Go on," Profitt said.

"The way it was explained to me," Kern said, "you run a Super-PAC, you're not supposed to talk back and forth with the pol you're backing. You're supposed to figure things out for yourself or some shit like that."

Kern gave Profitt the chance to say something. Like, "Yeah, that's right." He didn't. Guy just stayed clammed up. Told Kern the prick thought he couldn't be trusted.

He was right about that. Kern would have sold him out in a heartbeat if he had to.

But he didn't have to.

"Anyway, I shot pictures of Shady going into the building where McGill works. I uploaded them to the Internet right away. Shady was in there at least twenty minutes before I got pinched."

That got a response. Guy wouldn't have been human he didn't say something.

"What?" Profitt asked.

"Yeah, the Secret Service grabbed me. I was trying to shoot some pictures through the window of McGill's car. There were these papers on the back seat. Thought they might be something interesting. Never found out what they were. The feds deleted all my shots before they gave my camera back. They couldn't hold me because there aren't any laws against what I'd done. I was just taking pictures in public places of things anybody might walk by and see. My lawyer sprung me inside of two hours."

Kern waited to see if Profitt had any comment at that point. He didn't.

"Anyway, Bobby Beckley thought McGill and Shady weren't just talking sports when they met, and this broad name of Margaret Sweeney works with McGill is also Shady's girlfriend. She could pass tidbits back and forth, get around the rules, you know. If you want, you can see my pictures of Shady going to meet McGill."

The private investigator gave the speaker an URL where the images might be viewed.

"You can have the pictures for free," Kern said. "You want me to come see you at the Capitol, take an oath and all that, my time goes for five bills a day."

Profitt stood and fought off a smile.

Congress didn't pay lost wages when a witness testified.

Kern got to his feet and asked, "You want another dog? I'm still hungry."

The speaker turned and left without a word.

It would be a long time before he ate another hot dog.

Reserve Drive — Dublin, Ohio

Mather Wyman couldn't remember the last time he'd bought a television, wasn't sure he ever had. Now, he sat in the den of his home with his niece, Kira, looking at the large, flat screen, Internet compatible model his niece had ordered. Two pleasant young men from the store had spent fifteen minutes setting it up for him. The days of simply plugging a set into an electrical outlet apparently had departed with the rabbit-ear antenna.

Kira had offered the young men a tip. They'd politely declined and wished her luck with the birth of her children. Good manners were still in vogue.

Then Wyman and Kira sat down and watched the streaming video of the most recent debate between Patti Grant's celebrity surrogates and those representing ... not Wyman, possibly Howard Hurlbert but mainly the radical right views of the most volatile members of Congress. Two of the three members of the conservative side of the dialogue were Senator Darrin Neff of South Carolina and Representative Doak Langdon of Georgia. The third was preeminent conservative radio personality Bus Milbaugh.

The president's views were given voice by beloved veteran television actor Alan Alden, three-time Oscar-winner Beryl Green and *New York Times* columnist and Nobel laureate, Tad Klugman.

The moderator was Edward Cabot. He said he would introduce three topics. Each topic would be given twenty minutes of discussion time. An extra ten minutes could be added, at Cabot's discretion, if there were more points to be made.

Assertions of facts would be checked in real time by support staff, and if anyone got his or her *facts* wrong, Cabot would bring that to everyone's attention.

Likewise, any panelist quoting an outside person to buttress an argument would have that quote checked for accuracy and context. Misquotations and distortions would also be corrected by Cabot.

Profanity was discouraged unless accurately quoting a third party.

Everyone would be given time to speak. Talking over another panelist was to be avoided. Cabot would name the person who had the floor. Lengthy on-point responses were welcome. Speechifying was not.

Insults directed at other panel members or the moderator would not be tolerated.

Violators of this rule would be asked to leave.

Cabot's first topic was national defense: "The United States has a defense budget more than four times larger than that of China. China ran a $300 billion trade surplus with the United States last year. How do these two facts correlate and which side has the bigger strategic advantage?"

"Guns or butter?" Wyman said, watching from home. "Always a heated topic."

There was passion but no uproar and no invective. Both sides took Cabot's guidelines to heart. Even Milbaugh played by the rules, something that couldn't have been easy for him after Klugman shredded his argument for more defense spending with data showing that, historically, military overreach was the most common cause of decline for great powers.

The Times columnist also said putting the U.S. deeply in hock to its biggest economic competitor was a losing strategy.

The conservative side looked to the fact checkers, who were shown at work.

Klugman had his names, dates and numbers right.

"Smart guy," Wyman said. "He'd make a good Treasury

secretary."

Kira noted, "Alden and Green are sharp, too. So is whoever dressed them. They look good, but not glamorous. People you'd see at Starbucks not movie premieres."

Mather Wyman nodded. "That didn't happen by accident."

"No at all. They're playing roles. The common man and woman. Who just happen to be Ivy Leaguers, filthy rich and known by nine out of ten Americans. But don't mind that."

Cabot's second topic was sexuality: "Gay from day one? Is sexual orientation present from birth or a matter of choice? In either case, who does it hurt to be other than heterosexual?"

The third topic was population: "How many is too many? As the third most populous country in the world, should the United States consider setting an optimum population ceiling? If so, what should that number be and how would you keep it from being exceeded?"

On the matter of gaiety, there was partisan disagreement, within Cabot's parameters.

It made for good, lively and revelatory television.

The population question caught both sides off guard, never having been a major part of the country's general political discussion. Everybody agreed that a billion-person U.S. population would be a bad idea. Nobody wanted the country to face problems like those of India and China. Both sides felt five hundred million people might be the high end for a manageable population, certainly no more than six hundred million.

Keeping the number from going higher would mean examining the country's immigration policies and its fertility numbers. That meant border security and family planning. It also meant developing the economies of poor countries to improve domestic standards of living, relieving the pressure to emigrate . It further meant providing comprehensive sex education and continuing the empowerment of women to lower the number of births per family.

Topic three got its extra ten minutes. Had its moments of push and shove. Also came the closest to an unexpected sense of common purpose and bipartisanship.

By the time the show ended, Kira already had her smart phone out. She Googled the question she had in mind and told her uncle, "Reynard Dix chooses the conservative panelists."

Wyman grunted and shook his head. "That guy quit the party. He'll never —"

Kira's eyes went so wide they alarmed Wyman. "Are you all right, my dear?"

She bobbed her head and took her uncle's hand. "I'm fine, the babies are fine. I just had the most wonderful idea. How you can win the presidency. How you can beat Patti Grant and Howard Hurlbert."

Wyman had heard the hormonal flood of pregnancy could affect a woman's brain.

He didn't know that it conferred the gift of political genius.

He wondered if he should call a doctor for Kira.

"Mattie, there is nothing wrong with me," she said, knowing what he was thinking. "You said Reynard Dix quit the party, the Republican Party. Who else did that?"

Wyman saw where she was going now. "Patti Grant and Howard Hurlbert."

"So what does that make them?"

"Quitters?" Wyman said.

"They may or may not have good ideas, but you can't trust them because ..."

"They're quitters."

"With no way they can ever deny it," Kira said.

Wyman told his niece, "I could never call the president that name."

"Of course, you couldn't. You could, though, criticize her ... inconstancy."

Wyman nodded. That, he could do.

Maybe there was a connection between estrogen and genius.

Further advancing that theory, Kira said, "We'll let our surrogates call the president and Hurlbert quitters."

Florida Avenue — Washington, D.C.

When Putnam wasn't traveling, Sweetie lived upstairs with him. It was by far the grandest place she had ever called home. Too grand, really. Left to her own devices, she would have simplified the place to a point Puritans might consider underfurnished. But she'd already subjected Putnam to far more of her influences than he'd made her endure — if you excluded striking the spark that fired a renewed sex life for Sweetie.

Even there, she'd honed ecstasy to its glowing core.

At times like the present, with Putnam back in Omaha, Sweetie retreated to the one-room basement apartment she'd first rented from him. She felt more at peace there, more humble, more hopeful of receiving the Lord's mercy. She had the feeling she might soon need it.

Mercy, that was.

She had come right out and said she would shoot anyone who threatened the life of Jim McGill. There was no doubt in her mind she would live up to her word. Of course, if she were to kill someone, Jim would be the one counseling her on the need not to flagellate herself.

He'd be right, of course. Taking a life would be a last resort, probably. Sweetie had never told a soul but back in Winnetka, that time she'd jumped the gun on Jim and busted in on the kid who'd taken his girlfriend hostage and was threatening to kill her, she could have shot the little creep. Instead, she'd let him shoot her.

That might have been what Jesus would have done.

Then again the bible didn't say a word about Him kicking down doors.

Or being a cop, for that matter.

Now, still a newlywed, Sweetie honestly couldn't say she was certain she'd take another bullet for Jim. Putnam, yes. It was funny how wedding vows could change things. If she had a chance to get off the first shot, though, she would take it.

So killing someone might not be *absolutely* the last resort.

Hence the need for mercy.

And you never knew. People started shooting, it might not be a matter of stepping in front of anyone. It might be a question of wrong place, wrong time.

Hence again.

Seeking peace of mind, Sweetie said her rosary in the dark, bead after bead, decade after decade, in the dark, the way she always did. Catholic meditation. Her heartbeat slowed. The sounds of the outside world faded. She floated on a cloud of prayer.

And the moment she opened her eyes, she crashed to earth.

Looking out the window facing the street, she saw a big guy on the sidewalk out front. He looked up and down the street. Any cop in the world would know what he was doing. Checking to see if he'd be seen committing a crime.

The coast must have been clear because he ran up Putnam's front steps.

Her front steps now, too.

Sweetie eased out of her rosary chair. She opened the door to the apartment's only closet. Got her gun out of the floor safe. She heard footsteps above. The guy had broken into her home. She was about to go after the intruder. Would have if she was still single.

Stopped cold when she thought of Putnam as a widower.

She called Jim's cell number. He answered at the residence. Sweetie spoke quietly.

"Someone just broke into my house. He's upstairs, I'm in the basement. I need backup."

"I'll bring the cavalry with me," McGill said.

Sweetie said, "I won't go in by myself, but if he comes out, I'm stopping him."

"On my way," McGill told her.

Tom T's — New Orleans, Louisiana

Billionaire or not, Tom T. Wright, had stayed in the saloon business. Sure, he had a helluva lot nicer place than Dad had left him. Right on Bourbon Street. Everything gleaming wood, glowing brass and dark leather. Comfortable. Nobody was going to rush you out the door. It was a place to have a top shelf drink at a fair price. On weekends, Tom's music scouts brought in new blues, jazz and Cajun bands from all over the country. If the music really pleased him, he'd go as far as country or pop.

As often as not, the acts he booked drew attention from big name musicians who were playing in town or simply had come to New Orleans for the food and some fun. They'd get up on stage with the new talent and everyone would have a real good time.

Jean Baptiste and his genius at finding oil had made it all possible.

Well, that and his appreciation for Tom T. raising him right.

Tom knew the love between him and J.B. would never fade, but he wasn't too sure how much longer oil would be king in the energy field. Natural gas was coming on real strong. Electricity was on the rise with new battery technology advancing almost every day. He'd bet it wouldn't be much more than ten years before half the cars on the road in the U.S. were electric. After that, it'd be the blink of an eye before the rest of them were electric, too.

Of course, as rich as he was, the last drop of oil in the world could be burned tomorrow and he could live a thousand years and not go broke — unless all the banks collapsed and looked like they might take the government with them. Then Washington might call in all the old money and issue IOUs or something.

He didn't expect anything like that to happen, but between the crooks on Wall Street and the fools in Washington, he didn't put some mega-catastrophe beyond the realm of possibility. You grew up poor, there was always the haunting fear that poor was what you were meant to be. Where you'd wind up, long enough to make your life miserable before it ended altogether.

Tom never shared his fears with anyone, but they were the

reason he continued to believe in giving the little guy and gal a fair shake. Why he kept working at a trade he'd seen could carry him through tough times.

Sitting across a table from Senator Howard Hurlbert after the place had closed to the public, Tom poured Hurlbert a shot of George Dickel with a neat twist of his wrist. He did the same for himself.

"To noble ventures," Tom said.

Hurlbert nodded. They touched their glasses together and drank.

Tom said, "Bobby Beckley came by the other day, looking for money. I'd heard what he'd done to his wife, his second wife. Probably did the same to the first one. I told him to take his sorry ass out the door before I put some more hurt on it. I cannot abide a man who takes a hand to a woman. It's a despicable thing to do. My father had every reason in the world to bust my mother's nose, but he never touched her. I've followed his example."

"It was terrible," Hurlbert agreed. "I fired him immediately."

Tom thought the senator must have known what kind of man his chief of staff and campaign manager was. There had to be times when he'd seen Beckley's bruised knuckles and unmarked face. There was only one way a man showed that combination. He'd battered someone who never had a chance to fight back.

But Tom wasn't going to make that point. Not right away.

"The way I figure things," Tom said, "Beckley's going to find someone else to bankroll him and then he's going to come back to you. He'll want to run your campaign through a front man."

"I'd never allow that," Hurlbert said.

"Another way things might go is you find yourself another rich man to bankroll you. True South gained quite a few members when the senate rammed Governor Morrissey through to be vice president. It's not hard to imagine the same thing happening when the president gets her choices put on the Supreme Court. True South might become a real power, and you started it all. Money will be coming your way, Senator."

Hurlbert smiled and reached for the bottle. "May I?"

Tom nodded. "Be my guest."

The senator told him, "I expect you're right about the money, and with enough of it just about anything is possible. I might have a better chance of becoming president than even I would have thought possible."

"You might," Tom agreed. "The question is, what kind of president do you want to be?"

Hurlbert leaned forward. "I'm afraid Huey Long won't be my role model."

"Don't you feel anything for the ordinary working man and woman?"

The senator downed his drink and poured another shot without asking permission.

"I've never been an ordinary working man. I prefer the company of my own kind."

Before Hurlbert could drink, Tom took the glass out of his hand.

The senator was not pleased. Looked like he might get up and leave.

Tome held up a hand to forestall his departure.

"You should know, Senator, that before I invest my money in anyone, I have them checked out right down to the baby shoes their mamas bronzed for them. I did the same with you before we met up in Washington. My people delivered a big old file to me. I haven't read it yet because I figured I didn't need to know all your misdeeds if I wasn't interested in backing you. But then I saw you're a malleable fella. You'll go where the money leads you."

Hurlbert was stuck on an earlier point. "You had me investigated?"

"Thoroughly, like I just mentioned. So here's the deal. You're going to take my money and nobody else's. You *will* follow the gospel of Brother Huey Long. You'll do what I tell you or I will read that big ol' file of your sins and improprieties, and instead of spending a pile of money on getting you elected, I'll use it to destroy you."

Tom returned the glass to Hurlbert. Filled his glass, too, and raised it.

"What do you say, Senator? Shall we drink to our new understanding?"

Hurlbert saw no sign Tom T. Wright was bluffing.

He touched Tom's glass with his.

"Noble ventures," Senator Hurlbert said.

A half-hour after Senator Howard Hurlbert had departed the bar on Bourbon Street, Tom placed a call to Supreme Court nominee Senator Daniel Crockett in Washington, D.C.

Tom told him, "Hurlbert's our boy. We own him top to bottom."

Crockett responded, "Once the damn fool started his new party, the only thing to do was hijack it."

"You ought to be the one running for president."

Crockett laughed. "I thought about it. Then I asked myself, why would I want to be limited to four years or eight? I just got nominated to a lifetime appointment."

"Where you'll have only one of nine votes."

"Listen, Tom. Craig MacLaren is going to be the chief, but you just wait and see who's going to be writing most of the majority opinions."

"You saying you'll have a lot of influence?"

"I'm saying I'll leave my mark. One that's going to last a long time."

"How're you going to feel if Hurlbert winds up winning?"

Crockett said, "He won't, but he could make things interesting."

Florida Avenue — Washington, D.C.

From behind a tree, across the street from her townhouse, Sweetie saw Jim McGill walk down the street, using his cane. No cavalry. No Elspeth Kendry or Deke Ky. Not even Leo Levy driving Jim in the armored Chevy. He looked for all the world like a guy with a bum leg out doing his nightly rehab walk.

Sweetie didn't buy it for a minute.

That wasn't the point. People who didn't know better might buy it. Take a chance of doing him in while the opportunity presented itself. If someone made a move on him, she'd bet all sorts of people with guns would storm out of the darkness. Zero in on any threat and —

They might think she was one of the bad guys, if somebody got anxious.

Sweetie momentarily stepped out from behind the tree. A now-you-see-me-now-you-don't move. McGill saw her, gave a nod and tucked his chin to his collar and whispered something.

He walked right past her front door and kept going. Turned the corner and disappeared.

Sweetie watched her front door. Hoped that someone would come out and follow McGill. Or just leave with a pillow case filled with stolen goods. Either of those things would give her something to work with, but minutes ticked by and nothing happened.

Not until two Metro police cars pulled up in front of her house and put their spotlights on the front doors and windows. Several unmarked sedans, including McGill's Chevy, pulled up behind the patrol units. A SWAT truck was the last vehicle to arrive before more Metro cars sealed both ends of the block.

The SWAT team ran up the front steps behind their shields, knocked the front door off its hinges and ran inside. Lights went on inside, downstairs and then on the second floor. A moment later, the team filed out, their lieutenant calling out, "All clear."

Sweetie tucked her Beretta back into its holster and stepped out into the open with her hands raised. Always better to look foolish, she thought, than get shot by someone who was still keyed up. McGill saw her and smiled.

"Told you I'd bring the cavalry," he said.

Elspeth and Deke were there now. So was Special Agent Latz, recovered from when he'd been shot last year. It was good to see him again. Deputy Director Byron DeWitt was there for the FBI.

There was even a tech guy from the CIA who didn't give his name.

Sweetie told McGill, "I think you forgot the National Park Service."

"I did, but we've got the NSA listening in on everybody's phone calls, looking for any mention of your name or mine."

At first, Sweetie thought she was being kidded, but then she thought probably not.

DeWitt showed her several variations on an image of Olin Anderson. Some clean shaven, some bearded. Some with hair, some with a bare pate. All Sweetie needed to see was the scar.

"That's him," she said.

The CIA guy said, "I'll check to see if he planted any microphones or cameras inside. We'll leave them in place, piggyback their frequency and see where the transmissions lead."

"How about putting my door back on straight?" Sweetie asked.

"Not my job, but I'll make a call."

"Thanks."

"How'd you get across the street, Margaret?" Deke asked.

"Went straight out the basement door. Walked down to the corner just like Jim did, like I didn't know anything was wrong. Went around the block and came back sneaky."

Elspeth said, "Unless the guy was looking right at you when you came out of the building, acting innocent and ignorant was your best choice."

"Yeah," Sweetie said.

McGill said, "The important thing is, we know they're interested in you."

"They're after me as a way to get to you," Sweetie said.

McGill nodded. "Right. But they don't know we know what they're doing."

"Unless they've got their own spy satellite," Sweetie said. "Or maybe just somebody up on a nearby rooftop."

DeWitt shook his head. "The rooftops are clear. We checked that. With presidential authorization, we can find out if any satellite was overhead tonight."

McGill nodded. He'd see to it DeWitt got the approval he needed.

Elspeth asked Sweetie, "What would you have done if he'd followed you down the street? Or if you'd been upstairs asleep when he broke in?"

Her interest was professional. It would help the Secret Service know how to react if they were close enough to see Sweetie get threatened.

Sweetie said, "Shoot first and pray for his soul later."

Everyone said amen to that.

Ubiquity Cable TV — Nationwide

The ninety-second commercial ran at 3:14 a.m. Eastern Daylight Time embedded in an edited showing of the movie *L.A. Confidential.* The spot came on just before the film's climactic shootout. Neither the choice of the movie nor the commercial's placement within the movie's storyline was an accident.

The commercial was shot in the same film noir style as the movie, opening on a woman in a nightgown sprawled dead on a rumpled bed. An eddy of cigarette smoke drifted past, as if someone was sitting in the room with the woman's body. A deep male voice, sounding a lot like the late Jack Webb, began to speak in voice over.

"In 1986, aspiring film actress Jennifer Dean was on the verge of her big break."

The view moved closer to the dead woman's face. She'd died bloodlessly but in great pain.

"Jenny Dean was one of two actresses up for the lead in a major motion picture. The other actress was a former model and a newcomer to L.A. and to acting. Her name was …"

A smiling headshot, also in black and white, appeared.

"Patti Darden, now known as Patricia Darden Grant, president of the United States. Guess who got the part."

A photo of a radiant Patti attending the film's premiere filled the screen and then dissolved back to the image of the dead Jennifer Dean.

"Now, guess who the last person to see Jenny Dean alive was."

Another dissolve took the viewer back to the headshot of Patti Darden.

"That's right. It was the girl who got the part. Coincidence? The coroner ruled the death a suicide. So the case was closed. Officially. Thing is, a lot of people Patti Darden worked with in Hollywood didn't fare much better than Jenny Dean."

A photo of a damaged car on a stretch of sand appeared. A bloody blanket lay next to the car.

"Actor Jeremy Danvers was one of Patti Darden's co-stars. He drove his car off a cliff under the influence of narcotics. He managed to survive. The couple sleeping on the beach blanket wasn't so lucky."

An emaciated woman with leathery skin, desperate eyes and jarringly white teeth appeared live, blinking at the camera.

"Paige Nelson also lost out on a part to Patti Darden. She survived, just barely. But she's still anorexic."

Paige said, "The casting director told me Patti had the look they wanted. I've been trying to look like her ever since."

Pathetic Paige was replaced by a beaming President Grant, taking the oath of office at her inauguration. McGill stood at her side, his happiness obvious.

"A lot of people who don't know the whole story like this woman's looks. Once they find out who she really is, they know something else. She sure can put on an act."

The commercial ended with a one-line credit.

Paid for by Americans for Truth.

L.A. Confidential returned with the bad guys trying to shoot the shit out of the good guys.

Stephen Norwood, the president's campaign manager, was awakened by a phone call at 3:20 a.m. Neil Carrick, the campaign's rapid response chief, was on the line. He told Norwood to go to YouTube and search for a video called Presidential Confidential.

"You're not going to believe this one," Carrick said.

Norwood's computer was always on and he found the video in seconds.

"Jesus Christ," he said. The video had been posted only three minutes earlier and already had over five hundred views. Forget viral. The damn thing was going pandemic. Norwood had added his view of the video to the exploding tally numbers.

Carrick waited silently but not idly as Norwood took in the attack ad.

"You're ready to counterattack?" Norwood asked after watching the last frame.

"We already have the rebuttal on the first implication, that the president killed her rival for a movie role. Patti Darden was the last *known* person to see Jennifer Dean *publicly*. But Ms. Dean committed suicide in her apartment *nine* days after she auditioned. That was in an L.A. Times story. Nobody knows if anyone saw Ms. Dean in the interim."

"Was there any evidence of foul play?" Norwood asked.

"Not according to the medical examiner's report."

"Good, that's one thing. Now, how the hell does anyone get hold of a police photo of a dead woman?"

"Don't know, but I'll find out," Carrick said.

"Is there any information that the president and Ms. Dean exchanged words the last time they saw each other?"

"I'll look for that, too. You might ask Ms. Mindel to ask the president if she has any memory of what happened that day."

Norwood said, "Jesus. Yeah, I better. Neil, shoot this whole thing down as fast as you can, will you?"

"Nobody on my team sleeps until we do." Carrick clicked off.

Stephen Norwood called Galia Mindel, brought her up to speed. The White House chief of staff called Deputy Attorney General Linda Otani and gave her the particulars of the situation, told her be ready to indict the commercial's producers and

Ubiquity Cable on fraud charges.

Heaving a deep sigh, Galia called the White House and asked for the president. Just her luck, McGill answered the bedside phone. He was decent about it, though, didn't crack wise, just put the president on. Patricia Darden Grant listened closely to Galia's story.

"Madam President," Galia said, "can you possibly remember if you said anything to Ms. Dean the last time you saw her?"

The president said, "I'll never forget it. I said, 'Good luck, Jenny.' She said the same to me and kissed my cheek."

"Where did this take place?"

"On Melrose Avenue just outside the entrance to Paramount Studios."

"Did anyone see you and Ms. Dean?"

"People were coming and going. Nobody said hello to us."

Galia heard McGill's voice but couldn't make out what he said.

The president told her. "Jim says to see if you can find out who the guard on the gate was that day. He was paid to keep an eye on things, and two pretty girls wouldn't go unnoticed."

McGill added something.

"All right," the president said. "What Jim told me, verbatim, was the guard would have noticed two *gorgeous* women."

Galia had to agree with McGill's description. She liked the idea of finding the guard on the gate, too. Sometimes it paid to keep a private eye at hand. Not that she'd say so to McGill.

"I'm sorry for disturbing your sleep, Madam President."

"I'd have been angry if you hadn't. Let's get these bastards, Galia."

"Yes, ma'am."

McGill had one last suggestion.

The president told Galia, "Jim said to see if you can find Jenny Dean's phone records for the time between when I last saw her and the day she died. If the records are no longer available, look for Jenny's family and see if they called her during that period."

Okay, Galia thought, now McGill was just showing off.

Federal Correctional Institution — Danbury, Connecticut

Every morning, Erna Godfrey prayed on her knees with her face pointed at the wall of her cell and her eyes closed. She was a curiosity to both the inmate population and the staff. A murderess, a former death row prisoner, an attempted suicide, a widow, a woman who'd had a personal conversation with the president of the United States and now a student pursuing a master's degree in theology from the seminary at Northwestern University, her résumé was unlike anyone else's within the prison walls.

She prayed every day: morning, noon and night. Her prayers for the most part were silent, an exception being the saying of grace at the table where she ate her meals. The correctional officers paid close attention to what she said and reported to the warden that Erna only expressed thanks for the food that sustained her that she might work her way toward the path of righteousness.

The prison administration could abide that.

What Erna prayed for within the silence of her thoughts, no one could say. But that morning she rose from her posture of morning prayer and asked the correctional officer if she might speak with the warden. For the average prisoner, that request was not routinely granted.

Erna, however, was brought to the warden's office without delay. She had secrets the government wanted to know. Instructions had been given to the warden that if this particular prisoner ever started to feel talkative nothing should be done to discourage her.

Nonetheless, when Erna asked the warden for a pen and a pad of paper, he said, "No, I'm sorry but I can't let you have a pen or a pencil."

For a second, Erna couldn't imagine why in the world she couldn't —

Hold a pointed implement in her hand? The answer was obvious. An inmate might get to feeling suicidal or homicidal. Wouldn't be good for anyone's career to aid in either of those pursuits.

"My secretary takes dictation," the warden said. "Would that work for you?"

Erna nodded. Telling another person would add to the air of confession.

There remained one point to be resolved.

"I really should sign my name to what I have to say," Erna said.

The problem of providing a signature without the use of a pointed object was solved by the warden's secretary. She was the mother of a three-year-old. She had a red crayon in her purse. She snapped it in half and peeled the paper away from the blunt end.

The warden looked at it, smoothed the edge with a thumbnail.

He said, "I'll let you sign your name with this. Is that okay with you?"

"That'd be fine. Red's just the color for what I have to say."

Erna spent the next hour giving up every shred of information she had on the radical anti-abortion underground movement, including the identity of two people, like her, who had killed in the name of being pro-life. When she was done, her statement was entered into a computer and printed out. Erna read it and signed with the red crayon.

The document was scanned and sent electronically to the office of Attorney General Michael Jaworsky. It arrived as he was talking with Deputy AG Linda Otani. The preliminary federal investigation into the death of Jennifer Dean had revealed that in the last days of her life not only had Ms. Dean failed to get the movie role, her father had died of a heart attack and her boyfriend had left her for another woman.

Besides that, the woman on the bed in the commercial was not Jennifer Dean. The photo was a still shot of another actress, Haley Edwards, from a movie titled *The Wages of Sin*. Ms. Edwards had been alive at the time the photo was taken and remained so.

Deputy AG Otani wanted to indict the largest cable company in the country for facilitating a fraud: implying that Patricia Darden Grant was responsible for the death of Jennifer Dean. Otani also wanted to launch an investigation to find out just who was hiding behind the name Americans for Truth and indict them for fraud, too. And now Erna Godfrey had decided to come clean about the antiabortion underground.

All that in an election year.

Leaving Michael Jaworsky to think, Thank God I'm not president.

National Reconnaissance Office — Chantilly, Virginia

In return for McGill's suggestions that helped debunk the *Presidential Confidential* video, the president saw her way clear to provide a day-pass for McGill, Sweetie, Elspeth Kendry and Byron DeWitt to the nation's spy-in-the-sky agency, the National Reconnaissance Office. The NRO held the responsibility for monitoring the proliferation of weapons of mass destruction. It also kept tabs on the comings and goings of terrorist organizations.

Much of its work was done hand in glove with the Pentagon and various spy shops. But it also tracked the movements of drug traffickers and the doings of other criminal organizations. In less sinister but no less deadly circumstances, the NRO assessed the impact of natural disasters such as earthquakes, tsunamis, fires and floods.

Given this broad portfolio of responsibilities, it was less than surprising that the NRO did have a bird overhead taking photographs of the slice of Washington, D.C. that Sweetie and Putnam called home on the night in question. McGill and company were informed in no uncertain terms they should not ask why those photos had been taken. Just be grateful help was being provided.

The four of them sat around a small conference table in a room with bare walls and a two-way mirror. They'd had to surrender their cell phones. They would be allowed to view the photos in the room, but neither take them with when they left nor reproduce them. They were allowed to make notes with pens and paper provided by the NRO.

As if they couldn't guess, they'd been told they would be observed from behind the mirror.

To make sure they didn't try to slip a photo into their underwear.

McGill was okay with all the precautions. He knew they'd been given an extraordinary privilege. But he imposed one condition of his own.

"Look at us all you want, but no one listens in on our conversation."

An organization dedicated to snooping on others, the NRO didn't like its nosiness being curtailed in any way. They objected to McGill's condition.

He said, "Tough. Special Agent Kendry will sit with you to make sure you don't eavesdrop. You're not happy with that, I've got the president on speed dial."

He had to use it. The president gave her husband's NRO escorts a short earful of hell and they relented, but on her way out of the room, Elspeth cast her eyes to the ceiling. Her message was clear.

These were the people who spied from above. You think maybe they had cameras in the ceiling? DeWitt suggested they write any notes with their pads held in the vertical position.

Sweetie took things two steps further. No talking or writing, and McGill and DeWitt would sit on either side of her, hunching their shoulders around Sweetie like a mini football huddle. Once everyone was in place, Sweetie put the stack of photos to be examined in front of her.

"You think maybe I got a little too dramatic here?" McGill whispered.

DeWitt shook his head. "You're making a natural adaptation to the federal bureaucracy. Secrecy begets power, power is always hoarded."

"Spook fever," Sweetie said.

"No vaccine," DeWitt said.

They looked through twenty-two photos. The satellite caught

the guy she'd seen on the sidewalk outside her house. Sweetie tapped her finger on his image. McGill and DeWitt nodded. Another photo showed the same guy going out the house's back door. A sequence of shots showed him going down an alley. He got into a black sedan two blocks away. He sat in the front passenger seat. Someone else drove the car away. The angle on the car didn't allow for seeing whether anyone was in the back seat.

One pass through the photographs was all they needed.

Sweetie pushed the pile to the center of the table.

They put the unused pads and pens on top of the photos.

Got up and left the room.

On the way back to Washington, Leo told them there was no way anyone had bugged the Chevy while it was parked in the NRO lot. He'd been in it the whole time, awake and alert. No one doubted him, but they decided to wait until they were back at McGill's office to start making their plans.

However, that plan got interrupted.

A young guy in a blazer, khakis and boat shoes approached McGill on the sidewalk outside his office. He came to an abrupt halt when Elspeth pointed her Uzi at him. He put his hands in the air in the hope she'd understand he'd come in peace.

In his right hand he held a folded piece of paper with some sort of seal on it.

"Who are you and what do you want?" Elspeth asked.

"My name's Henry Davis. I work for the House Committee on Oversight." He waggled the paper in his hand. "This is for Mr. McGill. May I?"

He carefully extended it in McGill's direction.

A natural sense of curiosity led McGill to reach out. The piece of paper had barely touched his fingertips when Sweetie snatched the piece of paper away from him. Elspeth reacted by thrusting her weapon at Davis, very close to firing it now.

Davis backpedaled and said, "Mr. McGill, you've been served. That subpoena requires you to appear before the House Committee on Oversight and respond to such questions as may be asked of you. The date and time of your appearance are noted on the subpoena. Failure to appear will result in a charge of contempt of Congress being brought against you."

His spiel complete, Davis was the epitome of a smug bastard, smiling and victorious.

McGill told Elspeth, "Shoot him."

She flicked the Uzi's safety off. The click echoed like canon fire in Davis's ears. His face froze in horror. Elspeth *looked* as if she was about to follow orders.

But she turned to McGill and asked, "You sure?"

"Nah, I was just kidding."

They walked up the stairs to McGill's offices.

DeWitt said to him, "Remind me never to tick you off."

White House Press Room

The President looked out at the assembled press corps for ten seconds before saying a word. None of the reporters looking back at her fidgeted. Few of them did so much as blink. Patricia Darden Grant let very little get under her skin, but there was no question she was angry today.

That made it all the more unusual that there were four visitors in the room.

Three of them young.

Kenny and Caitie McGill sat along the side wall near the entrance to the room. Next to Caitie sat Cassidy Kimbrough. With Cassidy was her mother, Sheryl.

The president began, "I can't say Jennifer Dean was a friend of mine, but she might have become one, if she had not chosen to take her own life. When I knew her, she was young, beautiful and talented. Chances were good she would have had a life most people might have envied. But she got hit hard by three of the most daunting emotional traumas anyone can experience, and they came in quick succession.

"She suffered a professional setback when she failed to get a part in a movie that went to me. Her father died unexpectedly in his mid-forties. And the young man she'd dated for two years left her for someone else just when she needed him most. Family or a professional counselor might have pulled Jenny out of that awful tailspin, but she spent her last days alone. With no one to reassure her that things could get better, she took her own life."

The president's face turned hard. "Jennifer Dean's death was a tragedy. That it should be used as part of a political smear attempt all these years later is despicable. It renews the heartbreak all of Jenny's family members and friends felt when they lost her.

"An act of such cruelty should be punished, and Attorney General Jaworksy is going to see that it will. Trying to link me to the death of Jennifer Dean for political advantage constitutes a fraud upon the American public. Someone is seeking to gain a job for his or her preferred candidate that pays four hundred thousand dollars a year for at least four years and possibly eight years by deceiving the people who hold the power to make that decision.

"My administration will not tolerate such a fraud being perpetrated. The FBI is working right now to find the people behind the misnamed group Americans for Truth who paid for the fraudulent attack now popularly known as *Presidential Confidential.* When they are found, they will be arrested, indicted and tried.

"At this moment, Elton Galbreath, the chief executive officer of Ubiquity Cable Television, is being taken into custody for facilitation of fraud. He either knew or should have known his company has televised a fraudulent ad that sought to deny the American people their chance of having an honest presidential election."

The news that a corporate titan, a multi-billionaire, would be brought to trial for airing a political ad had every newsy in the room dying to leap out of his or her chair and shout a question, but all of them saw the president shake her head. The woman was still furious. Crossing her now could be professional suicide.

The president continued, "This loathsome attack commercial mentioned two other actors by name, one of whom was given a speaking role in it. Jeremy Danvers was said to be my costar in a film. He was a day player in a movie in which I was featured. I never met him.

"Day player is movie jargon for an actor who is hired for one day's work. It's an emotionally trying job done by people who passionately want to act for a living. Typically, they give their all to say no more than a single line of dialogue. They hope someone will see they are capable of so much more. For them, hope and disappointment are most often conjoined twins.

"I don't know whether the medication that caused Jeremy Danver's terrible auto accident was prescribed or taken illicitly. In either case, impaired driving is always unacceptable and often a tragic mistake. My condolences go out to the families of the young man and woman who lost their lives. I hope they and Jeremy Danvers can find some measure of peace, and that this vile attempt to smear me has not damaged them further.

"I never met Paige Nelson, never knew we competed for anything. But I understand all too well the tremendous pressure a young woman can feel to conform to impossible standards of beauty. There were times when I ate fewer than a thousand calories a day and thought that it was far too much. Fortunately for me, one day I looked at myself in a mirror and saw the structure of my rib cage all too clearly. I thought, 'Now, that is ugly. If that's what it takes to get a role, to hell with it.'"

The president shook her head, as the memory ran through her mind.

She said, "What Paige Nelson needs to do right now is to get some real help. Paige, if that's something you can't afford it, call me. I'll find someone to help you."

The president paused once more.

"The ad that slandered me did the same to the movie industry. It's true that Hollywood is not a place for the timid. Egos run amok and all too often they are supported by huge sums of money. Business deals can be cutthroat, friendships can be a matter of convenience.

"Despite all its warts, the film industry still manages to give us movies that entertain us. Some of these films approach the level of real art. In the face of great personal vexation, people both in front of the camera and behind it, strive to put aside their personal differences and get the best possible movie in the can. You can carp all you want about the movies that come out of Hollywood, but very few of us would want to live in a world without filmed entertainment.

"I will tell you frankly that some of my best friends are actors, and one of the people I love most in the world ..." The president gestured to Caitie, who knew a cue when she heard one got to her feet. "Caitie McGill will be acting in her first movie this year."

Caitie blew a kiss to her stepmother and got the only laugh of the press conference.

The president let her smile disappear before she brought her speech to a close.

"That was a moment of personal pride, but in a more serious vein let me say that no attack on me will ever cause me to abandon any of my friends, even if they make movies for a living."

The president exited the room with her guests.

Leaving Aggie Wu to handle all the questions shouted at the president's back.

The Chief of Staff's Office — the White House.

Galia Mindel clicked off the television in her office as the president left the press room.

Patricia Darden Grant had bared her soul.

Damn thing was as dazzling as the rest of her.

Fewer than a thousand calories a day? Just the idea made Galia's stomach growl. She wanted a Danish and she wanted it now. Only she was limiting herself to just under two thousand calories a day — and that was torture.

Galia's assessment of the speech was that the president had hit back hard. She'd bet any number of political trolls around the country had come to a screeching halt in the writing and filming of their attack ads. It put a real crimp in the old creative spirit to think that the FBI might come to pay a visit.

For Elton Galbreath, that had already happened. He was in custody. The plutocracy would be aquiver with terror that the revolution had finally come and they, too, might be hauled off to the calaboose. The upper reaches of the upper crust would also be enraged that one of their own had set this dangerous precedent. If one president could commit such an outrage, who was to say the next one wouldn't also? Just to show he was as much of a man as Patti Grant.

For the rest of the population, Galia thought Galbreath's arrest would play brilliantly. Nobody was above the law with President Grant in the Oval Office. Screw with her, she'd make you pay. Well, that was the way much of the country would feel.

For a large number of people, however, proof would never refute prejudice. They would believe every last lie in *Presidential Confidential* was gospel truth. They'd believe that until the day they died. In the meantime, they'd regurgitate the lies they'd swallowed whole.

Those people and their heirs were beyond reach.

Fuck 'em, Galia thought with a grim smile.

A more serious concern for Galia was the near certainty that she knew who was behind *Presidential Confidential:* Roger Michaelson. He'd been Patti Grant's political nemesis from the start. He'd lost his first race for a House seat to her. He'd thought he would be nominated to replace Mather Wyman as vice president. He'd lost every presidential primary election, save South Carolina, to her, having given up his Senate seat to pursue the presidency.

He was now done in electoral politics. So what could be sweeter than to take the president down with him. Accusing the president of murder would fit his mood perfectly. He'd probably thought he would get away with it, too.

No way in the world he'd have done it, or he'd at least have been more careful about *how* he did it, if he thought the FBI would be tracking him down. Galia had to plan for the way things would look when Roger Michaelson was caught. Not only would the president be advancing the radical notion that political lies were a criminal offense, she'd be bagging her biggest political enemy as only the second offender to be prosecuted.

That might look just a tad personal.

Galia would be the one who'd have to make it look completely justified.

She was about to get back to work when her phone rang. Either the president or —

McGill. Asking her, "Galia, what would the blowback be if I told the House Committee on Oversight to take the subpoena they sent me and cram it right up their heinies?"

The White House Mess

The president and her guests, Kenny, Caitie, Cassidy and Sheryl, had no trouble getting a good table. Service was excellent and Patti told her guests to order whatever they liked. If they weren't partial to anything on the menu, reasonable requests could be accommodated.

Caitie told Cassidy, "I know it seems like a kid thing, but the peanut butter and jelly sandwich is crazy good. The peanut butter is the best ever, and you can have your choice of three jellies or ask for all of them."

The president smiled. Caitie clearly had no concerns about counting her calories.

Kenny offered his opinion to their guests, "They do a great burger, too. It's not on the menu, but they're real nice about giving you what you want. I'm trying to eat a little smarter these days so I'm going with the grilled tuna salad."

Showing a flare for diplomacy, Cassidy said, "Yeah, the tuna sounds good, and maybe I could get half a deluxe PBJ to go?"

The president said she could. Sheryl ordered a Caesar salad.

Patti had the Oriental Mandarin Chicken Salad.

As they waited for their orders to arrive, Cassidy told Patti, "Madam President, I can't tell you how much your calls meant to all the other kids and me. We were all kind of in shock, and hearing from you, it was like all of a sudden the whole country was pulling for us."

"Thank you, Cassidy. We have many different political opinions in this country, but I'm sure you're right. Everyone was hoping and praying for your recovery."

A large number of Americans, Patti knew, would have thought she was exploiting the situation for political gain if they'd known she'd called the burn victims. But the president had kept that to herself. Just one more secret added to an endless list.

Caitie, in her usual fashion, bluntly asked Cassidy, "What were those kids doing on a college campus? They were only in high school, right? And why was there such a big fire?"

The memory was still not easy for Cassidy to deal with, but she said, "They told me they all hope to go to Indiana University. So they thought they'd drive through campus and shoot off fireworks to show off school spirit and then they'd write about it in their college application essays. The fireworks went off early, inside the car. That's what caused the crash and the fire."

Everyone at the table winced. Kenny gave Cassidy's hand a gentle squeeze.

She returned the gesture with a small smile.

Then Cassidy said, "Madam President, I listened carefully to what you said in the press room and I didn't hear one word of bull-puckey."

That got a laugh from Caitie and Kenny.

Sheryl Kimbrough turned bright red, but she found the nerve to explain her daughter's comment to the president. Patti laughed.

She said, "It's a good idea to be honest with the people who hired you. Sometimes you even have to put a little sting in your honesty. That's what happened today."

"It was mean, the lies that commercial told about you," Caitie said to Patti. "I'd like to sock someone."

Kenny told his sister, "We can't just go around whacking people, not with Dad teaching us Dark Alley."

"What's Dark Alley?" Cassidy asked.

Both McGill offspring turned to their stepmother, silently asking whether they should answer.

Patti took them off the hook. She told the Kimbroughs, "My husband, Kenny and Caitie's father, practices a little known form of self-defense. He's passing on his wisdom."

"Cool," Cassidy said.

The food arrived and the conversation turned to how delicious everything was. Lunch lasted just an hour, but Cassidy and Sheryl had acquired a memory to last a lifetime. Both of them shook Patti's hand and thanked her repeatedly.

"It's the least I can do," the president said. "Please say hello to your friends in Indiana for me."

Caitie bussed both Cassidy and Sheryl on the cheek.

Kenny shook their hands. He told Cassidy he knew something about kids going through tough times in a hospital. He didn't live that far from Bloomington. Maybe he could come and visit her and they could go see her friends together.

Cassidy said, "I'd like that."

A mess steward brought Cassidy's PBJ in a White House doggie bag. He said the chef just didn't know how to make half a sandwich. He hoped she wouldn't mind getting a whole one.

In the taxi, on the way back to their hotel, Cassidy told her mother in mock agony, "It kills me that I won't be able to vote for the president."

Sheryl only smiled.

She thought she might be the only person in the country to cast her vote as a citizen for Patricia Darden Grant and her vote as an elector for Mather Wyman.

McGill Investigations, Inc.

"Galia says I'll have to appear before the committee," McGill told Sweetie and DeWitt.

Elspeth and Leo were standing guard in the outer office and in the Chevy respectively.

Deke Ky was handing off his duties protecting Abbie McGill to Special Agent August Latz. Abbie, ever industrious, was taking two classes during the summer session. Not leaving her the time to have lunch with her sibs and Patti at the White House.

"That was pretty much to be expected," DeWitt said. "If a president is going to stiff-arm Congress, it has to be for a *big* reason."

"Not just keeping hubby happy," McGill said. "Well, it was worth asking."

"You could be the next one to get a subpoena," DeWitt told Sweetie.

"The Committee on Oversight breaks into my house, I'll start worrying," Sweetie told him.

McGill grinned and said, "Margaret has a point. First things first. We have to assume Todd and his friends are going to make a move to grab her soon."

"It might be simpler than that," DeWitt said.

"You're saying they might just shoot me?" Sweetie asked.

DeWitt said, "That's pretty much the way they've worked in the past, according to their files. They take out someone important whose death diverts a lot of official resources. Then they hit their main target."

"Me," McGill said. "They might even think I'd be so angry I could get clumsy."

DeWitt asked, "Is that a fair assessment?"

McGill said, "I'm pretty good at deferring grief and rage. That's how I got Erna Godfrey."

"Point taken," DeWitt said. "Another target of distraction might be … me."

Sweetie nodded. "You're a bigshot. You're leading the official investigation. Knock you off, it throws a monkey wrench into the effort to find them."

McGill said, "They might even go after Elspeth when she's off duty. Necessitate a change in my Secret Service protection. Even bringing Deke back, there'd be a little hiccup."

"What about Leo?" Sweetie asked. "Any driver who replaces him would be second best. Might give them an opportunity to attack from another car."

DeWitt liked that idea. "Yeah, could be. That car in the NRO photos, the one that picked up Anderson, it looked like a BMW to me. Some of them are damn fast beasts. Not as fast as your Chevy maybe, but if you have a new driver and the bad guys have recruited a hotshot …"

Everybody thought about the various possibilities.

DeWitt said, "We don't know how much Todd's guys know about us, but we have to consider each of us as vulnerable."

McGill nodded. "Yeah, but any of the scenarios we just raised assumes we're just going to sit tight and wait for Todd's side to make the first move."

"The FBI is doing all we can to find them," DeWitt said.

McGill said, "No criticism was implied, Mr. Deputy Director. I was only thinking of making the bad guys leap before they look."

Sweetie knew intuitively where McGill was going and smiled. "You want to reach way back into our bag of tricks, don't you?"

"If you don't mind, Margaret."

"I'm not as young as I used to be," Sweetie said.

"You've still got it, no question."

"Someone want to let me in on the gag?" DeWitt asked.

McGill told him, "Margaret is stylish when she wants to be, but ordinarily she's not —"

"Obvious about things," Sweetie said. "Never saw any reason to be a tease."

"Unless there are some lawbreaking creeps to sucker," McGill said. "Get them thinking with something besides their heads."

Strictly for law enforcement purposes, DeWitt looked at

Sweetie. Up and down. In a frank manner. He said, "I agree. She's still got it."

Sweetie laughed and said, "Men."

The foibles of the male gender taken into account, they worked out a plan.

Then McGill asked Sweetie and DeWitt for some privacy. He needed to talk to his lawyer about accompanying him on his date with the Committee on Oversight. He called Putnam Shady in Omaha and told him about getting the subpoena.

Putnam said, "Probably a good thing you didn't shoot the messenger."

The White House Residence

"You wanted to say fuck it on television?" McGill asked Patti.

"Has more punch than saying to hell with it, and it was what I really thought. When I saw how emaciated I'd let myself get."

"But you exercised masterful restraint."

"I save all my best material for you." McGill was about to reply when Patti held up a hand. "Just a moment, Jim."

She picked up the remote control for the television. After she had joined McGill in the Hideaway an hour earlier and told him of her moment of near four-letter honesty and, by the way, having Elton Galbreath arrested on a charge of facilitating fraud, she had turned on the television, curious to find out what the media were saying about her.

Two minutes was all she could take before hitting the mute button.

Up and down the dial, media creatures of all political stripes were railing against the arrest of one of their own, a CEO who couldn't reasonably be expected to know the content of every commercial his network televised. Aggie Wu, speaking for the administration, rebutted that criticism with an elegant socioeconomic equation. "The guy who gets the biggest paycheck bears the greatest responsibility."

McGill loved that idea.

It was playing well in flash polls, too.

"Galia came up with it," Patti said.

"Knew I saved her for a reason," McGill said.

The president swatted him, affectionately.

Disregarding public approval, the media continued to rant that the president was trying to cow the free press.

McGill said, "Not to mention killing the cash cow of TV time sales to political campaigns."

"The media would call your point of view cynical."

McGill sneered at the media's whining hypocrisy.

But when Ethan Judd appeared on screen, the president wanted to hear what he had to say.

The camera was close on Ethan Judd as he said, "Patricia Darden Grant is the most courageous president of my lifetime. She left a political party she believes has lost its way and possibly its sanity. She joined the opposition party, giving it the graft of a spine it so desperately needed.

"While we're on the subject of medical donations, let's not forget that she saved a young man's life by putting her own at risk. When was the last time we had a sitting president who did that? I'll leave it to our presidential scholars to make that call, but my guess is President Grant was the first to do that, too.

"She's been a groundbreaker in so many ways. She could have played it safe and chosen a man to replace Mather Wyman, aiming for gender balance, geographical balance and perhaps even someone who parts his hair on the opposite side of his head. She didn't do any of that. She made history again by choosing Governor Jean Morrissey, another woman, to join her at the pinnacle of the executive branch.

"Not content to leave any trail unblazed for long, the president decided that a campaign for public office does not confer upon a candidate a license to lie about his or her opponent. On the contrary, Patricia Darden Grant maintains that lying to obtain a public office constitutes a fraud because the winning liar is rewarded with the salary and other valuable benefits that come with holding the office in question.

"That legal theory will certainly be tested by the Supreme Court, sooner rather than later, but not before the president's two nominees to the high court are confirmed. Here again, Patricia Darden Grant moved in a bold way. She nominated a known liberal to be chief justice of the United States. In doing so, she'll change the direction of the way the Constitution is interpreted for many years to come, countering the steady rightward march we've seen since the Nixon administration.

"I applaud the president for both her daring and her bravery. I also want to say this will be my last day at WorldWide News. In my short time here, I've done everything I could to build a news organization whose purpose it is to bring the truth to the American people about their government, their country and themselves.

"When I went to work for Sir Edbert Bickford, I was skeptical that things would work out for either of us. To be blunt, I didn't trust the man. I thought he was too steeped in sensationalism and slanted news to ever change his ways. So my contract allows me to leave at a moment's notice. All the people I've hired at WWN have the same escape clause."

The camera pulled back to reveal dozens of people surrounding Judd.

"We've learned that Sir Edbert has planned to start another news channel. This one would be called WorldWide News in Review. It's purpose would be to take the reporting we do here and twist it to suit their own partisan agendas. Well, we're not having it. All the people you see here and many others working for WWN around the world have all resigned.

"The next few moments will be the last any of us toil for this network. So we'd like to take the opportunity to tell anyone out there with a lot of money and even more reverence for honest reporting that there's a news organization here that's ready to hit the ground running.

"My one regret about my time at WorldWide News was that I

was unable to persuade the president to do an interview with me. She didn't trust the idea of going on WWN and it turns out she was right. But, Madam President, we'll find ourselves a new soapbox and my offer stands.

"Thank you all and goodbye for now."

The image of Judd and his staff faded out.

A ten-year-old documentary on the life of Sir Edbert Bickford started to air.

McGill turned to Patti and said, "I like that guy."

Patti clicked off the television. "I should have trusted him."

"Judd, yes. Sir Edbert, never."

"There's always someone to slam the president."

"True. In some cases, it's even a good thing."

"*Et tu?*" Patti asked.

"I did say in some cases. And Judd said he'd be back."

"Let's hope it's before the election," the president said.

Aboard the Poseidon — Capital Yacht Club

Hugh Collier was summoned by his uncle, Sir Edbert Bickford, to come to his yacht with his passport and a wardrobe for two weeks at sea. Hugh came but he brought neither his passport nor more clothing than the weather and the dictates of fashion demanded. He had no intention of going cruising with a madman.

No bookie in the English-speaking world would take the bet that the evening news hadn't set the old boy free from the moorings of sanity. Elton Galbreath, a peer in wealth and power, was already in chains, and Sir Edbert had suffered a mutiny.

The man might think he was Captain Bligh by now.

Hugh had watched Ethan Judd's farewell to WWN. Judd had told him he would be leaving soon — a decision that was made immediately after Hugh had told the eminent newsman of Uncle's plan to launch WorldWide News in Review.

Hugh wasn't surprised by Judd's public love letter to the president. The woman was almost enough to make a gay man concede that being straight had its advantages. What did take Hugh aback was the mass resignation of the news staff.

He'd never have thought Judd or anyone else could inspire so many well-paid professionals to chuck their jobs. The more he thought about it, the more certain he was Judd had already found his next patron. Hugh had set his snoops to find out who that person was.

He made it all the way to the yacht club, though, before he thought of Ellie Booker.

That cunning little minx would know what was happening. She might even —

Hugh stopped ten feet short of the gated jetty to the *Poseidon*. There was no crew member standing watch. That was akin to Uncle leaving the front door of his London townhouse open to any street beggar who might pass by. Something was surely amiss.

Hugh peered at the gap between the dock and the yacht. Lights from the vessel illuminated dark water. No body floated there. That didn't mean some poor bastard hadn't been killed and weighted down before his body was dumped.

Unlike so many of the natives, Hugh didn't carry a gun in America. At home in Oz, he never felt the need. Most cobbers Down Under still felt they could settle their differences with their fists or, at worst, a blade. In the States, firepower was king.

That thought gave no small measure of concern to Hugh.

Unarmed but unwilling to retreat, he climbed the stairs at the stern of the craft. He tried to spot one of the yacht's officers or crew. He saw no one. Two-thirds of the way up to the owner's deck he stopped and looked about. No one was on the main deck below him. No floating bodies were visible from this elevated vantage point. Above him, one small pool of golden light glowed in the grand salon.

Hugh ascended the remaining stairs and stepped into the salon. There was not a soul to be seen. But another light shone softly on the spiral staircase that led up to the sun deck where Sir Edbert had his master suite. The lord of WorldWide News enjoyed starting his days at sea by pressing the control that opened his bedroom curtains and looking out at his female traveling companions as they reclined on lounge chairs and filled in their tan lines.

Sir Edbert was a dirty old man, to be sure, but when you had his kind of money nobody ever complained. Hugh wondered if he might find Uncle dead in his big round bed, having taken some poor unsuspecting bird with him. That would explain the crew having abandoned ship.

He was mildly disappointed to find out he was wrong.

Uncle was there, all right, but he was sitting out on the balcony that adjoined his bedroom. The glowing end of his cigar protruded from his face. Hugh stepped onto the balcony and took the padded chair opposite Sir Edbert. Uncle put his cigar down, but didn't offer Hugh a drink.

"You're late," he said.

"You fire someone, you can't expect punctuality," Hugh told him.

Sir Edbert grunted. "You left your luggage below?"

"I didn't bring any. Didn't see —"

Poseidon began to move. Dead slow ahead. The crew had come out of hiding.

"You brought your passport?"

"No."

"You've no identification at all?"

"A birthmark on my arse," Hugh said.

Uncle was not amused. He took a gun out from under a newspaper that rested on his lap. One of the newspapers he owned, of course. He pointed the gun at his nephew.

Hugh smiled. "Now, I understand about the passport. My photograph's in it. You want to make sure you shoot the right bloke."

"Shoot you, I shall. But we'll wait until we leave U.S. waters."

"Very wise. The water is so much deeper and colder twelve miles out. I don't suppose you'd consider giving me the chance to swim ashore from that distance."

Sir Edbert shook his head.

Hugh didn't beg for his life.

He made himself comfortable, extending his legs, resting his hands on his middle.

"Let me see if I have this right then. I didn't see anyone as I came aboard … and no one saw me. My luggage and passport are supposed to go into a stateroom. The crew is not to disturb me. I'm upset, no, distraught, about all the corruption I carried out, using your name to bend everyone to my will."

Sir Edbert looked as if he was trying to kill Hugh by the sheer force of his ire.

"I've anticipated this you know," Hugh said. "Not quite from the very beginning, but once you drove poor Colin Nedby to suicide just because he had the nerve to shag your third ex-wife. The man helped you make millions and … what was his sin? Getting above himself? Finding pleasure with a woman who'd once given you pleasure?"

Sir Edbert's face darkened. "We were divorced but I wasn't done with Portia yet."

"Ah, well. You might have put a notice in one of your news-papers, Uncle."

The nobleman extended his gun at Hugh. It was can't-miss distance.

"You won't shoot me now, Uncle. That would spoil everything. There would be blood, flesh and bone everywhere. The sound of the gun being fired would attract attention. Now, where were we? Oh, yes. Your plan. Once we're out on blue water, I become despondent and do myself in, going over the side in the bargain. You hit the man-overboard alarm. Like the one so close to your free hand.

"My body is never recovered, of course, because you smoke a cigar, enjoy a drink, do a crossword puzzle for all I know, before you sound the alarm. Poor me, my remains are many miles astern sinking into the deep, being consumed by sharks if you're lucky.

"Then, my heavens, any number of incriminating documents are found in my luggage. My passport is there, too, because it would be suspicious if it were not. Have I overlooked anything?"

"Only my great satisfaction that you will be the one to pay for my sins," Sir Edbert said.

Hugh drew his feet closer to the chair.

Sir Edbert rightly saw this as a possible threat.

It was much easier to spring with your legs tucked under you.

"I will shoot you, you know. I'll take my chances," he said.

"Of course, you will. I just wanted to lean forward to share a secret."

"I can hear you from where you are."

"Very well. Here's the thing, Uncle. Sorry to spoil your plans for me, but I left documents incriminating you with Ellie Booker. You might think of disposing of her, too, but the problem is you won't know where to find her. Not in time to stop her from putting your neck on the block."

"Why would she —"

Sir Edbert found the answer without assistance.

"That's right, Uncle, money. I paid her. Then there's the fact that she thinks you're a miserable old sod. Women are such good judges of character."

Sir Edbert looked as if he might sink into a pout, except that Hugh got to his feet.

He didn't try to attack his uncle. He leaned on the balcony railing and watched *Poseidon* turn toward the sea. The vessel increased its speed but only marginally. She really was a beautiful craft, Ellie's disparagement of her notwithstanding. Looking out across the river, Hugh saw the East Potomac Tennis Center on the far shore fall slowly astern.

Hugh wasn't certain how deep the river was at this point, but he did know the *Poseidon's* draft fully loaded was nearly thirteen feet. Even another ten feet of depth beyond that would serve his purpose. He'd have to move soon, though. Couldn't wait for the yacht to pick up much more speed. Wouldn't do to get sucked into the propellers.

The bloody minded old fool had thought he'd set a trap for Hugh, when all he'd done was —

"Look there, Uncle, I was wrong." Hugh pointed a hand. "Ellie Booker is right there under that street lamp."

Sir Edbert Bickford turned his head and that was the last mistake he ever made. Hugh grabbed the front of his shirt and his belt. Threw him off the balcony like a sack of dirty laundry. Hugh matched the splash Sir Edbert made with a landmark on the near shore of the river. Then he hit the man-overboard alarm and dived into the river.

Sir Edbert popped to the surface a moment before Hugh did, but being eighty years old and having experienced the terror of being flung into the sky and falling twenty feet into a cold dark river, he didn't stay above water for long. Just long enough for Hugh to grab him.

Grab him and take him under.

Like many an Aussie, Hugh was an excellent open water swimmer. He could hold his breath under water for two minutes. In the Potomac he didn't even have to worry about a great white shark stopping by for a nibble. All he had to do was wait a very few seconds for Uncle to suck in half his body weight in river water. Count to ten just to make sure. And surface, his heroic rescue attempt a tragic failure.

Emergency lights now flashed aboard the *Poseidon*.

Sirens began to clamor along both shorelines.

Help would arrive momentarily. Hugh cradled Uncle's head above water.

First impressions were so important.

Not having had the need to wrestle with so weak a specimen as Uncle, Hugh was sure he'd left no bruises on the body. There was no one who could say what had occurred under the river's surface. No way to say he'd done anything except try to save the life of Sir Edbert Bickford.

He wasn't sure what had happened to Uncle's gun.

No matter. His fingerprints weren't on it.

He looked at Uncle's face. Silly old sod.

Hugh had warned him he wouldn't be made a scapegoat.

7

May, 2012
Committee on Oversight Hearing Room — U.S. Capitol

The formal name of the body before which McGill was called upon to testify was the United States House Committee on Oversight and Government Reform. Its chairman, Representative Warren Rockland (Republican, 49th District of California), had a power unique in the House. He could issue a subpoena without a committee vote. In recent decades, the committee's chairmen had refrained from using that authority.

When Rockland took over, he reveled in its use.

He enjoyed banging his gavel, too.

Editorial cartoonists often drew him wearing a crown.

McGill's subpoena instructed him to be present at nine a.m. He and Putnam Shady arrived fifteen minutes early. McGill wore a navy blue suit, white shirt and marigold tie. Putnam went with a gray suit, blue shirt and red tie.

"So it'll be easier to tell us apart," Putnam said.

Henry Davis, the young careerist who'd served McGill his summons, stood behind the lower of the two tiers where the chairman and the committee members would ensconce themselves. Rockland's seat was front row center. His chair was slightly more thronelike than the others. In a moment of adolescent fantasy, McGill wished he could put a Whoopee cushion on it.

Davis directed other staffers in the placement of documents, coasters, glasses and pitchers of what McGill hoped was water. The young political climber avoided meeting McGill's eyes.

"He's probably still sore I told Elspeth to shoot him," McGill said to Putnam.

"A subject that might arise this morning," Putnam replied.

Good lawyer that he was, Putnam had checked out Davis down to his childhood vaccinations. He'd had them all. Had no criminal record. Graduated from Emerson College with honors. But in a college newspaper column Davis had been given a title: Most Likely to Piss People Off.

Anybody wanted to bring up McGill's little joke, Putnam was ready with the reply.

McGill and Putnam had done four hours of prep work. Both of them felt ready to deal with hostile questioning. Of course, it helped that the president had promised pardons to both of them if Rockland started throwing contempt charges around.

Neither of them wanted things to come to that, though.

McGill's testimony was already a piece of political theater.

The committee room was filled with newsies and cameras. Nobody was bothering McGill or Putnam at the moment. They'd wait until the end of the hearing and then pounce. Asking questions bearing on politics rather than substance.

In the lull before the storm, Putnam whispered to McGill, "Margaret was trying on a number of daring fashions when I got home, and by daring I mean things that made me think to call a cardiologist."

McGill smiled. "Yeah. She's something, isn't she?"

"She told me her fashion choices were work related."

"They are." McGill paused, then asked, "Has she ever told you about the undercover work we did in Chicago?"

Putnam gave McGill a long look. "No."

"There was nothing inappropriate between us, ever. But she left quite a few bad guys with their heads spinning. Within the bounds of department policy and her moral precepts, of course."

Putnam considered that. "The good-girl-bad-girl dynamic must have been mind bending."

"Pretty much."

"I wouldn't mind seeing more of it," Putnam said, "but not at the risk of any harm coming to Margaret."

McGill told him. "I don't love Sweetie the same way you do, but I have loved her longer. I'm happy the two of you are happy. We're doing everything we can to keep everyone safe."

Putnam nodded. "I'd probably be a nervous wreck if I'd known both of you sooner."

McGill was tempted to tell Putnam to talk to Carolyn about that, but he didn't want to make any comparison that might call his lawyer's masculinity into question. He looked at his watch and said, "We're already running five minutes late."

"The chairman is letting us know whose time is more important." Changing the subject, Putnam asked, "Did you see Ethan Judd's last moments on WWN?"

McGill beamed. "I did. I thought he was great. I hope he lands a new job soon."

"He has," Putnam said.

McGill understood the implication. "You had something to do with it?"

"I tried to make the best use of my time in Omaha. I got to know Darren Drucker quite well. His first job was delivering newspapers for the *Washington Post*. A humble beginning for the third richest man in the world. Before I'd even heard about Ethan Judd's dissatisfaction with Sir Edbert, I suggested to Darren he might want to return to the media business on a larger scale."

"So you didn't see Judd staying at WWN long?" McGill said.

"No, and Darren liked the job Judd was doing. I put a call into Judd to let him know Darren was interested. Things couldn't have worked out better. Darren hired a whole news organization."

McGill nodded. "The president hoped Judd would get back to work before the election. Thanks for the help."

"I do what ... well, I do what I think Margaret would like to see from me."

"She'll like this." McGill looked at his watch again. The inquisition was now running fifteen minutes late. He got to his feet and told Putnam, "Anyone wants to know where I am, tell them I have a small bladder."

"Rockland won't be happy if you're not here."

"Good," McGill said.

Men's Room — U.S. Capitol

McGill had just finished drying his hands when his cell phone rang. He'd deliberately left it on, hoping it might interrupt questions the committee would be directing at him. He intended to answer the call and ask the chairman to give him just a minute.

Putnam had been unable to find any precedent of a presidential spouse being called to testify before Congress for anything other than ceremonial reasons. McGill felt he owed it to those who would come after him to make Congress think long and hard before they dragged any future henchman or First Lady into its midst.

Byron DeWitt was calling. "We found the Buick Enclave that Todd and his friends bought in Virginia."

"Where was it?" McGill asked. He was sure DeWitt was only beginning his narrative. There had to be a greater reason for him to call than to report the recovery of a stolen vehicle.

"Mexico. Todd and his friends were down in Baja doing wing-suit flying."

Okay. That was a new one on McGill.

"Which is what exactly?" he asked.

DeWitt told him.

"You jump out of plane in a flying squirrel suit?" McGill asked.

"Great fun," DeWitt said.

The deputy director was from Southern California, a good thing as it turned out.

"The flying instructor south of the border goes by the name of Jaime Martinez. We're looking to interview him. In the meantime, we checked a number of jump clubs on our side of the border. We found a woman by the name of Angeline Woods who gives sky-diving lessons near Palm Springs. She picked Todd, Crosby and Anderson out of separate six-packs. Said Todd was a beginner but learned fast, was careful and polite. She said Crosby and Anderson had more experience than she did but were complete assholes."

DeWitt told McGill about the two CIA loons playing a game of chicken by seeing who'd wait longer to pull his ripcord.

"That's seriously crazy," McGill said.

"Well, all these guys broke out of the Funny Farm."

"Yeah, a point to remember."

"And now we know they might plan to parachute in — somewhere."

McGill was impressed by the work the FBI had done.

He complimented DeWitt.

"We have a lot of people working on this case, and we're spending money by the ton."

"You've got the budget for that?" McGill asked.

The deputy director of the FBI laughed. "It's all going on the CIA's tab."

Committee on Oversight Hearing Room — U.S. Capitol

A Capitol Hill cop reached for McGill's arm as he entered the room. The guy, who had a good ten years on McGill, told him sotto voce, "The chairman's ordered you to be placed in custody on sight."

McGill kept his voice down, too. "You try it and I'll have to hurt you."

He wasn't going to allow himself to be arrested in front of all the cameras in the room.

Talk about setting a bad precedent.

The Capitol Hill cop understood immediately that the threat was not an idle one.

He pulled his hand back.

McGill told him, "I'll buy you a beer the first chance I get."

Chairman Rockland gave the intimidated cop a dirty look. Then he curled his lip at McGill. "So glad you could finally join us, Mr. McGill."

"I was here on time. When you weren't here by nine-fifteen, I took the opportunity to visit the men's room."

Putnam didn't miss a syllable, but he kept his face impassive.

He'd intervene only when necessary.

McGill was sworn in, his testimony now being under oath, and he sat down.

"Do you have any further reason to delay the work of this committee?" Rockland asked him.

McGill said, "I'm not sure why the committee wants to see me at all."

There were forty members of the committee, Putnam had told him, twenty-three Republicans, seventeen Democrats. Looked like just about the whole gang had come to see him, too. Flattering in a perverse way, he supposed.

He hoped no one would ask for an autograph.

Rockland said, "We are the chief investigative committee of the Congress."

"I understand that, Representative Rockland. What escapes me is why you're interested in me. Perhaps I can save all of us some time and tell you right now I won't have anything to say that involves any communication between my wife and me. I also won't have anything to say about any communication between my lawyer, Mr. Shady, and me. Both types of communication are privileged, as I'm sure you know."

Rockland curled his right hand into a fist and used his thumb to tap the table.

McGill counted five taps before the chairman spoke.

"I don't suppose you'd care to waive either form of privilege, Mr. McGill."

"I would not, sir."

"You think you're really smart, don't you?" Rockland asked.

"You think you've found a way around Federal Election Commission rules and the Supreme Court's ruling that political campaigns and political action committees not coordinate their efforts."

McGill ignored the allegation and responded to Rockland's characterization of him, "As far as my intelligence is concerned, I did passably well in school and have received a number of professional commendations."

"Your manner is impertinent, sir."

"And yours is imperious."

Rockland leaned forward, his face red. "I represent the power of the federal government, Mr. McGill."

"But not well in my opinion. You were elected the last three times by a *plurality* in one of four hundred and thirty-five Congressional districts. In electoral terms, you arrived at your present position by receiving the votes of about one one-thousandth of the American *voting* public. I would think that a man in your position would approach his job with a great deal of humility. But I'm not getting that feeling from you, Representative Rockland."

The man's thumb was tapping the table furiously now.

"My title is Chairman Rockland," he finally said.

"Yes, *sir*," McGill replied, putting more than a little smartass into his tone.

Rockland was momentarily speechless but his number two, Representative Marvin Nokes, Republican of the 1st District of Kansas, said, "You're more than impertinent, Mr. McGill. You're insolent. Do you think we can't slap you with a contempt of Congress citation?"

"No, Representative Nokes, I don't think that at all. But I do have a question."

The gentleman from Kansas didn't care to hear what it might be.

But Representative Diana Kaline, Democrat of the 5th District of Michigan, asked, "What's your question, Mr. McGill?"

By parliamentary rules, both Nokes and Kaline should have

been recognized by the chairman before speaking, but Warren Rockland looked like he was busy fighting off an aneurysm.

McGill replied, "Why is it, Representative Kaline, that any American who comes before Congress may be cited for contempt of this body but members of Congress can't be cited for contempt of the American people? Isn't that an inequity that needs to be addressed, quickly?"

Putnam kept a straight face. McGill had thrown out their script from the beginning, had been ad-libbing the whole time. But Putnam was enjoying the show, and wanted to see how it ended.

Representative Kaline played along for one thing.

"I'm not sure what you mean, Mr. McGill. What would the grounds be to cite Congress for contempt of the American people?"

Not wanting to hear the answer to that question, now or ever, Chairman Rockland grabbed his gavel and pounded the table with a fury the late Keith Moon would have envied.

When the din subsided, a purple-faced Rockland said, "The gentlelady from Michigan is out of order. That question will not be answered. The witness is dismissed. Mr. McGill, you may leave."

McGill said, "Thank you, Mr. Chairman."

Comfort House — Arlington, Virginia

Damon Todd took the advice of Crosby and Anderson and cut off contact with any of his special friends. They would neither be taking shelter with them nor tapping any of their bank accounts. The three of them would have to get by on the quarter-million dollars they had on hand and would stay in public accommodations that valued and provided privacy for their clientele.

Comfort House catered to gay men who worked in both government and the private sector who were not yet ready to be forthcoming about their true natures. Many of the guests recognized each other. None of them said a word. All of them felt secure that none of the militant organizations that took pride in opening closet doors would dare expose them.

"Why is that?" Todd asked after hearing the first part of the story.

Crosby said, "Guy who owns the place is not only gay he's a snake eater."

Todd looked puzzeld. He wondered if —

Anderson recognized the misconception. "Not a figurative snake eater, a real one. Special forces. When they have to live off the land, they'll eat anything. The hardcore guys don't even bother cooking their serpents. Just skin'em and chomp'em down raw."

"Snake does *not* taste like chicken," Crosby said.

Todd knew better by now than to ask if Crosby's knowledge came from personal dining experience. Instead, he said, "The innkeeper has let it be known he's not a man to cross?"

Crosby and Anderson just smiled. They were sharing a room. Todd had one to himself, with a connecting door. At the moment, they were sitting in Todd's room. A complimentary copy of the *Washington Post* lay open to the Style section. A photo of Chana Lochlan and Margaret Sweeney graced the front page.

Each woman wore a form fitting dress with a slit up the side that ran from mid-thigh to the tops of their three-inch heels. Thus shod, both stood taller than six feet. Each of them looked like she could drop and snap off fifty pushups in less than a minute.

Ms. Lochlan was described as an award-winning television journalist about to embark on a ten-city speaking tour. Ms. Sweeney was said to be a partner in the Washington, D.C. private detective agency McGill Investigations, Inc., owned by James J. McGill, husband of the president of the United States.

For those who were interested, a list of the cities and sites where Ms. Lochlan would be speaking was provided.

Todd, Crosby and Anderson had all read the article more than once.

Anderson was particularly interested in the photo of Sweetie.

"Wouldn't have minded bumping into her when I dropped by

her place."

Not having had that opportunity, Anderson contented himself hiding half a dozen of the latest generation of miniature webcams around the townhouse. He was kicking himself now that he hadn't put one in the bathroom.

Todd told him, "She looks different these days."

The two former spooks looked at him.

"You've seen her in the flesh?" Anderson asked.

"In running shorts and a singlet. She passed me on the jogging path that encircles the National Mall. At the time, I thought she looked like the woman in the Apple computers commercial, the one who shattered the image of Big Brother."

Crosby and Anderson looked at each other. They'd missed that cultural milestone. The omission was quickly remedied by an iPad search of YouTube. All three men watched closely. The viewing reconfirmed Todd in his opinion; the actress looked like Margaret Sweeney.

Anderson looked back to the newspaper photo.

"You're right," he told Todd. "I see the difference, too."

Todd had the feeling he was about to be the butt of another joke.

Still, he asked, "What do you see?"

"First, you're right about the resemblance. But the broad in the commercial is carrying a sledge hammer. Margaret Sweeney on the other hand is wearing a wedding ring."

Todd turned his attention to the photo. He hadn't noticed it before, but Anderson was right. Sweeney was wearing a ring. It was understated but it was there. Marriage could often have a profound influence on —

"Getting laid," Anderson said, as if reading Todd's mind. "She's getting more than she used to. Some of the energy she might have used to kill dictators is being put to other uses."

Todd thought about that. "You may be right, but it would be a mistake to think this woman has been … domesticated."

Crosby chuckled. "Yeah, I don't think she'd trot up to you and lick your hand if you whistled, but Olin has a point. If she loves her husband, her willingness to take risks won't be the same. She'll probably hold back just a little."

"And that's when I'll take her," Anderson said.

The desk chair on which Todd sat had wheels. He pushed back and studied the two former covert operatives. Crosby and Anderson stared back deadpan.

Crosby said, "You know what he's thinking, Olin?"

"Yeah. Doc can't quite understand how we slipped out from under his thumb."

Todd clenched his teeth. He put a hand on each of the chair's arms.

"No need to run," Anderson said.

"We'll let you leave if you want," Crosby told Todd, "but if you go, you'll never know how we did it. Found the psychological loophole."

Todd relaxed, folded his hands on his lap.

"You're an interesting guy, Doc, but your technique needs refinement. Things had worked out different, the Agency might have helped you with that."

Todd was less than comforted. Upon seeing the photo in the *Post,* he'd been far more interested in finding Chana Lochlan than confronting Margaret Sweeney. He'd been trying without success to think of a way to do that. Now, he was hearing his work criticized.

Apparently with justification.

A true scientist, he was always willing to learn.

"How did you defeat the hypnotic suggestion I left for each of you?"

Crosby said, "You made us fear what might happen to us, if we hurt or killed you."

"That was a pretty good strategy, but there's this Hawaiian guy Arn and I know. Talking about his approach to life took the chains right off us," Anderson said.

Crosby told Todd the story of Danny Kahanamoku and his

plan to end his days by making love to Pele the Hawaiian goddess of volcanoes. All they had to do to stop worrying about what hurting Todd might do to them was to embrace the goddess, too.

"You're going to throw yourselves into an active volcano?" Todd found that hard to believe.

Anderson saw his incredulity and laughed. "Sure, it might sting a bit, but not for long, and think about the upside. Better to become a part of nature at its most powerful than turn into worm food in a bone yard."

Crosby smiled. "Look at that, Doc, you've turned Olin into a poet."

Anderson feigned a moment of bashfulness. Then he and Crosby laughed.

"No, Doc," Anderson said. "We don't have to go all the way to Hawaii. You've given us something much better to jump into, a final mission. For Arn and me that's the only good way to retire. So I'm either going to grab or pop Margaret Sweeney or die trying. I'll be on hand when that other babe does her first speaking gig in Washington. While Sweeney's pretending to be her bodyguard."

"It has to be a trap," Todd said.

"Sure, but that's what makes it fun," Anderson told him.

Crosby added, "If Olin fucks up, his worries are over and it's my turn at bat."

Todd could discern no sign that both men were anything but sincere.

So there he was, Todd thought, helping people again. His cell phone rang. Only one person outside the Virginia hotel room had the number. Todd answered and listened. "You're welcome. No just tell me, I'll remember. Good. Yes, goodbye."

Crosby said, "Jaime Martinez?"

"Yes, the mercenaries that you recommended and I paid for have freed his wife. She and Jaime have made it out of Mexico. No one at the drug lord's hacienda was left alive."

"Makes you feel warm all over, doesn't it?" Anderson asked.

First Street — Washington, D.C.

McGill, cane in hand, gave in and turned to talk to the crowd of reporters that had pursued him out of the Capitol. After some cajoling, he even changed places with the mob so they could have the grand building as the backdrop to their pictures. McGill looked at Putnam and asked, "Do I have anything stuck in my teeth?"

Putnam said, "No, you're good."

Addressing the newsies, McGill asked, "What can I do for you ladies and gentleman?"

A babble of shouts almost knocked McGill over, but he was able to make out the predominant question. The media wanted to know the same thing Representative Kaline had asked: What would the grounds be to cite Congress for contempt of the American people?

"Failure to do their jobs," McGill said.

He was asked for specifics.

"Well, there's any number of measures that could be applied. Over the course of a calendar year, has the unemployment rate gone down? Has the number of jobs paying a living wage gone up? Has the number of people with substantial health insurance gone up? Has the number of people using emergency rooms for their medical needs gone down? Has the number of U.S. made manufactured goods gone up? Has the number of imported manufactured goods gone down? Has the number of students graduating from high school gone up? Has the number of dropouts gone down? Has the number of admissions to colleges, universities, technical and trade schools gone up? Has the amount of student debt gone down? Has the number of cops on patrol gone up? Has the number of crimes against persons and property gone down? Has the number of people working their way out of poverty gone up? Has the number of whining fat cats gone down?"

McGill paused to catch his breath and collect his thoughts.

Then he said, "Maybe I can get in touch with Billy Joel and we can make a song out of all that."

As the newsies were laughing, McGill continued, saying that

if Congress failed in two or more areas of critical concern they would, *de facto,* be cited for contempt of the American people. Every member of Congress would have his or her pay reduced by twenty-five percent, they would receive no pension contribution for that year or health care coverage for the following year and members of the leadership would be confined at minimum security prisons during Congressional recesses.

The reporters were left in awe by McGill's vision.

How, he was asked, would such a situation come to pass?

"Congress would have to pass a law," he said.

The newsies laughed harder than before, and McGill shot the gap, slicing through the middle of the mob and made it to his Chevy. He let Putnam slide into the back seat first. Then he turned to face the crowd again.

He told the reporters, "The voters could make Congress do that, if they wanted."

He slipped into the Chevy. The moment the door closed, Leo sped away.

They hadn't made it a block before Patti called.

"That was quite the speech you just made," she said.

McGill, no longer surprised that his wife was damn near omniscient, replied, "What? You think Galia's the only one who can come up with good ideas?"

McGill Investigations, Inc.

FBI Deputy Director Byron DeWitt was waiting for McGill when he got back to his office, after dropping Putnam off at his townhouse on Florida Avenue.

"Your landlord let me in," DeWitt told McGill, "but I stayed here in the outer office."

"Dikki's a trusting soul. Am I going to have to make you a partner in the firm?"

DeWitt smiled. "I probably will leave government work someday, but not quite yet. Where are your Secret Service people?"

"Out having their earbuds cleaned, I think. They should be here soon."

The truth was, the Capitol Hill cops didn't allow anyone but themselves to be armed on their turf, and Secret Service agents just hated to check their Uzis at the door. Also, Putnam had thought the situation would be less confrontational — ha! — if McGill didn't appear with bodyguards who might seek to ignore the chairman's right to have the witness bound and gagged. Drawn and quartered.

Besides all that, everyone had been expecting the proceedings on the Hill to last far longer than they had, as one pol after another phrased his or her questions in the form of an eye-glazing speech. McGill's provocative behavior had cut things short and given him the opportunity, as was his wont, to go his own way.

He hadn't felt particularly vulnerable. Leo was armed, and he retook possession of his Beretta once he was back inside the Chevy.

Putnam had seen that and asked, "You think I ought to carry one of those?"

McGill remembered that Putnam had been shot at as he sat in his own living room, but he hated the idea that everybody needed to be armed at all times. The old saw that, "God made man but Colonel Colt made them equal," had several real-world flaws in its reasoning.

If someone attempting to use a handgun against an unarmed opponent wasn't quick enough to get the weapon clear of wherever it was being carried, disengage the safety and aim it accurately, then the unarmed opponent, should he be stronger, quicker and even trained in doing gun disarms, might turn the weapon on its owner.

Bang, I'm dead? No, bang, you're dead.

McGill had told Putnam, "Talk to Sweetie."

First Carolyn and now Putnam feeling the need to be armed, McGill thought.

What the hell was the world coming to?

As he and DeWitt went into his office, the deputy director told him.

"An FBI team searched a house in Ottawa, Illinois that Damon Todd and friends had used. It will be continuously monitored until we have all three men in custody. But we found a page of notes Todd wrote. He'd torn the page into many small pieces, but we have people who are very good at jigsaw puzzles."

"And you found?" McGill said.

"Todd used his hypnotic techniques on both Arn Crosby and Olin Anderson. He noted substantial improvements in the mental focus and physical response time of both men."

"Great," McGill said. "Refurbished killers."

"Yeah. What Todd didn't say but might be reasonably inferred is he might have managed to make both men susceptible to taking risks they normally wouldn't."

"Making suicide runs," McGill said.

"Yeah."

McGill shook his head. "I'm liking that sonofabitch less all the time."

Ruth's Chris Steak House — Kansas City, Missouri

Senator Roger Michaelson and Bobby Beckley sat opposite each other in the restaurant's Plaza Room, a private area that could accommodate up to twenty diners. There would be only the two of them that night. Beckley was picking up the tab, for Michaelson's travel expenses as well as the meal. The two men had never met before but they knew of each other by reputation.

They'd agreed on Kansas City for their first meeting because neither of them had been there before, and Michaelson had dropped out of the primaries before a campaign poster ever went up in Missouri. They were unlikely to attract any notice from the media. Their private dining planner had treated them with great courtesy, but had shown no particular awareness of their political standing. Under present circumstances, Michaleson was not irritated to be called mister instead of senator. The two men talked about the new baseball season until dinner was served and they requested an hour to themselves.

They each took it as a good sign that the other had ordered

a steak — New York Strip for Michaelson, Cowboy Ribeye for Beckley — rather than seafood or a veggie platter. The fact that both men also liked their beef blood red was another bond. The capper was neither minded talking business as he ate.

Beckley kicked things off.

"I'd never ask you to come out and say so, but if you had anything to do with that TV spot that got Elton Galbreath locked up for twenty-four hours, you have my sincere admiration."

Michaelson grinned and asked. "You wouldn't, by any chance, be working for Galia Mindel, would you?"

Just the idea was enough to make Beckley choke on his steak.

The senator continued, "I have to admit, it's not likely, but I've been burned underestimating that woman before."

Beckley cleared the obstruction in his throat, took a sip of water and collected himself.

"You're gonna have to give me fair warning, you keep talking like that. I would have laughed if I wasn't so busy choking to death."

"So, you're saying you don't work for anyone in the president's camp?"

"I don't, and I'll give you proof in just a little while."

"Why not now?" Michaelson asked.

"Okay, if you don't mind putting your knife and fork down."

"I'll make the sacrifice."

Beckley put his own utensils down and picked up the attaché case he'd brought with him. He popped it open and handed a manila folder to Michaelson. The senator opened it and looked at a black-and-white photo that lay atop a stack of printouts. Beckley closed his case and put it back under the table.

"Do you recognize either of those men?" he asked.

"Frank Morrissey, the new vice president's brother and her chief advisor, is the guy getting a hickey. Can't tell who the other guy is."

"His name's Soren Gilby. He's a state cop up in Minnesota."

Michaelson chuckled. "You don't say?"

Beckley said, "I do. Your people didn't find out Frank

Morrissey is gay?"

The senator's jaw tightened. "The guy who would have dug up something like that for me is now running for my seat."

"Bob Merriman," Beckley said. "Looks like he's going to win, too." He held up a hand to placate the senator. "I'm not trying to rub it in. I mention that only as a way of saying I can understand how you might like to get even with Patti Grant. The gossip on my side of the aisle had you becoming her vice president. Must've pissed you off pretty good when she chose Jean Morrissey."

"You think?" Michaelson asked.

"I do. So here's the proof I'm on your side. I've got more pictures. Frank's not the only one in the Morrissey family who likes to have a good time with his own kind."

Michaelson sat back in his chair and stared at Beckley.

He looked for any sign the man was lying to him.

"Are you still working for Howard Hurlbert behind the scenes?" Michaelson asked.

Beckley shook his head. He had taken a million dollars of Howard Hurlbert's surplus campaign funds as severance pay and deposited the money in his numbered account in Liechtenstein. The old bastard could have gone to the U.S. attorney about that, but then Beckley knew where Hurlbert hid his rake-off.

"No," Beckley said, "my days with the senior senator from Mississippi are a thing of the past. Tom T. Wright is running his campaign now."

Michaelson said, "Wright is rich, but he's an amateur. There's no way Hurlbert has a chance of winning with him running the campaign."

"If it was a one-on-one race, I'd agree. But you put three people in the ring, any crazy ass thing is possible."

Michaelson said, "I've heard that Beau Brunelle and the other people from the Senate and the House who've moved to True South won't have anything to do with the Huey Long populism Wright wants to peddle."

"True enough. They have a lot better chance than Howard

Hurlbert of getting elected. After things shake out, they can make of True South whatever they want. But don't underestimate the idea of Southern populism. You put some old-time soda pop in a new bottle people just might buy it."

Michaelson shook his head and said, "Shit, wouldn't that be something? But don't tell me it's what you're counting on. If you're not backing Hurlbert, and would never back the president or Mather Wyman, what's in it for you? You want to sink Patti Grant just for the fun of it?"

"Pretty much, yeah. It'd be something to feel good about in my old age. In the meantime, if you and I throw enough rocks through the big boys' windows, somebody might ask us to stop by and fix things."

"You've become an anarchist," Michaelson said.

"I prefer opportunist. So what do you think?" Beckley asked. "Do you have any interest in seeing pictures of the woman who beat you out for vice president having a good time with her girl-friend?"

Michaelson said, "I do."

Beckley picked up his case and passed another folder to Michaelson.

"Those printouts I gave you?" Beckley said. "They're the places Frank Morrissey likes to get together with his state trooper. Wouldn't be surprised if his sister, the vice president, uses some of them, too."

"*Still?*" Michaelson asked.

"Old habits and all that," Beckley said.

Michaelson didn't comment further. He'd put someone on it and let the gumshoe think he was working for Bobby Beckley. So if any of these dirty tricks came back to bite someone it wouldn't be him.

That was how one very angry gay snake eater from Virginia decided Bobby Beckley needed to learn a mortal lesson.

8

June, 2012
Q Street — Washington, D.C.

Carrying twins was considered a high risk pregnancy. Advising an expectant mother of that classification was a way to counsel her to take special precautions. It was also a way to keep both expectant parents on edge until everyone came through the pregnancy healthy, happy and ready to put in a lifetime of work to make sure all involved stayed that way.

Kira had more doctor visits than she would have had for a single-fetus pregnancy. She had additional ultrasounds to make sure all was progressing well. Welborn took her blood pressure readings daily throughout the third trimester.

Kira took care that everything she ate was approved by both her doctor and her nutritionist. She consumed extra folic acid to reduce the chance of neural tube defects. She applauded Welborn when he started eating better, too.

"The way we'll handle sleepless nights, flyboy," she told him, "is anyone who doesn't nurse the girls, gets up, changes diapers and comforts the colicky."

Welborn said, "Deal. As long as you prepare all my meals, too."

"Fine. As long as you don't want to eat them off my chest."

Welborn laughed. "Now that you raise the idea ..."

"Forget it."

The closer the due date came, each day that passed without cause for alarm, the more excited Kira and Welborn became. They were about to become Mom and Dad. They would have the most beautiful, brilliant, altogether wonderful girls in the world. They decided on the names. Aria would be the first born; Callista would be little sister.

By presidential order, Captain Yates was placed on detached duty for the last three month's of Kira's pregnancy and the first three months of his children's lives. Any work that came his way would be limited to what he could do from home using a secure computer. Welborn set up shop in the bedroom the twins would use.

His workload was light but he still had trouble focusing.

He kept imagining all the things he'd want to teach his daughters.

Kira worked for Mather Wyman's campaign at a desk that had been placed in the master bedroom. She also wrote longhand on legal pads while lying propped up in bed. She spoke at least once a day with Mattie to tell him, yes, she was fine and still up to helping him.

Welborn and Kira avoided any stress being placed on the girls or their marriage by not discussing the fact that they supported rival candidates for the presidency. That plan worked well until the time came for Kira to go to the hospital.

With the permission of James J. McGill, Leo Levy was on call to them.

"I'll ride with Elspeth, if there's a conflict," McGill told Welborn.

So everything was in place the night Kira told Welborn, "It's time. Call Leo."

The former NASCAR driver arrived before any jitters could set in.

He announced himself with a brief chirp from the siren McGill's Chevy featured.

Welborn escorted Kira down the front steps of their townhouse to the car and got her situated comfortably in the back seat. He was about to join her when Kira grabbed his arm and told him, "My bag, it's on my desk. It has all my necessities."

Leo said, "Go get it. I'll get you to the hospital in time."

Welborn ran back inside. The bag was right where Kira said it would be. He grabbed it — and saw a legal pad that had lain beneath the bag. He saw at a glance what was written on the top page.

Debate Strategy. Criticize President's Inconstancy. Call Her Quitter by Implication.

Those words, written by his wife, hit Welborn like a kick to the gut.

He flipped the pad face down, so Kira would find it that way.

Welborn ran out of the house with Kira's bag, barely remembering to lock the front door.

Leo got them to the hospital on time. He waited with Welborn in the new dads' room until the girls were born. With the delivery of twins, it was suggested Welborn not be in the birthing room. When the nurse came in and told him his wife and daughters were all doing fine, he wept for joy. Leo hugged him and told him to go see his ladies.

The twins lay in small transparent cribs each with her name on it when he entered the birthing room. So tiny, so pink, so perfect, he thought as he marveled at them. He moved on to Kira who looked like she'd just run a marathon — and won. He kissed her.

Unable to resist, he said, "Remind me to have all my children with you."

Kira laughed and winced. "I am so sore. I need a little rest. Would you mind giving Ari and Callie their first feeding?"

A nurse held up two bottles with clear liquid in them. "Water with just a touch of sucrose."

She nodded to a chair. Welborn sat. Another nurse brought his girls to him, settled each one in the crook of an arm. They were so small he had no trouble cradling them and holding the bottles to their mouths. They took the liquid without hesitation.

Welborn had never known a feeling of such joy and fulfillment.

It lasted until he remembered Kira's note on debate strategy.

Call the president a quitter? How could Kira have thought of something so awful?

More important, what should he do about it now that he knew?

Betray the president or the mother of the two little angels he held in his arms?

United States Senate — Washington, D.C.

One of the great powers of the Senate majority leader was he got to schedule when a bill or the confirmation of a nominee was debated and later came to a vote. With the Democrats holding a fifty-three to forty-seven majority, Majority Leader Wexford scheduled the vote to confirm the nomination of Craig MacLaren to be chief justice of the United States first.

Public opinion had hit the Senate Republicans hard for walking out on the vote to confirm Governor Jean Morrissey as vice president. Fox News held fast and defended the GOP, but all the other major media outlets called the Republicans crybabies and worse. A popular movement called DockTheir-Pay had begun online to withhold a day's pay from any member of Congress who boycotted a vote because the outcome was unlikely to be the one he or she wanted.

So far ten million "signatures" had been collected and electronically transmitted to Wexford in the Senate and Speaker of the House Peter Profitt. Neither man had yet to respond publicly. The DTP movement said if the pols wanted analog petitions they'd find a way to bury them in paper. It looked as if the voter's ability to make their elected representatives vote against their personal interests would soon be put to the test.

James J. McGill was invited to sign the petition in front of TV cameras in Washington.

He did, though allowing in only a pool camera and the movement's founders.

They all smiled and shook hands.

The president told her husband, "You might have new career opportunities."

"Perish the thought," McGill said.

After the nominees appeared before the Judiciary Committee, the judgement of every senator who would speak for the record was that Judge MacLaren was an unabashed liberal who thought it was high time someone who saw the Constitution from his perspective headed the high court again. His boldness had sent three conservatives to the hospital with atrial fibrillation. Senator Daniel Crockett was seen as a moderate conservative, an acceptable choice had the nominee for chief justice been a staunch conservative, but was dubious in the present context.

The American Bar Association's Standing Committee on the Federal Judiciary rated both men as well qualified. That meant not a damn thing to a hard right wing that wanted the two "strong" conservative justices who'd died to be replaced with "even stronger" conservative justices. They didn't give a good goddamn if the Democrats controlled the Senate.

The only nuclear option they cared about was one that nuked all Democrats.

Some of the fire-breathers held seats in the Senate. Majority Leader Wexford and Deputy Leader Bergen weren't sure if they might try something drastic or even criminal. The Capitol Hill police and fire departments had both been alerted. No one truly thought the Capitol would be burned down as the Reichstag had been in 1933 Germany, but why take a chance?

Every Democrat in the Senate demanded a roll call vote, far more than the one-fifth of those senators present required to force the issue. The clerk called the senators' names in alphabetical order, requiring a yea or nay in response. A running tabulation was kept.

Several Republicans and every member of True South *shouted* nay to the nomination of Judge Craig MacLaren, but no actual violence occurred. The nomination was confirmed, fifty-three to forty-seven. Senator Daniel Crockett, Republican of Tennessee voted for his fellow nominee. Senator Roger Michaelson, Democrat of Washington went the other way.

Senator Crockett's nomination was confirmed ninety-four to five.

The senator abstained from voting for himself.

Once the Senate's business was concluded, the losers walked out again.

Nobody had yet started a petition to penalize a bad attitude.

9

July, 2012
The Royale Hotel — Washington, D.C.

Olin Anderson decided that the place to either kidnap or kill Margaret Sweeney was in the ladies room just off the rear of the hotel's Plaza Ballroom. He and Arn Crosby had gone over the video Damon Todd had shot of the hotel and the ballroom with a tie-pin camera. Crosby agreed with his friend's choice.

Wanting to have a role to play, Todd had persuaded Crosby and Anderson that he could visit the hotel and pass himself off as a convention planner for the American Psychological Association. He'd say he was looking for meeting space for next year's national conference. He'd say he had a five-year contract to offer the right hotel. For the kind of money that would involve, they'd let him see their chef's secret recipes.

With a new suit and a fresh haircut, wearing tinted glasses, knowing all the professional jargon and having the bearing of the actual doctor he was, Todd had been able to pull off the deception. He'd told the hotel's sales representative that he was favorably impressed and would let her know of his decision within a week.

Todd had shot footage of everything Anderson needed to see, including service entrances, corridors and elevators, the three-stall ladies room at the rear of the ballroom and the uniforms hotel maintenance people wore to work. Prep work was critical to the success of any covert operation and both former CIA spooks had been impressed by Todd's thoroughness.

"Helluva good job, Doc," Anderson told him.

"First class," Crosby agreed.

Todd accepted the compliments with a nod and stepped back to watch the pros lay out their plan. He thought Anderson's idea was overly optimistic, but he didn't comment. The one time he'd tried to take McGill on it hadn't worked. He didn't have license to criticize.

He'd wait and see what happened.

What happened was Anderson, in a knockoff hotel uniform stitched together by a Korean seamstress, made his way into the hotel. He carried with him a large tool bag and a three foot length of brass pipe with a six-inch elbow at one end, as if he was working on a plumbing job. He elicited no questions on his activities from any of the people he passed. There were times when Anderson's tough face was an asset. After knocking on the ladies room door and receiving no reply, he went inside.

Todd and Crosby watched and listened to Anderson's progress compliments of the camera and microphone he wore. Both instruments were embedded in the U.S. flag pin he'd affixed to his uniform shirt. Placed over his heart.

No one would dare question a public display of patriotism.

Anderson entered the large wheelchair accessible stall at the end of the row and closed the door. The door and walls of the stall ended six inches above the floor. Anderson unscrewed the cap of the brass pipe and withdrew a black wooden cylinder. From his tool bag, he took a rubber tip and put it over the bottom end of the cylinder. The object now resembled a cane with a brass handle. Anderson leaned it against the door. The section visible to an outside observer showed that the occupant had a legitimate reason to use the special needs stall.

To complete the illusion of a gimpy old broad using the facilities, Anderson took two mannequin legs sawed off at mid-calf out of his bag. Each appendage wore shoes similar to those Anderson remembered his grandmother wearing. He positioned the legs so the left foot pointed straight ahead and the right foot was splayed outward at forty-five degrees.

The way Anderson normally sat on the throne.

Now he squatted with both feet up on the seat. He could hold the position for hours. You spent years working in Asia, you learned to sit like the natives. It actually got to be comfortable once your muscles stretched out.

From where Anderson had perched, he couldn't see anyone who might come in, but he'd spent hours watching and listening to videos of Chana Lochlan. When she and Margaret Sweeney entered the room, he was sure they'd be talking. Broads talked everywhere, and they loved company when they went to the john.

Of course, he was betting they'd take a pee before Lochlan gave her speech.

If they didn't … nah, they would. A woman speaking in public, it was probably in her DNA to use the john first.

So he'd recognize Chana Lochlan's voice. Sweeney would say something back, sounding tougher, like the bodyguard she was, and he'd be all over them in nothing flat. Lochlan would have to get conked, knocked out. A damn shame, a babe like her getting treated that way. Of course, normally Anderson would have killed her, but if he did that, there'd be no living with Damon Todd.

If Anderson caught Sweeney looking the other way, he'd knock her out, too, and take her with him. Hostages were valuable. If she was ready to put up a fight or started screaming, he'd kill her.

Of course, some other broad, maybe more than one, might come in, but if one of them didn't sound like Chana Lochlan, he'd just sit tight. But he was betting the peeing public would be using the big rest rooms off the main corridor near the entrance to the room. The little relief station back here, that'd be for the star of the show.

He hoped anyway. Worse came to worse, the target never showed, he'd just hold his water.

Leave the way he came.

He settled in to wait for Lochlan and Sweeney to arrive, letting his mind drift but not too far.

Be something if he wound up buying it in a ladies' loo. People who knew him would say, "Yeah, they tried to flush old Anderson right there, but he clogged the drain and they spent a month trying to —"

The door to the room opened. He heard just one pair of footsteps. Fuck.

Some broad needing a tinkle, he hoped. Not the other stuff if he was lucky. Some women … he thought he should have heard a stall door close by now. He thought it should have been the far one. Given a choice, people didn't like to crap too close in public.

Anderson was surprised to see a square of blue paper float under the door to the stall.

Fall to the floor right in front of him.

What the fuck?

He wasn't going to give himself away to anyone he didn't have to kill. He'd just sit quiet and … something was written on the blue paper. He had good vision and the writing was nice and clear. What it said was —

Should've given your legs a few varicose veins.

Shit!

Then a woman's hand reached under the door and grabbed his cane.

Goddamn!

Anderson jumped off the toilet and threw open the stall door. He saw Margaret Sweeney all right. James J. Fucking McGill, too. And some dark-haired broad he'd never seen before. McGill had Anderson's cane now. Pulled on the brass handle and revealed a gleaming thirty inch blade.

McGill said, "Not as broad as a Roman sword but nearly as long." He tested the edge with his thumb. "Sharp, too."

Anderson reached up a sleeve and came out with a switchblade knife. He popped it open.

"Come on, McGill," he said. "You're any kind of man, you'll

fight me, sword to knife."

Without taking his eyes off Anderson, McGill told Sweetie and Elspeth, "Shoot him."

They did. Sweetie with a beanbag round, Elspeth with a Taser.

Sweetie shot for the gut and knocked Anderson on his ass.

Elspeth nailed Anderson in the chest.

The combination bounced him on his backside like a bronco buster.

Until he lost consciousness and toppled over sideways.

Anderson would be turned over to Daryl Cheveyo, who was back with the CIA on a short-term contract, for questioning. One down, two to go.

McGill picked up Anderson's knife. Looked at it and noticed something. He pushed open the door of the nearest stall with his foot. Pointed the knife blade at the roll of toilet paper. Pressed the knife's blade-release button. The blade shot free of the handle and embedded itself in the roll of toilet paper.

He looked at Sweetie and Elspeth and told them, "The next time someone reaches for something, we don't wait for anyone to say shoot."

The Oval Office

Circumstances being what they were, McGill had the privilege of preempting anyone when he needed to see the president. When he presented himself to Edwina Byington, she said, "The president is conferring with the vice president and the chief of staff, but I'll let her know you're here, Mr. McGill."

"You're a marvel, Edwina."

"So I've been told," she said.

Less than a minute later, the door to the Oval Office opened and Jean Morrissey stepped out. She extended a hand to McGill. "Mr. McGill, so nice to finally meet you."

"Madam Vice President, the pleasure is mine."

"Rory Calhoun," she said.

McGill smiled. There weren't many who saw the resemblance so quickly.

"My brother Frank is a fan of old cowboy movies," she told him. "He says when I get out of politics he's going to open a dude ranch out west."

"Well, good for him. We don't have enough people going into dude ranching these days."

Jean Morrissey chuckled as if he'd said something funnier than he knew.

She said she hoped they'd meet again before too long and went on her way. When McGill entered the Oval Office, closing the door behind him, he saw he was alone with Patti. Galia must have left through the side door.

McGill knew Patti had anticipated the wisdom of having just the two of them in the room.

The advantages of spousal privilege already having been made clear to Warren Rockland.

"We got Olin Anderson," McGill told Patti. "Took him alive."

"Without so much as a scratch on you." Patti nodded in approval.

"I had Sweetie and Elspeth shoot him with sublethal measures."

"I might swoon. Smart man, powerful women working toward a common goal. May I sit on your lap?"

McGill laughed. "Later. We wouldn't want to rumple your power suit."

The president contented herself by sitting next to her husband and holding his hand.

She said, "So everything went as well as possible?"

McGill sighed. "It went well. Not as well as possible."

"What do you mean?"

"We should have set up our snooping equipment sooner. It's the newest gear. Elspeth and Byron DeWitt went out and bought it from a high-end spyware shop here in town. Anderson, from the way things went, never noticed he was on camera from the moment he entered the hotel."

"But?" Patti asked.

"But he wore a hotel uniform that was picture perfect, and he knew the least obvious way to get to the ladies room where we grabbed him. That means somebody had to blaze the trail for him, give him the information he needed."

"Crosby or Todd?" Patti asked.

"Todd is my guess. He has the civilian, white collar background. He's used to manipulating people. He probably got the hotel people to give him a guided tour. DeWitt's checking on that."

Patti added her sigh to McGill's.

"Would've been nice to catch him first," she said.

"Or even follow him back to bad-guy central. Grab all of them."

"Nobody's perfect, Jim." She squeezed his hand.

"Don't I know it?" McGill said.

"The goal, then, is to be less imperfect than the other guy."

"Yeah, that's the goal for both of us."

McGill kissed his wife and let her get back to the business of running the country.

That and thwarting the ambitions of lesser politicians.

When McGill left, Edwina buzzed the president.

"Madam President, your chief of staff asked to know when the coast was clear. Is it?"

"Yes, Edwina. Please send her in."

Galia returned. Patti gestured her to a chair.

"Do I want to know?" the chief of staff asked.

"You might, but it wouldn't be good for either you or me."

"Well, then. I believe there was one item left on our agenda."

They moved on to how they should respond to the president being called a quitter.

Interstate 80 Westbound — Iowa

Crosby was driving now, had been for the past fourteen hours. He showed no signs of fatigue yet, no signs of amphetamine use either. For a man in what was certainly the last quarter of his life, he exhibited amazing endurance. In the absence of Anderson's adolescent gregariousness, a streak of deep bitterness had also emerged in Crosby.

Todd, forcing himself to remain awake for fear Crosby would drift off at the wheel and kill them both, saw several instances when Crosby would have liked to inflict pain on drivers who passed them. None of the targets of his ire had come close to side-swiping them or cutting them off once they'd passed. They simply had the freedom to speed while Crosby felt obliged to hew closely to the speed limit.

That had produced in Crosby a hair trigger sense of road rage.

Not that he necessarily intended to shoot anybody.

He had his Vietnam tomahawks under the driver's seat.

If a cop pulled Crosby over for any ticky-tack offense, things would get ugly.

Out of the blue, he glanced at Todd and said, "Thanks, Doc."

The expression of gratitude made Todd feel uneasy. He asked, "For what?"

"For not saying Olin fucked up. Which we both saw he did."

They'd agreed to wait twenty-four hours for Anderson before leaving Virginia. But when the camera in Anderson's flag pin showed them that he'd been shot at James J. McGill's direction they'd left Comfort House without bothering to check out.

They headed west. Crosby explained that was the direction Chana Lochlan's speaking tour would take her. His idea was to wait until just after the last stop on the tour to strike. That was the most likely time for the other side to let their guard down. Then he lapsed into grim silence.

Todd was far from sure he agreed with Crosby's reasoning.

But he wasn't about to debate the point at the moment. Todd turned his attention to his iPad, looking for any news online of what had happened at the Royale.

He found no mention of Anderson, but he came across a replay of a D.C. television station's interview with Chana Lochlan. Todd couldn't take his eyes off her. Margaret Sweeney stood just behind

Chana, but he didn't care a whit about her. Not with Chana in the picture.

"What good would criticizing Anderson have done?" Todd asked.

"Only improve gas milage, I guess," Crosby said with a sour smile.

"I don't understand."

"The less weight a car carries, the better its mileage."

"Indeed." So Crosby *was* in a mood to lash out.

He'd have to look for opportunities to make a quick getaway.

Crosby said, "Olin didn't like you much at first, but he came to respect you by the end."

"And you?" Todd asked.

"Jury's still out. You don't try to fuck me over, we'll be okay."

"You think they killed Anderson?" Todd asked.

"Olin will be lucky if they only kill him."

"They shot him twice."

Crosby's practiced eye had seen *how* his friend had been shot. He explained to Todd. Then he added, "A Taser or a beanbag can kill you. Getting hit with both increases the chance of dying. But Olin is one tough bastard, and my guess is those two broads knew where to shoot to keep him alive."

"You think he'll be returned to the CIA?"

Crosby shook his head. "He'll go to a supermax prison under a new name. All the necessary paperwork will show he killed somebody in some awful way. It'll also diagnose him as —"

"A paranoid schizophrenic?" Todd asked. "Someone with delusions he was a covert operative for the Central Intelligence Agency?"

Crosby gave Todd a look. "You are one smart SOB, Doc. That's just what I was going to say. Maybe now you can see why I'm a bit cranky."

Todd nodded. "I do, but please remember, I want to see James J. McGill die."

"Then we're on the same page. We work together, we'll get

him."

They were not quite halfway to their destination, the last stop on Chana Lochlan's speaking tour, San Francisco.

Bellevue Hospital Prison Ward — Manhattan

Ever since the 9/11 attacks, the CIA had maintained a collegial relationship with the intelligence units of the NYPD. For the most part, the Agency got along better with New York coppers than it did with their federal brethren at the FBI. When the CIA needed a private space in a locked psych ward, they found one at Bellevue. For an appropriate fee, of course.

McGill and Daryl Cheveyo were sitting opposite Olin Anderson in a private room when he awakened. He saw McGill and said, "You pussy."

McGill kept a straight face and didn't say a word.

Anderson was strapped into a hospital bed. His wrists were chained to metal railings on either side of the bed. An IV line was attached to his right arm. Cheveyo liked the irony of using ketamine hydrochloride as a sedative to keep Anderson calm. An antihistamine had been administered to dry out Anderson's mouth. He wouldn't be spitting at anyone.

"Interesting choice of insults," Cheveyo said.

"Who the fuck are you?" Anderson asked.

He was trying to work himself up, but the IV sedative drip kept him from getting far.

"I'm the CIA shrink who recommended not hiring Damon Todd."

"Asshole."

"We'll get around to that. Right now, what I'd like to know is whether you're interested in helping us find Dr. Todd and your friend Arn Crosby."

Anderson didn't even bother cursing Cheveyo. He just turned his head away.

McGill said, "He's a tough guy. Of course, his reputation's

going to suffer when people hear a couple of women brought him in."

Anderson turned his head back. McGill could tell he'd wanted to put some snap into it, make the movement dramatic, but the drugs had left him sluggish.

"You should fucking talk. You needed to bring those broads with you."

McGill shrugged. "I'm just an easy-going guy."

"Olin's going to be a lot easier-going soon," Cheveyo said.

Anderson managed to smile. "You think you can scare me? Shit."

"So you know you're going to spend the rest of your life in a cell, right?" Cheveyo asked. Not waiting for an answer, he continued. "I think you'd be able to endure that better than most, but what I was wondering, how would you tolerate having to sit down to pee?"

"What the hell are you —"

The implication filtered through Anderson's foggy brain.

"You can't do that," Anderson whined. "You can't mutilate me."

"We've already made preparations. Sterilized your package for surgery. Want to see?"

Anderson shook his head, "No."

"Of course not. That's the last thing you'd want to see, but take a look."

Cheveyo crossed to the bed, lifted the hem of Anderson's hospital gown and held a mirror at just the right angle. Anderson had been shaved clean. His genitals had been painted orange with mercurochrome. It wasn't a pretty sight.

Anderson had to look, though, if only to see Cheveyo wasn't bluffing.

When he began to tremble, Cheveyo let the gown fall.

McGill was standing now. He asked, "You want to talk?"

Anderson pressed his lips together and shook his head.

"Your choice," Cheveyo said without rancor. He held up a small audio recorder for Anderson to see. "Voice activated. I'll leave it on the chair here. You start talking, we'll cancel surgery. But don't wait too long. A surgical anesthetic is going to be introduced into your drip line. Don't know exactly when because suspense is part of the fun. Once you're under, that's it. Into the OR you go."

Cheveyo gave Anderson a nod and left.

McGill stepped over to the bed.

He said in a quiet voice, "Just so you know, asshole, I'll get your buddy and Todd, anyway."

Then he left the room. He rejoined Cheveyo in the hallway. "You think it'll work?"

"I think so. I'm not supposed to tell you this, but Anderson and Crosby used the same gambit on an assignment. When they didn't get the information they wanted, they followed through."

McGill winced and said, "He has to know that you know that."

"I sincerely hope so," Cheveyo said.

10

August, 2012
Democratic National Convention — St. Paul, Minnesota

For a recent arrival to the Democratic Party, Patti Grant was given a rousing welcome. Vice President Jean Morrissey, the former Minnesota governor, brought down the house with the ovation she was given. Movement feminists were in ecstasy over the all-female ticket. Of greater significance, every poll taken in every corner of the country showed that women of all ages and political leanings were more enthusiastic about voting in the upcoming election than they'd ever been before.

Patti Grant won cheers, laughs and applause when she told the convention, "My beloved American sisters, our day has come, and we promise to make the most of it. My dear American brothers, we promise to take very good care of you, and treat you with the utmost respect. My precious American children, our every thought will begin with concern for what is best for you."

It was only after the party's two nominees were affirmed by a vote of the delegates with the president's adopted home state of Illinois putting the ticket over the top, that any controversy arose. The vice president visited a Sunday morning talk show on the new Drucker Direct Network and was interviewed by editorial director Ethan Judd.

DDN had caused a stir in the broadcasting community with

its brash slogan, courtesy of Putnam Shady's chosen ad agency, Wheaton & Kennerly. *DDN: Get your news from journalists not propagandists.*

Judd asked Vice President Morrissey how the newly constituted Grant ticket would deal with tough issues, like national defense, the economy and second amendment rights, on which the Republicans accused them of weakness.

Morrissey had been well briefed on national defense.

"You'll remember, Mr. Judd, what the president said about defending our country when she ran for the presidency the first time. 'If another assault is launched against the United States by any foe, we will determine the countries that supported the attackers and destroy their capital cities, without warning or mercy. If the United States is attacked with a weapon of mass destruction, that will trigger a nuclear response. Any aggressor nation involved in any way will be obliterated.'

"I couldn't have said it better myself, and I agree with the president completely. If it were ever my choice to make, I'd do the same thing."

The president's words had been stunning in their day, but now it became the vice president's turn to shock the nation's sensibilities.

"It's interesting," Morrissey told Judd, "that you should mention jobs and guns in almost the same breath. We have to do a lot better for the American worker. We have to create more jobs with higher pay. We also have to find a way to connect work with government guaranteed health care insurance. There's nothing more important to people than having a real opportunity to provide for themselves, their families and their futures.

"Prosperity is also of critical importance to the continuity of the United States government. When you see widespread joblessness and despair in other countries, you'll see people throwing rocks, maybe even Molotov cocktails. If we get to the point in this country where Dad has lost everything but his assault rifle, we'll be in real trouble.

"The lunatic fringe militias we see now will be Cub Scout troops compared to millions of armed, long-term unemployed who don't see any future for themselves. Facing a prospect like that, we have no choice but to reestablish the middle class as the secure bulwark of our society."

Judd questioned whether things could get that bad.

"Mr. Judd, there are more guns than people in this country. The gun lobby has a long record of having its way with Congress and state legislatures. We've already seen too many tragedies where distraught people turn their guns on their families and their coworkers. If we ever see widespread economic desperation, I think other targets will present themselves."

The vice president refused to specify those targets.

It wasn't hard to figure out whom she meant, though.

The conspicuously wealthy and the pols who tilted the playing field their way.

Galia Mindel placed a call to Jean Morrissey the minute she was out of the DDN studio and had a few choice words to share about the political firestorm she'd just started.

Jean Morrissey wasn't about to be intimidated by *anyone's* chief of staff.

She said, "I thought I was fairly subtle, Galia. I mean, I wasn't the one who talked about obliterating entire nations."

Republican National Convention — St. Louis, Missouri

Mather Wyman, like everyone else in the country, had heard Jean Morrissey speak on the subject of jobs and guns. He refused to take the advice given by several party leaders and condemn Morrissey for inviting anyone with a grudge to shoot a rich person.

Wyman said, "She was careful not to say that, and *we* don't want to be the ones to put that thought into anyone's head."

The party leaders persisted. It was time to attack.

Wyman countered, "We open that can of worms, and there

will be talk of gun control linked to demands to repatriate jobs from abroad. Is that what you want?"

Wyman's running mate, Rosalinda Fuentes, backed him forcefully.

In private, she told Wyman, "We'd better hope your idea of calling Patti Grant a quitter works. If it doesn't, we'll have a *big* hill to climb."

When Governor Fuentes was introduced to speak to the convention, all the women in the hall did their best to match the vocal enthusiasm given to the Democratic candidates. A beat later the men joined in for an effective two-part roar if not harmony. Watching from his hotel suite, Mather Wyman, sitting alone, whispered to himself, "Without you, Rosie, I'd be sunk."

He'd already heard rumors that some of the party's big donors were calling for a last-second coup. The plan was they'd put together a big enough pot of money to bring Howard Hurlbert back into the party as their nominee. If it had been anyone but Hurlbert, Wyman would have been worried.

On the night Wyman was to speak, the giant video screen behind the podium came to life with a field of sky blue. A single puffy cloud gave the viewer an impression of great height. After a moment of quiet, a deep rumbling sound began, as if something immensely powerful was about to appear from over the horizon. The rumble built to a roar, the roar became a deafening din and then a shock wave made things start to shake.

In the blink of an eye, a formation of dots appeared on the screen. With incomprehensible speed the dots took on raked geometric lines and grew in size. They sped toward the eye of the beholder with a sense of both awe and menace. For the briefest moment, they were recognizable as U.S. Navy fighter jets. Just as it seemed they would burst free from the screen, they pulled up into a steep climb and there was an enormous bang.

A sonic boom.

When the lights went up, Mather Wyman was standing at the

podium. Everyone understood what they'd just witnessed, the kind of force Acting President Wyman had unleashed on the militants at Salvation's Path. They roared in approval, loving the fact that their nominee had been the man to unleash such overwhelming power.

More than one person in the hall, and not just the men, had the same thought.

Seeing something like that made you want to go out and bomb somebody.

Three minutes passed before Wyman had the silence he needed to start his speech.

"My fellow *Republicans,*" he said, "I'm so happy to be here tonight as *your* nominee."

The cheering resumed.

Wyman continued, "I had thought I'd be here to support the renomination of the president."

Boos rang out now. People would be going to bed with sore throats tonight.

"The president, however, had other plans."

More boos filled the convention center. Sore throats and ringing ears.

"A number of other former colleagues also went south on us," Wyman said.

That round of boos almost matched the one for the president.

Wyman thrusted his chin forward and said. "I'll tell you this. A Republican won the presidency in the last election and a Republican will win the presidency in this election."

Now, the cheers went on longer than any of the boos had.

"And I'll tell you why we will win. Because you can say the same thing about every last person here tonight: We are not quitters!"

Wyman thought he could actually hear voices crack now, the cheers were so loud.

He hadn't said the president was a quitter.

He'd said he wasn't one.

But the meaning was perfectly clear.

As every politician knew, there was a time for subtlety and a time for red meat.

Tonight, the carnivores had to be fed.

True South Convention — Dallas, Texas

The one thousand delegates to True South's first national convention fit comfortably in the ballroom at the American Airlines Training & Conference Center. The new political party also had the distinction of holding the first convention that would be covered by the new TV outlet Drucker Direct Network. It was an honor they could have lived without.

Word had gotten around quickly about DDN. Try to play fast and loose with the facts around them, and they'd nail you for being the charlatan or ignoramus you were. In the blink of an eye, DDN came to be feared and loathed by spin doctors everywhere.

If the party's presidential nominee had his way those speak-the-truth-to-power bastards would have been kept outside the building, preferably no closer than Oklahoma. But Tom T. Wright said let them in and Tom was paying for the hall. He'd also paid for the infrastructure that got True South on the ballot in all fifty states, was buying TV time in major markets and had been busing volunteers to the far reaches of the country to set up a ground game.

When you paid the piper you called the tune.

You could also turn off the lights, if you wanted.

More important than any of that, Howard Hurlbert feared that Tom T. Wright had the kind of dirt on him that could lock him away for the rest of his life. Look at who brought Wright to him in the first place, that miserable wife-beater Bobby Beckley. If there was anybody who knew where Hurlbert was vulnerable it was Bobby.

What the law would call the two of them was coconspirators.

Put them in the same cell and Hurlbert knew he'd be the one

getting cornholed.

So Senator Howard Hurlbert followed the directions Tom T. Wright had set out for him, but he'd yet to buy into being a latter-day Southern populist. It wasn't necessary to improve the average man's lot in life to win his vote. All you had to do was give him an enemy to hate and he was happy.

Divide and conquer had been a favored strategy forever because it worked.

Populism pretended it was about bringing people together, Hurlbert thought, and to a degree that was true. It brought the mob together. Instead of turning against each other for reasons of skin color, culture or language, the lower orders directed their resentments against their betters, people with more money, land, toys and the time to enjoy them all.

Bigotry taught hate of the poor; populism taught hate of the rich.

That was the way Hurlbert saw matters, anyway.

He also saw the evil seed that blonde witch Jean Morrissey had sown. If the people of means didn't make sure everybody got his piece of the pie, and a scoop of ice cream, too, they damn well better build moats around their mansions and learn how to drive armored personnel carriers. Because ol' Billy Bob does, in fact, own an assault rifle and hunting the rich might prove to be more fun than bringing home a twelve-point buck.

The notion made Hurlbert shudder, but he didn't put it beyond happening. Things got too far out of hand, you'd have some hillbillies *eating* the rich. Then what the hell good would having a lot of money be? No good at all if you weren't free to enjoy it.

One of Tom T. Wright's young people knocked on his door.

Pretty young lady, graduated top of her class at Rice.

Ought to be thinking about getting rich herself. At least marrying a young man who was going to make his fortune. Instead, she was working for a fool's crusade, trying to get him elected president. What were young people coming to these days?

Of course, the latest polls showed he was doing better than he'd ever expected.

Within five points of Mather Wyman.

Only eleven behind Patti Grant.

The young lady told him, "You're on, Senator."

He gently clasped her hand in both of his and said, "Thank you."

The smile she gave him was so warm he almost thought he was doing the right thing.

He waved to the delegates as he stepped to the lectern at the front of the ballroom. They seemed genuinely enthused, too. Made him think they were all high on the same drug, hope.

The applause kept him smiling long enough to make his face sore.

As soon as he got the chance, Senator Hurlbert started to speak.

"Huey Long," he said, "told us that in this country every man should be a king. Me, I don't think we need any kings at all. What we need is a country where every man, woman and child can *live* like a king."

The message wasn't a tough sell. Every-damn-body got to his feet and cheered.

Except for Tom T. Wright. He just kept his seat and smiled.

The Oval Office

Galia Mindel said, "I tried to make clear to Madam Vice President before we left the convention that picking an unnecessary fight with the most powerful lobby in Washington was not a good idea. She responded that it was small potatoes compared to the obliteration of entire countries."

"She's right about that," the president said.

"Of course, she's right, but that's irrelevant. We don't need that debate."

"Maybe it's just what we need. Not right now. After the inauguration. It might be useful."

"Useful? How?" Galia asked.

The president said, "Sometimes people need to get a look at scary possibilities to help them see sense. If we ever again have unemployment levels like those of the Great Depression, how close do you think Jean's shoot-the-rich scenario would come to reality?"

Galia needed only a moment to decide. "Very close. Could well be real. Truth is, she didn't go far enough. If the rich become fair game, elected officials will, too. Then we'd have anarchy."

The president nodded, "And whose efforts put weapons of war into the hands of people who have neither military training nor discipline?"

"Our old friends, the gun lobby."

"Exactly. Now that Jean has opened the conversation, we'll be asked to continue it."

"You're going to confront the gun lobby head on?"

The president laughed. "Charge into the canon fire? No, I don't think so. But I do have another idea."

"I'd love to hear it," Galia said, not really sure that she would.

"What is it that women do ever so much better than men?"

Galia said, "The list goes on forever."

Patti laughed. "Well, maybe a mile or two anyway. What I was thinking about, though, is our ability to start a conversation and keep it going."

"Okay," Galia said, waiting to see where the president was going.

"At the moment, proposing much less passing gun control laws makes no sense. It would be like trying to bring Prohibition back. Even if you could pass the law, people would not abide by it."

"Not that the gun lobby would ever let it pass. Not that a supermajority of the Senate wouldn't filibuster it," Galia said.

"Exactly. That's the way things are now. The gun lobby runs the show. Congress is in its pocket. But you know what, Galia, nobody can filibuster a national conversation. After Jean raised everyone's hackles, I did a little checking on my own. You know how many people belong to the NRA? Four million. You know how many American adults own one or more guns? Fifty million. So more than ninety percent of gun owners *don't* belong to the NRA. You do a little more research and you find well over a hundred million American adults *don't* own any firearms at all."

Despite her misgivings, Galia started doing the political calculus in her head.

The president continued, "So what I think we should do next term is start the discussion from right here in the Oval Office. What does responsible gun ownership look like? What carries the right to bear arms beyond anything the authors of the Constitution might have imagined? How do we look at the Second Amendment in light of advances of firearm technology far beyond the days of muskets and flintlocks?

"We ask these questions and a hundred more and we get an idea of what the country at large, not just the gun lobby and the voices in its choir, thinks are the right things to do. Then, if we can arrive at a consensus on what the Second Amendment should mean in the twenty-first century, we go to Congress and propose laws that reflect the will of the people."

Galia said, "That's absolutely subversive, Madam President."

"Thank you."

"I'm not sure I meant that as a compliment. I meant that you'll turn things upside down."

Patti Grant smiled. "I've been meaning to ask Jim how he'd feel if I got a tattoo. *'Born to Cause Upheaval.'*"

"I think I'll leave that one alone," Galia said.

"There's one very important question I want to raise when we have this discussion," the president said. The expression on her face said it was the *most* important question to her.

"What's that, Madam President?"

"How could anyone try to justify owning a rocket launcher like the one Erna Godfrey used to kill Andy?"

There was, of course, no justification for that.

The president's question raised one in Galia's mind.

Had the president used her new VP to raise the gun issue in the first place?

11

September, 2012
Bellevue Hospital Prison Ward — Manhattan

Cheveyo had been lent the use of a staff doctor's office. He and
McGill sat and listened to a recording of the confession Anderson
had provided. Nothing like letting a prisoner think he might
become subject to the same cruelties he'd visited upon others
to get him talking.

Anderson had begun with a plea for mercy. "Don't castrate
me! You want to kill me, go ahead. You got to show me you're
serious, just take one nut. But not both and not my dick."

Anderson had paused, as if waiting for a reply.

Cheveyo shook his head and said, "Shows you how people
organize their self-images. I surely wouldn't want to lose my
genitals, but I'd fear a lobotomy more."

McGill said nothing, thought it'd be a toss-up for him.

Sounding anxious that he might be anesthetized at any
moment, Anderson continued, "Okay, here's what I know."

He told them that the plan he, Crosby and Todd had come
up with was to follow Chana Lochlan's speaking tour and grab
Margaret Sweeney or kill her. But McGill and the others had to
know that because they had a trap ready for him. He and Crosby
had both figured Chana Lochlan was being used to bait the two of

them, but they thought they could beat the trap. They were pros competing against amateurs.

Anderson paused to take a breath.

"A sense of grandiosity," Cheveyo said.

"What I've read, these two used to be really something," McGill responded. "Maybe they'd just lost a step. Although, we thought Todd might've been upgrading them."

Cheveyo nodded.

Anderson had more to give. He told them Crosby and Todd would be traveling at least for a little while in a black BMW. He gave them the license plate number. He honestly couldn't say what Todd wanted more, to kill McGill or run off with Chana Lochlan. Anderson said if McGill and Cheveyo didn't kill him, he'd find a way to commit suicide. Death was what he deserved for betraying Crosby. Betraying Todd, too. Who wasn't such a bad guy and the moronic CIA damn well should have hired him.

The only thing he asked, no matter who killed him, was to go out as a man.

Anderson moaned, "No, no!" He felt himself losing consciousness.

His ketamine hydrochloride dose had been elevated.

But he wasn't going to be castrated.

Cheveyo was going to have a go at hypnotizing him. He'd be told to forget he'd ever been threatened with the loss of his penis. Wouldn't do to have that testimony come out before Congress. He'd also be coaxed into forgetting about suicide. Persuaded he deserved a life sentence in a supermax prison.

McGill thought Cheveyo had a lot of work cut out for him and didn't envy him any of it.

"They bonded," McGill said. "Anderson spoke respectfully of Todd."

"But the three of them didn't come at you together. So there was still a hierarchy."

"When there were three of them. Two people tend to pair off."

Cheveyo shook his head. "Anderson and Crosby were the

natural pairing, and they didn't use that."

McGill had to agree. "Todd could be hanging back, seeing how the pros do it, learning from their mistakes."

"Or he just doesn't want to lose to you again. He might be content to kidnap Ms. Lochlan while Crosby is keeping you busy."

That was an idea or part of one McGill could buy.

He said, "Todd wants both, me dead and Chana for himself. He might use Crosby's attack on me as a distraction to make a kidnapping attempt. But does that mean Margaret Sweeney is out of danger?"

Cheveyo said, "No. Anyone close to you might be a target. If not for distraction then torment. If Todd can't reach you —"

"I understand," McGill said. He didn't need to hear more. "Let me know if Anderson gives you anything more that's useful."

McGill decided he couldn't allow Todd to focus on anyone but him.

Well, him and Chana.

He'd have to do for Chana what he'd refused to do the first time she came to him. Become her personal bodyguard. Let Elspeth be *his* visible protection. See if he could lead Todd and Crosby to think they were more than a match for a female Secret Service agent and him.

Everyone else would have to hang back to suck Crosby in.

Let him think he could beat the trap, even if Anderson hadn't.

In the Chevy with Leo and Elspeth on the way back to D.C., McGill received a call from Byron DeWitt. He told McGill, "The flag pin Anderson was wearing, it was a webcam. Todd and Crosby must've seen you when you bagged Anderson."

McGill thought about that. "Is it still working?"

"Yes."

"So there's a chance I might use it to send a personal message?"

After a moment's silence, DeWitt said, "Maybe."

McGill said, "Let's give it a try when I get back to town."

Q Street — Washington, D.C.

The moment Aria and Callista Yates were tucked into their facing cribs, lying on their backs, Welborn assuring Kira the baby monitor was activated and operational, Mom and Dad dragged themselves into their bedroom. Welborn fell backward onto the marital Tempurpedic king, not bothering to remove his shoes.

He thought he could yield to unconsciousness within minutes had he landed on a bed of nails. He didn't remember Air Force Academy basic cadet training being as grueling as the first days of fatherhood. A fifty-pound rucksack was a trifle to carry compared to bearing the burden of assuring a bright future for two six-pound baby girls.

Welborn was sliding down the slope of conscious responsibility into the soft warm sea of sleep when he heard his name called. Kira asking for attention. Not now, please. Not even for the enticing exercise that had led them to this very moment.

"Welborn," Kira said again. More iron in her tone than silk.

He conceded one raised eyelid to her. "What?"

"There's a legal pad on our dresser."

He let the eyelid close. "Property of a burglar who makes notes?"

"My legal pad," Kira said.

Now, he remembered, but he kept his eyes closed, said nothing.

"It was face down. I *never* leave anything face down."

Welborn still hadn't heard a question, but he felt Kira join him on the bed. More than that, he smelled her hovering above him. He hoped the lactating Mrs. Yates didn't drip on him.

Still longing for rest, eyelids steadfastly shut, he said, "I'm sure everything will look better in the morning."

"It is morning."

"I worked the night shift," he reminded her.

"We need to talk, now."

Welborn responded with a jaw-cracking yawn, hoping his breath was stale enough to make Kira retreat. She was made of sterner stuff. He gave up and opened both eyes.

Kira told him, "I know you saw what I wrote on my pad. If I wasn't so busy having twins, I'd never have left it where you could see it. What I want to know is, did you rat me out?"

Welborn told the mother of his children the truth. "No."

Kira looked for any sign of a lie. She studied his eyes. They were bloodshot with exhaustion but were not evasive. She saw no tremor of deceit anywhere in his body. But then he didn't have the energy for that. Aware that she'd never caught him in a lie, or even suspected him of one, for as long as they'd known each other, she had no choice but to accept his word as true.

"Thank you," Kira said. "That must have been hard for you."

"It was, but I found a way to rationalize my inaction."

"That being?"

"Telling myself that Galia Mindel must have anticipated such an attack the moment she learned the president was going to change parties. Your idea was not only unworthy of you, but you unwittingly placed your Uncle Mather in a very bad spot. To put it bluntly, if he should raise the topic of quitting in a presidential debate, I would bet our girls' college money the president will hand him his ass. If he doesn't raise the topic, it will be raised for him. For example, your Uncle Mather did *resign* his position as vice president. Galia won't overlook that."

Kira looked stricken. *She* had overlooked that.

"Why didn't you tell me?" she asked.

"I believe your scheme was hatched before Aria and Callista were. I didn't have the chance. After your uncle raised the issue of quitters at his nominating convention, it was too late. For future reference, please bear in mind, it's never a good thing for an amateur to take on a pro."

Tears formed in Kira's eyes. Welborn pulled her down into his embrace.

As they fell asleep together, he hoped he wasn't overrating Galia Mindel.

August Coppola Theatre, SFSU — San Francisco, California

Damon Todd felt at home on the campus of San Francisco State University. He'd spent much of his career, pre-Funny Farm, in academia. Arn Crosby hated the place. He liked tech schools, the ones that taught useful skills. Like how to kill the other guy before he killed you. A university, with all the snootiness that word implied, in San Francisco, where you couldn't kill the '60s if you used cyanide, gave him nothing but bad feelings.

But Todd was the one who clenched his teeth when he saw the notice at the front of the theatre. Crosby showed no emotion despite seeing …

An Evening with Chana Lochlan had been canceled.

Refunds should be requested online.

Crosby had instructed Todd earlier that they shouldn't pay more than casual attention to any aspect of the theatre. There might be people watching for them on campus. They had to be ready to run or fight. If they stopped and gawked, they'd deserve to get caught.

They kept walking and no one tried to stop them. They got into the BMW and drove south to San Bruno. Crosby said he was in the mood for Italian food because that was harder to fuck up than any other cuisine and if someone served him a bad meal he was going to start shooting. They stopped at a place called Toto's.

The pasta was terrific, the beer was cold, the service was excellent.

Crosby didn't shoot anyone and after Todd said he'd drive the next leg and Crosby could drink all he wanted the mood mellowed. Sure, they were both still sore that McGill, that bastard, had to be behind getting them to drive all the way across the country for nothing.

Until Anderson had been caught, Crosby hadn't had any personal animosity against McGill.

Now, all that had changed.

He not only wanted to kill the guy, he wanted to make him suffer.

Todd, no less emotional, sat nibbling his pizza and sipping a Coke.

He'd been surfing the web on his iPad since the food had been served. Crosby thought Todd was probably hoping to find some paparazzi photo looking up Chana Lochlan's skirt. He'd been leching after her ever since they left the East Coast. Todd could fool you, though, and that was what he did to Crosby after the waitress had brought him his fourth beer.

He handed the tablet to Crosby.

McGill's face was right goddamn there, looking at him.

Crosby stuck Todd's earbuds into his auditory canals. Didn't worry about hygiene.

A tap on the screen started the video.

McGill told him, "The first thing Olin Anderson said after he woke up in custody was to call me a pussy."

That made Crosby smile.

McGill continued, "Kind of ironic, I thought, because that was *my* opinion of him. Same way I feel about you and Todd. Couple of ex-CIA hotshots and a mad scientist sneaking around, hiding out, taking your own sweet time to work out your master plan. Can't even make a simple run at a retired cop who's working on a private license just to fill his time."

Much as he hated to do so, Crosby thought the guy had a point.

If you forgot about all the Secret Service agents the prick had watching him.

McGill hadn't. He brought that up, too.

"Most of the time, I've got one special agent looking out for me. Lately, that agent has been a woman. She and my friend, another retired cop, another *woman*, were all I needed to take down your pal Olin. He's been singing like a canary, by the way. Must've held out for all of fifteen minutes."

Crosby grimaced. He was going to make this fucker pay.

"So the way I figure it, if you've got any stones at all, you should just come for me. I suppose you could try a long-range shot. I hear you've got — or had — that skill. But if that's the way you go, you really are a pussy. Just come get me. We can do hand to hand, edged weapons, blunt objects. Something up close and satisfying. Blood and muscle. You know, the way a man would do it.

"Todd tried that once. Didn't work out at all for him. But maybe he's grown a pair since then. So here's how you can find me. I'll be providing personal bodyguard service for Chana Lochlan. How's that for motivation for you two dimwits? You don't have to call back. Just show up.

"If you're not too busy mailing in applications for your AARP cards."

Crosby removed the earbuds and looked at Todd.

"Tell me he's not as good as he thinks he is."

Todd said, "You know he's baiting us."

"Of course, he is, but how good is he?"

"Good enough he can tell two women to shoot Anderson and not let it bother him."

Crosby thought about McGill's challenge as he finished his pasta and beer.

"He's right about both of us being motivated, isn't he?"

Todd nodded. "The bastard knows his enemies."

Cheltenham Drive — Bethesda, Maryland

With the death of Sir Edbert Bickford — How the hell had the old bastard managed to fall off his yacht and drown? — Reynard Dix was down to one job. The way he was doing it, it looked like he was working for Patti Grant, for God's sake. No matter whom he picked for the celebrity debates with the damn liberals, his people came off looking like stuffed shirts and gasbags.

The richer-than-Midas liberals always managed to act like regular people who just happened to have Aaron Sorkin, if not Will Shakespeare, feeding them lines. They knew just how to dress, too. Wore designer casual clothes with price tags that would be a stretch, but not completely out of reach, for the average voter. The overall effect was aspirational. These were the people the viewers wanted to be, and when you saw them on your computer or replays on TV, that seemed like a reasonable ambition.

When voters saw Dix's panelists, what'd they think?

Banker looking to foreclose on my house.

Shit. The real problem, Dix had come to realize, was he was playing out of his league. Patti Grant had an army of Hollywood pros backing her side. His side had ... him. It was like sending a T-ball team out to play the Yankees.

Goddamn job didn't even pay a salary. The only reason he kept it was in the hope he could parlay it into something better. But even that possibility was looking remote. He was having a hard time finding anybody on the right willing to go up against the president's shills.

It was pathetic. Conservatives were supposed to be the badasses. Liberals were supposed to be the pansies. Couldn't any-damn-body remember their parts anymore? People were watching these days just to see how bloody the Republican road-kill would be.

It was morbid but funny, if you weren't Reynard Dix.

Things got any worse, he was going to change his name.

In that frame of mind, he took a phone call from a guy calling himself Rick Tuck.

Being a political junkie since birth, Dix picked up on the familiar sounding name.

"Any relation to Dick Tuck?" he asked.

Dick Tuck had been a political consultant and a practical joker who had loved nothing better than driving Richard Nixon crazy. In 1968, Nixon's campaign slogan was Nixon's the One. So one day when Nixon was speaking to a white bread audience, Tuck hired a very pregnant African-American woman to wander through the crowd.

She wore a T-shirt that said: *Nixon's the One.*

"Only as a kindred spirit," Tuck said. "He was the godfather of dirty tricks, I'm the future. I've got a proposition for you."

"You know my politics, don't you? I *liked* Nixon, from what I read about him."

"Sure, I know. I feel about Patti Grant the way Dick Tuck felt about Nixon."

Dix told him to come right over.

Rick Tuck looked geeky enough but barely old enough to be an Eagle Scout.

"How old are you?" Reynard Dix asked, letting the kid into his house.

"Old enough to make serious money and cause serious problems for people I don't like."

"Are you threatening me?" Dix asked.

Tuck laughed. "Don't get your tighty-whities spun around."

The kid handed Dix a certified check for twenty thousand dollars.

Manna from heaven, Dix thought. Well, breathing room anyway.

He'd no sooner slipped the check into his sport coat than he thought of the *quo* that had to go with the *quid pro*. "What do I have to do for this money?"

Tuck handed him a manila envelope. "There's a photograph in there. What you need to do is get it into the hands of whatever mainstream media goon you trust most to make the biggest splash with it. Time it so the photo goes public around mid-October."

Dix asked, "May I —"

"Look at it? Go right ahead."

The former RNC chairman did. He saw a young Jean Morrissey in bed with another young woman, lying together spoon fashion. Morrissey, raised up on one arm, was kissing the other woman's cheek. Their faces and shoulders showed, but no other bare skin. Even so, it was clear they were in love.

Dix had to sit down.

Revealing that Patti Grant's new vice president, her running mate, was a lesbian would be an October surprise that would blow the president out of the water. But who would the election go to,

Mather Wyman or Howard Hurlbert? And … oh, shit. He was going to be the cutout.

He'd be the one holding the bag, if things went wrong.

Dix looked at the kid. He was wearing horn rim glasses and a blonde wig. His buck teeth didn't look real either.

"Your name's not really Rick Tuck, is it?" he asked.

"Nom de guerre," the kid admitted.

"Is the check real?"

"Good as gold."

"So I do this, I'm stuck with whatever happens."

"You do it right, someone gives you a big job."

That was a possibility, Dix thought. On the other hand, "If I screw up?"

"If it's an honest screwup, no comeback from me. If you try to do a fakeout, I'll know, and I already have access to your bank accounts, credit cards, computers and BlackBerry so you'd probably be better off killing yourself. Of course, you could just give me that check back and forget I was ever here."

Dix kept the check.

A plain white van with mud-smeared plates picked up Rick Tuck. In ten seconds the vehicle was out of Reynard Dix's sight. Tuck was happy Dix hadn't asked where he'd gotten the picture. So many dopes wanted to know. Like he'd give away a trade secret.

It was pretty simple, really.

Millions of Americans loved to put together photo albums online. As long as the images didn't appear to be of someone getting laid or killed, the software said okey-dokey and slapped the album together. It got shipped to a mailing address and everyone was happy.

Thing was, more than a few famous people used the online album services. They didn't try to sneak anything pornographic or incriminating into their albums but they revealed plenty of dumb stuff. The pictures they thought fit to put between two covers had started divorce proceedings and ended business deals.

Rick Tuck's old man, the guy behind the wheel of the van, had been your classic low-rent gumshoe. His specialty had been cheating spouses. He'd photographed a thousand of them. Then his son Rick had come along, tech savvy as hell, and said, "Hey, Pop, let's see if these dopes take their own pictures, ones that'll cook 'em good."

He started hacking the servers of online photo album sites.

Hit paydirt first time out.

Jean Morrissey was just one big name they had on file.

Tuck et Pere had been paid a lot more than twenty grand for Morrissey's picture.

Funny thing was, they didn't know the identity of the guy who hired them.

12

October, 2012
Hillside Drive — Bloomington, Indiana

On a beautiful early October weekend, Kenny McGill and his mother Carolyn Enquist drove from Evanston, Illinois to Bloomington, Indiana. Kenny and Cassidy Kimbrough had been Skyping and e-mailing each other since their meeting at the White House. A mutual interest had developed that was clear to both their mothers and met with both mothers' approval.

The field was also cleared when Kenny and Liesl Eberhardt decided to be just friends.

A cordon of Secret Service special agents traveled with Kenny and Carolyn.

They kept a measured distance.

Close enough to be effective, not so close as to be oppressive.

Carolyn had told Sheryl ahead of time the Secret Service would be on hand.

She hoped the Kimbroughs wouldn't mind.

"We'll just pretend *we're* special enough to need them," Sheryl said with a laugh.

Cassidy had shared with Sheryl the story Kenny had told her about almost dying and being visited in his hospital room by Congressman Zachary Garner at a time when all the nurses and doctors said that would have been impossible. Kenny told her that

Garner had been one of the people who gave him the strength to go on living.

"You think that story's true, Mom? I know Kenny thinks it is, but could it really be?"

Sheryl had to shrug. "I'd like to think so, but I don't know. I've never really been religious. I like to work out my own sense of morality. Maybe that's a drawback of being agnostic. Things are always a bit uncertain, a little scary."

Cassidy nodded. "I'm the same way. So I think, maybe, it'd be comforting to have someone around who has a different way of seeing things."

"Could be," Sheryl said, thinking how some young man would soon displace her as the most indispensable person in her daughter's life.

That happened and she'd have to reexamine her own life.

When Kenny and Carolyn arrived, Sheryl served lunch.

Kenny said everything was great. "There was a time," he added, "when I'd be glad to finish anything somebody else couldn't eat."

Cassidy told him, "You look pretty slim now."

"Yeah. After I got out of the hospital, I kept reading how keeping a normal weight is a great way not to go back into the hospital. There's motivation for you."

"The scare-the-hell-out-of-you diet?" Cassidy asked.

Sheryl scolded her daughter, but Kenny said it was true.

Cassidy said, "Sounds like your diet is closely related to my waiting-for-early-college-admission-decision diet. I can hardly eat a thing lately."

"Fasting becomes you," Kenny said.

Cassidy blushed.

"Snacking probably would, too," he added.

Cassidy laughed.

"He's just like his father," Carolyn told the Kimbroughs.

After the lunch dishes were washed, a chore handled by the younger people, a tour of the IU campus was next on the schedule, to be followed later by dinner and a movie.

Sheryl suggested Cassidy show Kenny the campus without any helicopter moms hovering nearby. Carolyn agreed. Kenny took Cassidy's hand and said, "Quick before they change their minds." The two young people trotted off together.

The Secret Service detail, given advance notice this might happen, smoothly divided itself in two and with fewer agents to protect each package moved in closer.

Ten seconds later, Carolyn sighed.

"Something wrong?" Sheryl asked.

"Their timing probably."

Carolyn gestured. Kenny and Cassidy were walking now but still held hands.

Carolyn said, "Kenny tells me Cassidy is going to Stanford."

"She hopes to. She has wonderful grades, top test scores and one hell of a college essay. But who knows with selective schools? She might wind up right here. Where's Kenny thinking of going to college?"

"Georgetown. He'd like to be on campus with his sister and near his father, assuming there's a second term for the Grant administration."

The two women came to a shaded bench and took a load off their feet.

Sheryl asked, "Would you mind if I asked you a personal question?"

Carolyn smiled. "You mean, how do I feel about having been married to the man who's married to Patti Grant?"

Sheryl laughed. "Okay, we can start with that."

"I fell in love with Jim McGill the day I met him in grade school. I love him still. But when we were married, his being a cop worried me sick. I couldn't take it. I'm a much better fit with my husband, Lars, whom I love even more than Jim."

"That's good."

"Now, what question did you want to ask?"

"How well do you know Patti Grant and what do you think of her?"

Carolyn had no idea Sheryl Kimbrough was an Indiana elector.

She said, "Patti is the kind of woman another woman might look at and ask, 'Where does she get off being so rich and so beautiful? And by the way, what is my ex-husband telling me by marrying someone like her?'"

Both women laughed. Then Carolyn turned serious.

"Patti also saved Kenny's life and almost lost her own in the effort. You know how they say Secret Service agents will take a bullet for the president?"

"Yes."

"Well, I would, too. For this one."

www.pattigrantwins.com— *World Wide Web*

The craggy, world-weary face of global movie star John Marsden stared at the camera as he sat at a bar with a beer sign in the background. A click on the arrow superimposed over his image started the video. Marsden got right to the point.

"I am one lucky sonofabitch. I was feeling thirsty when I got off of work at a construction site one day. I was just a kid. So I went into a bar for a beer. Some silly bastard tried to grab the bottle the bartender had just set in front of me. A short right to his jaw told him that was the wrong move."

The memory brought a smile to the actor's face.

"Turned out the guy I clocked was the cinematographer for a movie shooting down the road. Right about then, the movie's director stepped into the bar and saw his right-hand man sprawled on the floor. He shouted, 'Who the hell laid that man out?'

"I raised my hand. Oh, yeah, I also caught the bottle of beer the guy had tried to swipe. Hadn't lost a drop. The director shouted at me, 'You know how much money you just cost me?'

"I replied, 'You know how little I care?'

"The director kinda liked that. He was a fan of attitude and ad-libbing. Never did worry too much about the health of his employee. I started to feel a little sorry for the guy I'd hit, having to work for a prick like that. So I took a drink of my beer and poured what was left on the face of the guy I'd decked to see if he'd wake up.

"He not only regained consciousness, the last few ounces went right into his open mouth. He looked up at me and said, 'Hell, that was all I wanted. You didn't have to slug me.'

"What I had to do was love a guy like that. Bob Purdy went on to shoot ninety percent of my movies. I even made four films with the director, Conrad Tucker, who I never did like. And buying rounds with those two guys in a blue collar bar was how I got into the movies.

"If you're as lucky as I am, it doesn't matter who the hell gets elected president. But if you're one of the guys I used to work construction with, if you're one of the craft people who works behind the camera on a movie or if you're married to any working stiff, it damn well matters who you give your vote for president to.

"You know why I'm going to vote for Patti Grant? Because I almost went straight home from work that day, and if I had she'd be the one looking out for my interests right now."

Marsden raised a beer bottle in salute to the president.

WorldWide News Headquarters — New York City

"Bloody brilliant," Hugh Collier said.

He'd just finished watching the rebroadcast of the Marsden video on WWN. Every major television network, broadcast or cable, had been showing it all day. Even Fox. They'd put their own spin on it, of course, saying Marsden's interests as a young construction worker weren't the same as those of the wealthy actor he was now. The fact that he'd failed to recognize the difference cast grave doubt on his political judgment.

They sure did like his movies, though.

Turning to Ellie Booker as she sat next to him in the WWN

chairman's office, Hugh asked, "What do you think of the video, Ellie?"

"On its own, it's terrific. You think about its implications, that's where things get really significant."

Hugh had spent the past week begging Ellie to come visit him in New York.

He'd told her he'd get down on his knees and do anything she liked from that position, if only she'd see him again.

She'd told him the things she liked were best accomplished from other postures by guys who had a different point of view. She did confess, though, that having someone grovel just to see her did have its appeal. Especially when that someone was the new chairman of WWN.

Sir Edbert Bickford's will had left controlling interest of his media empire to his nephew. Hugh had been shocked when the estate's solicitors in London called him the day before he'd intended to fly home to Australia. Hugh had been told him he was Sir Edbert's principal heir, and would inherit all of his uncle's stock in WWN.

Hugh had said, "Christ, when did all this happen?"

The solicitors said Sir Edbert had changed his will one week prior to his tragic death.

That was when the fog lifted. The old sonofabitch had been trying to protect himself. He shoots Hugh and dumps his body into the ocean. Then he plays the grieving father figure.

"The poor chap. So distraught over the troubles the company faced. Thinking he'd failed me. I wanted to show him how much faith I had in him. Tell him we'd emerge victorious and go on to even greater glory. That the keys to the kingdom would soon be his. If only I'd told him when I had the chance."

No doubt Uncle would have managed to produce a crocodile tear or two.

No one would ever think he'd murdered the nephew he'd just made his heir.

Then Sir Edbert would be beset by another tragedy as he discovered Hugh had been the misguided soul who'd bribed officials in the U.S., the U.K. and around the world. Poor, poor Sir Edbert. Best to let him off the hook with a token fine and let him wallow in his misery.

Of course, the inheritance might have been seen as a motive for Hugh to kill his uncle, if anyone could prove he'd known about it. Hugh quickly arranged for a lie detector test to be administered to him with police officials looking on. Other than the control questions used to establish the baseline for an honest response, Hugh had allowed only one query: Had he known that he would inherit the bulk of Sir Edbert's estate before his uncle had died?

He answered no and that was shown to be a truthful response.

Sir Edbert's solicitors swore that they had not communicated the recent change in Sir Edbert's will to Hugh Collier.

There was no physical evidence that Hugh had done anything other than try to save his uncle after he fell into the Potomac River. There was no one to contradict him when he said Sir Edbert had been on the balcony of his stateroom when Hugh went inside to get himself a drink, and when Hugh had returned Sir Edbert was gone.

Hugh had no idea of how his uncle had gone over the side.

Only saw him flailing in the water when he looked.

Pleading ignorance, he had no details to keep straight.

There was no way for a clever detective to trip him up.

In short, he was now golden.

"What are the implications and when do things get significant?" Hugh asked Ellie.

"The big implication is that Putnam Shady is emerging as a political mover and shaker. First, he launches a lobbying fund for the common man, ShareAmerica. Next, he gets Darren Drucker, the third richest man in the world to set up a liberal Super-PAC, Americans for Equity. Then he persuades the ad agency with the best reputation in the country for doing creative work to sell Patti Grant's candidacy. Still not done, he talks Drucker into starting his own broadcast network."

"It helped that Drucker owned twenty TV stations already," Hugh said.

"Yes, it did, but Drucker didn't put them together for a purpose other than earning money until Shady came along."

Hugh smiled. "I can't help but like that chap's name."

"Just wait until he starts eating WWN's lunch. See how you like him then."

"Point taken. What else do you see for our future?"

Ellie said, "The president's campaign is showing us television will go the way of the printed book. It will continue to exist, but it will play second fiddle to Internet video, the same way hardcover novels have fallen behind ebooks in sales and consumer preference."

Hugh steepled his hands and looked over them at Ellie.

He said, "Name your price, Ms. Booker."

She smiled and answered, "Freedom."

Hugh understood that. Once Sir Edbert had died and the trumped up documentation that Hugh had been WWN's bribemaster had been disposed of, he'd paid a fine of a hundred million dollars to the government with no admission of guilt. That ended the DOJ investigation and the feeling of relief had been immense.

Hugh had also passed the word throughout the company that he'd chop the balls off any employee who ever paid a bribe to anyone.

Then he'd set about rebuilding the news organization that Ethan Judd had stripped bare. He followed a two-prong approach. He brought ten of the most esteemed names in television news out of retirement and hired scores of the brightest journalism school graduates from around the country. The network still used too much filler but it was coming on strong.

He'd even been able to sell off the contracts of Mike O'Dell and the other mad dogs who'd been hired to staff WorldWide News in Review. Satellite News UK, SNUK, was launching a new division, Satellite News America, SNAM. They'd snapped up the whole motley crew.

The competition in TV news would be fiercer than ever in the coming years.

That was why Hugh felt he had to have Ellie Booker on board.

"Financially rewarding freedom?" Hugh asked her.

"Beaucoup bucks, yes. You pay on delivery. I remain an independent contractor."

"We always get first look," Hugh said.

"Unless you pass on two consecutive projects."

"You promise not to bring me any poison-pill projects."

"You promise not to pay any other independent source or in-house employee more than you pay me."

They shook hands on the deal. Ellie passed on drinking to it.

After she left, Hugh looked at the portfolio of television pilots Uncle had commissioned. Only one stood out. *Woman in Command* by Carina Linberg. The story of a female Air Force pilot who blasted her enemies to bits. Metaphorically or otherwise. He liked it.

Felt the market for tough women dramas would continue to grow.

He took a phone call just before leaving for lunch.

Former RNC Chairman Reynard Dix had a photo he said Hugh should see.

"I'm afraid we don't do that sort of thing anymore," Hugh said.

He gave Dix the name and phone number of a chap at SNAM.

The White House

McGill told Edwina Byington he could wait to see the president this time. The president was meeting with the vice president, the Democratic Congressional leadership and her chief of staff; the meeting had been unscheduled and was very urgent. McGill knew better than to ask what was up — most of the time.

With Todd and Crosby on the loose, though, the thought occurred to him those two pricks might take it to mind that a bit of domestic terrorism could be just the thing to disrupt the hunt for them and maybe even distract his Secret Service protection.

He asked Edwina, "Nobody's been setting off bombs, have they?"

The president's secretary shook her head.

"It's not that bad, but it is serious." Edwina looked around to make sure no foreign potentate or tabloid reporter was drawing hear. Seeing the coast was clear, she beckoned McGill to come within whispering distance. He complied.

"It's political," Edwina said. "An October surprise. Targeting the vice president."

McGill sighed. This damn town, he thought.

Having shared one confidence, Edwina gave McGill another nugget.

"Before this meeting, the attorney general was in with the president."

McGill held up a hand. He didn't want to know. He took a seat.

Thirty minutes later, doing nothing more than sitting and staring off into space, trying to work out his own problems, McGill was starting to make Edwina fidgety.

"Is there something I might help you with, Mr. McGill?" she asked.

He said, "I'd like to see a certain Marine, have him come here. I don't know whether I should make the request of the commandant of the Marine Corps or the secretary of defense."

"I'd think the commandant. It would be better form to respect the individual service branch if it's not an overarching matter."

"No, it's nothing that big. You have the commandant's phone number?"

"Of course." Edwina hesitated before asking, "Is this something of which you'd think the president would approve?"

McGill thought Patti would go along, if not approve.

He told Edwina, "Chances are, yes. If not, I'll take the heat."

Edwina looked as if she were offering up a silent prayer. Then she asked, "Would you like me to make the call for you?"

"I would."

Edwina called the commandant's office at the Pentagon. She was put through immediately.

"General Abel, this is Edwina Byington at the White House calling on behalf of James J. McGill. Do you have a moment to speak with Mr. McGill, sir? Thank you."

Edwina extended the phone to McGill. He took it.

She whispered the general's name to McGill. "Patrick Abel."

McGill nodded and said, "General Abel, thank you for speaking with me, sir. I was wondering if I might have a few hours with one of your men, First Sergeant Ciro Vasquez. I met him last year when he was stationed at Camp David."

The commandant asked if he might know why McGill wanted to see Vasquez.

"Certainly. I want to know if First Sergeant Vasquez would like a rematch."

DOJ Press Room — Washington, D.C.

Attorney General Michael Jaworsky stood behind a lectern at the front of a packed Department of Justice press room. Deputy Attorney General Linda Otani stood to his right. To Jaworsky's left was a forty-two inch flat screen television.

The Grant administration had its own October surprise.

One whose timing had been anything but planned.

An announcement that legitimately could not be put off until after the election.

"Good afternoon," Jaworsky said. "The federal government was provided with information that led to the arrest this morning of thirteen people on charges of first degree murder, capital murder, conspiracy to murder and destruction with the use of explosives.

"More specifically, the individuals who will be named are charged with the bombings of medical clinics in Wisconsin and Ohio. Both of these facilities provide legal terminations of pregnancies. In the Wisconsin bombing, a security guard was killed. He was married and the father of three children. In the Ohio bombing, a nurse staying on the premises late to catch up on her paperwork was killed. She was the single mother of two children, both under five years of age."

Jaworsky paused to take a sip of water.

"All the persons taken into custody surrendered peacefully. No harm came to them or to the special agents of the FBI who made the arrests. The evidence recovered not only connects the people taken into custody to the Wisconsin and Ohio bombings, it also shows they planned to continue their bombing campaign, despite knowing they were already responsible for the deaths of two people.

"After consulting with the president, I will take the unusual step of telling the American people now that their government will not seek the death penalty for these defendants, even though the heinous nature of their crimes make that a legal option."

The attorney general saw that every newsy in the room was wondering why capital punishment was being taken off the table. He would have been disappointed if they hadn't been curious. He had an explanation he wanted to sell them.

"The reason we are not seeking the harshest punishment available is that both the president and I do not want to see this chain of tragedies claim any more lives. Murder must be punished severely and we will seek sentences of life imprisonment without the possibility of parole, but the government does not wish to add to the body count.

"Deputy Attorney General Otani will now provide you with the names of those people arrested and the charges that have been brought against them. Neither she nor I will answer any questions. All the information we are prepared to share at this time is contained in the press releases you will be given."

Jaworsky was telling them they shouldn't ask whether Erna Godfrey had provided the information that led to the arrests. Erna's betrayal of her former comrades in zealotry had resulted in a problem for the Bureau of Prisons. There was no doubt her actions would make her a target for death. But the system didn't have anywhere to put her that would be safer without also being a far harsher place to live.

For the time being, a special detail of correctional officers watched over her.

The attorney general looked on from the sidelines for a moment as his deputy ran down the names of the people arrested that morning. Three of them claimed the title reverend. Two of the pastors looked penitent in their booking photos; one was clearly defiant.

Jaworsky wondered if any of the reporters was smart enough to see the other half of the strategy for announcing that he wouldn't seek the death penalty. There was a presidential election right around the corner. A new administration might not be so lenient in its approach.

The death penalty might be more politically appealing.

That point would be made clear to those with their lives on the line.

The hope was most if not all the defendants would cop a plea.

Wrap up this awful mess before the administration either left office or started a new term.

The White House

First Sergeant Ciro Vasquez wasn't able to make it to the White House until the following morning. When he entered the White House exercise room McGill extended a hand to him. Vasquez, wearing combat boots, utility pants and a green T-shirt with the word Marines on it, gave him a look. Then he shook hands.

"You have a good trip, First Sergeant?" McGill asked.

"Military transport, sir. It's familiar."

Vasquez had come from Okinawa, his posting after requesting a transfer from Camp David.

"What I'm curious about," McGill said, "is whether you're well rested and not hungry."

"I'm good, sir."

"Still pissed off at me?"

Vasquez repressed a flip answer. He was in the White House, and there were two women watching him and McGill. One blonde, one dark haired.

"Permission to speak frankly, sir?"

"Of course."

"No, I'm not pissed, but I am a guy who likes to even the score."

"Maybe even come out ahead?"

"Yes, sir."

"Why'd you try to brain me?"

Vasquez shrugged. "Just a reaction. After seeing what you did to Captain Wolford."

"You know that Captain Wolford is doing just fine now, right?"

"Yes, sir. He's stayed in touch. You don't mind my language, he told me I was a dick for not accepting your invitation to Thanksgiving dinner at Camp David last year."

"You were. So how are your hands?"

"Both good, sir." Vasquez extended his fingers, curled them, brought them back out.

McGill nodded. "All right, First Sergeant, here's the reason I had you travel halfway around the world. There's a guy looking to kill me. I made sure he's good and mad at me, too. I don't know if he was ever in the military, but he was a field op for an intelligence agency so there might be some overlap in training. What I'd like to do is spar with someone else who has a gripe with me. You came to mind. I'll use my shillelagh. You'll use a shillelagh, a staff and ... we never did get to the knives last time. Do you know how to use them?"

Vasquez nodded, allowing himself a small smile.

McGill said, "We'll go at each other hard. Injuries are acceptable. Fatalities are not. Agreed?"

"Yes, sir."

"I bet you've been studying my stick work. Looking at videos and whatnot."

Vasquez frowned, as if McGill had spoiled his surprise.

"Yes, sir. I saw some stuff, but none quite like yours."

"Well, let's get started. Maybe you can pick up a few tricks."

Without taking his eyes off the Marine, McGill said, "Margaret?"

Sweetie tossed a shillelagh to Vasquez. He caught it neatly, attacked immediately.

The session lasted ninety very hard minutes. McGill used only the stick, Vasquez changed weapons, showing a natural feel for the long staff. Both of them had bruises splashed from ankle to shoulder. McGill had a black eye. Vasquez had a broken nose. McGill would have had a slash on his left arm, probably disabling, if the knives Vasquez had used didn't have plastic blades.

Both men were breathing hard and the floor was getting slick with blood from Vasquez's nose when McGill called a halt. Elspeth gave the Marine a look of warning: no late hits. Sweetie was doing the same. Vazquez politely gave Elspeth his plastic knives.

Flashed McGill the peace sign and a grin.

Told him, "You sure know some tough ladies, sir."

McGill saw the toughest of them all enter the room.

Vasquez turned his head and saw the president. He snapped to attention.

"At ease, Marine," the commander in chief said. "Did you give my husband a good run for his money?"

"Yes, ma'am. A real good run."

"He's holding up all right for an older man?"

"Probably need some ibuprofen, ma'am. Otherwise, he's holding up fine."

"You came here from Okinawa?"

Clearly, Patti had spoken with Edwina.

"Yes, ma'am."

"Take seventy-two hours leave before you fly back."

Vasquez gave a picture perfect salute. "Yes, ma'am!"

The president handed the first sergeant a fresh tissue.

"Try not to bleed too much on your way out."

"Yes, ma'am."

The president opened the door and everyone except McGill filed out.

"You are a sight," she told McGill.

"I do my own stunts."

"You'll also do your best not to get hurt?"

"I'm still willing to have Elspeth shoot people for me."

"Good. Will you join me for lunch in the residence, after you clean up?"

"I will. I'd like a couple of steaks."

"One for your eye?"

"Exactly."

When McGill got out of the shower, starting to feel the hurt, there was an envelope waiting for him on the vanity. In it was a note from Vasquez, penned by Elspeth. The Marine had talked with the Secret Service agent. Elspeth had given Vasquez a rough idea of the guy McGill was baiting. Based on that information, the Marine offered a few ideas as to the kinds of weapons someone like that might use.

A very helpful guy, Vasquez, when he wasn't trying to kill you.

The Residence

Patti was having a Cobb salad and White House ice tea for lunch.

McGill had a steak and a baked potato. A Goose Island Lager for lubrication. He was going to have a hot fudge sundae, too. He'd worked out hard enough to pile on some calories.

"You came to bed last night after I was asleep and you got up before I was awake," McGill told Patti. "Either that or you didn't come to bed at all."

"I did, but I was very tired and you were sleeping peacefully."

"You can always wake me. Any time you need to talk, I'm happy to lend an ear."

"I wasn't ready, but I am now."

But she wasn't, not for another two minutes by the count McGill kept in his head.

"This time," Patti finally said, "it's Vice President Morrissey's turn to be … slandered would only be the legal term. She's being mischaracterized in a way that will play on some people's prejudices, and will make too strong a denial anger other people. The intent is not only to cost us votes but also to play people off against each other. The hoped for result would leave the country more divided and antagonistic than ever."

McGill was physically drained but he felt his temper rise nonetheless.

"What happened?" he asked.

"Someone found — or stole, as Jean put it — a private photo belonging to the Morrissey family. Taken at face value, it shows Jean at age eighteen in bed with another young woman. There's barely any skin showing. There is certainly no sexual contact taking place. There is a kiss, though. Jean kissed the cheek of her sixteen-year-old cousin, Molly, who was like a kid sister to her. She did it to comfort her. Molly died a month after the photo was taken … She died of leukemia."

McGill felt as if he'd been hit harder than any blow Vasquez had delivered.

"Bone marrow transplant wasn't as effective or accessible thirty years ago," Patti told him.

"Sonofabitch," McGill said.

"Indeed."

"How are you going to hit back?"

"We're going to try to preempt."

Patti told McGill that Hugh Collier had quietly passed the photo to Aggie Wu. It had been offered to him. He'd passed on it without having seen it. Then he'd thought maybe he should take a look. He requested a copy. When he saw what he had, he'd turned it over to the White House press secretary and warned her that another copy might have gone to Satellite News America.

That news outlet would soon be hearing from the office of the United States Attorney for the Southern District of New York. An assistant U.S. attorney and special agents of the FBI would have a judge's order to seize the stolen photo.

What both McGill and Patti knew but neither of them said was there could be thousands of copies of the photo in circulation by now, and once it hit the Internet, the ballgame was over. Everyone in the world would have the opportunity to see Jean Morrissey's private act of kindness and misinterpret it, if they so chose.

"Who started passing out the pictures?" McGill asked.

"As far as we know right now, Reynard Dix, the little weasel I handpicked to cast the conservative voices on a certain Internet talk show."

McGill extended his hand to Patti, trying to transfer to her what little strength he felt at the moment. She took it and held tight for a moment. Then she let go.

"Hold a comforting thought for me," she said. "I'll be back tonight before you go to sleep. Between now and then there's a presidential debate waiting for me."

McGill had planned to attend the debate, but with his new black eye ...

Greenberg Theatre, American University — Washington, D.C.

The debate between President Patricia Darden Grant and former Vice President Mather Wyman had reached the end of its first hour. The moderator was the university president Dr. Vincent O'Neal. His function was to see that the debate kept to the mutually agreed upon ground rules.

The debate would last for two hours. There could have been as many as eight topics of fifteen minutes duration or there might have been one topic of debate that consumed the entire two hours. As it was the candidates decided to give thirty minutes each to the economy and national defense. As he had at every fifteen-minute interval, O'Neal asked whether the two candidates wanted to continue with the topic being debated or move on.

Both candidates had to agree to continue a topic already under debate.

Representatives of the two campaigns had compiled the list and sequence of the topics to be debated. In the second and final presidential debate, the topics would be selected by the public. Otherwise, the structure would follow the same rules.

O'Neal was tasked with making sure neither candidate tried to dominate the discussion either by the raising of a voice or the status of current government position. Given the mutual respect between the president and her former number two, O'Neal had to rap no knuckles in the first hour.

The debate was streaming live on the Internet and was available to any broadcast entity on the planet that cared to televise it. The estimated viewing audience for the evening was well over a billion people worldwide.

O'Neal introduced the third point of debate. "What role does personal character play in determining whether a president is a success or a failure? Please specify the elements of character you feel are most important and tell the country how you exemplify those traits better than your opponent."

Wyman said, "Courtesy is very important, and that's why I insist the president go first."

The audience in cozy Greenberg Theatre laughed.

Patti gave them time to enjoy the moment.

Then she said, "Thank you, Mather, but I believe it would have been more courteous to ask me if I'd like to go first."

The president got her own laughs and more than a few female cheers.

"I would happily have said yes. So with your kind permission I will begin."

Wyman gestured for her to proceed.

Patti looked past the cameras at the people in the audience. "The most important quality for any president to have is bedrock courage. When you ask to assume responsibility for the welfare of more than three hundred million people you cannot be timid."

She turned to Wyman. "Mather Wyman is a courageous man. When I had to invoke the twenty-fifth amendment and hand the powers of the presidency over to him, I felt confident that he would do a fine job and he did. He put a swift end to an act of lawlessness at the Salvation's Path Church in Virginia, and he did so with a minimum of force and no lives lost. I applaud what acting President Wyman did."

Patti Grant put her hands together and the audience followed with enthusiasm.

Wyman, however, knew that criticism would not be lagging far behind.

"There are other kinds of courage, however," the president said, "and that's where I think I have the upper hand. Half the world's population — the female half — knows it takes real bravery to think you can win a job that only men have ever held. To make a plan to do that, to put in the backbreaking work and to come out on top, you have to wake up fearless and go to bed just as resolute. There's no end to the people who will tell you it just can't be done. You've got to have the courage to prove them wrong. As president, you also face a multitude of voices — many of them in Congress — who tell you the things you want to do to help the American people just can't be done. You've got to have the courage to prove them wrong, too."

The audience applauded loud and long.

Both Patti and O'Neal knew it was time to let Wyman have his turn.

He got off to a good start by being gracious.

Wyman said, "Never doubting for a moment that all the president's words were completely sincere, let me say she's a hard act to follow."

The laughter was loud enough to sound bipartisan.

"Courage is essential to any president who hopes to succeed, and let me commend the president for saving the life of young Kenneth McGill. As we all know, Patricia Darden Grant put her own life in peril to save her stepson."

The round of applause was for the president, but it also helped everyone warm up to Wyman.

He went on, "As important as courage is, I think judgement matters more. A president has to be able to see the whole world while understanding the circumstances of any given American, any of you here with us or the millions of us across this great land. Individually, collectively and even globally, the president has to understand the world he confronts and choose the best way forward."

The president made a note. It was a subtle movement, but Wyman paused to look at her. He knew the moment he did it that he'd made a mistake. His reaction was that of a subordinate looking to see what the boss was doing.

Trying to recapture his thoughts and regain his rhythm, Wyman took a drink of water.

"In my view," he said, "I have the better sense of judgment. It comes from experience. Some might call the way I look at things practicality. Sounds pretty boring but it avoids taking unnecessary risks, the kind that might cause the economy to melt down and throw people out of work. It refrains from sending our armed forces to fight other people's conflicts. It focuses on providing life's basic necessities, because once we have what we need to get by then we have the freedom to dream, to reach for more distant opportunities that require not just our skills and talents but also our passion.

"When the president speaks of courage, she's also talking about daring. She dared to run for the presidency and won. Her place in American history was assured by that victory. But since then she's also dared to leave the party that helped to make her the president. She's now running on the opposition party's ticket. It's reasonable to assume she would finish out a second term as a Democrat, but precedent says that's not a sure thing.

"If the people here and across the country want to elect a Democrat, the president is your candidate. But if you want someone you're sure will still be a Democrat at the end of the next four years, you might be out of luck."

The Wyman partisans in the auditorium applauded.

The Grant partisans waited nervously to hear what their candidate had to say.

"Vice President Wyman's memory is off just a bit. The way the last presidential election went, I won more votes from independents and Democrats than Republicans. Certainly, there were Republicans who voted for me and I thank them for that. I had hoped the party would rally around me, but opposition from Republicans in the House during my first term only grew in intensity.

"In the words of one senior GOP member of Congress, I was 'an accidental president.' If it hadn't been for the sympathy vote I received after my dear first husband, Andy Grant, was killed, I never would have been elected."

The crowd booed that assessment. O'Neal asked them to remember their manners.

The president continued, "I was asked by the former head of the Republican National Committee if I planned to run for reelection. At the time, my favorability rating was sixty-three percent, but my own party, of that time, didn't assume it might be good for them or for me to want a second term. I think it's fair to say my former party left me before I left it.

"If you look at Mather Wyman's record both as the governor of Ohio and as a member of that state's legislature, you'll see his positions on several important issues were well to the left of where the Republican Party is today. I think it would be a serious error of *judgment* to think the Republicans in Congress will rally around their current nominee any more than they did for me. Either Mather Wyman will toe the hard right line or he will become a figurehead."

O'Neal looked as if he was about to toss the ball back to Wyman but —

Patti said, "Just one more thing, please. Speaking on the matter of judgment, Vice President Wyman said that a president has to understand the world he confronts and choose the best way forward. From my experience in the Oval Office, I can say sometimes there is no best way forward to choose. Sometimes you have to *create* a new way forward. That's where courage is required. The same kind of courage Democrats had when they made me their nominee, and as long as they continue to show that bravery I will be with them to the finish and every inch along the way."

Patricia Darden Grant's backers jumped to their feet and applauded.

She gave Mather Wyman a cool look and he knew just what it meant.

By bringing up his days in Ohio, she had reminded him he'd told her he was an Eisenhower Republican. That same day, he'd told her he was gay.

The president would not break her promise and expose him, but her paean to courage was her way of telling him he didn't even have the guts to let the voters know who he truly was.

The remainder of the debate did not go well for Mather Wyman.

Howard Hurlbert chose not to take part in the presidential debates. In truth, Tom T. Wright decided he would not participate. He knew his handpicked candidate would not be able to speak extemporaneously on the same level as his opponents. He'd been groomed over his long career in politics to regurgitate talking points. At best, he'd sound stiff. At worst, he'd remind people he was still looking for a running mate.

The joke going around the country had it that Howard Hurlbert's vice president would be the guy right behind the last man drafted by the NFL.

Tom T. figured the best way to present Howard to the voting public on debate night would be at a party in his New Orleans' bar where there would be plenty of free food and drink, and folks would be feeling real happy. The debate between the president and

Mather Wyman would be on TV sets throughout the bar. Howard would offer his responses to points made by Patti Grant and Mather Wyman.

Not that he'd come up with his own jokes or observations. His lines were being fed to him via the iPad he held in his hands. They came from a poly-sci professor who hadn't quite made tenure and a standup comic fresh out of rehab, working from Tom T.'s office.

As an act, it went over just fine with the crowd at the bar. To reach a wider audience in the desired demographic, Tom T. had pursued his own innovative media strategy. He'd bought time on the Real Movies for Real People Channel. RMRP featured a lot of early Eastwood, early Arnold and Sylvester and everything Vin Diesel had ever done.

Howard Hurlbert, broadcasting live from New Orleans, was a hit with action movie fans, too.

RMRP started playing unpaid reruns and offered Hurlbert free time to do five more broadcasts from New Orleans before Election Day.

Inevitably, his YouTube video went viral.

Several brewers and distillers vied to become official campaign sponsors.

Tom T. told them to wait just a little while.

McGill Investigations, Inc.

With the presidential election less than two weeks away, McGill, Sweetie, Elspeth, Daryl Cheveyo and Byron DeWitt were trying to work out the best way to lure Damon Todd and Arn Crosby into a trap without McGill or anyone else getting killed. All of them were sure that overconfidence on the part of the bad guys would no longer be one of their advantages.

There were other problems, too. The possibility still existed that Crosby might go after Sweetie first, hoping to make people look the wrong way at the wrong time. Everybody else McGill cared about had protection by the platoon.

Celsus Crogher had even been dispatched to Evanston to over-see the Secret Service detail that worked with the Evanston PD to protect Kenny, Caitie, Carolyn and Lars. In years past, none of the McGill children liked SAC Crogher, but a call home had reassured McGill things had changed.

Crogher, he'd been told, had mellowed. *Mellowed?*

Caitie had even told him, "Dad, you should see the way this guy can dance."

McGill wondered what the hell was going on.

The problem with an attack on Sweetie was countered by having Deke Ky become her constant companion. He was the only Secret Service special agent Sweetie would agree to have in her hip pocket, as she put it. She said Deke was also the only one, except maybe Elspeth, she trusted not to shoot her by mistake if a gunfight broke out.

Deke told her, "Stop it, Margaret. You'll make me blush."

DeWitt said that with a shove from the president the National Reconnaissance Office had eyes in the sky watching McGill's office building, using software developed by another spook shop to detect the presence of vehicles or individuals surveil-ling it as a potential target.

"So far, no one has given your building more than a passing glance," DeWitt said.

Dikki Missirian, McGill's landlord, had been used as a lure by Damon Todd the last time he and McGill had clashed. So now at McGill's expense, Dikki's Armenian cohort of personal security had off-duty Metro cops backing them up.

What had to be worked out now was how to draw Todd and Crosby out into the open. That and how much space to give McGill to make the bad guys confident they could take a crack at him and get away. McGill wanted more elbow room; Elspeth wanted to give him less.

While they wrangled about that there was also the problem of finding a suitable Secret Service decoy for Chana Lochlan. Coming up with a woman who could shoot, fight, and pass for someone once known as the "most fabulous face on television" was no easy task.

Then the genuine article walked in, looking as fabulous as ever. Deke asked right off, "You know how to shoot, Ms. Lochlan?"

Chana told him, "As a matter of fact, I do."

Chana informed McGill and the others, "It was part of my therapy. I've always been athletic, so learning hand-to-hand self-defense came naturally. I even got Graham to take jeet-kun-do lessons with me. He's pretty good, too. But after what Dr. Todd had done to me, I still felt vulnerable. My therapist had worked through her own issues, ones similar to mine, and told me she had learned to shoot. She said she never carried her weapon, but having it at home, knowing she could hit what she wanted to, reassured her. I tried it. It helped me, too."

Everyone in the room looked at Chana.

"What?" she asked.

McGill told her, "A good cop hates putting civilians at risk."

She replied, "You've told me I'm already at risk. That's why Graham and I have been in hiding all this time. We're tired of it. I felt liberated when you asked me to raise my public profile to see if we could trap him. Finally, I was being proactive. I came here today to see if there was something more I could do."

Sweetie asked, "Is Graham downstairs? Do you have a body-guard with you?"

Chana shook her head. "Graham is at our home in California. He said if anything happens to me, he'll call on some very danger-ous friends and they'll hunt Dr. Todd down like a dog. I thought it would be better if I helped you get the job done."

"So you came here alone?" McGill asked.

"Got in my car and went for a drive, like anyone else," Chana said. "But I am armed."

The others looked at one another.

Daryl Cheveyo brought up a point he'd meant to raise earlier. "It's possible the man working with Dr. Todd, a former undercover intelligence operative, could be feeling suicidal. He might attack without regard to his personal safety."

Chana shrugged. "I'm not an expert, but shouldn't that make him easier to kill?"

Old Canton Road — Jackson, Mississippi

Bobby Beckley's house went for north of a million dollars. In some places, that price tag would buy a starter house or even a tear-down. In Jackson, it had bought Bobby five bedrooms, three fireplaces and a forty-foot pool on two acres of manicured lawn and custom landscaping. Five minutes by golf cart from the first tee. Bobby didn't have to worry about losing his Southern mansion because he'd paid cash for it, and had numbered accounts in four different countries.

He could have sat back, sipped bourbon and had a different hooker delivered every night for the next forty years. He partook of all those pleasures and hustling suckers out on the golf course, too. But that wasn't enough for him.

He wasn't happy unless he was messing with people on a grand scale.

There was no place better for doing that than Washington, D.C. The combination of nation-building sums of money, hordes of people who were greedier than they were smart and the pretense that each scam was for the benefit of the public provided everything a cynical predator could want.

Bobby had no intention of resting until he was back in the thick of it. To help him in his efforts he was funneling money to a kid who'd lived in a house a quarter-mile down the street. Rupert was a smart boy who'd earned his degree in chemistry from Tulane, graduating with honors. He'd approached Bobby about getting in on the ground floor of a great business opportunity.

Bobby knew a shitter when he heard one, and he'd learned of Rupe's academic major from his boastful father on the golf course. He'd also heard about the kid's run-ins with the law, ones that had been made to disappear by Daddy's money and lawyers.

The boy wanted Bobby to provide seed money for a meth lab. Being involved with the manufacture of illegal drugs was something he couldn't have gotten away with even when he'd had Howard Hurlbert to protect him. Hell, you couldn't even skate on beating up your old lady these days.

So Bobby took a pass on going into the meth trade, but he had a counterproposal. What the world needed, he felt, were recreational drugs made entirely from chemicals that were one hundred percent legal. There could be a whole range of new leisure time pharmaceuticals.

Something to give you extra energy for pickup basketball, something else to make music sound extra good, something to distort your girlfriend's eyesight so she thought you had the biggest ding-dong in the world. You got your line of products patented and trademarked, hired a lobbying firm to make sure the FDA and state legislatures were on board and you'd have yourself a goldmine.

Rupe had said that was the best idea he'd ever heard. In fact, he had one project just like that already in the works. He took the hundred grand Bobby gave him and said he'd be back with a sample in two weeks. Rupe was as good as his word. He came back with a key of crystal meth he'd colored with brown food dye, sweetened with sucrose and formed into tiny tablets. He called the product Super Brown Sugar, SBS for short.

"You just pop a tab under your tongue," Rupe said, "let it melt there and it'll go right into your bloodstream, give you a real energy boost."

Bobby had been doing SBS ever since Rupe had dropped off his first batch.

Couldn't stop popping the delicious little fuckers into his mouth.

He preferred to let them melt on his tongue.

Damn, if they didn't let him work for three days straight without having to sleep. He'd used the extra time to come up with some amazing plans for getting back to Washington. Hell, for taking over the whole damn place. Now, if he could only remember where he'd put his notes.

Didn't matter. He knew where he kept his SBS. In the fridge.

He liked the taste of it better cold.

On his way to his kitchen, though, he looked out through the French doors and saw somebody lounging next to his pool. At first, he thought he might have imagined seeing a stranger in his backyard. He'd seen a few things lately that hadn't been there. His daddy, for one, who'd died more than twenty years ago in another man's bed with another man's wife.

Pure Southern Gothic.

Only Daddy had been a shadow and had disappeared when he turned a light on.

Out back, though, there was nothing but sunshine, and pressing his nose right against the glass didn't make the stranger go away. It would have been okay if he'd been a neighbor who stopped by and decided to take a nap. But Bobby had never seen this dude before — some old guy with closely cropped white hair — and when he saw Bobby, he got up off the lounge chair, whipped his dick out and peed in the pool.

Sonofabitch.

Bobby grabbed a handy fireplace poker and ran outside. He charged the intruder, the poker cocked high over his right shoulder. He meant to split the asshole's head like a ripe melon. The guy didn't seem to take the threat with the least bit of concern. He appeared to be looking over Bobby's shoulder. At the last second, the trespasser pulled a gun with a sound suppressor from under his jacket and shot.

The bullet passed so close to Bobby's head he felt it go by. He heard a grunt behind him and a body fell. Bobby skidded to a stop and turned to look. Rupe lay in a growing puddle of blood on the pool apron. In one dead hand, the kid from down the street held a gun. In the other, he held the bag of SBS Bobby had ordered.

The thought hit Bobby then. Not only was Rupe dead, the

secret of how to make SBS might have died with him. Bobby roared and whirled to smite the stranger. Only the bastard plucked the poker from his hand and shoved him into the pool.

Bobby got a mouthful of water and, from the taste of it, some pee, too.

He popped to the surface and was immediately struck by the poker the intruder threw at him. His forehead split open and blood ran into Bobby's eyes and the pool. Stunned, partially blinded and having trouble keeping his head above water, Bobby wailed, "Who are you? Why are you doing this to me?"

The intruder lowered himself into a crouch. He was a mean looking sucker.

He said, "Frank Morrissey was my guest. No one fucks with my guests' privacy."

That was it? As far as dirty tricks went, that was kid's stuff.

Bobby could not believe it ... especially when the guy took a large water-filled baggie out of a pocket. There was something moving inside it.

"What the hell is that?" Bobby cried.

"Aquatic pit viper," the intruder said. "Just a baby, but he still has a hemotoxic bite. Orients himself to blood in the water."

Bobby added to the urine content of the pool.

"No, don't. Please."

The intruder opened the baggie.

Knowing his fate was sealed, Bobby did what came naturally.

He tried to take others with him. "Roger Michaelson helped me."

The bastard dropped the snake in the pool.

"Reynard Dix, too."

Bobby tried to outswim the snake and lost.

He was bitten on the neck before he could also blame Howard Hurlbert.

Greyhound Bus Terminal — Oakland, California

Arn Crosby decided it was time for Todd and him to put some miles between them. Not stop working together. Just make sure they both didn't get caught or killed at the same time. They would stay in touch electronically. When Crosby went for McGill, Todd would be able to watch the same way they had watched Anderson, by means of a web cam.

But this time Todd would do more than observe. He'd have Crosby's back.

Warn him if he saw trouble coming. Let Crosby decide in real time whether to go for the kill or abort the mission.

The former CIA operative would lay the groundwork for his attack as he crossed the country by bus, making sure as he went that they hadn't already given away their location. Crosby suggested that Todd abandon the BMW in favor of another vehicle. Todd declined. He felt the risk at this point would be greater in obtaining a new car, and he wasn't about to buy a used vehicle from a private seller.

"You might be right, Doc," Crosby said. "Olin and I might have passed our best-used-by date while we were in The Funny Farm. If you don't hear from me in four days, you're on your own. Go after McGill or forget all about him, it won't matter to me."

Todd only nodded. The two men didn't shake hands.

Crosby got on the bus to Salt Lake City. Todd started driving to Lake Tahoe.

He thought Crosby's plan stood a better chance of success than Anderson's had. It was also more likely to result in Crosby dying rather than being taken captive. Todd had come to agree with Crosby that death would be the preferable alternative.

Todd didn't want to be incarcerated again. He didn't want to have to take refuge in another personality. If he couldn't kill McGill, if he couldn't possess Chana Lochlan, what would be the point of going on? Assuming Crosby didn't succeed, he would need his own plan to get at McGill. By the time he approached the western slope of the Sierra Nevada he thought he had an idea that might work.

He used the handsfree phone in the BMW to call the number Jaime Martinez had given him.

McGill Investigations, Inc.

After seeing how Chana Lochlan shot — very well, thank you — Elspeth Kendry still had a critical point to make. "If you draw your weapon, you use it. You don't deliver a corny speech, you just shoot."

"To kill, I assume," Chana replied.

Elspeth nodded. So did Sweetie. And Deke.

"You, too?" Chana asked McGill.

"The death panel is unanimous. No half measures now."

"All right then."

She walked out the door and down the stairs. McGill caught up with her and, shillelagh in hand to continue his bad knee ruse, was the first to step out into —

The view of a guy across the street pointing a cell phone at him, taking a picture of him and Chana standing close to one another in the building's doorway. The guy was grabbed at the corner of the block by two Secret Service agents and thrown into the back of an unmarked car. He was gone in a matter of seconds.

But well after he'd have been able to empty a clip of ammo into McGill and Chana if he'd been carrying an automatic weapon instead of an iPhone.

"Not reassuring," McGill said. His body mike was supposed to pick up his every word.

He opened the back door of his Chevy and let Chana enter the back seat of the armored vehicle first. Leo was just putting his Beretta back in its holster as McGill got in and closed the door behind him. He said, "Damn near plugged that fool, boss."

"Won't happen again." Elspeth's voice told McGill through his ear bud.

That made him feel better than if she'd said sorry.

Elspeth sounded pissed and was undoubtedly going to chew some Secret Service ass.

That made McGill feel better, too.

"You still up for all this?" he asked Chana.

She tapped her chest with a fist. Like everyone else she was wearing body armor.

"He'd have gone for center mass, right?"

"If he knew what he was doing."

"You're right. It's the klutzes that'll kill you." She gave McGill a smile. "No harm, no foul. Let's hope the picture that jerk took turns out blurry."

With that, they set off on an *ordinary* day of work for a television journalist. With a presidential election drawing near, Chana was putting together an hourlong show on people who weren't going to vote, asking them why not and what might get them to change their minds and cast a ballot. They'd meet up with a camera operator and a sound man and start shooting interviews around town.

McGill would make sure Chana didn't try to chat up Arn Crosby or Damon Todd, and watch out for incidental hazards. All would go well.

A moving ring of Secret Service agents encircled them, Elspeth Kendry would exercise her judgment as to just how tight the cordon should be at any given moment. She'd gotten McGill to respect her decisions by asking Margaret Sweeney, in McGill's presence, whether he'd trusted her in the days when they were both Chicago cops.

"Absolutely," Sweetie said.

Elspeth had given McGill a look that said it all. *So what's the deal, buddy, there's only one woman in the world you can trust to look out for you?*

Until that very moment, McGill's answer would have been yes.

But Sweetie was giving him a look, too, and a wise man knew when to adapt.

"All right," he said.

Now, he was hoping he wouldn't regret his decision.

He was glad Sweetie would be monitoring their every move by means of the Metro Police Department's closed circuit TV cameras. He thought it was a good idea that they had air support, too. In spite of all the backup, McGill said a silent prayer none of the good guys would get hurt.

The Peninsula Hotel — Chicago, Illinois

Todd heard from Crosby the same morning McGill and Chana had their unwanted picture taken. On his way east, Todd knew he could not return to the secluded farmhouse in Ottawa. He was also looking at things from a different point of view now. He didn't know whether he had a long-term future anymore. If he didn't, he wanted to spend his remaining time living as well as he could. So he chose a five-star hotel just off the Magnificent Mile as his place to lodge.

His room had a view that encompassed both the city's skyline and Lake Michigan. The room service was superb, and the long list of amenities included Wi-Fi. So his iPad's connection to the Internet was rock solid, and the link Crosby had sent him was plugged directly into the live transmissions of the Metro Police Department's CCTV cameras in Washington, D.C. Even better, Todd could choose which of the cameras interested him most at any given moment.

He had Crosby on the phone, both of them using throwaways.

"How did you manage to hack the D.C. cops?" Todd asked.

"I didn't. I'm not that good. But I know where to find people who are, and I had something to barter."

Todd said, "Something you can tell me?"

"At this point, why the hell not? I traded the hack for Putin's cell phone number."

"*Vladimir* Putin?"

"Yeah. How's that for fun? Olin and I got a guy out of St.

Petersburg. He wasn't supposed to have that number, but he did. Wouldn't have done us much good if dumbass Putin changed the number and his password once in a while, but he never does. Guy's arrogant like you can't believe. Thinks his security can't be cracked. Anyway, the Company and the Pentagon have been overjoyed to listen in on his calls."

"What will the people you gave the number to do with it?" Todd asked.

"Hell if I know. Maybe record all Putin's calls and sell them to the highest bidder."

"Spoil things for the CIA and the Pentagon."

"Yeah, well, fuck them, too. So you understand what I want you to do?"

"Look for McGill to show up on one of the D.C. closed circuit cameras and look for whatever kind of security he has around him. Let you know what I find."

"Exactly. As soon as you get a fix on things, I'll know how to make my move. I'd like to get this job over fast."

"You're feeling well?" Todd asked.

"I get edgy when I work. I stay wound up too long, my performance drops."

"I'll watch closely," Todd said. "I'll let you know the moment I have something."

"Thanks, Doc. Damn shame we didn't get to work together sooner. You'd have been a killer."

Todd was already that, but Crosby's compliment made him glow.

He kept a sharp eye on his iPad.

Metropolitan Police Headquarters — Washington, D.C.

Sweetie and the two techs at the Synchronized Operations Command Center knew which monitor displayed the whereabouts of McGill and Chana Lochlan. The local cops had to watch all the other monitors, too. Sweetie concentrated on just the one.

If she spotted a threat none of Elspeth's people saw, she could warn McGill directly.

At the moment, nobody saw anything menacing.

Chana was asking pedestrians in the area of Union Station if they had a moment to stop and talk with her; Sweetie could hear McGill and Chana as well as speak to them. Just about everyone Chana approached was happy to speak with her. Many of them knew of her. All of them knew they'd have a good story to tell family and friends.

Yeah, Chana Lochlan, from TV, wanted to know if I was going to vote.

And you know who was with her? The president's husband. No, really.

Lots of people were taking pictures of McGill with Chana now.

Sweetie paid close attention to Jim. He was guarding Chana. Sweetie was protecting him.

When the cluster of people around them grew thick, Sweetie could see Elspeth's special agents get right up close, too. As people moved on, the Secret Service fell back. Smart cookie, that Elspeth, Sweetie thought.

After a break for lunch, Chana would move the show to Wisconsin Avenue in Georgetown. Tomorrow morning they would be on the National Mall and then over to the Pentagon. Sweetie settled in for a long surveillance job.

Without losing focus on her task and without her beads in hand, she began to say the rosary silently, one decade after the next, losing all sense of time, banishing boredom, gathering grace.

Catholic Zen.

The Oval Office

Galia had brought the president the latest news and numbers, both being more than a little surprising. "Rosalinda Fuentes' mother was taken to the hospital this morning."

"What happened?" Patti asked. "Will she be all right?"

— Joseph Flynn —

"She had a heart attack. She's resting quietly, but you know that's no guarantee."

The president did know. Her own mother had survived a heart attack that hit her at home; the one that followed at the hospital had killed her. Patti Darden had been estranged from her mother for years, but when she'd heard the news of the first infarction, she'd gotten on a studio plane in L.A. to fly home to Connecticut. Her mother died while she was in the air.

Old wounds hurt all the more once you learned they'd never have the chance to heal.

"What has Governor Fuentes decided to do?" the president asked.

"She sent her regrets to Vice President Morrissey. She'll be unable to make the debate."

"She has her priorities right," the president said.

Only one vice presidential debate had been scheduled, for the following night.

Now there would be none.

"Please send the elder Ms. Fuentes my best wishes."

Galia nodded and made a note, even though she had already done as the president had asked.

She moved on to the next item on her list.

"The assistant U.S. attorney for the Southern District of New York reports that Satellite News America willingly surrendered the photo of the vice president and her late cousin, Molly. They said that after the print had been analyzed by their photo experts they had decided not to use it anyway."

"Something was faked?" Patti asked.

"Something was removed. A spaghetti strap. As the vice president told us, both she and her cousin were wearing nighties. They weren't nude. But when Satellite News America called Reynard Dix demanding their money back, they said he told them they wouldn't get it and he'd find someone else who would run the picture."

The president shook her head. "Have the FBI visit Mr. Dix and talk to him about being a party to a fraud. Ask the agents if they can find out who gave Dix the photo. He didn't come up with this on his own."

There was a moment of silence in the room. Both women were thinking they knew the name of the culprit, the man who hated the president more than anyone else, now more than ever, since he felt he'd unfairly been denied the vice presidency: Roger Michaelson. Neither of them was willing to say the name aloud for now.

Moving along, Galia said, "Bobby Beckley was found dead in the swimming pool at his home in Jackson, Mississippi. He'd been struck on the head, apparently with a fireplace poker that was found in the pool, but the cause of death was snake bite."

The president gave Galia an incredulous look.

"A dead water moccasin was also found in the pool. Done in by the chlorine. There was a second human body found dead of a gunshot wound at the edge of the pool. The victim was identified as Rupert Beauchamp. In a plastic bag next to his body, the police found a kilo of crystal methedrine that had been cut with sugar and food coloring and formed into small tablets. More of the same were found in Beckley's refrigerator."

"A drug deal gone wrong?" the president asked.

"That's the preliminary theory, but the snake has muddied things for the police."

"Must make life complicated for Howard Hurlbert, too," Patti said.

"He's issued a statement expressing his sorrow that a one-time friend and colleague had come to such a bad end."

"One-time being more important than the sorrow or the bad end."

"Of course," Galia said, "and that brings us to the latest poll of likely voters, and things are much closer than either of us would like. You stand at forty percent, Madam President. Mather Wyman is at thirty-four percent and Howard Hurlbert at twenty-six percent."

"How do we look for holding the six point lead through election day?"

"Everyone's support, including ours, is soft around the edges. And there's one last thing that might stir the pot. Word is that Tom T. Wright has agreed to become Howard Hurlbert's running mate. The announcement is expected to come later today. Now, we have a rich guy who's jumped into the race with *both* feet."

"You mean *another* rich person," the president said.

"Stephen Norwood expects a flood of money from Wright to give Hurlbert a big push, starting any minute now."

"I have at least as much money as Tom does," the president said. "Have Stephen let me know what he needs, and Galia ..."

"Yes, Madam President?"

"See to it that we get a bigger bang for our bucks."

The White House Residence

McGill got back to the quaint cottage he called home just after eight p.m. He hadn't been hungry at lunch, but now, after dropping Chana off and letting her small private security army take over for the night, he was starving. He called Blessing, the White House head butler, from the Chevy and asked for an extra large serving of king crab legs, a pound of shoestring potatoes, a green salad and three bottles of Bell's Lager on ice.

"Will that be all, sir?" Blessing asked.

"A slice of devil's food cake or a brownie, whatever's on hand."

"Very good, sir. When should the meal be ready and where would you like it served?"

Leo, hearing every word, flashed the fingers of his right hand three times.

"Fifteen minutes. In the residence dining room."

"Will the president be joining you, sir?"

"I don't know. Please give Edwina a call. Say I'd love to have her company for dinner. The president's, not Edwina's."

"Yes, sir."

McGill ended the call.

"Quite the life, huh boss?" Leo asked.

McGill shook his head. "Never in my wildest dreams did I foresee anything like this, Leo."

"Me either."

Patti arrived one minute before dinner did. Blessing's sense of timing, no doubt. First the head of the free world, then the food. McGill got up from the table to greet his wife with a kiss. They took their seats and dinner was served.

Would that the whole world ran so well.

Patti had used her authority as chief executive to divvy up and amend McGill's food order. She took one-third of the crab legs, two-thirds of the salad, cut the potato order in half and divided it evenly, took the brownie, gave McGill the devil's food cake and took one of the Bell's Lagers for herself.

McGill said, "I won't say I'm getting too old for all this stuff yet, but here's to the twenty-second amendment."

The one limiting a president to two terms in office.

The president and her henchman tapped their bottles and drank.

They ate in a companionable silence, each of them hungry and more than comforted by the presence of the person he or she loved most. By the time they put their forks down after dessert they were ready to discuss the rough and tumble of their respective days.

McGill went first.

"I can't say I ever wanted to be a worm on a fishing hook, but that was what I felt like today. It got to be wearing after a while. I felt like hitting someone with my shillelagh just to show I could."

"Of course, you didn't."

"Too close to the election," McGill said.

Patti laughed. "Thank you for your consideration and political insight."

She gave McGill the same run down of misfortune, death and horse race politics Galia had given to her earlier in the day.

"You're sure you want to do all this another four years?" McGill asked.

"I'm just getting good at the job, and I don't have any gray hair yet."

"Oh. I thought your stylist took care of that."

The president threw her napkin at McGill.

Cat quick, he caught it and returned it.

Patti asked, "Have I saved you from overeating?"

McGill patted his abdomen. "Svelte as a teenager."

"Randy as one, too?"

McGill smiled. "Now, I see your little plan. Amour shall not be thwarted by indigestion."

"I could use some close company tonight. How about you?"

"You know me," McGill said. "The closer the better."

The President's Bedroom

The bedside phone rang at six a.m. As usual, Patti was already out of bed and McGill had to reach across the bed and grab the damn thing. He said hello. Not even half-awake, he didn't sound like himself. Thought, God, is that what my voice will be like when I get old?

"Mr. McGill?" It was Galia.

"The last I checked," he said.

"May I speak with the president, sir?" Formal Galia.

McGill thought, Oh, shit.

"Just a minute. I'll get her."

McGill saw a sliver of light coming from under the door of what used to be the president's dressing room. The space still partially served that purpose, but Patti had cut her wardrobe in half last year and used the liberated area to do both yoga and Pilates. Darn stuff worked so well he was tempted to take it up.

He tapped on the door and when it opened he saw his wife in a black unitard flushed with excellent circulation and showing muscle tone a gymnast would admire.

"Galia's on the phone," he said. "Sounds serious."

Patti didn't whine. She sucked it up and took the call.

McGill started to head to the shower but Patti tapped the bed next to her.

Ever attentive, McGill sat. Waited to hear what the problem was this time. The presidency was the world's busiest complaint window. Maybe one term, six years like they did it in Mexico, would be long enough, McGill thought. Nobody should have to run for this job twice.

"Thank you, Galia . I'll be in the Oval Office in thirty minutes."

Patti looked at her husband and asked, "Did you know I'm a lesbian?"

"Last night's activities notwithstanding?"

"Not only am I gay but Jean Morrissey is my lover."

McGill stopped cracking wise. He knew what was coming next.

"You are just my front man. A prop to keep up appearances. You attend to your own needs, of course, with your many girl-friends. The foremost of whom is —"

"Chana Lochlan," McGill said.

Patti nodded. She told McGill the story of the stolen picture of Jean Morrissey.

"This whole cock-and-bull story came from one photo ripped off from the Internet? And it must be true because it's *on* the Internet?"

Patti kissed McGill hard. "Just one more week," she said.

Eight days, but who was counting?

McGill watched Patti run into her bathroom to shower.

He ought to be pissed, he thought, but he found an unexpected silver lining.

If every nitwit in the world was talking about this sordid sex scandal, it ought to reach Damon Todd and Arn Crosby before long.

Jealous fellow that Damon Todd was, maybe all the publicity that McGill and Chana were an item would prompt some action.

Maybe he'd get to hit someone today.

Peninsula Hotel — Chicago, Illinois

Damon Todd awakened an hour before he was scheduled to call Arn Crosby. It was still dark when he got out of bed. Lights were on in all the high rise buildings he could see from his room but the lake was a sea of blackness. He sat at the desk in the room and turned on his iPad. He'd set up Google Alerts for both Chana Lochlan and James J. McGill.

He wanted to know whatever anyone had to say about either of them, as soon as it hit the Net. He was flabbergasted, though, when he saw how much there was to choose from that morning. Nearly a hundred people had posted candid photos they had taken of Chana and McGill in Washington. Each of them was a wound to Todd.

Time had left no insult on Chana's face. If anything, it only seemed to reveal a deeper beauty. Todd longed to hold her. Explain to her how much he loved her. Tell her he'd do *anything* for her. What McGill was doing was obvious. He was protecting Chana. Todd had seen other armed bodyguards yesterday as he'd carefully watched the CCTV video. But McGill was always the one closest at hand.

He was Chana's last line of defense. So close she was able to — and did — reach out to touch McGill. Whisper in his ear. Make him smile. McGill, too, had worn well with time. The whole situation made Todd all but insane with anger.

He wanted to look down from his window and see McGill about to enter the hotel. Swoop down on him in a flying suit like a BASE jumper. Alight before a stunned McGill and do him in the worst way imaginable. He wasn't quite sure what the method of demise would be, just something agonizing and bloody.

Todd was trying to work out the exact details when his disposable cell phone rang. Crosby calling. Damn. He'd been the one who was supposed to make the call. He clicked the answer button.

Crosby said, "Something wrong?"

"Diarrhea. Must've eaten at the wrong restaurant."

Todd hoped the lie passed muster.

There was a pause, but Crosby said, "Yeah, well, that's the shits. What do you have for me?"

Todd told him, "I counted eight people, five men, three women, whom I think are Secret Service. They appeared from off camera and formed a circle around McGill and Chana any time the crowd around them got heavy. Four of them were looking at McGill and four of them were looking outward. Twice, I saw one or more of them looking up at the sky."

Crosby said, "That's real good, Doc. Tells me a lot. They've got air support and evacuation nearby. Give me all you can about what the people you saw looked like: age, hair, eyes, skin color, physique, clothing and anything else you can remember."

Todd searched his memory and was surprised by the amount of detail he was able to recall.

"Damn, Doc," Crosby said, "that is *good*."

"You think you'll be able to get to McGill?" Todd asked.

"Will he be out and about again today?"

"The National Mall in the morning. The Pentagon in the afternoon."

He'd found that information on a Google Alert last night.

"Perfect," Crosby said. "I'll get him this morning. You watch on your tablet, you'll see it. Raise a glass to my memory when you get a chance. See you in hell, Doc."

So Crosby was going to sacrifice himself to kill McGill.

He'd certainly sounded confident he could succeed.

But then so had Anderson.

Just in case things didn't work out, Todd still had Jaime Martinez on call.

He rented a car and mapped out a drive up the North Shore to Winnetka.

Reserve Drive — Dublin, Ohio

Mather Wyman was the first person outside the immediate Fuentes family to hear that Maxina Fuentes had succumbed to a second, massive heart attack in a hospital in Santa Fe. Governor Rosalinda Fuentes, her siblings, their children and numerous friends all grieved the passing of a good woman.

"I don't know that I'll be of much help before the election," the governor told Wyman. "One sorrow begets another now, and we all need comforting."

"Don't think about politics for a minute," Wyman told her. "Please accept my condolences and extend them to everyone who loved your mother. Family comes first, always."

"Thank you. I'll call back when I can."

Wyman sat alone in his house. The place was way too big for one old man. He'd have put it on the market already if he hadn't thought Kira and Welborn and their two darling girls might come to visit a few times a year. He'd need to have room for them.

He had made the time to stop in Washington and meet Aria and Callista. It almost broke his heart to see them; he knew how much his beloved Elvie would have adored these beautiful children.

Then Kira had introduced him to the infants and he couldn't hold back his tears.

"This is your Grandpa Mattie, girls. You're so very lucky to have him in your lives. He'll do all sorts of fun stuff with you. Give you your first pony rides like he did with me."

Thinking about it now, he wanted to take his own advice.

Put family first. Be a presence in his grandchildren's lives from the start.

Who the hell needed to be president anyway? Look at the outrages a person holding that office had to endure. Like the rest of the country, he'd seen the reports of the accusation that Patti Grant and Jean Morrissey were lovers, and James J. McGill was a philandering front man. The whole thing was despicable.

The official response had come from Press Secretary Aggie Wu.

She'd told the world, "The president and Mr. McGill will say no more about their marriage than they've already said. However, both the president and Mr. McGill condemn the idea that to say a person is a lesbian or gay should in any way be thought of as an insult. The measure of any person should be his or her character, and how it is expressed both publicly and privately.

"I'll make no mention of Vice President Morrissey's reaction, and take no questions concerning her, because she will be making her own statement later today.

"Mr. McGill also asked me to inform the people behind these malicious lies that he is a former police officer and currently holds a private investigator's license. He intends, after the election, to find the people responsible for spreading lies about the president and see that they are brought to answer before the appropriate court."

Wyman thought about what he'd heard. The president had condemned the idea that calling someone gay was an insult. There was a statement that was long overdue.

Would that he'd have the nerve to say the same thing, if by some chance he won the election.

But how could he, if he was still keeping his secret.

Losing the White House didn't scare him, but the chance that he might lose Kira, Aria and Callista terrified him. He had deceived Kira her whole life. There was no way he could bring himself to do the same with Aria and Callista. But what if Kira rejected him?

Well … Patti Grant had it right. If you wanted to be president or even a decent human being, it took courage.

Mather Wyman called Kira and said, "I'll be coming to Washington today. Would you mind if I stopped in for a brief visit?"

The National Mall — Washington, D.C.

"The president isn't mad at me, is she?" Chana Lochlan asked.

Like everyone else in the country, she'd heard the rumors about McGill and her.

McGill said, "No. How about Graham? Is he going to come looking for me?"

"No, he said after all you've done for me, I owe you a good time or two."

McGill grinned. "That's pretty California of him."

"He is a native, and we've been married more than three years now."

"Maybe we've taken this line of discussion as far as it should go," McGill said.

He looked around, saw the security cordon was hanging loose. There was a nip in the air of the late October morning. Tourists and locals were sparse on the ground. Kids, on a school day, were nowhere to be seen. The few people on the footpath coming their way filtered through the line of Secret Service special agents without challenge.

A harmless lot. Harmless *looking* anyway.

Disregarding Satchel Paige's advice, McGill looked back. More special agents. A few more middle-aged to elderly types out for a stroll despite the chill. The only person who stood out was a monk with a tonsure and a beard. His face was sun-browned from years of exposure. McGill thought he remembered hearing of a nearby monastery in Virginia ... Holy Cross, he thought it was.

The guy might have seemed suspicious if he'd had his cowl up, but his face was exposed and the expression on it seemed almost beatific as he worked his way through the beads of the rosary in his right hand.

McGill turned his head forward. He and Chana were heading to the Lincoln Memorial. Chana's camera operator and sound man were already there, waiting for the *talent* to show up. Even on a less than perfect weather day, Mr. Lincoln was always a big draw on the Mall. Chana was sure she'd find people to interview there.

Chana asked McGill, "You see anybody to shoot while you were looking around?"

Metropolitan Police Headquarters — Washington, D.C.

Sweetie spotted the monk behind McGill at the same moment he did. She saw something he didn't. The guy looked right, but he didn't walk right. There was no sense of humility to the way he moved. His pace certainly didn't fit with someone saying the rosary. Moving in cadence with prayer, his step should have been relatively slow and constant. You didn't rush the rosary.

This guy wasn't jogging exactly, certainly wasn't running, but he was closing the gap between himself and Jim and Chana. Hadn't the Secret Service people noticed? Or did they think the monk simply wasn't a threat?

Sweetie saw a patch over the heart of the monk's vestment.

It looked familiar but she couldn't quite make it out.

She nudged a tech. "Can you zoom in on that monk?"

She pointed to the monitor that interested her.

"Sure. How far in you want me to go?"

"Waist up. I want to see that insignia on his chest."

"No problem." Then the tech said something that gave Sweetie a chill. "That old boy's got some big sleeves on that rig of his. You could hide a country ham in there."

The patch was clear now. A black rectangle above a white rectangle. A red cross with flared ends smack in the middle. The flag of the Knights Templar. A Christian society of knights formed to fight the Crusades and to drive the Muslims from Spain. The guy on the Mall wasn't a monk.

He was a killer.

Sweetie yelled into her mike, "Jim!"

The National Mall — Washington, D.C.

One word was enough. McGill recognized both Sweetie's voice and its tone of alarm. He turned to look behind him, bringing up his shillelagh as he did. He saw a spinning object flying straight at his face. Flicking the fighting stick in an arc, he batted it aside.

McGill didn't try to see what he'd deflected because the monk he'd noticed before was sprinting toward him holding a weapon in his right hand. It looked like a hatchet with a blade on one side of the haft and a spike on the other. McGill turned sideways to present a smaller target. Blocking another throw, from a shorter distance, wouldn't be easy.

He shouted to Chana, "Run! Zigzag!"

McGill didn't want the sonofabitch to nail her with a thrown weapon.

He needn't have worried. The monk came for him. His present intent was to chop or impale McGill with his weapon. He raised his right arm high, as if hoping to bring the edged side of his weapon down through the middle of McGill's skull. The same type of strike Ciro Vasquez had attempted with his pugil stick.

This weapon, though, was more versatile. It had two ways to kill; Vasquez's note had told him about it. The thing was called a Vietnam tomahawk, and one of the favorite ploys of the men who fought with it was to get an opponent to bite on a feint from one side of the weapon, pull it back and strike backhand with the opposite side.

Forewarned was forearmed, McGill opened with a feint, too. He pretended to raise a roof over his head to stave off the attack from above, but as the monk pulled his weapon back, McGill stepped back and to his right, pulling the shillelagh to his shoulders and parallel to the ground.

When the monk's backhand swipe with the spiked end of the tomahawk came, McGill hollowed out his midsection, sucked in his gut and arched his back to make a sideways U. The spike missed by millimeters. Meeting no resistance from flesh or bone, the weapon continued onward, the momentum of the stroke turning the monk's back to McGill.

A skilled fighter could often recover from a missed blow in one fluid movement, but not if his opponent was as quick or quicker. McGill swung a backhand of his own and the knobbed end of his shillelagh connected solidly with the back of the monk's shaved head.

He dropped like he'd been shot.

Then Chana Lochlan, no retreat for her, stepped up and shot him for real.

Eyes wide she asked McGill, "Everyone told me shoot to kill, right?"

They had … and there had been no corny speech.

Peninsula Hotel — Chicago, Illinois

The sense of revelation Damon Todd felt was stupefying. Chana Lochlan — his Chana — had just *executed* Crosby. He'd seen the whole thing on his iPad. McGill, acting as if he'd just heard a warning from God, had whirled a moment before the tomahawk Crosby threw would have cleaved his skull. He knocked it aside. As if he'd practiced the trick a hundred times a day.

Crosby charged and attacked. Todd saw the opening move. Crosby looked as if he hoped to bring his blade down on the crown of McGill's head. McGill seemed as if he would parry with the stick he held and then … Todd could not reconstruct what happened next.

It all happened too fast.

It seemed as if Crosby went from targeting McGill's head to going for his gut, but somehow Crosby missed and the next thing he knew Crosby's face was in the dirt.

And then Chana appeared and delivered the *coup de grace* with a handgun.

How could she have been so cold blooded?

It chilled him just to think about it. He wanted to see a replay, sure it wouldn't show the same scene. He'd only *thought* he saw Chana kill Crosby. But the CCTV feed didn't offer replays.

He tried to find coverage on commercial television. Surely some bystander with a cell phone must have shot —

No, the pictures came from a video cam operator said to be part of the news team with which Chana had been working. The cameraman had been coming across the mall looking for Chana and had captured the whole event. But it was not all to be seen. The thrown tomahawk and the execution were left out. All the public was allowed to see, in slow motion, was McGill whacking Crosby on the head with his stick.

Even slowed down the movement was hard to follow.

Todd took two lessons away from that morning's reality television.

Chana Lochlan would never be his; she'd kill him at the first opportunity.

And he'd never best McGill at anything approaching a fair fight.

Picking up his rental car minutes later, he planned accordingly.

Indiana University — Bloomington, Indiana

Sheryl Kimbrough had been sitting alone in her classroom, thinking about how much she was going to miss Cassidy, newly admitted to Stanford, when one of her students ran in and clicked on the television.

"Ms. Kimbrough," the student said, her voice trembling, "you've got to see this."

MSNBC was playing the video of McGill whacking Crosby on a video loop.

It showed neither the beginning nor the end of the fight on the Mall.

A political commentator speaking in voice over supplied those details. It also said the dead man was a monk from Bulgaria who'd entered the country on a tourist visa. After attacking James J. McGill and being knocked to the ground by him, he'd been shot by well known television journalist Chana Lochlan.

Why the man had attacked the president's husband and why Ms. Lochlan had been carrying a gun had not yet been explained. Mr. McGill had been using a cane recently and a walking stick the past several weeks because of a sore knee.

As the rest of the class filled in around the television, Sheryl fielded a call from an excited Cassidy, speaking a mile a minute, "Mom, did you see what just happened with Kenny's dad? I got permission from school to call Kenny, but his cell phone was off. Then I realized he must be in school, too, but what if he was home with the flu or something? I called there and got Mrs. Enquist. She said Kenny's fine and his dad is, too. She said Mr. McGill knows how to protect himself like nobody's business. What she didn't understand was why Ms. Lochlan shot that guy. What she saw, Mr. McGill had already knocked him out."

Now, that's interesting, Sheryl thought.

For the moment, though, she contented herself with calming her daughter.

Getting Cassidy back into class. Getting back to her own class. The events on the Mall, though, caused the vice president to push back her announcement, and then the hour was up and Sheryl's students had to move on to their next classes.

She told them she'd record Jean Morrissey's statement and they'd discuss it next week.

A moment later, the vice president of the United States addressed the nation.

She spoke from the Vice President's Ceremonial Office in the Eisenhower Executive Office Building, located opposite the West Wing of the White House. She sat behind the desk that was first used by former Rough Rider Theodore Roosevelt in 1902. The Stars and Stripes flanked her to the right and the left. A photographic portrait of Patricia Darden Grant hung on the wall behind her right shoulder. The choice of location and furnishings was no accident.

Jean Morrissey looked formidable, and she got straight to the point.

"As I'm sure most of you have heard, some no good skunk has accused me of being the president's lover. That is a lie. The president and her husband, James J. McGill, love each other. I've seen them together and it's obvious. Anyone who knows them will tell you that's true.

"The same no good skunk also called me a lesbian. I do not consider that to be an insult, but it is also untrue. If I were a lesbian everyone would have known it long ago. People in Minnesota can tell you, I'm not one to hide my light under a bushel.

"Now, here's something I've never spoken of before because it wasn't my place to do so, but I asked for permission to say what I'm about to tell you, and I received it. My brother, Frank, my chief of staff and the finest human being I know, is gay. That isn't a secret to anyone who knows him. Frank just reached the conclusion at an early age that if straight people didn't have to take out a newspaper ad announcing their gender orientation, he didn't have to do so either.

"So allow me to recapitulate. I like men and so does my brother. That's the long and short of it. Except for one other thing. Mr. McGill said he's going to find the dirty skunk behind these lies and bring him into court. Well, you better hope he finds you first, Skunk. Because if I do, I'm going to bust your nose for you.

"Thank you and good day."

Sheryl Kimbrough smiled and applauded.

"That ought to put Minnesota in the president's column," she said to herself.

13

November, 2012
Cornell University — Ithaca, New York

McGill and Patti waited backstage at Bailey Hall. It was five minutes until curtain time. In truth, the curtain was already up. The moderator was onstage chatting with the audience. The room had once been described as having "acoustics by God and seats by Torquemada," but it had been beautifully renovated and none of those seated appeared to be squirming.

Mather Wyman would appear from the opposite wing, wave to the audience and shake the moderator's hand. Then the president would be introduced. Everyone would shake hands, wave to the audience some more and get down to business.

"Tell me again," Patti told McGill.

McGill had told her several times already, and there'd been no slippage in the president's power of recall, but when you were about to speak before the country and the world, you wanted to be sure you had everything exactly right.

McGill told Patti once more, "Chana said she thought she saw Crosby trying to get up. He still had the Vietnam tomahawk in his hand."

DNA testing had determined the *Bulgarian monk* was Arn Crosby. His fake passport and visa, it was supposed, were to be used to get out of the country if he'd somehow managed to kill

McGill and elude the Secret Service. As Crosby had brought no cloak of invisibility with him, his chances of escape were nil to less than. Still, a guy could hope.

Crosby's true identity would be revealed ... sometime after the election.

"Did you see Crosby try to get up?"

"No," McGill said.

"How hard did you hit him?"

"Very."

"Is it possible you killed him?"

"Possible, yes. Will we ever know, no."

Chana's shot entered Crosby's skull, near enough as made no difference, at the same point McGill had clubbed it. Quite the pickle for any medical examiner.

"Is it possible, Ms. Lochlan saw a movement you missed?"

"Possible, yes. Did I miss something? I honestly don't know. I was a bit keyed up, too."

"Is Ms. Lochlan suffering from PTSD?"

"Nobody's made that call yet. I think she was helped by the fact that nobody put any cuffs on her and Elspeth looked her straight in the eye and told her she'd done exactly the right thing. I called California earlier today, and Graham Keough told me she's doing well. Hopes to get back to work after the first of next year."

"What's your dimestore psychologist's view of what happened?"

"Chana hated the fact that Damon Todd had reentered her life. He represented a threat to her and Graham, and if Crosby was helping him ... maybe she wanted to see him getting up."

And who could blame her, Patti thought.

What she said to McGill was, "Thank you."

"You really think you'll be asked about Crosby?" he asked.

"I can't say, but being unprepared wouldn't do."

McGill pointed his chin at the other side of the stage. "There's Wyman."

Patti gave her former VP a polite nod. He returned it.

"He looks relaxed," McGill said. "Like the two of you are going to talk to the Kiwanis."

Patti agreed. Did her best to assess what was going on in Mather Wyman's mind.

"We'll have to see if Mather has brought his A-game tonight," Patti said.

Then it was showtime.

The format was the same as the first debate except this time the questions had come in from around the nation by e-mail. All the queries had been stored in a data base and thirty minutes before the start of the debate had been queued at random. The moderator, Anthony Winsted, the dean of the College of Arts and Sciences at Cornell, read the first question to the candidates and the rest of the world.

He said, "Ms. Helen Wagner of Holland, Michigan says, 'I'm a junior at the University of Michigan. I'm a dean's list student majoring in computer engineering. My fiancé is a senior at Michigan, a top student, and a drama major. The two of us will start our married and working lives with over one hundred thousand dollars of combined student debt and uncertain job prospects. What can either of you do to persuade us you'll keep the American Dream viable for us and all the other young people of our country?'"

Mather Wyman, having deferred to his opponent in the prior debate was first up.

The former vice president paused, as if he'd had something else on his mind, but then focused on the matter at hand. He said, "Thank you for writing, Ms. Wagner. Congratulations on your academic achievements and your upcoming wedding. You have every right to be concerned about your future. The prospects for young Americans today don't look nearly as bright as they did twenty or even ten years ago. The sad fact is the private sector of our economy is not creating enough good jobs for your generation. I have some ideas to remedy that situation. These ideas go against the recent orthodoxy of my party because they involve the federal government's participation.

"If elected president, I will submit to Congress plans for two programs aimed at creating full and meaningful employment for young people in the United States. For graduates of our colleges and universities, the program will be called America's Interns. For graduates of our technical schools, the program will be called America's Apprentices. In both cases, the federal government will pay fifty percent of your hourly wage up to ten dollars per hour for your first two years of employment. That will give smart businesses a subsidized labor force and encourage hiring. It will also give graduates a foothold in the labor market, the ability to move up in the company that hires them or the ability to move on to a company that's smart enough to scout first-rate talent elsewhere.

"In addition to providing help with salaries, the programs would also offer a dollar of credit toward repayment of student loans for each dollar earned on the job. That would enable our young people to get out from under their debts while they are still young. That would give Ms. Wagner and others the chance to buy their own cars and homes which would help the economy to expand and produce still more jobs.

"These programs will be funded by a one-dollar tax on every stock transaction that is made in the United States. That way, every time someone buys or sells securities, he or she will also be investing in our country's future.

"I have to admit, I hadn't specifically thought of drama majors, and maybe that area of endeavor would be better addressed by the president, but thinking on the matter now perhaps a third program could be added for graduates engaged in creative pursuits. We could call it America's Protégés."

Bailey Hall, the concert venue of Cornell's Department of Music, erupted in applause.

TellMeTrue.com, a website created to track national and global responses to the answers the candidates provided, both in terms of direct responsiveness to the question and appeal as a new solution to an existing problem, gave Wyman ninety-nine points out of a hundred.

The president came up to bat. "I applaud Vice President Wyman's ideas. I would happily embrace them in a second term. I would go further, though, and look at education as a whole as a means to building a good life. Between kindergarten and high school graduation, going to school each day should become an occasion for joy. College, for those who aspire to it, should be the educational adventure of a lifetime.

"To realize that vision, to provide the programs Vice President Wyman has suggested, to secure the future for Ms. Wagner, her fiancé and other young Americans, there is one reform that must come first. We must end the influence of special interest lobbyists. As long as legislation and votes in Congress can be bought by campaign contributions, the government will not serve the people.

"Giving a hand up to Ms. Wagner will never be possible as long as special interests are busy carving out tax loopholes and preferential treatment for themselves. I agree that a one-dollar tax on every stock transaction would be a fitting way to fund the programs Vice President Wyman has suggested, but that legislation will never pass Congress while Wall Street's lobbyists are on the job.

"Unless ..." The president took a dramatic pause. "Unless you, Helen Wagner, and millions of other Americans demand that the link between campaign donations and favored legislation be severed.

"I have suggested that legislation be passed prohibiting any member of Congress from voting for or advocating for any person, company or cause that has made a campaign donation to that member of Congress. I proposed that no member of Congress be allowed to become a lobbyist or adviser to lobbyists for a period of ten years after leaving office. No staffer to a member of Congress would be allowed to become a lobbyist or adviser to lobbyists for five years after leaving his or her government job. I proposed that no former member of Congress be allowed to enter the House or

Senate chamber except on ceremonial occasions.

"If I am returned to office, I will make this the first challenge I take up. Jesus said the corrupting influences of money changed the temple into a den of thieves. That's pretty much the situation in Congress today. Ms. Wagner, my fellow Americans, tell your representatives and senators to get behind lobbying reform or get out. Do it at a shout if necessary. That is the surest way to make the government work for you again and to restore the American Dream, whether Mather Wyman becomes your next president or I remain your president."

The president received an ovation to equal Wyman's.

TellMeTrue.com gave the president ninety-nine percent, too.

The debate continued through the subjects of the separation of church and state and the proper way to achieve social change: moral persuasion or the force of law. Both candidates gave detailed, thoughtful answers. Each was interrupted by applause several times. In horse racing terms, the debate looked as if it would be a photo finish.

Then came the closing statements, and the country was given something new to think about.

Mather Wyman went first. "I thank all the kind people here at Cornell for hosting the president and me tonight. I thank all the people who have worked with and for me through all my years in politics. I especially thank my beloved niece, Kira Fahey Yates, for her unqualified love, going so far as to think of me as her surrogate father, and grandfather to her and Captain Welborn Yates' dear baby girls, Aria and Callista.

"When a man or woman enters politics, he or she is supposed to make all sorts of disclosures, and I have complied with the letter of the law but not with its spirit. There is something else I must tell the American people before I can ask any of you to vote for me to be your president."

The room went completely still. Mather Wyman drew a deep

breath.

"I am … a gay man. I'm sorry it took me so long to tell you. I lacked the courage. President Grant knew my secret. I told her last year. Another competitor might have used that knowledge for political advantage. She did not. On the contrary, listening to her speak of courage at our last debate helped me to come to this decision.

"If you were to elect me to be your president, I would have to show great courage to do the job properly. I know that for a fact because for a short time I was acting president. To do the job right for four years, the president needs the support of the country. To ask for that support, he or she must be honest with you. That is what I'm doing now. I have no other secrets to conceal and I hope you will judge me on Election Day by what I want to do for our country."

There was a long moment of silence before the moderator said, "Madam President?"

Patti Grant looked at Mather Wyman and then out at the audience.

"Either of us here on this stage will do our best for you. If you choose me, you should know I will ask for Mather Wyman's wise counsel on many issues. Thank you, all."

Air Force One — En Route to Andrews AFB

After conferring with her staff, Patti took the seat next to McGill in the president's private suite. He turned off Sports Center to share the moment with his wife.

"When will you leave for Winnetka?" she asked.

"Tomorrow morning. Abbie has decided to come with me. She cleared it with her profs at Georgetown."

"They probably trust her to keep up with her work."

McGill grinned. "Yeah. She wants to cast her first vote for president at home with Carolyn."

"You know who she likes?"

"Well, it's a secret ballot, but I have my suspicions."

Patti asked, "You'll have all your security people on hand?"

"Sweetie, Elspeth, Deke, Leo and assorted hangers-on."

"I'd hate to win the election and find out something bad has happened to you."

"Me, too. It was a closer thing than I like to remember, seeing that tomahawk flying at my head."

Patti took McGill's hand. "Good thing you've got quick reflexes."

"And Sweetie warning me in time."

"And Sweetie. You think Damon Todd will make an attempt after two professionals failed?"

"The guy is smart, but he's not straight on the rails."

"You're saying he might act against his own best interests?"

"More colorfully, yes. We'll put the word out where I can be found. He'll come."

Patti didn't ask what the outcome would be for Todd. She didn't want to know.

"You're not upset I didn't tell you about Mather Wyman?"

McGill wanted to know one thing before he answered.

"Did you tell Galia?"

"No."

"Then I'm not upset. In fact, feel free to tell Galia things I don't know. Most of them, I probably wouldn't want to know. Mather Wyman's lifelong masquerade being a fine example."

"So you're comfortable having me keep secrets?"

"I've read Khalil Gibran and taken his advice to heart," McGill said.

"'Let there be spaces in your togetherness?'"

"Exactly."

The North Shore — Northeastern Illinois

Global warming was doing a bang up job prolonging the fall color season. McGill decided to keep his Secret Service people on their toes by getting out and about, visiting not only his kids and Carolyn and Lars, but also his mother and father. He sang duets with Mom after a family dinner and went fishing at Chain O' Lakes State Park with just his dad — and his security detail dotting the shoreline, and a helicopter on station out of sight and hearing.

Sweetie also visited with her family, and Putnam flew in to meet his new in-laws.

Norman Rockwell, had he not died thirty-four years earlier, might have worn out a paint brush capturing the All-American good times. He probably would have left all the ladies and gents wearing sunglasses and carrying automatic weapons for Edward Gorey to fill in along the margins.

What an artist to be named later had yet to seize upon — along with all the feds and local cops — was sight of the main villain of the piece, Damon Todd. McGill felt sure that was due to the obvious show of force around him. He didn't think for a minute that Todd had given up the hunt or would be content to go off and scheme in isolation for a year or two.

When Election Day came, McGill's platoon of security personnel had vanished. He showed up at his old polling place, St. Simon's Catholic Church, in Evanston with just Elspeth Kendry for company. The election judges and the other voters on hand, all of whom had seen replays of McGill's tussle on the National Mall, gave him a warm welcome. Handshakes and hugs. Great to see you agains.

But one wise guy had to tell him, "No electioneering at the polling place, pal."

He pointed to the *Reelect Patti Grant* button on McGill's lapel.

McGill told Elspeth, "Shoot him."

The wise guy was uncertain just long enough to draw a smile from McGill and laughter from everyone else. Except Elspeth. She thought McGill ought to retire the line.

McGill stepped into the voting booth and punched the ballot cleanly for his wife.

Thankful it would be the last time.

— Joseph Flynn —

The Oval Office

The president, Galia Mindel and Stephen Norwood watched the reports of voter turnout and exit polls come in from around the nation. The weather was mild and dry throughout the country. Turnout was much heavier than normal.

"We might set a record for total votes cast," Stephen Norwood said. "The percentage of women voting will be very high and that should be a good thing for us."

Galia said, "Turnout in the South is high, too. We know who that's going to help."

Norwood said, "There was no way anyone could have foreseen the rebirth of Southern populism. It has introduced a whole new dynamic to American politics, and Tom T. Wright joining the True South ticket gave Howard Hurlbert a big lift."

"Sure," Galia joked, "especially after he promised to make every Tuesday, year 'round, an honorary Mardi Gras with two for one drinks."

Norwood laughed, but when the president didn't her two top political counselors looked at her. Galia said, "Madam President?"

"You think I'll win?" she asked.

"It will be close, but yes," Galia said.

"Very close," Norwood said, "the counting might not be done tonight. Worst comes to worst, you should have a majority of the Supreme Court."

That made Patti Grant smile.

"Let's hope it doesn't come to that. Do you think Mather Wyman will finish third?"

Galia sighed. "What he did was very brave. I think it will open minds and opportunities in the years to come but, today, I think he did himself in. He'll finish third."

"My opinion, too," Norwood said.

"What a shame," the president said.

Chicago Executive Airport — Wheeling, Illinois

Jaime Martinez had never jumped out of an airplane so far north. He was used to warmer skies with different wind conditions. He was used to landing on soft beaches in sunshine. The return to earth he'd make tonight would be unlike anything he'd done before.

Still, he owed Damon Todd more than even his life. The men Todd had hired had freed his wife and killed the *cabron* who had taken her. Todd had arranged for both of them to flee Mexico. The cartel could look for them in the United States until the end of time and would never find them. Jaime and his wife were resettled on a small *finca* in Uruguay. It was a beautiful place, and tonight would be the last time he would set foot north of the equator.

Jaime had completed one jump that day, just to be sure all would go well tonight. For him, the temperature at ground level, sixty-two degrees, was cool, but seeing all the local people walking about in short sleeves, smiling in the sunshine, he knew he was lucky. The weather, his research showed, could be a lot worse, much colder, windy, even snow was possible.

His test jump showed him it was possible to fly here. He saw the great city and the vast lake to the southeast. He saw the residential neighborhoods along the shoreline to the north of the city. He didn't know which of the lakefront mansions would be his target, but tonight there would be a beacon to guide him.

Chicago Executive Airport lay just outside the airspace of the vastly larger airport called O'Hare. The flight tonight would be only a few minutes to the lakefront. His jump would be even shorter. With just a bit of grace from God, all would go well.

Todd would be repaid and he would be free.

After his test jump, Jaime had been picked up and driven back to CEA. He and the pilot both inspected the aircraft they would use that night. Everything was perfect, including the amount of money the pilot would receive to not mention that a man had jumped out of his plane that night.

"Everything good, Mr. Donato?" the pilot asked.

Jaime was pretending to be Italian.

His skin was fair enough to pass and he had blue eyes.

"*Si, molto buon.*" He even knew a few words of the language.

Jaime went back to his hotel and called Todd. Told him everything was ready.

The Grant Mansion — Winnetka, Illinois

Only a handful of lights were on in the mansion Patti and Andy Grant had once called home. The property was walled off along Sheridan Road and from the neighbors on either side. The steel beams that had been sunk into the lake bed to keep boats from landing on the private beach were still in place and holding firm.

Beyond that, no other security measures were visible.

Neither guards nor dogs patrolled the grounds.

All was quiet along the lakefront nearing the end of Election Day.

McGill sat alone in the room where Andy Grant had died. Had been blown to bits by the rocket-propelled grenade Erna Godfrey had fired. So much had happened since that awful night, but the pain of Andy's death remained one of the threads that bound McGill and Patti together. The room had been restored and filled with awards and mementoes Andy had been given.

Photographs filled all available wall spaces. There was only one of Andy standing next to a politician and a celebrity. In that case it was Patti who filled both roles. The two of them smiled like little kids who shared the best secret in the world. It was their wedding picture.

All the other photos were of Andy with his friends. People with whom he'd worked. People to whom he'd extended a helping hand. Many of those in the latter category were too busy hugging him to be bothered looking at the camera.

In the early days after Andy's death, McGill had told Patti that high among his regrets was that he hadn't had more time to get to know Andy better. So, in an act of both generosity and trust, she'd given him access to both his business correspondence and his diaries. McGill would be the only one to receive that privilege while Patti still lived.

McGill had learned that Andy had come from a family that was affluent but nowhere near as rich as Andy would later become. After graduating from the University of Chicago with a degree in mathematics, Andy went to work as a trader at the Chicago Mercantile Exchange. Possessing both an ability to analyze hard numbers and an intuitive grasp for which way the markets in pork bellies and wheat would move, he'd made millions.

Then joining with two college classmates who'd moved to California, he was a founder of a venture capital firm, and that was where his billions had been made. In the last years of his life he spent the majority of his time managing The Grant Foundation.

Giving money away wisely, as he'd told McGill.

Getting to know Andy's life better, McGill regretted his inability to save his life all the more.

An ironic sentiment, he knew. Had he saved Andy, he never would have married Patti.

Might have become an old bachelor content to live off his two pensions.

Wondering how to fill all the hours he didn't spend with his children.

Or he might have married Clare Tracy.

The way things had turned out, he was watching the returns of the presidential election come in from the eastern third of the United States. He had not only a rooting interest but a personal interest. A civic interest, too. He was biased, sure. But even if he had become an old bachelor, he'd still have thought Patti would do the best job for the country.

The sound level of the television was low enough that McGill heard a beep on the alarm console next to his chair. He silenced the alarm and turned off the TV. The alarm had indicated a threat from above. Once the FBI had learned that Todd had taken sky diving and wing suit flying lessons, the Secret Service had installed a radar system. Just like at the White House.

Something or someone had entered the estate's no-fly zone.

Then McGill heard the rumble of marine motors come to life. Through the room's east-facing windows, he saw lights appear on boats stationed on the lake. McGill smiled. It would be funny if Todd overshot the mark and wound up in cold water. Be hilarious if one of the special agents held his head under until all their troubles were over.

While there was activity on the lake, if the plan was holding, the grounds around the house would remain dark and quiet. Allow Todd to feel safe, if the activity overhead had been a fake-out. And that seemed to be the way of it.

McGill heard the front door of the house open.

He'd made it easy and left it unlocked.

He clicked his Beretta's safety off and called out, "That you, Dr. Todd? I'm up here. First door on the right at the top of the stairs. Great view. We can watch the show you set up out on the lake."

A man with any sense of reason would know he'd been suckered. Would have at least attempted to get away. McGill heard footsteps on the staircase. The chair in which he sat was in line with the doorway. The gun in his right hand was pointed at Todd's head as it came into view.

A little voice in McGill's mind told him to do what he'd instructed Elspeth so often.

Shoot him.

McGill would have had to make it a head shot. As Todd stepped into the second floor hallway, McGill could see that under a formfitting black Lycra top Todd was wearing a vest. Well, McGill had dressed in Kevlar, too. Fair was fair.

Only Todd's hands were empty. No gun, no knife, no stick. Unless the SOB had become an overnight master of empty-hand combat, that was suspiciously cocky of him. The muted creak of a floorboard sounded from the first floor.

Todd turned to look. McGill knew what he saw, Sweetie and Elspeth climbing the stairs, completing the trap, herding Todd toward McGill. It was too late to commit cold-blooded murder now. Elspeth might look the other way. Sweetie's conscience would never let her do the same.

Todd raised his hands and asked McGill, "May I join you?"

McGill said, "Sure. Just like old times."

Except he hadn't had backup the last time he'd faced off with Todd.

And Todd had been anything but submissive.

As Todd entered the room, McGill studied him. The recessed lighting was set in the midrange of the rheostat. Seeing Todd was no problem at all. Missing some small detail was still a possibility. Sweetie and Elspeth entered the room. They kept their weapons pointed at Todd.

Todd had stopped fewer than ten feet away from McGill, between him and the windows that looked out on the lake. Close enough to tackle, if a sub-lethal counterattack was called for.

Close enough to study for a hidden weapon, too.

The bastard had to have something up his sleeve.

Todd saw McGill's concern and offered a mocking smile.

"Well, Marshal, ya got me," he said.

Todd started to lower his hands.

McGill said, "Keep them up."

"What's the matter? Do I scare you?"

"Never have. That's what bothers you about me. I just don't want to get gore on the furnishings."

Todd saw that McGill wasn't kidding and kept his hands up.

McGill studied him, searching for a place Todd could have hidden a weapon.

Didn't see a damn thing. The only imperfections in Todd's garb were the bulge around his torso from the vest and a dangling loop of stray thread at the hem of his shirt. He had to be missing something.

"Sweetie, Elspeth," McGill said, "you see any sign of a weapon?"

"Turn around," Elspeth ordered.

"Keep your hands up, too," Sweetie told Todd.

He obeyed both orders. Gave it a minute. Turned back to face his captors.

"How is Chana?" he asked McGill.

"Sorry she didn't get to shoot you, too."

Todd frowned. "You've changed her," he told McGill, "and not for the better."

The old combative Todd was creeping back into sight now, putting McGill on edge.

He had to be missing something. He moved to the edge of his chair, the better to see Todd, and closing the gap if he had to go for the man.

He thought that provoking Todd might throw him off his game.

"Chana is very happy with her life, her work and ... her husband. Graham was her first boyfriend, you know. Her first love. Her *true* love."

Any semblance of humanity fell from Todd's face like a rockslide.

He revealed himself as a beast about to strike.

McGill pushed him one last step.

"You figured out the reason you need to kill me, right? To show Chana you're the better man. But you've never been able to do it. Even with the help of two playmates from the —"

Todd likely expected McGill to say CIA, but McGill didn't. He bolted from the chair while Todd was waiting for him to complete his sentence. Todd had finally given himself away. He'd dropped his head and lowered his eyes. He was looking for the loop of thread hanging from his shirt. It wasn't a stray piece of fabric at all.

The loop was a triggering ring. Todd wasn't wearing body armor; he was wearing a bomb. He was willing to kill himself as long as he could take McGill with him. Getting Sweetie and

Elspeth, too, would be a bonus.

McGill grabbed Todd's right arm as he tried to bring it down — hoping neither Sweetie nor Elspeth shot him by mistake — and yanked it back up, putting an arm-bar on Todd's triceps. Using the submission hold, McGill ran Todd headfirst toward the windows facing the lake. Shoving Todd as hard as he could, McGill sent him crashing through a window.

He spun and threw himself to the floor, yelling to Sweetie and Elspeth, "Get down!"

For just a heartbeat he thought he was going to look like a horse's ass if —

The explosion shattered the windows not already broken and made McGill's ears ring. Todd must have triggered the bomb with his free hand a second after taking flight. Maybe it was an un-stoppable continuation of effort begun as McGill still held him. Maybe he hadn't wanted ever to be held in confinement again.

It didn't matter to McGill. Callous bastard that he'd become, he was simply glad Todd was dead. He was happier still to see Sweetie and Elspeth step back into the room. They'd been smart enough to duck out while the ducking was good.

Obeying an impulse he'd later regret, McGill looked out through the shattered window frame.

Damon Todd's remains bore no resemblance to any human form.

McGill turned around and found one consoling thought.

He'd saved Andy's room from getting blown up again.

Washington, D.C.

McGill had assured everyone back home in Illinois that he was fine, but he wasn't. His ears still rang, though not as bad as at first. The more serious pain came from learning that once again he'd been too late to save an innocent man. Deke had told him that Todd had spent an unknown amount of time hiding out at the house of the neighbor who lived just to the north of the Grant mansion. Had used the neighbor's ladder to scale the wall between the two estates.

Todd had timed his entry onto the Grant property with seeing Jaime Martinez zoom past overhead and the lights of the security boats going on. Martinez had been caught, explained he knew nothing of what Todd had planned. The expatriate Mexican had no criminal record, but it looked like it would be some time before he got back to his wife in Uruguay.

Perry Hardwick, the late neighbor, had been a retired ad exec, something of a snoop when it had come to seeing if he could peer into Patti Grant's bedroom window and reputedly stingy with the dispensing of Halloween candy. But he'd deserved a better end than meeting up with Damon Todd. He'd been found tied to a chair in the basement of his home. He'd suffered no ghastly torture or even mild abuse. He simply hadn't been given his heart medicine and had died from the neglect.

No big deal to Todd. Hell, he'd planned to kill himself. He was going to worry about a stranger? The sonofabitch. McGill was kicking himself for not getting to Todd sooner.

He dropped Abbie off at Georgetown and took some comfort from the hug and the words with which she'd left him. "Dad, you did your best. Who could have done better?"

McGill promised Abbie he'd pull himself out of his funk

He didn't want her to worry about him.

Besides that, he had to give Patti moral support.

It took two hundred and seventy electoral votes to win the presidency.

Patti had won two hundred and sixty-nine.

Patti won California, Illinois and New York, the new early primary states. Thanks to Jean Morrissey, she also won Minnesota. That had given her a great head-start with a hundred and fourteen electoral votes from just four states.

As counting continued through Election Night, Patti added Connecticut, Delaware, Florida, Massachusetts, New Hampshire,

New Jersey, Ohio (a blow to Mather Wyman), Oregon, Pennsylvania, Rhode Island, Vermont, Virginia, Washington and Wisconsin. Total electoral votes: two hundred and sixty-nine.

Howard Hurlbert won Alabama, Alaska, Arkansas, Georgia, Idaho, Kentucky, Louisiana, Mississippi, North Carolina, Oklahoma, South Carolina, South Dakota, Tennessee and Texas. Total electoral votes: one hundred and forty-three.

Mather Wyman won Arizona, Colorado, the District of Columbia, Hawaii, Iowa, Kansas, Maine, Maryland, Michigan (the irony), Missouri, Montana, Nebraska, Nevada, New Mexico (thank you, Rosalinda Fuentes), North Dakota, Utah, West Virginia and Wyoming. Total electoral votes: one hundred and fifteen.

That left one state, Indiana, where the vote was still too close to call.

A recount was a certainty in the Hoosier State.

McGill sat in on the Wednesday morning quarterbacking that took place in the Oval Office with Patti, Galia Mindel and Stephen Norwood. Everyone inquired after McGill's health, but attention quickly turned to coming so close yet remaining far away. The race in Indiana was between Mather Wyman and Howard Hurlbert. Patti Grant had finished a distant third.

Galia shook her head and said, "I just don't know what we can do."

"Update our résumés," the president suggested.

The two staffers in the room gave thin laughs.

"Jim?" Patti asked.

"Play 'til you hear the buzzer. Go out with your heads high, if it comes to that."

"Stephen?" the president asked.

"It may well come to that. Our electoral votes are solid. So are the other guys' votes from everything I've been able to find out. If there's no winner in the Electoral College, the election goes to the House of Representatives."

"The goddamn House," Galia said, "where we have *so* many

friends. We might as well start packing now."

The president shook her head. "No, we keep working. Out of respect for the people who put us here the first time."

Galia and Norwood nodded and went back to work. The First Couple were left with each other.

"How do you feel, loyal henchman?" the president asked. "Is this all small potatoes after what you've been through?"

"Not small potatoes at all," McGill said. "You make more life or death decisions than I do."

"Maybe I've had enough of all that."

"Who could blame you? Whatever happens, you'll still be my girlfriend?"

"Sure. My prospects are few these days."

McGill got up, leaned over the president's desk and kissed her.

"Back to work," he said. "The taxpayer expects value for his money."

14

December, 2012
Indiana State Capitol — Indianapolis, Indiana

Mather Wyman carried Indiana by nine hundred and twenty-two votes. That added eleven more electoral votes to Wyman's tally, giving him a total of one hundred and twenty-six. Not enough to move him out of third place.

On the Monday following the second Wednesday in December, the seventeenth day of the month, Indiana's eleven electors met to cast their ballots. Each elector had to complete and sign six Certificates of Vote. Two would be sent by registered mail to the President of the United States Senate. Two would be sent by registered mail to the Archivist of the United States. Two would be delivered by hand to Indiana's attorney general.

In addition to the Constitutionally mandated requirements, each state was free to add non-conflicting obligations. Indiana chose to have each elector give an oral declaration, stating his or her name and the name of the candidate who would receive that elector's vote. The declarations would begin with the most senior elector and conclude with the most junior elector.

Sheryl Kimbrough was sick to her stomach at the thought of what would happen if the election was sent to the House of Representatives. There was no way Mather Wyman was going to leapfrog Howard Hurlbert to become president by a vote of the

House. The country at large had shown it wasn't ready to elect an openly gay president; the members of the House certainly weren't going to blaze a new trail.

What did that leave?

It left New South cajoling Republicans into voting with them. Heck, they'd say, we're all really Republicans at heart. That was how things would work out, along with New South picking up a chick-enhearted Democrat or ten. There were always Democrats willing to sell out their party. They were famous for it.

Then the House would vote and Howard Hurlbert would —

"Sheryl, it's your turn." Her old boss, Senator Charles Talbert, tugged her sleeve. "You're the last one to vote, my dear."

She got to her feet, went to the lectern and looked out at all the faces looking back at her.

Looked at the television camera that would record her words for history.

She said, "I'm Sheryl Kimbrough and I cast my ballot for ... Patricia Darden Grant."

ABOUT THE AUTHOR

Joseph Flynn has been published both traditionally — Signet Books, Bantam Books and Variance Publishing — and through his own imprint, Stray Dog Press, Inc. Both major media reviews and reader reviews have praised his work. Booklist said, "Flynn is an excellent storyteller." The Chicago Tribune said, "Flynn [is] a master of high-octane plotting." The most repeated reader comment is: Write faster, we want more.

You can read a free excerpt of each of Joe's books by visiting: *www.josephflynn.com.*

Find out what Jim McGill will be doing next and meet other friends of McGill at *www.facebook.com/TheFriendsofJimMcGill*